A SHIELD OF C(

Marion Molteno grew up in South Africa, spent some years in Zambia where her daughters were born, and since 1976 has lived in Britain. She has pioneered community education projects, written and lectured widely on inter-cultural issues, and was a founder of the Refugee Project Croydon. Since 1993 she has been an advisor on children's rights to Save the Children, supporting projects with disadvantaged children in over 50 countries.

A shield of coolest air was her first novel and was received to critical acclaim, winning the David Thomas Prize for fiction. *If you can walk, you can dance* won the Commonwealth Writers Prize for the best book in the Africa region, and was selected in the top 20 books of the year for the Women's Book Festival in New Zealand. Her volume of short stories, *A language in common,* set among Asian women in Britain, has been translated into five languages and *The Bracelets* won the London Short Story award. Her most recent novel is *Somewhere more simple.*

A SHIELD OF COOLEST AIR

Marion Molteno

A shield of coolest air

Longstone BOOKS
LONDON

A shield of coolest air
was first published in 1992 by Shola Books
This edition published in June 2008 by Longstone Books
33 Theatre Street, London SW11 5ND

Copyright © Marion Molteno

Cover design by Andrew Corbett
Cover photo © Pat Marsden
Set by Long House Publishing Services, Cumbria
Printed and bound by Biddles Ltd, Kings Lynn, Norfolk

Distributed by Central Books
99 Wallis Road, London E9 5LN

A catalogue reference for this book
is available from the British Library

ISBN 978-0-9554373-4-2

www.longstonebooks.co.uk

Now you depart, and though your way may lead
Through airless forests thick with hagar trees,
Through places steeped in heat, stifling and dry,
Where breath comes hard, and no fresh breeze can reach –
Yet may God place a shield a coolest air
Between your body and the assailant sun ...

———

From a Somali poem by
Sayyid Mohamed Abdille Hassan

PART ONE

Arrivals

They arrived in midwinter, with almost no winter clothes. In the airport building the children clung around her, restless in their insecurity, as they shuffled with the slowly moving queue to the desk marked ALL OTHER COUNTRIES. When finally it was their turn she found it difficult to speak, to answer the questions of the man with the impassive face. His fingers twitched in silent irritation round the rubber stamp in which was invested the power to let them in or turn them away. Back.

Once they were through she felt momentarily at a loss. All her energies had been concentrated on getting her past that point. She became aware of one of the children tugging at her hand, pulling her towards the baggage collection point where the suitcases lurched out through rubber flaps to flop heavily on the conveyor belt and begin circling slowly round.

Alistair met them. That in itself seemed a miracle, that he should really be here half way across the world, waiting for them. They travelled for what seemed hours through interminable, congested streets, with buildings crowding on top of each other, leaving no room to breathe. They stopped finally at a house which looked exactly like all the others, the home of the people who had taken Alistair in when he had arrived so suddenly two weeks before.

Afterwards Rachel remembered little of those first few weeks. Their hosts could not have been kinder - they were themselves products of an earlier political exodus - but with five extra people the house was impossibly crowded, and full of carefully arranged possessions which she was constantly having to keep the children from touching. People kept coming to the house to talk to Alistair, people with cameras and microphones and recording equipment, people asking questions and scarcely listening to the answers. How long were you detained?

Tortured? Police repression, South African regime, refusal to be silenced... And against the background of this continuous stream of male voices - propounding, disputing - confident, articulate - her own thoughts swirled ineffectually. Where could they go after this? How would they support themselves? How would they ever get past the state of living on short term permits in someone else's country?

Eventually Alistair found a flat for them to rent, in a place she had never heard of called Battersea, miles away in South London. The week after they moved in Alistair set off on the first of many travelling assignments, as photographer accompanying a journalist on a three week tour of Angola.

And there she was, stranded, in a place where she knew no one. A place of miserably wet, grimy streets where it was dark by mid-afternoon, imprisoned in a depressingly furnished upstairs flat with three confused and unusually demanding children, who were used to playing outside most of their waking hours and had little idea of how to amuse themselves indoors. A place, above all, where she had never imagined she would have to live.

All those first months she felt as if she were operating through her body but not in it. The real Rachel was still in South Africa, still waking to the sun each morning, her feet touching that earth. More clearly than her Battersea flat she could see the familiar objects of the home she had had to leave so suddenly, saw herself again on that evening only a few weeks ago, calling the children in from the garden where they were playing under the sprinkler, to come in for bath time. 'Where's Daddy?' Kate had asked as they sat down to supper. 'Working late,' she had said and hoped it was true. But already she was afraid. He had been photographing a demonstration outside a police station in Soweto, and it should have been over hours ago. She waited until the children were asleep before phoning friends who had also been at the demonstration. None of them had seen him. There had been thousands of people, they said, though only a handful were white. Once the police had started shooting it would have been impossible to find anyone. But Alistair would be all right, he always was - don't worry. She made herself lie down but by now the panic had gone to her bladder. Each time she returned from the bathroom she checked that the children were still safe and as she had left them, Kate's fair hair slipping softly over her face, Simon's wispy ginger curls damp with night perspiration, the one-year-old Ben on his tummy with his bottom humped up in the air.

Eventually, well after midnight, Alistair appeared. His clothes, usually so consciously casual, were dishevelled, his large body tense but excited. 'Where the hell have you been?' Rachel said, but whispering, as if someone were listening. But the anger had already given way to relief. Even the smell of cigarette smoke on his shirt was comforting. 'At Andy's place,' he said. 'I thought you would have guessed.' She didn't ask, Why didn't you phone? He would not have risked the police tracing the call. 'Where's the film?' she whispered. He could scarcely contain his triumph. 'On its way to London, courtesy of Geoff!'

But before it was light they came for him, knocking repeatedly on the door till Rachel woke, to stare in terror at Alistair who was already up and moving to the door. 'Don't open it!' she hissed, though she knew that would have been pointless. The security police took over. Grey suited and silent, they emptied every drawer, pulled all the books off the shelves. Then they began on Alistair. He refused to answer their questions, insisting on his right to have a lawyer present. The police became abusive and hustled him into their waiting car. The car drove away. Rachel stood watching, alone on the doorstep in the first thin strands of morning light.

She was totally unprepared for dealing with the weeks that followed. Not that she had been politically blind. On the contrary, all the years she and Alistair had been together she had known that this would happen, had been waiting for it, almost. She had taken to reading accounts by people who had had long periods of detention without trial, as if learning how they had coped would somehow help her when their own turn came. But when it happened it was of course Alistair, not she, who had to deal with the terrifying hours of interrogation, the mental torture of solitary confinement. Not physical torture, thank God. Perhaps being a foreign journalist did at least save him from that. But nothing Rachel had read or heard had warned her of what it would be like on the outside, of something as simple as that her ability to sleep would disappear almost completely, and with it her hold on reality. She seemed to move, zombie-like, through days that had a bizarre resemblance to normality. The children still needed to be fed and taken to school. Friends would arrive to comfort her or bring her meals they had cooked. Yet all the time the only person of whose existence she was absolutely convinced was Alistair, and he was not there.

Alistair was suffering and she could do nothing to help him. More than that, it was her fault. Why, she could not have explained, but she did not question that it was so. Alistair was in detention because he had publicly challenged the authorities. She had not, and she was free. She saw him being made to stand for thirty six, forty eight hours without a break, deprived of sleep while they questioned him - and her own eyes would not close. She saw him alone in his cell, all sense of time and reality retreating - and she discovered that she too was cut off, that she could not remember what anyone had said to her all day.

Two weeks later Alistair was released, as suddenly as he had been detained. Presumably they had decided that a foreign journalist was less trouble to them out of the country than in jail. It was almost as difficult to adjust to his return as it had been to his disappearance. Detention without trial can last indefinitely; in that sense every detention is forever while you are experiencing it. Yet here he was, out, and extraordinarily unscarred - and with only forty eight hours before he had to be out of the country. And now she and the children stood huddled together, watching and waving through the plate glass of the airport observation lounge as he disappeared into the aeroplane. And then they were back in the desolate house which had suddenly ceased to be their home, where her mother looked after the children while Rachel packed, bought plane tickets, made arrangements for the sale of their house and most of its contents, the transfer of bank accounts, and five hundred other nightmarish tasks which she scarcely understood, and in a daze said goodbye to her friends whom she had never expected to have to leave.

For much of their first year in London Alistair was away. His detention had hit the headlines, giving him an instant reputation for being able to get to where the news was being made. After Angola there was an assignment in Colombia, and then another in the Phillipines, and then... In the flat in Battersea Rachel waited for him to come back and tried meanwhile to remake a home. Each small task was a first-time and that made it seem a major undertaking. Winter clothes - she stared at the prices of coats. One for each of the children would take all she might have for two months. It was months before she found out about jumble sales. Later she could not imagine how that was possible, for there was one almost every week in the church hall at the end of their road. But there had been too much new to notice, she must have been automatically cutting out from most of it, concentrating on the next step. A doctor - it seemed inconceivable afterwards, but it was only when Simon woke in the night with a high temperature that she realised she had no idea how to find a doctor. There must be some emergency arrangement. She searched the telephone directory. Doctor? Hospital? Medical? Nothing. Did no one get ill in this country? Emergency Services, Ambulance. She could not call an ambulance just for a child with a temperature. She did not know her neighbours. They passed on the stairs, coming in or going out of their doors. A brief nod, perhaps a smile, 'Cold today, isn't it?' Certainly not enough for her to be able to wake them in the night and say, 'Where can I find a doctor?'

A school for Kate and Simon - did she just walk in at the gates of the first school she saw and ask to see the head teacher? Would any school take them, children from another country? In the middle of term? The building seemed tall and forbidding, the small asphalt playground impossibly overcrowded. She edged Ben's pushchair through the melee of small bodies. Simon's hand held tightly onto hers. Kate walked close beside her, her back straight with concentration. A football whizzed past them. A group of boys rushed at them, nearly knocking them down as they yelled urgently to each other to Pass! Pass!

Alistair was back. They would greet him with excitement and relief, would tell him about the school, the doctor, the jumble sale, and he would listen and laugh with them, but as if he were listening to someone else's story. And then he would be off again to yet another part of Africa or Asia, taking photographs, meeting the leaders of liberation movements, making friends in half the major cities of the world. Rachel kept explaining to the children - or to herself - that he was busy with his important work and would be back as soon as he could. But in her more vulnerable moments she knew. She would wake in the middle of the night, cold from the dream that had pursued her since before Alistair had been arrested - to find the place in the bed that he should have occupied empty. Alone in the dark she could not

7

avoid facing the knowledge that Alistair was in no hurry to get back, too caught up in the drama of being constantly at the centre of things. In the increasingly brief periods when he was back his presence brought not the longed-for companionship but only an uncomfortable awareness that he could not bring himself down to their level, hers and the children's. He was simply using them as a convenient stopping-off place from which to plan his next departure.

Each time he left she filled the evenings after the children were asleep by writing to her friends back home. Her humorous, apparently confident descriptions of her adaptations to her new life disguised what the length of the letters gave away, that she needed desperately to hang on to the closeness that had been so suddenly snatched away from her. Her friends replied, briefly. The gaps became longer, their letters more detached, like round-robins at Christmas to people you never see. She knew it was inevitable. Their lives continued as before, caught up as hers and Alistair's had once been in the immediacy of political events. Her small dilemmas must seem very remote.

Perhaps because her own sense of loss was so great she worked passionately to help the children feel that this life was the real one, not a poor substitute for the one they had left behind. She got to the school early each day to fetch Kate and Simon, to stand in the playground alongside the other mothers, watching, listening, learning. She attended every open day and parents' meeting, overcoming her sense of being an outsider to introduce herself to the mothers of the children her own had talked about. She filled the bare walls of their cramped little kitchen with a collage of the children's paintings and drawings, took them to museums on wet Sundays, invited other children home after school. Within a couple of years she realised she had succeeded almost too well. Ben had been less than two when they had come to Britain and remembered nothing of the time before. All Simon appeared to retain was a handful of memory-pictures, unconnected, frozen into myth. For Kate the memories were clearer but so was the pressure to be like other children. From her first day in the new school she had suppressed any part of herself that did not fit in. She learnt the playground rhymes the children here used and forgot as quickly as possible the ones she had known before. She would eat only the kinds of food her friends ate, watched the same television programmes, spoke as they did. Only in the privacy of home did she allow herself to keep contact with what had been before, to draw pictures to send to Ouma, her grandmother. To say to Rachel, 'Do you remember the time I got that huge thorn in my foot, the time Oupa took us all up onto that hill behind their house - what was it called?'

'Duiwelskop. And do you remember how Ouma got it out?'

'Soaking my foot in vinegar!' said Kate. 'Ugh!'

Rachel was grateful that there was at least one other person who could remember and laugh with her, and keep it alive. But like Kate she too needed to concentrate first on survival, and too much thinking about what had been lost made it harder. When they moved from that first small flat into a house with a patch of garden she began to plant, having no idea what would grow in this strange climate or which time of year it was appropriate to do what, just planting in faith, letting the pansies and geraniums she bought from the street market put down roots for her, for the children. And when she found that they died, that everyone else brought their geraniums in for the winter, she tried again the next spring with shrubs whose names she had never heard, having no idea what kind of flowers they might produce or when. She knew only that she had to grow something, something that would still be there next year.

The garden grew. Daffodils in the window boxes to greet the spring. A honeysuckle rising like Jack's beanstalk to trail over the kitchen window. An apple tree that had been only four foot high when she put it in produced its first four apples. 'One for each of us!' said Simon excitedly. And no one said, 'Except Daddy,' since he wouldn't be back until long after the apples had been eaten. Alistair's earnings were erratic, but adequate. Rachel found a mornings-only job in a wool shop, leaving Ben with Evelyn, one of her friends from the school who worked as a childminder. If it had not been for the dream, Rachel could almost have been lulled into thinking the adjustments were over.

But the dream would not leave her. It had a terrifyingly eerie quality. No conversations, however surreal. Nothing visual. Only a mounting tension that expressed itself rhythmically, an impersonal tread that came crunching towards her, becoming steadily louder and more ominous, nearer and nearer to where she stood, watching, waiting, helpless. And she would wake - always at three in the morning, the hour they had come for Alistair - and she would be icy cold and trembling with a sense of impending loss. She would switch on the light, make herself tea, read, anything to cancel out the relentless pursuing rhythm that lurked somewhere in her subconscious, waiting to pounce again the moment she stopped being vigilant and let herself drift into sleep. When finally she felt calm enough to turn out the light, she would lie in the dark wondering what on earth she was doing here, six thousand miles from everyone who mattered to her, in a place that was neither her home nor Alistair's. How had she let herself do something so irreversible, without stopping to think what she was losing? Alistair had been in trouble, and she had dropped everything to be with him. The sentence of exile had been pronounced on Alistair, and she had assumed, blindly, that it was for her too. And now it turned out not to have been exile for Alistair at all but a new lease of life. While she...

She would wake next morning to the alarm. The present took over. The children to get ready. Walk to school, Ben to Evelyn's. Hurry, to be at work by nine-thirty. Fetch Ben, shopping, Simon and Kate from school, chat to the other mums. About Simon's new teacher, about the sponsored walk around the common, the PTA meeting on Monday - now, today, tomorrow, never about anything that had been before.

2

They had been in Battersea for three years before she first walked into the Reference Library. She had been intrigued by the building from the first time she had seen it. It was tiny, scarcely wider than any of the Victorian terraced houses alongside it, and stuck away in a side road behind the backyards of the Lavender Hill shops. Yet it had a sort of toy-town grandeur, with its diminutive frontage full of angles and sweeping curves, and its clock-tower topped with a ridiculous little pyramid-shaped roof. An absurdity, built of toy bricks with no regard to function but simply a delight in shapes for their own sake. But Ben was dragging at her hand and it was time to fetch the other two from school so she didn't go in that day, nor did she make time to do so later, though almost every week she took the children to change their books in the lending library just round the corner.

Finally it was for Simon, not for herself, that she first went inside. He had made a card for her mother's birthday, no ordinary card but a collage of fabric and bottletops and pieces of string, and by the time it had been padded to prevent damage in the post it was a fair-sized parcel. He got into one of his nothing-is-right states, insisting that no one but he was to post it, but clearly not confident enough to go alone. Rachel capitulated, abandoning the Saturday morning chores to say, 'Let's you and me go together then,' and left Kate in charge of Ben for half an hour.

She was rewarded by Simon being in one of his most chatty and confiding moods. 'How many miles does it have to go?' he asked, as he licked the stamps and carefully stuck them on.

'About six thousand,' she said.

Simon held his parcel up to the gaping mouth in the wall and hesitated before dropping it in, suddenly loath to part with all those hours of careful handiwork, to be sent six thousand miles to a grandmother he could scarcely remember. They came out into the early April sunlight and waited at the zebra crossing. Simon said, looking across the road to the lending library, 'I like the way it's got church windows and red and white stripes over the door,' and she thought how he would love the toy-town reference library, and wondered why she had not before gone those few hundred yards out of her way to show it to him. She said, 'There's an even nicer library round the corner. Do you want to see?'

So they went. She watched his face as they rounded the corner, his intense concentration as they climbed the three curved steps that would have done credit to a town hall. She followed his eyes, down to the shiny green stone inlay that waited to receive their feet, up to the carved stonework above the entrance, an elaborate design of lions and a dove holding a coat of arms. 'What does that say?' he asked, 'those old-fashioned letters?' She read, *'Non mihi, non tibi, sed nobis.* It's Latin. It says, Not for me, not for you, but for us.'

'Are we allowed?'

'Of course - it's a library!'

Heavy wooden doors, each side bearing a polished brass plate, PUSH on one and PULL on the other. Simon stared at the notices, intrigued at being offered a choice. He pushed, and they were inside.

Her eyes took a moment to adjust. When they did her first impression was of the colour of dark wood - wooden bookshelves lining the walls of a small, beautifully proportioned hall that rose to a vaulted ceiling; all available floor space was filled with dark wooden

11

tables for people to study at - an extraordinary range of people from all over the world, each quietly concentrating. It was the most crowded library she had ever seen, and also the calmest.

She could imagine no place she would rather work. She could feel already how it would be to be welcomed each day by the deep warmth of the wood, to sense the years of continuity as she climbed up to the wood-panelled balcony to reshelve old volumes; to escape each day as these people studying at the desks did, from the noise of the traffic-filled streets, the pressure and isolation of life in this overcrowded city that drew people from all over the world and then left them, unconnected, to find their own way.

She saw the advertisement for a part-time library assistant only two weeks later. Nothing had been further from her mind than looking for a new job. She could have done with more money of course, but how could she work two afternoons and until nine one evening a week? Yet something beyond logic made her intensely excited at the idea of once again spending her working time among books. She applied. She did not tell anyone she was doing so, not even Kate. Alistair, of course, was thousands of miles away - Burma, this time - so the question of talking it over with him didn't even arise. She wrote off for the application form and filled it in late one night after all the children were asleep. It was the first genuinely impulsive thing she had done for a long time. Perhaps that was why, afterwards, it seemed so significant.

She was called for an interview and was offered the job. At each stage of the process she was surprised - surprised that men in suits who spent their days making decisions and allocating budgets should have taken her crazy impulse seriously. She began to understand that she must seem a desirable candidate. They were not expecting applications from people with librarianship qualifications and several years of experience. They explained that, the post being what it was, they could not unfortunately pay her in accordance with her qualifications. She had never expected them to. The only other time she had applied for work in Britain was when she had been desperate to get some income of her own, however small, so that she would not have to depend entirely on Alistair's. She had accepted the role of beggar, and here were people behaving as if they were lucky to get her.

When she realised that the job was hers to accept, she went into a sudden panic. Thrusting fantasy firmly aside, her over-responsible self took the matter in hand. She phoned the head librarian, who had been on the interviewing panel and had seemed reasonably human. She said thank you very much but it was all a terrible mistake. She had had no business wasting their time by applying, there was no way she could manage the hours. He said, 'Come in and see me and we'll talk about it.' She had by now confessed to the children. Kate said, 'Go on Mom, you want to do it. We'll find a way.' And within four days it was done. The librarian agreed to waive the requirement of one late evening duty a week. Rachel asked, 'Why is it worth it to you?' He said, 'If I appointed anyone else I'd have to start by teaching them the Dewey system before they could reshelve a single book.' Having been offered so large a concession she did not dare to say that she could not manage the afternoons either. Instead she spoke to Evelyn, who already had Ben in the mornings. Two afternoons would be no problem, Evelyn said, and she could collect Simon from school on those days. That left only Kate, to come home to an empty house. 'Don't be so silly, Mom,' was all Kate said. 'I am twelve, you know.'

So that was it. On the first Monday morning she walked in through the wooden swing doors to start work, feeling no nervousness, only an oddly peaceful sensation that this had been intended to happen; as if this library were a place she had known in some previous life and was now, finally, to recover.

She was taken through her first morning's routine by a woman called Pat - in her early twenties, Rachel guessed, with hair cropped close and a large earring dangling from one ear. Rachel followed her up the stairs that led to the balcony, watching the confident swing of her long cotton skirt. She wasn't exactly slim but supple as a cat, relaxed with her own body. She knows who she is, Rachel thought, and felt pleased that she would be working alongside her. Pat said, 'You've worked in a reference library before?'

'Yes,' said Rachel, 'but years ago, before I came to London.' Instinctively her voice had conveyed a warning, don't ask me where that was. She regretted the tone immediately, but it was too late. She couldn't start in on all those explanations. Simpler to close it off, start this new life clear, without debris from the old. At the top she and Pat stood for a moment looking down over the rows of dark bent heads -

tight African curls, sleek black Indian hair, all varieties in between - and around at the book-lined walls. 'I love the wood,' she said; then, pleased to be able to offer some innocuous personal information, 'That's why I applied for the job, to be able to work in a place like this!'

Pat seemed amused. 'I hope the magic lasts. The dust's pretty unbearable, whatever the shelves look like!'

'I don't mind dust,' Rachel said, and despite herself was assailed for a moment by images of that other, lost life. Dust and the freedom of bare feet, her soles toughened from earliest childhood to the pressure of small gravelly stones and the prickle of thorns. Dust blowing into the kitchen from the back yard, through wire screens that kept out the flies but let in whatever breeze there might be on the long summer afternoons. Dust that settled on everything, on the stones her father collected and kept on the ledge by the window, each one with its own miraculous pattern, structure of the rock from which it had been severed by centuries of torrential rain, the fierce heat of the day, the unprotected cold of cloudless winter nights.

And it was on that same afternoon that she first encountered Anab, who had also grown up with dust. It was at the school, at children-collecting time. The moment Rachel walked into the playground she noticed her, a tall, poised African woman, strikingly beautiful. Her skin was a glowing dark brown and she had unusually long features, almost Arab. Her face was framed by a large headscarf, intended for Islamic modesty perhaps, but with one end flung gracefully over her left shoulder it created an air of freedom and movement that enhanced her beauty rather than hid it. Her full-length robe, made of something light as chiffon, blew around her legs, making Rachel feel suddenly short and shapeless in her jumblesale dungarees. The woman stood near the gate, not shyly to one side as one might expect of someone new to the school but straight and tall and proud, as women walk who carry pots of water on their heads. The playground was full of mothers waiting to collect their children. No one spoke to her. No one would have had the nerve.

The children began to tumble out of the school building, lighting up the bare asphalt with their exuberant energy, the constantly moving colours of their clothes. Simon appeared, talking and laughing with a girl Rachel had not seen before, who ran past them to where the tall woman in the flowing robe stood just inside the playground gates.

'Who's your new friend?' Rachel asked Simon.

'Oh, just someone,' he said, and she knew better than to ask any more.

The next day Evelyn followed her eyes. 'Sado,' she said, watching the child.

'Do you know where they're from?' Rachel asked.

'Tooting,' Evelyn said. 'Mark's teacher was telling me. They've been in a bed and breakfast place there for six months. Just been rehoused on the estate near the station.'

'Where are they from?' Rachel asked again. But that Evelyn didn't know. Africa was too far away, mentally as much as geographically.

Eventually Rachel asked her herself, overcoming the awkwardness of speaking to a stranger because something about the way the African woman stood there, so apparently self-contained - cut off - reminded her almost painfully of her own first few months in Britain. She could feel how this woman must be seeing the others around her as she herself had once done, almost as if they were part of a film she were watching, something outside herself. English women in shoes with worn down heels, others in what she later came to realise were clothes of the latest fashion, though it was months before her eye became accustomed to such subtleties; Pakistani women in loose trousers and tunics of highly patterned eastern fabric, half-hidden under Woolworth's anoraks; the Ghanaian woman who wore African print cotton dresses all through the winter, so that Rachel wondered how she didn't freeze. And she, Rachel, there yet not there, going through the motions of everything that had to be done, yet not part of it. Not even wanting to be...

'I am from Somalia,' the woman said. 'My name is Anab.' The moment she spoke her remote, almost aristocratic air vanished as her face opened into an extraordinarily lovely smile, calm and lively at the same time. Somalia. Somewhere near Ethiopia. Rachel knew nothing else about it. The child Sado appeared, a bright faced girl with skin as shiny brown as her mother's. Anab bent to speak to her in a vigorous flow of Somali. So confident, so normal - What was it about Anab then that made it so clear that she and her daughter were alone, survivors of some traumatic event?

Perhaps Anab sensed her awareness, for without any further conversations about where either of them had come from, they gravitated towards each other. They found themselves serving tea together at the school fete. They sat next to each other on the afternoon of the sports day on the common, and again at the end of term concert, laughing together afterwards at the pompous speech of the chairman of the Board of Governors - 'Like a politician,' Anab said, her tone making clear what her experience of politicians must have been. On the first day of the next term they arrived at the school gate at the same moment, and both laughed with pleasure as they put out their hands to take hold of each other's and exchange news. Their friendship was immediate, warm, reliable - and confined as if by unspoken agreement to the present, to this life that revolved around the children and the school. They were simply two women alone with children in a country that wasn't theirs. Without husbands, without relatives. Cut off from whatever had gone before.

Before... Sitting on the verandah of her parents' house in Lourensrus. The hum of insects, a blur of afternoon heat. Aunt Anna saying, 'It's a mercy your father is not alive, Rachel, he would have died of shame'... Rachel had wanted to get up and walk away but the years of family training made her say instead, 'Aunt Anna, just leave it,' - *los dit maar* - let me be, I'm too tired to fight.

None of her relatives had ever liked Alistair. 'Why do you have to marry a New Zealander, with all our South African boys to choose from?' Aunt Anna had asked, and though her tone had been jocular both she and Rachel knew it was meant in earnest. 'I can't understand these people who come from other countries and all they can do is criticise. If he thinks we're all so terrible, why doesn't he go back?' The others were more oblique but their reservations were just as clear to Rachel, who was adept at interpreting family code. 'Maybe Rachel will improve him,' she overheard Daniel say mildly, which made her laugh to herself and save it to tell Alistair, for if anyone was being changed it was she.

'Forget them,' said Alistair, 'they're your past, about which you can do nothing. You make your own future.' And she had tried to, escaping with relief back to Johannesburg where there were no relatives to watch and comment, where she and Alistair were surrounded by friends who thought as they did; leaving behind the confusing tangle of emotions that Lourensrus evoked in her.

That Alistair, like Aunt Anna, suffered from no uncertainties was of course one of his attractions for Rachel. After growing up in the isolated backwater of Lourensrus, where there seemed no way to challenge the poverty and injustice that surrounded her, it had been exhilarating to find in him and his friends a circle of people who were so sure of what to do, who organised, held public meetings, distributed leaflets, made speeches. She was at his side in all the demonstrations at which he doubled as an activist and photo-journalist, ensuring that the outside world would know what was going on. She was drawn into the cameraderie, and when Kate was born went along with Alistair's insistence that a baby should make no difference. Kate came too, the youngest protester.

But underneath Rachel felt uneasy. What did all this urgent activity achieve? She knew, surely the others must know, that the government would be unmoved by the demonstrations. They would imprison the people making the speeches, ban the newspapers, and go on mowing people down as before. And - it was years before she could admit this to herself - she felt increasingly ambiguous about Alistair's role. Despite her admiration, she began to see that he thrived on the sense of drama, that photographing police atrocities seemed to excite him more than the atrocities themselves depressed him; and she felt less and less inclined to be there with him. After Simon was born she said, 'It's impossible with two children,' and left Alistair to go alone on the demonstrations.

'It's Lourensrus again,' Alistair flung at her in one of their arguments, and he meant, you're succumbing to pressure from those conservative relatives of yours. But the effect of her visits back home worked in precisely the opposite way from what he assumed. It was there, in a town so small that people could not screen themselves off from each other, that Rachel had her most direct encounters with black poverty. Each time she returned to Alistair she found it harder to see any connection between all that bustling, self-important political activity among well-off white people in Johannesburg, and the black children of Lourensrus who would continue to have no shoes in winter, or the women like Martha, who for so many years had worked as a servant in the home Rachel had grown up in, living, like all black servants attached to white homes, in a cramped little room at the back of the garden, not allowed to have her own children with her. From early childhood, long before she could find words to argue with her family, Rachel had known that this was wrong but now as she cared for her own young children it became for her the epitome of all South African crimes. Black parents were separated from their children simply for white convenience - surely this above all was an issue Alistair's friends ought to be making speeches about? Yet they seemed to take the Marthas of the world as much for granted as anyone in Lourensrus, to assume that their own personal Martha would be there at all hours to cook meals and clean and take care of their children, while they were out night after night at meetings, making speeches.

Despite herself she began to feel resentful that Alistair was never at home to help with the children. His work could not be adjusted, he said. If she was feeling trapped by domesticity why didn't she get a maid? She flared up furiously, feeling he was betraying something of fundamental importance on which she had thought they were both agreed. For them to employ a servant would be the ultimate defeat, the acceptance that nothing would ever be different from the way it had been when she was growing up. Alistair said coldly, 'For God's sake, Rachel, don't be so emotional. We're not going to exploit anyone. We'd be offering employment when people are desperate for it.' Could he not see that if she once set off down that road, the laws, the society around her, even the person she employed, all of them would trap her in the destructive pattern of white madam/black servant? How could she accept a style of life that was dependent on some other woman having no chance to be with her own children?

And then the police had started visiting the house to confiscate Alistair's photographs, cutting across the furious arguments, closing them in on each other in a tight, defensive knot. Of course she had told no one in Lourensrus, and how could they possibly have heard, stuck away in the middle of the western highveld, hundreds of miles from anywhere? But the very first time it happened, before she and Alistair had even finished packing away the papers the police had turned out of drawers in their middle of the night foray, she had begun to get phone calls. 'We've been so worried about you,' said Aunt Anna, but Rachel knew it was more than worry. When she next went back to visit, Aunt Anna took her aside to tell her bluntly what the scandal was doing to her parents - as if, thought Rachel indignantly, I'd personally asked the police in! 'We are respectable members of the community,' Aunt Anna said, speaking pointedly in Afrikaans to remind Rachel of who she was. 'None of the family has ever been in trouble with the government.' Alone with her mother afterwards Rachel demanded to know what people had been saying. Her mother said, 'It's all a lot of nonsense. Anna should know better than to be giving you further worries at a time like this.' Then she changed the subject; so Aunt Anna had been right.

And then the thing they had known was coming finally happened, and Alistair was in prison. And of all those tensions and strained loyalties she could remember only that through him she had been offered the chance to take political action and she had backed away from it. The police had taken him and had left her. At some level beneath rationality that made her guilty...

A few months after she had started work at the library and met Anab, Alistair finally left. As he later never tired of pointing out, it was Rachel who told him to go, but she simply put words around the separation that he himself had created by never being there. After years of trying not to admit to herself how little it bothered him that he scarcely saw her or the children, something cracked and she saw with sudden clarity that he would never be back again in any meaningful sense. What brought about this revelation was, oddly enough, the prospect of a new and more secure job for Alistair - based, this time, in New York. There was something about the quality of his self-absorbed excitement - Fantastic opportunity! A journal with a world-wide audience, excellent reputation! And Rachel saw herself uprooted once again, landed in yet another strange city, to cope on her own just as she had had to here, while Alistair continued to rush around the world. More than that, she realised, perhaps for the first time, that she was no longer just coping, she had made a new life of her own - and it was here, in this place she had never chosen to come to but which had now become her home. And the children, she was not again going to move them from their activities, their friends, just to make another base for Alistair in another city. Let him go to New York. He could stop over and see the children from there, it could scarcely be less often than it was now. But whatever he did, she was staying put.

And from now on, she said, her anger riding strident on the wave that had taken so long to break, she wanted it recognised that their lives were entirely separate from each other, except in relation to the children. She didn't mind about the legal things, she just wanted to be free emotionally, to learn to face the fact that she was unimportant in his life, and to try to make him unimportant in hers. So would he please get out, make a clean cut. Nothing could be more painful than this slow, agonisingly slow decay.

It was interesting how few people she spoke to about the separation. Alistair had been with her so little that few of her friends from the school had ever seen him. They had accepted her as she already was in practice, a single parent. It seemed pointless now to make announcements about it. She wrote to her mother, of course, overcoming a certain resistance to providing Aunt Anna and the others with such fruitful material for saying I told you so. What did it matter? They were thousands of miles away, she would not have to listen to them or decide whether to argue. The only people who were involved in the question in any real way were Hymie and Lillian, the South African friends in Golders Green who had taken them in when they had first arrived. They were Alistair's friends more than hers, a generation older than her and with his kind of political involvement, and she talked to them perhaps for that reason, needing to explain to someone who knew Alistair and valued him, and would yet be able to accept what she had done. They were sad but not very surprised, and moved immediately to practical support. Alistair would need somewhere to stay when he stopped over in London to see the children, and of course he must come to them.

She did tell Pat, her colleague in the library. Pat said simply, 'You're better off without him. Who needs men?' The briskness was helpful, though Rachel was far from being able to match it herself.

3

A November day, miserable and blustery. The door to the Infants School kept blowing open, letting in a gust of cold air as each new mother and child arrived, to begin taking off coats and wiping noses. Rachel was trying to get Ben to stay still long enough for her to get his wellington boots off. The door blew open again. She looked up to see Anab, bringing with her another woman.

'My friend,' Anab was saying, 'from Somalia.' Then she added, unnecessarily, for the woman's face made it clear, 'She has just arrived.'

Rachel straightened up to say hello, leaving Ben to slip out of her grasp. She felt, as on the first day she had seen Anab, an instant, painful recognition. The woman stood as if she had been placed by someone else. Her clothes, superficially like Anab's, hung limply around her. Her face seemed to shrink into the surrounding headscarf, as if to escape from the world's buffetting. Two children stood silently next to her, a girl of seven or eight with fat little plaits all over her head, and a boy a couple of years younger, holding tightly to his mother's long skirt. Anab said, 'Her name is Haleemo. Her boy Ahmed is coming into Ben's class.'

Ben was holding his new dinosaur up to the face of the big-eyed child, saying, 'Look, it came in the post from my dad!' The little boy stared, but did not back away. Rachel thought fleetingly, Ben will go bananas if the child thinks he's giving it to him; but her attention was not on the children. She was watching Haleemo's shell-shocked face.

Rachel asked, 'Does she know any English?'

'She can understand. It is only that she is not used to speaking it.'

In that case, thought Rachel, we should stop talking over her head as if she weren't here. But it was difficult to believe that Haleemo did understand, for her expression did not change; not when she turned her eyes vaguely down towards her son, nor in response to Rachel's smiling Hello, nor even when Anab spoke to her in Somali. She just stood, looking as if she did not know where she was, or why, or what to do about it.

Afterwards Rachel found it difficult to remember exactly how it had happened that her life had become so entangled with Haleemo's. That Haleemo needed support in those first weeks was obvious, but Anab provided that, taking her to the Housing Department, the school, the doctor, interpreting not only the language but the system. Rachel did nothing more than chat to her in the playground on the afternoons she fetched the children, and even that was of the most minimal kind, what she thought of privately as the 'Cold today, isn't it?' level. Then Anab announced that she had enrolled for a computing course, to start after Christmas, which meant that her daughter Sado would get herself home after school and Anab would no longer be part of the daily gatherings of mothers in the playground. Yes, that must have been when things began imperceptibly to change, with Haleemo beginning to turn to her with the questions she might once have asked Anab.

And then there was the day Haleemo nearly fainted. It was a Monday, a week or two after the start of the January term. From the moment Rachel arrived at the school she knew something was wrong with Haleemo. Her headscarf was pulled over her forehead lower than usual, and she was standing right up against the school building, almost leaning against it. Rachel went up to her. 'Is anything the matter?'

'I feel -' Haleemo put her hand to her head and swayed slightly.

Rachel said, 'Come and sit down,' and led her by the arm to the nearest bench - grimy, wet with rain; never mind, she needed to sit. 'When did you start feeling like this?'

'Few weeks,' said Haleemo, and sat down abruptly. Rachel sat next to her and took hold of her hand. It was icy cold. A couple of other women began to gather round, peering anxiously. 'She looks really poorly,' said one. 'You ought to be in bed,' said another, speaking loudly as if that would ensure that Haleemo understood her English. Evelyn said, 'She can't possibly walk home. I'll go and ask Sophie if she can give her a lift.'

Rachel thought, But the children? She's not capable of looking after them. She turned to Haleemo, still sitting with head drooping, passively allowing them to take charge. 'Haleemo, shall I take your children to my house for an hour or two?'

For a moment there was no response. Then Haleemo's head moved, a minimal nod. She said, 'Yes. I want rest.'

Ben came hurtling towards them, calling, 'Me and Ahmed fed the rabbit!' Ahmed raced past, landing up with a thump on the seat next to Haleemo and starting to talk to her in rapid Somali. Now Asha was there, quietly standing near them before Rachel had noticed her coming. Haleemo spoke briefly to the children. The little girl looked up at Rachel, anxious, undecided. Rachel went down on her haunches to bring her face to the same level as the child's. 'Asha, your mum is not well. We'd like you and Ahmed to come and play at Ben's house this afternoon.'

All the way home the child Asha held on to Rachel's hand, saying nothing, looking solemn. Not so Ahmed; he could hardly have

22

understood most of Ben's chattering but he let it roll over him, tuning in when it suited him and interrupting periodically to say things of his own, isolated words from both languages, strung together by excited gestures. When they got home Ben took Ahmed up to the room he and Simon shared, and within ten minutes they had invented a game which required no words, driving toy cars into each other and roaring with laughter when they crashed. Asha perched tentatively on the edge of Ben's bed and watched from the sidelines, clearly with no intention of taking part. Simon had ostentatiously collected a pile of his books and gone to shut himself in Rachel's room, making it plain that if his mother wanted to invite seven year old girls home for the afternoon she could not expect that he was going to entertain them.

'Come,' said Rachel to Asha, 'let's see what you'd like to do.' They went down to the kitchen where she tried to interest Asha in drawing with coloured pens. Asha performed obediently for about three minutes, then stopped and sat staring with her large dark eyes. What is she seeing? Rachel wondered. The profusion of children's paintings on the wall in front of her? The brightly coloured magnetic letters on the fridge door? The window above the sink, looking out onto the garden where the light was already disappearing, making the long stems of the climbing rose stand out, angular and gaunt?

'Would you like to help me cut up the tomatoes?' Rachel asked, and put the chopping board and knife and washed tomatoes in front of her, cutting one and putting it in the bowl to show her what needed doing. The child risked a quick smile that lit her brown face and seemed to stretch the skin over her high cheekbones. Her hair, that was usually held firmly in place by little fat plaits, was today a mass of springy curls. I'd love to touch it, Rachel thought, and was surprised by the power of the picture this awoke in her. Where - when - had she done just that? The memory must be coming from far back, when she was a very young child. Now she could see it more clearly. She was standing on a table and being allowed to pat a head of just such springy African hair. That was it! The kitchen table in her childhood home in Lourensrus, and Ellen, the woman who had looked after her, taking off her neat red headscarf to let the child Rachel touch her hair...

Kate arrived home, and the problem of how to keep Asha entertained was solved. 'Come to my room,' Kate said, leading Asha off as if she were the one person she had been waiting to see. 'There's something I want to show you.' When Rachel went upstairs ten minutes later she found them both on the floor sorting through all Kate's earrings and hair bands.

She hadn't intended to stay long at Haleemo's. She was conscious of having left Kate in charge and of all the clearing up still to do. But when she walked in with Asha and Ahmed to the dark, depressing hallway of the divided house, and saw how bare and miserable were the two rooms they occupied - an armchair that looked as if it had come off a skip, cardboard boxes against one wall, a double bed that almost filled what was clearly both bedroom and living space, a television on the floor in a corner - she was shocked into feeling that she couldn't just deposit the children and go. So she accepted Haleemo's offer of tea.

Haleemo still looked far from well. She directed at the children a couple of rapid sentences in Somali - telling them to keep out of her way, to judge from the tone. The children went straight to the television and Rachel followed Haleemo into the kitchen. It was even barer than the first room, not only of furniture but also of food. She buys what she's going to cook each day, Rachel guessed, and probably saves on food for herself to get the children what they need.

'Have you seen the doctor?' she asked. 'About feeling faint?'

'Yes,' Haleemo said, her voice flat. 'Two weeks before.' She shrugged. 'He say, not serious.' She was pouring the tea, which she had made by boiling up everything in the pan - water, milk, sugar, tea. She put the mug in front of Rachel, went to the cupboard to get out a packet of cardamoms and dropped two into each mug. The sweet steam curled up into Rachel's nostrils, strange yet pleasant.

'Did he examine you?' she asked.

'No.'

'He didn't take any blood tests?'

'No.'

'Didn't he give you anything? Any tablets? Or tell you what he thought was the problem?'

'No. He just say, Maybe you worried about something.'

'That's hopeless!' Rachel flared, far too incensed to bother about whether she was interfering. 'You should go back, the doctor must examine you, that's what they're there for. There may be some illness, like anaemia. If they find what it is, they can put it right.'

Haleemo made no reply.

Rachel tried another tack. 'I'll be happy to have Asha and Ahmed home again if you'd like me to. They had a good time today.' She realised she was thinking of the children's needs as much as of Haleemo's. What did they do all afternoon, in this bare flat with almost no toys, and a mother who was too tired or too preoccupied with her own anxieties to give them much attention?

Haleemo sipped her tea. She didn't say yes and she didn't say no. Rachel sat quiet too, her hands cupped around her mug, the sugary-spicey after taste clinging to her palate. Her eyes travelled over the dampstained wallpaper. From the next room came the sound of the television - canned laughter, hilarity at the press of a button.

*

The librarian listened coldly as Rachel told him that she would have to leave at three because her childminder was ill. 'If there's no other arrangement you can make,' he said curtly, 'I suppose there's nothing to be said.' But his eyes had plenty to say. I've already made concessions to you about evening duties, I didn't expect to have to make any more.

She walked back to the section of the stacks she had been straightening up, passing Pat on the way. 'Well?' asked Pat.

'It was like being up in front of the headmaster for smoking in the toilets.'

'Forget it,' Pat grinned. 'He'll recover.'

She left work at the last possible moment, though the librarian wasn't even there to observe - he had gone off to some meeting. She just missed a bus and had to run most of the way, feeling irrationally angry with the librarian, the memory of whose cold eyes had prevented her from leaving sensibly five minutes earlier. You can't win, she thought. Either you cheat work or you cheat the children. She arrived, puffed, two minutes after three fifteen, to be greeted by Ben, saying, as he now did every time she collected him, 'Can Ahmed come?'

Ahmed came. And when Ahmed came Asha came too, because it was impossible to let her stand there next to him, with her neat tight plaits over her beautifully moulded head, her enormous eyes looking up at Rachel, and not include her. Once they were home she would hover in the kitchen while Rachel worked, tackling with intense concentration whatever little task Rachel suggested, and giving a shy

25

proud smile when she was complimented. Compared to Ben and Simon, who made such specific emotional demands, neither she nor Ahmed appeared to expect individual attention. That made them easy to look after, but it also made Rachel wonder about Haleemo.

It was hard to say what she felt about Haleemo. Certainly not the kind of immediate friendship she had with Anab. At first Haleemo had seemed glad to let the children come alone, but increasingly she chose to come too. Rachel felt slightly trapped by her presence, unable to get on with her housework, which always had to be crammed into her afternoons off. Haleemo drank the tea that Rachel made for her, and then she simply sat. Maybe that was what she would have been doing at home anyway, but it felt wrong to leave her to do that here. She tried asking Haleemo about her life in Somalia. She was told that both Haleemo and Anab were from the biggest town in the north, Hargeisa. No, they had not known each other before they came here, but they were relatives. When Rachel asked what kind of relative, Haleemo indicated that this would be impossible to explain to an English person; and then she lapsed into silence again.

Another time Rachel learnt that Haleemo's husband had been a businessman with several shops in Hargeisa. She had lived in a big house with relatives all around her, including, it seemed, one who lived in their house and whose sole function was to help with the housework. 'I never doing too much work alone, like here,' Haleemo said with considerable feeling. Rachel tried to conjure up a picture of Haleemo in a large house with a servant, a member of a privileged class. It was in fact easy enough to do. She saw her own mother, her aunts, all the white households in Lourensrus; just change the colour of the madam.

Filing away journals in the library she came across a stack of National Geographics, going back years. She would love to be able to take these home for Kate to see, the colours in the photographs were amazing. Kate had just joined the photography club at school; modelling herself on Alistair - and Rachel pushed away an irrational stab of - what? Jealousy? Rejection? Why on earth shouldn't the girl want to be like him in that way? Heaven knows, she had little enough of her father to hold on to.

Camel herders of the Horn, page 37. That must be Somalia, surely. She turned to page 37; a full page photo of camels standing near a deep well, waiting to be watered. They crowded in close, yet held their noses absurdly in the air as if this was all no concern of theirs. Young men naked to the waist bent over the rim of the well to receive the containers of water being passed up by a boy who had climbed half way down into the well. Their bare limbs shone with sweat. The landscape around them was semi-desert, nothing much growing except for a few scrubby bushes. Not unlike the drier bits of the Karoo.

Another picture, this one of Hargeisa. She looked with sharpened interest - Anab and Haleemo's home. Low white buildings, the earth cleared around them. An umbrella tree. Beneath it marketeers sat on the ground next to their spread-out wares. Men stood talking, dressed in long white cloths wound round the waist to make three quarter length skirts, with shirts loose over them. Some wore another long cloth draped over one shoulder. Many of them carried walking sticks - young men too, oddly, as if the sticks were items of fashion.

A place called the Haud. *The Haud before the rains*. Little sign of life. Scratchy remains of last year's grass, yellow and brittle. One dried up tree in the foreground that looked as if it would never produce a leaf again. On the left a pile of massive boulders, like those at the top of the hill behind her childhood home. *The Haud after the rains*, a savannah landscape with tall, gently waving grass, stretching away to the distance; enticing, life-giving. A thorn tree in the foreground, silhouetted against the immense sky - Good Lord, it was the same tree, the same spot exactly. Those rocks on the left, identical. Amazing.

And extraordinary also that looking at photographs of a place she had never seen should make her homesick. Hargeisa was at the other end of the continent from Lourensrus, yet as she looked she could feel on her skin the dry heat, she could smell the dust, could feel the scratches on the soles of her bare feet as she climbed Duiwelskop, clambering over rocks to get to the top, to look out over the drought-stricken veld that stretched away to the west. There was so little grazing that each farm spread for miles, yet the land was never, to her eyes, barren. And the sky arched above it, an immense dome of cloudless blue that dwarfed even the immensity of the land...

Perhaps it was the pictures of Hargeisa that caught her; perhaps the child Asha's springy hair and solemn eyes, latching on to a corner of her affections with her silent, concentrated gaze, and refusing to let go.

Perhaps it was none of these things, but sheer indignation at the woman in the DHSS office.

Know Your Benefits, the leaflet had announced confidently, and then given no concrete information, just a lot of waffle about making sure if you were on a low income that you were getting the financial help you were entitled to from the Department of Health and Social Security. 'These leaflets aren't worth the paper they're written on,' Rachel said to Pat. 'I don't know why we bother to keep them in the library. How is anyone supposed to find out what they're entitled to?'

Pat said, 'By going to the DHSS office and sitting in a queue.'

'You speak from personal experience, I gather!'

Pat nodded, her earring swaying in emphasis. 'I was unemployed for six months when I first came to London.'

'I was hoping there was a short cut. Haleemo's asked me to go with her - the last time she went she didn't understand what they were saying. But it means taking the children with us and I can think of nothing worse than spending hours in a waiting room while Ben and Ahmed charge all over the place.'

'See if you can get someone to give you an answer on the phone,' Pat suggested. 'The Citizens Advice Bureau should, even if the DHSS won't.'

The DHSS wouldn't. 'We don't answer questions about particular cases over the phone,' the woman said. The Citizens Advice Bureau couldn't. 'I can tell you the general regulations,' the woman said, 'and we can work out what we think she's entitled to. But if she's getting less than she should be, she'll have to get the DHSS to reassess anyway. You might as well go straight there.'

Waiting at the DHSS took as long as she had imagined it would. She alternated between teaching Asha finger games and trying to provide amusements for Ben and Ahmed, other than seeing how far the chairs would tip back without falling over. Meanwhile she worried stupidly about having left Kate and Simon alone at home all afternoon. When they finally got to see someone, it was to be told that Haleemo's pitifully low weekly allowance was all she was entitled to. 'But look,' Rachel said, 'these figures you showed me for a single mother with two children, that's more than she's getting!'

'Yes, but she's a refugee,' the young woman said. 'Until she has her proper papers she's not eligible for the full rate.'

Rachel stared. 'Do refugees need to eat less than other people?' she demanded.

The young woman took defence in formality. 'It's the regulations,' she said. And Rachel gathered up the children and Haleemo and left, fuming, as in her childhood she had fumed helplessly at the regulations of that other government, and her mother had said, mildly, 'That's just the way things are Rachel. You've got to learn to be sensible.'

4

For Hassan, the first sign of things to come, or rather that he was to be drawn into them personally not just professionally, was the phone call from his cousin Nuh in Somalia. October 4th, 1987. He remembered the date precisely. A Sunday. He had been out all evening at his friend Jeyam's flat in Camden, talking, listening to music, lazing about. Jeyam, with his straight black hair dangling over his eyes, had been reading The Observer and entertaining Hassan with a stream of caustic comments about politicians in general and Sri Lankan and British politicians in particular... It seemed a long time ago. He had forgotten that he had ever been capable of such complete relaxation.

He had got back to his own flat late. The house was in darkness, except for the blue light of late-night television flickering through the thin curtains of Mrs. Holden's flat on the ground floor. He let himself in - anonymous stairwell with its worn patterned carpet, gas meters on the wall by the entrance - and went up the stairs in his normal style, two at a time and without bothering to put on the landing light. As he reached his door he heard the telephone ringing. Probably Jeyam with some final wisecrack to impart; no one else would phone at this hour. The key seemed to need more fiddling than usual, he must get a new one cut. The door finally moved. He pushed in, flicked the light switch, flung down his things and made a dash to pick up the phone. 'So what's the hurry, mate?' he said.

It was not Jeyam. It was a voice speaking in Somali. His cousin Nuh, phoning from Mogadishu.

His first feeling was one of sharp joy, a greedy slaking of thirst. It was so long since he had had proper news from home. But almost immediately this was overlayed by apprehension. 'I've been trying all night,' said Nuh. The line was fuzzy. 'I was out,' Hassan said, his chest tight. 'What is it?' His words echoed back at him. There was a burring noise. He caught the words, 'My uncle -' then Nuh's voice disappeared. Fear began to creep over him, starting like a pain in the groin. 'Nuh, is it *Aabahay*?' - my father? It seemed a long time before Nuh's voice replied, 'Hargeisa prison. Three days ago. My father sent someone from Hargeisa with the news.'

The fear had exploded, become a wild anger. 'Why?' Hassan yelled, and in the echo he could hear his voice was out of control. 'Why? Why? Why him?' The line crackled, cutting out Nuh's answer; and then went dead.

He sat by the phone all night, drinking one cup of coffee after another, waiting in case Nuh might phone again. By ten o'clock next morning he remembered that he ought to have been at work. He telephoned the office. Barbara answered, 'Advice Centre for Refugees, can I help you?' Her familiar voice seemed a long way away, crossing miles of barren desert to reach him. 'It's Hassan,' he said. 'I'm not coming in today. Something's happened.'

He flew to Djibuti the next day. He could not risk flying in to Somalia itself, not with his job. But Djibuti was near enough, the border only a couple of day's journey from Hargeisa. He would get across somehow.

In Djibuti he managed to trace an uncle, Ismail - closer to his own age than to his father's, and Hassan could not remember ever having met him before, but that made no difference. Ismail accepted without question that he would take Hassan in, give him the names of people who might be helpful to him, and arrange a lift for him on a truck that was heading south for Somalia the next day.

It was only as the truck neared the border post that Hassan's mind started functioning normally again, and he began to tense up at the prospect of the difficulties to be overcome. The whole of northern Somalia was a militarised zone. Even for the people who lived there, trying to move from one place to another was hazardous; for someone coming from outside it might prove impossible. In Djibuti he had heard contradictory reports of what to expect. One of Ismail's contacts had insisted that the only sure way to get in was to use his British passport, pretend not to speak Somali, and claim to be part of an aid agency based in Hargeisa. With his light skin he would get away with posing as a foreigner. 'The man's mad,' Ismail had said. 'Everyone knows the aid agencies are pulling out of Hargeisa.' Don't do nothing to draw attention to yourself, he urged. Dress casually, use your Somali passport, speak only Somali from the moment you get on that truck. If anyone wants to know, tell them you've been buying things in Djibuti and you're going back to your uncle's house. There's nothing in the shops in Hargeisa anymore, people are always coming across the border to stock up. And as for not looking like a Somali, that's nonsense. You're exactly like your father. If anyone says anything about your colour, just tell them it's Arab blood.

In the event the border was less of a problem than Hassan had feared. Another truck had arrived shortly before them. The people who had travelled perched on top of the goods at the back had all piled off and were standing talking, chewing, sharing food they had brought wrapped in pieces of cloth, while the border guards stripped the truck of its contents and insisted that the driver open every sack and box. They were clearly more interested in goods than in people. The driver was reacting with what Hassan thought foolhardy haughtiness, but even that had its uses, for it meant the guards paid scant attention to the truck Hassan was travelling on.

Across the border, the road to Hargeisa seemed interminable. It was the end of the hot, dry season and the rains were late. A bad year, the man next to him said. People were being driven further and further afield to find grazing for their camels, then having to trek back thirty miles or more at the end of every few weeks to the nearest wells. Hassan had never been in a place as dry as this. His childhood memories of visits to Hargeisa were nearly all from a time of year when there had been grass left over from the spring rains, and the land still looked like a place that could sustain life. This was something different, a vast, empty land of stretching sand alternating with dramatic rocky outcrops. Barren, hostile. And hot, suffocatingly hot. The heat was an onslaught from which there was no escape. He sat squashed between his fellow-passengers on a lumpy sack from which something hard pressed into his thigh. His legs, forced at different angles into the only available spaces, had lost all sensation. One arm was stretched out to push against another sack in a fruitless attempt to lessen the jolts as the truck rattled and bumped over the almost non-existent road. Every part of his body ached, but the discomfort was as nothing compared to the scorching attack of hot air that battered him, unceasingly. Thought became impossible.

They slept that night by the roadside. The men spread out cloths on the earth, the women lay crumpled together in the back of the truck. The next day was like the one before, interminable, punctuated only by army checkpoints where soldiers arrogantly pointed and poked with their rifles. Hassan's initial tension had by now been replaced by a heat-induced passivity. With all the others he would pile out of the truck and simply wait for the senseless ordeal to be over.

It was the afternoon of the third day before the truck finally began to struggle up the perilous mountain pass to the plateau, and into Hargeisa itself. Hassan had thought that he was by now past caring what happened to him, but this turned out not to be the case. As he unfolded his cramped limbs and stumbled off the truck for the last time he experienced an almost overwhelming fear of the power of the soldiers coming towards them. When the search was over and he had got away with no more than the usual amount of attention, he felt weak, as if his legs might give way under him. For a moment or two he was incapable of movement. Then he began walking, as slowly as he could manage though he wanted to run, towards uncle Ali's house.

He spent two weeks in Hargeisa and achieved nothing. Anyone could have told him he was wasting his time. If he'd given it two minutes' thought before booking his ticket he would have known it himself, but he would probably have gone anyway. It was terrible enough having to live with the knowledge of his father shut away in prison; at least he knew he had been there himself, had been to see every possible official, had, through uncle Ali's perseverance and the passing of a substantial sum between him and the head of the prison, been permitted finally to see his father for himself. Once, for twenty minutes.

'My son,' said his father. 'You shouldn't have come.'

'I had to, *Aabo*,' Hassan said. *Aabo* - Dad - to be using the word again, and in these circumstances! It was over five years since he and his father had seen each other, that last summer in Mogadishu. Five years! Of course since then there had been no more long university holidays, but that shouldn't have stopped him. Yet every time he had suggested coming back his father had written to say, Not yet. Things are tense. Wait a while. And by the time he had waited a while he had started work at the Advice Centre, and his father was writing, Not now. Not with your job. Until here they were, more than five years later and meeting in a prison, while an armed guard stood two feet from his father, listening to every word they said.

His father stared at him blankly. 'There is nothing you can do,' he said.

'There has to be.'

His father smiled, a tired smile. 'You haven't changed,' he said. Hassan wanted to say, 'Nor have you,' but it would have been a lie. The words would not be spoken. He stretched his hand out to touch his father's face, as if by doing so he could bring back to the skin the warm dark glow that he remembered, and see his eyes laugh, and then the laugh spread to his whole face.

'Aabo, do you get the food we're sending in?'

His father shrugged. 'I get food.'

The guard behind him moved slightly. Hassan asked, 'What about books? I brought you some in case you haven't got any.' He started to hand them to his father. The guard stepped forward and took them. Hassan said loudly, 'According to the regulations you're allowed reading material.' His father looked past him, making no reply. Hassan switched to English and spoke softly, fast. 'Aabo, uncle Ali is doing everything he can. There's a senior officer he spoke to yesterday. Something may come of it. Don't give up, neither of us will rest until you're out of here.'

The guard was right next to his father now, breathing down his neck, and Hassan was suddenly terribly afraid of what would happen after he had gone, when no one was there to see. Every time he took a risk it was his father who would pay.

His father said in Somali, slowly and clearly, 'I want you to go back, and be safe.'

He had come back. Not because his father had told him to, but because in the end there was nothing else to do. 'Go back,' uncle Ali said. 'The last thing your father needs now is to hear that you too have got yourself into trouble.'

He had come back. Back to an English landscape that just three days earlier had been devastated by the great October hurricane, that in the space of a few hours had flattened millions of trees, shattered boats into pieces of driftwood, thrown caravans over cliffs. The debris of destruction was all around when he returned. Everyone was still talking about it, about the suddenness, the terror of waking in the early hours to hear a tree crashing onto the roof, a home destroyed. For Hassan it was comforting, in an odd way, to find the calamity that had befallen him reflected here on a cosmic scale, in this quiet island where people thought such things could never happen to them. But within a few weeks the shattered glass from the office-block windows was swept away and new glass installed. The staff of the insurance companies worked overtime, processing claims. The trees that blocked the roads were hauled onto the pavements and eventually sawed into logs, neatly stacked, awaiting collection. On the commons new trees were planted to replace the old. People found other things to talk of. Only he was left with his private trauma undiminished, the picture of his father's suffering face carried constantly within him, while he sat in his safe office behind a desk - as his younger cousin Mohamed later so accurately described it.

He found it impossible in the weeks after his return from Hargeisa to cope with evenings alone in his flat. He took to staying on later and later at work, telling himself he had no choice, he had to get through the backlog. But he seemed unable to keep up with his own cases, let alone supervise or support anyone else's. Mike, for instance. Hassan was irritated at the mere sight of Mike's desk. He really must tackle the man. If Mike chose to leave three days' worth of unwashed tea mugs on the windowsill that was his affair, but the files stacked one on top of each other in no particular order represented other people's lives and one day some crucial papers were going to get lost - But he had done nothing about it. Like so many other things.

Eventually he would lock up the office, long after all the others had gone, and depart armed with piles of paper to protect himself against the evening. Or he would go straight from work to the community centre in Whitechapel, once again joining the evening rota to give free legal advice as he had done in the years when he was doing his artricles and had needed to escape from the suffocating atmosphere of a city law firm. If his friends in the centre wondered why he suddenly had time for this, and to attend extra meetings, they accepted it without comment; probably they were all too busy to question it. Then after the meetings he would go down to the canteen, to sit talking with whoever was there, delaying the moment of going home to his empty flat, of confronting once again his fundamental impotence.

'It's up to you,' uncle Ali had said. 'We can do nothing.' And Hassan had seen that it was so. Uncle Musa, the oldest of the brothers, had not even tried. Hassan had expected to find him raging, invoking the name of the Almighty to destroy his enemies for this assault on the family honour, but he appeared to have withdrawn from worldly combat; suddenly an old man, he sat for hours together reciting verses from the Qur'an. Uncle Ali had behaved more normally, springing into immediate action, brother defending brother. By means known only to himself he had arranged, for a price, that his brother would not be kept in the worst of prison conditions and that, for the moment at least, he would be protected from torture. But beyond that, the wealth which would once have bought his brother's freedom was powerless. And Hassan, watching, saw that in uncle Ali too there were subtle but disturbing changes. Now when he was not negotiating with officials he was talking to distant cousins whom he had summoned from the interior, and the talk was of camels. He was quietly converting his capital into the oldest kind of wealth, the only one to be relied on for ultimate survival.

'It's up to you,' uncle Ali had said. 'Tell people over there. Get them to make a fuss internationally. It's the only way to get him out.' Over there! If uncle Ali could only have seen what the reality was like over here. His father was unknown outside Somalia, his detention no more dramatic than that of thousands of others. Hundreds of thousands. How could he, Hassan, one equally unknown person in this huge, impersonal city, expect to make even the slightest impact on the awareness of those millions of busy, self-concerned people who swarmed to work on the underground every morning? He had given his father's details to Amnesty International. He had harried their staff to accept him as one of their Prisoners of Conscience. He had galvanised his own local branch (all thirteen people) from its moribund state into taking part in the letter-writing campaign on his father's behalf. Together he and Jeyam had written an article about human rights violations in Somalia, which Jeyam had managed to get published in a student journal (circulation two hundred?) Nothing. It amounted to nothing. And meanwhile there was his father's face, shutting him out - 'Go back, and be safe.'

35

I don't want to be safe, Hassan wanted to yell, alone in his flat at night with no one to yell at. Not when you're not. Aabo, Aabo.

His mother, as he might have expected, was unable to help him in the way he most needed. He had hoped that a crisis of this magnitude might break the habit of years and make it possible for them to talk more openly about his father, but it seemed to have the opposite effect. What had always been a difficult area between them had now became a terrifying one, to be avoided at all costs. He had wanted to see her before he flew out to Djibouti, but after trying all day to reach her on the phone had in the end only got through to her from Heathrow. She had been teaching at the college all day, she said, and had gone straight from there to a concert with a friend. Over the phone it was impossible to expect of her anything more than she gave, an agonised 'Oh no!' when she heard what had happened, followed by a difficult silence when Hassan told her that he was about to fly out. 'Take care of yourself,' she said, and though the strength of her caring was obvious in her voice, it was impossible to gauge what she thought about his going. She sent no message to his father.

At that stage Hassan was still scarcely aware of what he was feeling. He was simply acting, proceeding to the next thing with a single-minded determination that could waste no time on peripheral emotions. But once he was back and all possibilities of action had dried up, the hurt opened up again. It was four days before he phoned her. Not that he did not want to speak to her - on the contrary, there was no one else here who knew his father, no one else to whom it would have been possible to talk. But the very intensity of his need made him afraid to say much, in case she could not respond. When he finally went to see her, he told her what had happened so briefly and, he realised it himself, in a voice so defensive that it was scarcely surprising she did not press him for more details.

And really, there was very little to tell. His father had seen some soldiers roughing up a young boy, who was creating a fuss at their taking away his uncle. It happened every day, but this time Hassan's father had given way to the indignation that years of exposure to such crimes had not dampened. He had confronted the soldiers. So stupid, uncle Ali said, for of course the boy had taken courage from finding himself supported. He had lurched forward, beating his fists wildly and ineffectually at the armed men who held his uncle, until one of the soldiers had settled the matter by pointing his rifle at the boy and shooting him. Hassan's father had gone straight to the army commander to insist that action be taken against the soldier. So unbelievably naive, said uncle Ali, shaking his head. After all his years of working in government offices in Mogadishu, watching the ways of those in power...

They had arrested him on the spot. He had had a ten minute trial; the charge and his guilt were announced almost simultaneously.

Hassan's mother sat very still, and despite everything he was comforted by the concentration with which she listened. Every now and then her hand would move to flip some strands of her long soft hair off her face. It was a gesture he associated with her from his earliest childhood, for she alone in his family had the kind of hair you could flick in that way. Each time she did it he felt a longing that he did not know how to express. Her eyes were afraid, but neither of them could talk about that fear.

5

'Cold today, isn't it?' said Mrs Holden as Hassan left for work, almost colliding with her on the doorstep as she brought in her milk. He agreed that it was cold today, which it certainly was, the first real attack of winter. He had seen bulbs sprouting in sheltered corners of the park. Now they would be killed off again. Did they get a second chance when that happened, he wondered? He didn't like it when even the weather went wrong.

At work the central heating chose that morning to break down. Sod's law. Fortunately it had been on for a couple of hours before it gave up, otherwise they would all have frozen, spending the day in that Victorian building with its high ceilings and draughty floorboards and windows that didn't fit their frames. Barbara found a couple of electric bar heaters in the bottom of a cupboard in her office. One she had to keep in reception, where the queue was building up - people huddled in inadequate coats, already chilled from standing waiting for buses to get here, people whose needs were urgent and who would rather wait in an unheated room than be told to come back tomorrow. But that left five case workers' offices to be warmed from the one remaining heater.

'We could move it around,' Barbara suggested doubtfully, 'give each of you a turn.'

'No,' Hassan said, feeling for once clear and decisive as he had been before his father's arrest; perhaps it was the air of crisis, but a crisis of manageable size. 'Tell Mike and Juan to take their papers home and work from there. Jenny and Gita and I can take clients in the common room.'

So that was what they did, all huddled as close to the one ineffectual bar heater as possible. 'The pure refugee experience!' laughed Jenny in one of their brief pauses between clients. And in fact, although it was crowded and they kept having to go back to their offices to fetch other files, there was a cameraderie about the morning's work that he found comforting. It was Gita's first week in the job and Hassan saw that it was helpful to her to be in the same room as him and Jenny, able to get a quick answer to any query. Why hadn't he thought of that himself, instead of waiting for the heating to break down?

At lunch time the heating came on again. The moment Hassan was alone in his office he felt once again bowed down by an impossible task. He surveyed the morning's haul of paperwork. So much follow-up on each of these cases - when would he ever get to it? And what would it achieve, anyway? Advice Centre for Refugees and Asylum Seekers, they called themselves, but what was the point of giving advice when the rules were always stacked against the people they tried to advise? With an effort he made himself start sorting the papers into piles. Done. Not yet done. Urgent, to be done. Bala Shivanaratnam, Tamil refugee from Sri Lanka, granted leave to remain for only one year, leave now expired, application for extension. Why the hell hadn't the Home Office given him refugee status? He'd been in prison, tortured, his family terrorised by the army, what more evidence of persecution did they want? He dumped the papers wearily in his intray and turned to the next. A Zairean asylum seeker who had arrived without contacts, no address to go to - so he had spent the weekend in detention at the airport; now released on temporary admission. Emergency housing to be sorted out, letters to the DHSS, the housing department.

This one, a pathetic young man trying to get his wife and child out of a refugee camp in Afghanistan. Application for family reunion turned down by the Home Office. Could he appeal? the man had asked. Hassan had looked at the desperation in his eyes and explained as best he could that no, he could not appeal. He had only temporary permission to be here and therefore had no right to bring dependents in.

Nothing to be done.

That evening he went from work to the Whitechapel centre. There was no meeting, no special event, but there would be people. The canteen-bar was noisy, the air thick with smoke and the acrid smell of beer; or something else, an indefinable awareness that made him start looking to see where the Somalis were. *Qaat* leaves being chewed -

Yes, over there in the corner. A group of men sitting talking, keeping themselves separate from the beerdrinkers over at the bar, Hassan noticed wryly. As Muslims they did not touch alcohol, just got themselves high on chewing qaat instead! Most of them were his father's age, tall, thin, but wiry and tough; men of the interior who had grown up herding camels and living off camel's milk only for months together, and had then become seamen, taken on to British ships in Berbera or Aden. Stopping off in Cardiff, Liverpool, London; for a few months, a few years, half a life-time.

He heard his name called and recognised Aadan, a college friend of his cousin Mohamed, years ago in Mogadishu. They shook hands in the Somali way - full hand grasp, holding thumbs, back to full hand - and Hassan submitted to the pleasure of being drawn into the group. Having included him they went on with what they had been discussing. Politics, as usual. But there were more than enough people wanting to do the talking, so no pressure on him to join in. Just what he needed, to sit and listen to the familiar sounds, to feel himself being carried on a wave of talk, back, back...

It was just as his father had described it to him, long before Hassan himself had ever started coming here. His father must have been one of the first Somalis to be sent abroad to study. Hassan could picture him, leaving his room near the university when the homesickness became unbearable, to hang around near the docks in the hopes of encountering Somali seamen; and through them discovering the cafes where they used to spend their time between voyages, where the cafe proprietor was himself a Somali, receiver and conveyer of news, unofficial banker. He imagined his father's face, alive with pleasure at having found again the kind of company he loved, sitting with them to drink tea, chew qaat, and talk, talk, almost as if they were back in Hargeisa. The pleasure was not simply hearing Somali spoken again, but the kind of talk - conversation as an art form, never using five words if you could say it in twenty, with companions who were accomplished orators or poets; men who could not read and write but who from boyhood onwards had loved to sit and listen to long poems being recited, and could memorise them with a facility that literate people have lost. They would return from a voyage to Berbera with the latest political poems that were circulating among people back home, with poems of clan hostilities, poems against the British and the Italians, poems demanding independence. Love poems -

Woman, lovely as lightning at dawn,
Speak to me even once

they sang, and remembered the plains of the Haud, where lightning held the promise of rain, longed for. As now they longed for home -

Your bright mouth and its loveliness,
Your fragrance, the look of you,
Ubah, flower-named, for these
My journey is forgotten.

And now thirty years later here was he, Hassan, sitting with these men just as his father used to. The thought comforted him.

They offered him qaat, but as usual he refused. 'Qaat takes away the need for sleep,' uncle Musa used to say, 'makes your mind sharper than by day.' He didn't want his mind to be sharper than by day. He wanted to be able to sleep, to blot out the pain that seemed now always to lurk, ready to pounce.

Back alone in his flat he saw that it was still far too early to go to bed. He picked up a book and began to read. A thriller, totally useless. He threw it down and reached for another. Translations of Somali poetry...

For as long as he could remember he had been mesmerised by the sonorous, alliterative phrases, not understanding them but wanting to possess them. 'Explain it to me, Aabo,' he used to demand, when the complex poetic vocabulary was beyond him. His father would say, 'Just listen and memorise. It has a power of its own whether you understand it or not.' But it didn't work that way for him, he knew it couldn't when he was away ten months of the year and had only the summers in Mogadishu, to sit on the verandah where his father and the other men talked for hours, and wait for the moment when someone would start reciting -

'Aabo, tell me about that one you were reciting tonight.'

Uncle Musa, who had never been to school, would start his usual rumblings about how the boy had been ruined since his mother had taken him off to England - 'Taught to use pen and paper for everything. Forgotten how to use his memory.' Aabo would turn it aside with a joke, or get angry and argue, depending on his mood. But at a certain point he seemed to recognise that Hassan was not going to absorb poetry as he himself had done as a child, and so he began to teach him. He would recite the poem slowly, line by line, explaining the detailed allusions and multiple meanings. Once Hassan understood, he found them easy to memorise, the easier perhaps because poetry now had an additional power for him - the power to keep him connected to his father's world, from which he was constantly being taken away.

By his mother.

He slammed the book closed, got up with a sudden restless movement, and went into the kitchen to put on a kettle. He stood over it waiting for it to boil. It was time he phoned his mother, he hadn't seen her for weeks. Nor had he thanked her for that cutting she had sent, the review of a new book on African literature; an intellectual offering where she couldn't manage an emotional one.

Was there nothing left that she could share with him of that world? Of the love that had given her the courage to defy the disapproval of her uncomprehending parents, and marry an African, someone from a remote desert colony they had never heard of? He tried to imagine his parents as students together. It was easy to see why she would have loved him - Abdillahi Dahir Farah, tall, proud of bearing, full of laughter; avid student of history, with an independence of mind that would have swept like clean clear air through the dusty collection of worn-out ideas that was all her parents had ever offered her, living their lives out behind carefully drawn net curtains in the small town in Hampshire that they had never left.

They had refused to meet him. Only after Hassan was born, his mother had told him, did they relent and invite her to bring the child for them to see. She said, not unless they would meet Abdillahi too. So they finally did, sitting tensely on the edges of their chairs and being scrupulously polite; three days before their daughter was due to leave for Somalia.

Now as an adult, knowing his mother in the life she had chosen to make for herself, he could understand why she had not been happy in Somalia, how the constant presence of all those other people in his father's house must have been a penance for her. But for him that was what made it home, all those people. Mohamed and the other Mogadishu cousins, Nuh and the countless others from Hargeisa, hundreds of miles away; but that did not stop them journeying to and fro to see each other; and just because it was such a long journey, they would stay weeks, months, long enough for the children to forget, almost, who belonged where. His aunts, nagging, scolding, with collective authority over any child who came within their reach; his uncles - Mohamed's father, Omar, impressive in his army officer's uniform yet spontaneous and fun loving, half a boy himself; the older uncles from Hargeisa, Ali and Musa, who would arrive in Mogadishu without notice in one of their huge long-distance trucks, bringing back stories of what had happened on their journeys. His father, his eyes alive with the pleasure of being with them all, sitting talking for hours, arguing vigorously, laughing.

His father had more brothers and sisters than Hassan could keep track of. Only gradually did he realise that many of them were half brothers and sisters, children of his grandfather's three wives. But to his father there was no distinction between them. Even if twenty years separated them and they had scarcely known each other in childhood, any of them and any of their far more numerous offspring were entitled to arrive at any moment and claim the hospitality that was automatically given to family members. And all the time they stayed they needed not only to be housed and fed and talked to, for hours on end, they also needed money, to taste what Mogadishu had to offer. Their brother (or uncle, or cousin) Abdillahi Dahir Farah had a good job in a government office, so it was assumed that he would provide it; which he did. 'You want me to turn away my own family?' Hassan would hear his father shouting when his mother objected. 'You don't know what you're saying, woman.' And Hassan too was ashamed that she was not more generous. Only after years in England did he come to understand how insecure she must have felt at the loss of control over her own life that his father's perpetually open purse represented.

42

But it wasn't only money. While the other women sat together in the courtyard, talking as they worked, or inside in the hot weather or the rains, Hassan's mother would withdraw into the one room she insisted on keeping as a private space. If she kept herself away too long his father would shout at her, flashing that quick anger of his that was gone ten minutes later. Hassan, watching anxiously, could see that his mother had no way of dealing with anger except to withdraw even further, shutting the door on herself and her books. Those books, that room, the need to be alone, all those made her different from the other women, more different even than her white skin or the fact that she spoke Somali so strangely. Alone together, his parents used English; as soon as the relatives appeared it had to be Somali, and she was immediately at a disadvantage, able to undertand most of what was going on, but never a part of it. His father changed, too. He became - not exactly distant towards her, but not prepared to show before others the intimacy that he expressed only in English. Hassan saw it, and with instant loyalty felt her hurt; but he also saw how his uncles behaved with their wives, and knew that his father could not do otherwise.

When his mother had told him that she was taking him to England, to school, Hassan had been completely bewildered. Why could he not keep going to school here in Mogadishu?

'Because,' said his mother, in that tense voice which made him wish she would sometimes get angry as his father did, 'because your father and I both want you to go to an English school, to get a good education.'

But if the school in Mogadishu was good enough for his cousins, why not for him? And when would they be coming back?

'In the summer,' she said, 'when the school has holidays.'

To Mohamed and Jama he repeated all this, and was beguiled for a while by their envy. Hassan, going to England! Through their eyes he began to see a place of great power and wealth, to which he was unexpectedly being given privileged access. But at night, watching his mother pack up his small collection of personal possessions, the confusion and sense of loss swept over him again. 'But why?' he pleaded. 'Why do we have to go?'

His mother packed all her books, but only some of her clothes, the English ones, leaving behind the long Somali skirts and headscarfs.

And then they left, so suddenly despite all the warning, going by boat to Aden and from there by plane to London, to a flat that seemed to him incredibly confined after the big open rooms and courtyard of the Mogadishu home, with no cousins, no one else at all in the flat except him and his mother, and no possibility of roaming around outside as he and his cousins had always done.

And then his English school - He could not have said what he had imagined, but certainly not this place, where there was no one to whom he could speak. His mother had always used English with him, but he hadn't liked it when she had done so in front of his cousins, and he would always answer in Somali. 'Hassan, speak in English,' she would say, 'you know perfectly well how to.' But he couldn't, not with Mohamed and Jama right there. And now here, in his English school, it was the teacher saying, 'Speak in English, Hassan,' and this time he found that he really couldn't, he did not know how to say the things he needed to. Nor could he understand half of what the children said, though he could tell that a lot of the time they were saying things about him, and they weren't complimentary, either. He became aware that being brown-skinned made him different from most of the children in his class, as his mother had been different from his family by being pale-skinned. The other children pointed at him, and stopped talking when he came near. 'Why don't you wash?' taunted one of the boys, calling across the playground to where he stood, alone. An older girl said, 'Leave him alone,' but his gratitude at having a protector soon disappeared, for she and her friend made a game of touching his curly hair, as if he were a doll to be played with. In class one of the boys refused to sit next to him. 'My dad says he's a nignog,' he said. The teacher gave them a lecture about not using nasty words, which drew more attention to Hassan than ever and made him feel even more excluded. But his need for company was stronger than all his other confused feelings; he wanted desperately to join in the playground games of these strange children. Only once he had learnt to understand what they were saying and then to talk as they did, did the remarks about blackies and the jungle cease.

Eventually summer came, and they went home. Of course it was still home; he was exhilarated to be there, to see Mohamed again and Jama and all the others, and of course his father whom he had missed terribly, feeling that London would have been different if his father could have been there with them. His older cousin Nuh was visiting from Hargeisa, now fifteen and almost one of the adults, yet always with time for him; and Sabah, Nuh's younger sister, alert and lively, bursting to swop stories. 'You missed the worst family argument ever,' she said, her eyes wide with drama. 'About me! Uncle Musa told my dad he would give up working with him if he wasted the business's money sending a girl to school!' His cousins wanted to hear all about his life in London. It was impossible to tell them. They had images of wealth and magnificence, and he had to find things to say to fulfil those expectations. He described the underground trains, the electric lights in all the streets, things that had fascinated him when he had first arrived but which had distracted him for only the briefest time from the awfulness of having to live with only his mother in a cold, wet place with closed doors everywhere.

And beneath the pleasure of being back was the knowledge that he was a visitor here now, no longer a proper member of the family. In a few weeks his mother would take him back to the place she now called home. He tried to block out the thought but it crept back to confront him on the rare occasions when he was alone; at night, just before he fell asleep...

As now he saw his father.

Every night. So clearly. But still he managed to block out the worst of the pain, for he did not see him as he had been in the prison, but rather as he remembered him from all the years in Mogadishu - his long face alive with energy, a strong dark brown; his eyes full of that quiet humour that could flare into huge laughter when he was surrounded by people he liked; his hair rising turban-like above his high forehead, just as Hassan's did; his sonorous voice reciting, in the chanting tones that were reserved for poetry -

Yet may God place a shield of coolest air
Between your body and the assailant sun...

He remembered still the excitement of showing his father the English translation of that poem. He had discovered the slim, unassuming volume in a sale of old books in the local library; until then he had not known that any Somali poetry had been written down, let alone translated. He had bought the book and rushed back home to shut himself in his room and devour it. For some reason that he did not try to think about he had kept it hidden from his mother. The next summer he had taken it back to show his father, whose amazement had exceeded his own. For an hour his father sat reading right through the book, saying nothing but every now and then recognising from the English something he knew in the original, and reciting it to himself in Somali as he read. Hassan went to get a book of his own and sat near him, wanting to be there the moment he finished. Eventually his father looked up, handed him the book and said, 'That one. Recite that one in English.' Hassan read,

> Now you depart, and though your way may lead
> Through airless forests thick with hagar trees,
> Through places steeped in heat, stifling and dry,
> Where breath comes hard, and no fresh breeze can reach,
> Yet may God place a shield of coolest air
> Between your body and the assailant sun -

'A shield of coolest air,' interrupted his father. 'Do you know what that is in Somali? *Hagoog layr ah.*' Hassan knew what *hagoog* was, protecting yourself against the sun, the wind, the dust, from your enemies; with a shawl wrapped around the head, perhaps, covering the whole body except for the eyes. 'But hagoog made of air!' his father said. 'That is the image of a great poet. This poem you should memorise, Hassan.' And in case he should forget, his father had recited that poem for him when he had left to return to England that year -

> *Now you depart...*

and again the next year and the next, till it had become a private ritual between them, repeated each time Hassan had to leave.

A shield of coolest air - It was his father who had needed that protection, not him; and God, as usual, had done very little to provide it.

The phone rang. His mother. Damn, he should have got in first. 'I was just about to phone you,' he said, stretching the truth considerably.

She sounded so pleased that he felt even more guilty. 'I've got tickets for Brahm's violin concerto,' she said. 'Would you like to come?'

'Great,' he said, and thought, 'That will be easier than a whole evening talking.'

He asked about her work - her college teaching, her research. She told him about the article she had just finished writing. Then she said, 'What about you? Any news?'

Come on, Hassan, he thought, tell her. Say, It never stops. I have Somali refugees arriving in my office every week, and each time I hear yet another terrible story of why they had to leave, it is as if *Aabahay*, my father, is talking...

He said, 'Oh, nothing much. Been pretty hectic at work.'

6

It was Rachel's turn on duty at the enquiries desk. A quiet time, usually, updating index cards between queries. A man came in, wanting the address of some organisation, a tall thin African in late middle age, with Anab's long features and confident bearing. A Somali, thought Rachel, he must be. He didn't know the name of the organisation, but he had heard they were people who helped refugees. CADAS, NACAS, something like that. It was the kind of task Rachel enjoyed, looking things up in reference books and having to use a bit of guesswork. The man joined in the spirit of the search and laughed in triumph with her when she finally handed over the slip of paper with the address and telephone number. His laughter made her momentarily homesick - African laughter, large and uninhibited, not necessarily for something humorous but just from pleasure. In the warmth of that feeling she chanced it and asked, 'You're from Somalia, aren't you?' He was delighted. 'You know some Somalis then?'

ACRAS, it had turned out to be. She had reckoned that if it had something to do with refugees there would be an R in it. Advice Centre for Refugees and Asylum Seekers.

Hassan pushed the ACRAS button and waited for the buzzer to open the door. He stopped briefly in reception to tell Barbara he was back, and then went to find Jenny. 'How did you get on?' she asked.

'Appeal postponed,' he said.

'Not again!'

'On my insistence this time. The interpreter spoke the wrong language. I ask you, in a deportation appeal!'

The clerk had not even been aware there was an issue as he had told Hassan blandly, 'Couldn't get a Kurdish interpreter for today, but we've got Arabic.'

Hassan had stared at him in disbelief. 'They're not the same language.'

The clerk said defensively, 'Your client's application states that he knows Arabic.'

'It's not his first language,' Hassan said, his anger rising once again at this vast impersonal system that sent people back to almost certain imprisonment and possible death, and left you no one to vent your anger on but an ineffectual clerk. 'It's like offering you a French interpreter who knows no English, and saying you ought to be able to cope because you once learnt French at school!'

In his office Gita was waiting to see him. 'I need your help,' she said. 'This one's beyond me.'

He dumped his case next to his desk, took the file of papers she handed to him, and sat down to look through it.

I have given directions for your removal...

Another bloody deportation. A nineteen year old, this one, arrested for supposed anti-government attitudes while still at school. Managed to get out, entered Britain on a student visa but couldn't raise the fees so worked illegally in restaurants. Only discovered he could apply for asylum once his visa had expired.

You do not qualify for entry under any of the immigration rules...

The rules, the rules. The rules were blind, deaf. Kurdish, from Iraq, his entire family exterminated by chemical weapons, but the Home Office didn't consider that he had any reason to fear persecution. Quite happy to send him back. Forget about the fact that he'd already spent over a year in prison, and been tortured.

'His room mate came to see me this morning,' Gita was saying. 'Apparently he kept saying he would die rather than go back and face torture again. When he got the removal letter he tried to disappear.'

Hassan saw that her small hands had gone white at the knuckles. 'Go on,' he said.

'The police found him and took him to the airport. He tried to run away but they caught him. Then he tried to commit suicide. He's been in hospital, he's alive, but only just - Hassan, now they've taken him back to Pentonville prison, they're still going to send him back!'

'They're bastards,' he said softly. For a moment neither of them said anything else. Then Gita asked, 'What do I do?'

'There is nothing you can do. He was an illegal immigrant at the time he applied for asylum, and that means he has no right of appeal.'

'And even a suicide attempt makes no difference?'

'I've already told you,' he said, far more sharply than he intended, 'in terms of the law there is nothing anyone can do.'

The phone rang; Barbara, from reception. 'Someone with an enquiry about benefits. Can you take it?'

'Ask them to hold on a minute.' His hand over the mouthpiece, he turned back to Gita. 'Listen, our only hope is on a technical point. If he can come up with some new information which wasn't presented in his original application, you could see if you could get his MP to raise it with the Home Office. But you'll have to move fast.'

'OK.' She got up to go.

'And Gita -' He had been going to say, Don't get too hopeful, there's very little chance. But when she turned in the dooway he changed his mind. 'Let me know what happens.' He lifted his hand off the mouthpiece. 'OK,' he barked. 'Put it through.'

A woman's voice. 'I'm enquiring on behalf of a friend who's a refugee. We're not sure whether she's getting the right benefits.'

'What's her status?'

'Status?'

He felt irritated that she did not immediately know what he meant. He wished suddenly never to have to answer any more questions. He said, 'Are they still considering her case or has she been accepted as a refugee?'

'All she's got is a piece of paper they gave her when she arrived.'

'Temporary Admission.'

'I think that's it. And the DHSS say she's only entitled to 90% of what other people get. I can't believe that's right!'

'Depends what you mean by right. If you mean, Have you been correctly informed? the answer is yes. If you mean, Is it just? I agree with you. It's not.'

There was silence at the other end. Then, 'And there's nothing that can be done about it?'

'I wish there were. I've been doing this job for four years and I haven't discovered anything yet.'

Rachel put the phone down. 'Extraordinary,' she said.

'What?' asked Pat.

'The person I was talking to. He didn't sound at all like someone in an advice office.'

'What do you mean?'

Rachel thought for a moment how to say it. 'He was angry. Like someone who has passed the point where he can be bothered to hide it.'

*

There were crocuses out on the common as she and Haleemo walked home with the children that day. 'Look,' she said to Haleemo, 'aren't they amazing?' Brilliant splashes of purple and orange after all those dreary months. And the light was different. 'It's wonderful when the days start getting longer again,' Rachel went on. 'I don't mind the cold so much but I don't think I'll ever get used to it being dark in the day.'

Haleemo was looking at her oddly. Of course, Rachel realised, she probably thinks I'm English!

She started laughing. 'Didn't you know I come from Africa too?'

That afternoon Rachel looked out some early photographs of the children, before they had left South Africa. Water glistened on their naked bodies as they played with a hose and sprinkler in the sun of the Johannesburg garden, which seemed to Rachel's now-English eyes far more spacious than she had remembered it. Haleemo was interested, but still, Rachel could see, unconnecting. She searched the drawer of her desk until she found some earlier photos, snapshots from her childhood in Lourensrus and then later ones of visits there with the children. The baby Kate, the one-year-old Kate, the eighteen-months-old Kate, taken again and again to visit her proud grandparents. Then, in diminishing profusion, the baby Simon. There was Dad, watching Simon strutting jerkily across the *stoep*, the open verandah that ran along one side of the low white painted house she had grown up in. Dad again, bending down to put something into the four year old Kate's hand, absorbed in her absorption in whatever he was showing her; one of his rocks, probably.

Haleemo was rivetted by the photographs. The people could mean nothing to her, but she was staring at the scratchy yellow grass of the veld that stretched out beyond the edge of the straggly garden, at the granite ridge of Duiwelskop rising behind. 'This where you live?' she asked, amazed.

'When I was a child,' laughed Rachel. 'It's South Africa.'

Haleemo laughed too and put out her hand to touch Rachel's arm. 'Like Hargeisa,' she said, 'like my house in Hargeisa!' The connection seemed to have woken something inside her. She looked at Rachel curiously and asked, 'Your husband? He is in prison?' as if that were the normal place for absent husbands.

'No, we're separated. He lives in New York and travels from there to other countries. But he was in prison, before we left South Africa.' And then, suddenly not sure how much would need explaining, 'We didn't like the government.'

Haleemo brushed this aside. 'How long?' she demanded. 'How long he was in prison?'

'Two weeks.'

Haleemo looked unbelieving. 'He very lucky. In Somalia if the government put you in prison they never let you out quickly like that. Military government, you understand? Army, very bad. They come in your house, they beat the boys, they take the women, they look for the men to kill them. People have to run away. Because we are Isaaq.'

'Isaaq?'

'It is our clan. The people who live in north. In my town, Hargeisa. The military government not liking Isaaq people. Soldiers come our house with guns, they look, Where is SNM people?'

'SNM?'

'They are the people who fighting the military government. Somali National Movement. Soldiers come many time for my husband. They say, Where is he? We know, he is with SNM. But he is not. He is away, with the trucks.'

'What trucks?'

'He have business with trucks. They bring from Berbera, from the sea port, to the towns and the small villages, for the shopkeepers to buy. But the soldiers they say, We know he is with SNM. Tell us where he is, we want to shoot him. Then he have to run away to SNM, otherwise they put him in prison.'

Gradually Rachel pieced Haleemo's story together from the rush of confusing detail that now seemed to pour from her. Haleemo had been away from home with Asha and Ahmed, visiting her sister in Mogadishu. She had received a message that it was too dangerous to go back - one of her husband's brothers had been arrested, the other beaten up. The family had fled from their houses and taken refuge with more distant relatives, some elsewhere in town, most in the villages nearby. She waited until eventually another message came, from her husband in Ethiopia this time, instructing her to try to get to London where his younger brother Yusuf was working for the SNM and should be able to look after her.

'Thank goodness you had the children with you,' said Rachel.

'But only these two,' Haleemo said miserably.

For a few seconds Rachel could not take in what she meant. 'You have other children?'

'Two more.' Haleemo sounded almost offended that Rachel had not known something so obvious. And now Rachel began to see that it should have been. Haleemo must be several years older than her, certainly old enough to have children Kate's age or more. And there was something about the way she dealt with Asha and Ahmed that Rachel had always felt was slightly odd but had never been able to place. Now it was clear - Haleemo's relationship with Asha had none of the intensity that is focused on a first child. They were younger children of a large family, in which no one can expect a lot of individual attention.

'Nafisa and Abokor,' Haleemo was saying. 'My two big children. I leave them in Hargeisa when I go to Mogadishu. Now I am afraid. Nafisa she is fourteen. I am afraid when the army come to the house. And Abokor he is twelve, he is a big boy. Maybe they think he going to join SNM like his father. Maybe they shoot him.' She stopped, as if unable to get past that thought.

Rachel felt paralysed. 'Who is looking after them now?' she managed.

'The wife of my brother-in-law, the one who look after my husband's business. But she have many children to look after. And now the soldiers they take my brother-in-law, there is no man there. What she do if the soldiers come again?'

A girl, fourteen, and a boy, twelve; Kate and Simon in two years time. At that moment Simon came in to the room and straight to Rachel's lap, asking for a cuddle in that way which he had never lost from a much younger age, wordless, just needing to touch base for a few moments and then be off again. She felt a surge of protective anxiety for him, almost as if he were threatened with the terrible things that had happened or that might still happen to Haleemo's children.

'Can't you get them out,' she asked Haleemo, 'to join you here?'

'Out of where?' asked Simon. 'Who?'

'Asha and Ahmed have another brother and sister,' Rachel said. 'Their mum had to leave in a big hurry like we did, and the older children were in another town so she couldn't bring them with her.'

Simon sat still, saying nothing. Rachel kept her arms firm around him as she turned to Haleemo again. Haleemo looked tired after her long speech, and helpless, all the stuffing once again taken out of her. 'Now is too difficult. The military government tell the British Embassy, you not give visa, these bad people, they are SNM. Only if Somali government say yes, the British Embassy give visa.'

'But they're your children! If they've let you in, you must be entitled to have your children with you?'

Haleemo looked helpless again, and depressed. 'I not understand these all British government rules. My brother-in-law, he try. He say it is not possible.'

That night Rachel's dreams were confused, with images of army lorries and tanks rumbling ominously through a deserted town of low white houses, on a plateau where the yellow-grassed land stretched, hot and dry, into the distance. And then the houses were no longer white, but the grey and rusty brown of corrugated iron and salvaged pieces of wood, patched and held together by God knew what, the houses of the African township at Lourensrus - and now of the slums outside Johannesburg, erected by people driven into town from the barren rural areas yet not officially allowed to be there. The same army lorries were still rolling on threateningly, coming nearer and nearer to the makeshift houses until they rolled right over them, crushing them as effortlessly as if they had been made of paper. Right in front of where she was standing a young girl and boy ran out of a house that was collapsing around them, ran screaming, holding on to each other, until they were forcibly separated by the crush of people running to get away from the tanks that rolled relentlessly on.

She woke, jolted awake by her own voice calling out. It was dark, the house silent. She waited for her heart to stop thumping and the pictures to go away. She made herself lie quietly in the bed that still felt empty each time she woke, afraid of her own fear, in the middle of the night. Breathe deeply, she told herself, deeply and evenly. Gradually she drifted off again. Almost at once the dreams were back;

but this time, thank God, there were no army lorries, just Auntie's battered old car driving along the potholed dirt road to the township outside Lourensrus. And then they were next to the low concrete-block school building, and Auntie was talking to Mr Moseko, the African social worker, while Rachel - the child Rachel - drew patterns in the dusty earth, waiting for Auntie to finish. A bell rang. She watched as the brown children emerged from the school buildings, their uniforms several sizes too small for them, their legs exposed in the cold highveld winter. A girl her own age came up to her. '*Wat is jou naam?*' - What's your name? - she asked in Afrikaans, Rachel's language, the white people's language, which the African girl knew though Rachel did not know hers. Together they began to collect stones and arrange them in piles to make little buildings. She noticed with surprise that the girl had unusually long hair, African hair all tightly curled, but done in black plaits in a style she had never seen in the Lourensrus of her childhood. And then she realised that this was Asha, and she, Rachel, was no longer a child but herself, Rachel now, with the child Asha looking up at her solemnly as if waiting for her to say something. She heard herself say, 'I'm sorry about your sister and brother, Asha.'

And only then after she had said it did she understand that of course it was they who had rushed screaming out of the corrugated iron house in Lourensrus, as the army tanks rolled over it.

*

For several days the weather had been blowy. Not a particularly strong wind, but since the October storm every wind carried a hint of threat. This time it blew in Mohamed Omar Dahir, arriving without warning on Hassan's doorstep after it was already dark, and ringing continually at his bell till Mrs Holden downstairs peered out of her window to see who it was, and eventually went out to tell him to go away. Couldn't he see there was no one in at 24 B ?

'Standing there with his suitcase, he was,' she told Hassan next day, making as much as possible out of this chance for a chat. 'Telling me he was your cousin. Well, how was I to know if he was telling me the truth? You could be anyone, I said. Then he showed me this letter you'd written him, almost a year ago, it was, and all written in funny words I couldn't understand, but it was your address all right on the back so I thought you wouldn't want me to keep him standing out there in the wind.'

She had let him in. In, that is, to the hall, not of course to her own flat. She had shown him up to the first floor landing and gone back to finish watching East Enders, leaving him there. In the dark.

Hassan finally got home at about eight. He started up the stairs, two at a time as usual, and not bothering to switch on the light - and at the top collided with Mohamed's suitcase, landing sprawled on top of him. He cursed in Somali as he extricated himself, and reached out a hand to the luminous push-button on the wall that would light up the landing and show him the face of this intruding stranger. And then he saw that it was no stranger, but Mohamed.

For a moment his heart was thumping so violently that he had to stand still to contain it. Then his mind came to terms with the extraordinary but indisputable fact that his favourite cousin stood here, in England, in his house. He flung his arms around Mohamed's shoulders, saying 'Walaal!' - brother! - and it felt like a celebration merely to be using the word. They began talking and laughing simultaneously, the excitement bursting out of them, till their one and a half minutes were up and they were once again surrounded by darkness.

'Why does it keep doing that?' Mohamed demanded.

'It's a dastardly English plot to confuse foreigners,' said Hassan, feeling lighthearted and joyous as he had not done for months. 'Bring your things in and I'll get you some food.'

Mohamed watched curiously as Hassan busied himself in the kitchen. 'I never thought I'd see you cooking, Hassan!'

'Your turn will come,' Hassan laughed. 'You've left the land in which there are always women to take care of your needs. Hungry?'

'I could eat a camel. I've been four days in transit, and it cost me so much getting the visa, there was no money left. That airline food is nothing.' He watched Hassan chop onions and peel garlic. 'You're making proper food then?'

'Proper as I know how. Stop distracting yourself. Get on and tell me how you got here!'

It had been a normal, slow, Hargeisa afternoon. Mohamed had been in a teashop with some friends when an officer newly posted to the town had come in. He heard someone use Mohamed's full name, Mohamed Omar Dahir, and knew who he must be. 'You are the son of Omar Dahir Farah?' he demanded, and then began to taunt Mohamed. He had known his father years ago, for they had been in the same army unit in Mogadishu. What a crazy decision, deserting like a coward! And look where joining the SNM had landed him! Years wandering around in the desert of Ethiopia, then creeping back with a bunch of pathetic, deluded stragglers and a few stolen rifles. And why? To attack a prison! To let out the riff raff and traitors. What a way to meet your death!

Mohamed went beserk. He sprung at the officer, who was so used to being the aggressor that he was taken by surprise and didn't have a chance to reach for his pistol before Mohamed had knocked him out. By that time the teashop had emptied. Everyone knew that the army would be there within minutes, ready to shoot without asking questions. Mohamed ran. He hid that night in the nearby village where their eighty year old grandmother lived, from where a message was sent back to the family in Hargeisa. In the early hours of the next morning he was heading north in one of uncle Ali's trucks, almost suffocating beneath a pile of sacks.

He had gone via Djibuti, managing somehow to get to Aden, the port across the narrow tip of the Gulf. He had got work at the docks, enough just for basic survival, and spent the rest of his time working with the local Somali National Movement group. But within less than a year Somalis who were known to be SNM sympathisers were being harrassed, some imprisoned, some threatened with being sent back. 'I decided to move before they moved me,' Mohamed grinned.

Hassan asked, 'What did you do about a travel document?'

'Djibuti passport. Ismail fixed it up for me.'

'And the visa? How on earth did you get that?'

Mohamed said, 'Money buys anything in Aden.'

'How long is it valid for?'

'You sound like an immigration officer! Why does it matter?'

'Because this isn't Aden,' Hassan said sharply. 'You're unlikely to get that visa extended, and if you try and live here without valid documents you're asking for trouble.'

'Relax. I told them I had no passport. I applied for asylum.'

The word, so familiar to Hassan in his daily work, triggered off intense anxiety now that it applied to someone close to him. No state could be more insecure than the one Mohamed had launched into with such apparent nonchalance. For months ahead, even years, he would have no right to be anywhere, just a single sheet of paper reminding him that at any time while his application was being considered, he was liable to be detained. But Mohamed's confidence was infectious, and at least he had had the sense to dispose of his false papers and not to try to use them on the British immigration officials. 'What did you do with the Djibuti passport?' Hassan asked. 'Flush it down the aeroplane toilet?'

Mohamed grinned and looked down at his feet, an odd expression on his face. 'I need to unpack,' he said, and bent down to untie his shoe laces. Hassan watched as he took off a shoe, then a sock. A passport fell to the ground, squashed and discoloured with sweat, but intact.

'Might still come in handy,' Mohamed said, smoothing out the curled up corners. 'And it cost a lot. A pity to waste it.'

They talked late into the night. Hassan followed Mohamed's eyes as they travelled around the flat, taking in the trappings of this new incarnation of his cousin - the bamboo blinds rolled down to close out the long northern night, a Somali mat on the wall, woven by some nomadic woman for her husband to sleep on, an object so ordinary Mohamed would never have dreamed of valuing it; the shelves filled with books Mohamed would have no interest in reading, books on African art, African music - perhaps Hassan himself would not have needed them had there been more continuing contact with the thing itself. So much had happened to separate them, yet their brotherly closeness had been as instantly resumed as in each summer of their childhood, with their loyalty unaffected by the arguments that constantly flared up and died away just as quickly. In the family they joked about Mohamed having inherited his father Omar's temperament, ready to fight at the slightest provocation. The army was the right place for Omar, Hassan's father used to say; before the coup, that was, when people could still joke about the army.

Mohamed was still asleep on the sofa when Hassan set off for work next morning. When he got home he found, what he should have expected, that the flat was full of young Somali men, summoned by phone from Whitechapel. Aadan, Mohamed's college friend from Mogadishu days, two others from Hargeisa, and a whole group of SNM hangers-on. Empty coffee cups and the remains of tandoori take-away were scattered around the room. They stayed until nearly midnight, leaving only to get the last train.

After they had gone he and Mohamed talked for another couple of hours till Mohamed said, 'You're falling asleep. I should have brought some qaat from Djibouti to keep you awake!'

Hassan laughed, 'I haven't used the stuff for years. Never mind, to be continued tomorrow evening. I'll be back about seven. I've got a late meeting.'

Mohamed was uncomprehending. 'We haven't seen each other for six years. Why don't you cut work for a couple of days?'

'I can't. It's not like that here. I have a full-time job.'

'Tell me how to get to Whitechapel, then.'

'Wait till I get back, we'll go together. I need to show you how to use the underground.'

'You tell me how to get there, I'll walk.'

Hassan laughed, 'It would take hours.'

'Since when have I been afraid of walking for a couple of hours? Uncle Musa would be shocked to hear you talk like that!'

'There isn't much about my present life uncle Musa wouldn't be shocked at. And I'm not afraid of walking. I just prefer to do it where I don't have to breathe carbon monoxide and be deafened by traffic. Uncle Musa never had to contend with that!'

Beneath the banter there was a pang of something that almost amounted to jealousy. He could see what would happen. Once Mohamed set foot in the SNM office, that would be it. Aadan's place would be filled with Somalis day and night, unemployed and with all the time in the world to sit and talk. Mohamed would phone Hassan to say, 'I think I'll sleep here tonight,' and after that he would never get round to moving back.

7

She was inside a shapeless bubble, big enough to move around in without noticing that the bubble was there. Then she would find herself unexpectedly looking through it and would realise that there was another world out there, clearly visible but cut off from her. She knew it was pointless trying to reach it, for the bubble was as impenetrable as it was invisible. The knowledge that she was trapped was deeply troubling to her, though inside the bubble she had everything she needed, security, love, laughter; her children, friends. What was outside the bubble was hard to describe and kept changing, but always it emanated a quality of fear, of anxiety.

She woke, to the deep dark of her silent room. She was burdened by an almost intolerable sadness. She switched on the light and reached for the novel she had been reading before going to sleep. She read for more than an hour and though the sadness did not lift, it shifted sideways a little where she didn't have to deal with it for the moment. Eventually she put her book down and turned off the light. She did not feel ready for sleep but she would have to try, otherwise tomorrow would be hell.

For several days she kept seeing pictures of Martha in the Lourensrus of her childhood. Once she was with Martha in the back yard, handing pegs up to her as she hung out the washing. Martha was telling her one of her long stories and Rachel was watching the way her large buttocks spread sideways and flattened out as she bent to pick up the next shirt and then reformed themselves like a shelf sticking out backwards when she stood up again and reached her arms up to the washing line.

Another time she saw herself in Martha's room, the outhouse at the bottom of the garden. The servant's room, her mother called it. On the covered applebox next to Martha's bed was a photograph of two children, one about Rachel's age, one a little younger. She had not thought of the possibility that Martha might have children of her own, and the knowledge made her insecure. Who looked after them while Martha was looking after her and Matthew? 'Don't tell your mother,' said Martha. 'She wouldn't like it if she knew I had shown you the photograph.' How absurd, Rachel thought, the grown up Rachel, Martha wouldn't have said that. But there were no longer clear dividing lines between memory and fantasy, for now she had a picture of her mother being there with them in Martha's room, which she was sure had never happened. The child Rachel was asking, 'Why can't Martha's children come and live here with her?'

'Where would they sleep?' her mother asked, mildly. 'This room is far too small.'

'In the house with us,' Rachel said, and then realised that that wouldn't work because if the children were in the house and Martha was out at the back she still wouldn't be with her children.

'It's our house not hers,' her mother said in a firm, matter-of-fact voice. 'That's just the way things are, Rachel. You have to learn to be sensible about it.' Rachel looked from her mother to Martha, needing one of them to comfort her with a hug but not knowing how to go to either without appearing to take sides.

She remembered, and this she was sure was a real memory, the first time she had seen Martha's children. She had gone with Auntie to the African township some miles outside white Lourensrus. Martha had come with them because it was after lunch on Sunday, her time off, and Auntie was giving her a lift home. Martha sat in the front next to Auntie, which Rachel knew by now was not how it would have been in anyone else's car. Auntie as usual didn't bother to stop at the stop sign at the end of the road. 'It's there for the bad drivers not for me,' she said, 'I can see perfectly well if anything's coming,' and it seemed logical that there should be special rules for Auntie. Now they were bumping over the dirt road out of town, descending slowly into each pothole and climbing laboriously out again. They reached the township. The car stopped. Martha got out. Two children ran out to greet her, the children of the photograph. Martha lifted the younger one up onto her ample hip and put her arm out to draw the bigger one up against her, and from the joy in her face Rachel understood for the first time something that should have been obvious but that had never struck her before, that Martha had a life of her own in which she, Rachel, had no part. Rachel's home was only the place where she worked. Her real home was here, this shack that was scarcely bigger than Martha's room at the back of their garden, made of sheets of corrugated iron balanced one against the other, with another on top for a roof, held down by stones; here where her children and her old mother slept rolled up in blankets on the floor with only a skimpy curtain to divide the space into two small rooms. This was Martha's home. And because she was busy looking after Rachel's family she could only be part of it one half-day and one night a week.

News from Hargeisa. One of Haleemo's brothers-in-law had been shot for resisting arrest. Her sister's daughters, aged fifteen and twelve, had been taken away by the soldiers. Presumed raped, maybe dead. 'I must bring my children out,' Haleemo said, her voice rising in panic.

Someone had to do something, and quickly. Rachel had no idea who or what, but it was impossible to go on as if nothing had changed. She watched Asha and Ahmed, normal, healthy children playing noisily with her own, small people whose large personalities filled the house and whose needs determined the time-table of the day, children whose noses ran when they had colds and who squabbled over which television programme to watch. And then she tried to imagine those other two children whom she had never seen, surrounded by terrible dangers. Try as she might she could not give them faces or personalities. They were abstract, symbols, almost, of children in danger, children in terrible need. Children left behind without their parents in a city where the army was at any minute likely to walk in and rape or kill. The children who were right now being mowed down by the police and army in townships all over South Africa, for attending funerals of their friends, similarly mowed down.

'I must bring my children out,' Haleemo said, her voice urgent, needing comfort. No, needing action. But what? In all the years of living in South Africa Rachel had never found a way. The challenge had been there constantly in the eyes of the black children of Lourensrus who used to stare curiously at Auntie's car as it passed, while they stood in the dust of the roadside, their legs and arms spindly from malnutrition; in the children at the school who came shyly in little groups to talk to her while Auntie was busy with the headmaster, asking her how old she was and if she was Miss Faure's niece, touching her clothes in envy as they gathered round. It was there in the stories she heard Auntie tell her mother and Aunt Anna, of the children she worked with in the clinic; a girl who had tuberculosis, a girl called Rachel, like her - in another life it could have been her - 'She ought to have been sent to a sanatorium,' said Auntie. 'It's probably too late now.' The grown-ups nodded and sympathised and said wasn't it a shame. Rachel was raging. 'Why didn't they send her?' she demanded. 'They didn't have the money,' Auntie said.

As simple as that. Rachel's anger drained away, replaced by helplessness.

What could one do? What could anyone do? Auntie held street collections and shamed her relatives into parting with money they would much rather have spent on other things. By constant effort she managed to raise enough to provide each child in the township school with one meal a day, but even that was a tiny patch of watered grass in the vast expanse of dry veld. When later Alistair took Rachel's political education in hand he explained to her that you can't solve problems of that magnitude with charity. Women like Auntie, he said, achieved little except perhaps making themselves feel better. Rachel sprung to Auntie's defence, knowing that he had fundamentally misunderstood her, not having bothered to meet her more than once. But she also knew that while Auntie's way was right for Auntie, it provided no simple pattern for her to follow. She would perhaps have argued less vehemently if she had been clearer about what she herself could do.

Haleemo was looking at her with urgent eyes, saying, 'I must bring my children out, to me!'

'There's an organisation that helps refugees,' Rachel said. 'Maybe they know a way?'

*

He had spent half the night with Mohamed and his friends, at Aadan's place. They had offered him qaat and for once he had accepted. He could not think afterwards why he had. He should have known that after so many years it would have had an unusually powerful effect on him. But there seemed no good reason to refuse and he wanted for once to be part of the group.

While he was there Aadan managed to get through to Mogadishu on the phone, to an SNM contact called Abdi. At one point he handed the receiver over to Mohamed. 'Abdi wants to speak to you.'

Hassan listened as Mohamed spoke, cheerfully at first and then falling silent to listen. 'OK,' Mohamed said eventually. 'Let us know if you hear anything.' By now Hassan was feeling blank with panic. No more, please, no more.

Mohamed handed the receiver back to Aadan and turned to Hassan. 'It's Nuh,' he said. 'He's disappeared.' Nuh, their older cousin, mentor of his boyhood. The panic had been replaced by a familiar, helpless fury. It had to happen, thought Hassan. Nuh was too good to stay unscathed in that den of thieves. Mohamed was saying, 'As far as Abdi knows he hasn't been arrested. It seems he was tipped off about possible trouble and went into hiding.'

'What about Amina?' Hassan asked. 'And the child?' Alone at night, with Nuh gone and the army or security police arriving at the door in the small hours -

'They're OK,' Mohamed said. 'Sabah's taken them in.'

Sabah, Nuh's sister, who had always stuck to her work as a doctor and refused to get involved in politics - 'It's not worth fighting them,' she used to tell Nuh. 'If you get rid of them there will only be more like them to take their place. And you take too many risks.' Now she was taking the risk, sheltering Nuh's family; as Hassan's father had taken in uncle Hirsi's family and then uncle Omar's. Sisters, brothers, cousins, they all got drawn in, one generation after another. Who was left now in Mogadishu to run around trying to find out what had happened to Nuh? Of the older generation, only aunt Khadra with her husband uncle Hirsi - a cabinet minister before the coup, now a broken old man, mentally unbalanced after serving a sixteen-year sentence in prison.

The country is snatched and divided by whosoever is stronger -
he heard again the men on his father's verandah, reciting the poems of resistance that had been composed about the colonial powers, now used against their own Somali government -

The country is sold piece by piece without our knowledge;
And for me, all this is the teeth of the last days of the world.
The teeth of the last days of the world, devouring relentlessly.

When he had to leave that night Mohamed walked with him to the station, through deserted streets littered with the debris from the day's street market. He took Hassan on a detour via the SNM office. Mohamed had a key; they let themselves in, climbing the stairs to the first floor. Inside Mohamed handed him a copy of a duplicated report in Somali, an SNM memorandum marked For Internal Distribution Only.

Hassan grinned. 'So you're contravening the Movement's rules by showing it to me!'

Mohamed said, 'Since when are you an outsider?' No, thought Hassan, not this one again. But Mohamed was already launched. 'We need you Hassan. Things are bad in the Movement. The leadership is behaving like a bunch of women, delaying, delaying. We need to push them to act now, before things get even more difficult. It's that Habar Tol Ja'lo crowd. We let them take leadership positions because we didn't want the others to say the Habar Awal were trying to dominate. But they do nothing -'

'Listen,' Hassan cut across Mohamed's rising voice. 'You ought to know by now I'm not interested in that kind of tribal accusation.' He wanted to add, I don't react like a Habar Awal because of who my father's family are, any more than I react like an Englishman because of my mother's. But it was pointless, Mohamed would not understand. He seemed genuinely puzzled that Hassan should not feel the same unquestioned loyalty to the Movement that he did. Perhaps he put it down to cowardice, and perhaps it was? As a boy Hassan had shied away from the physical fighting which came so naturally to his cousins. But if he was afraid now it was not the kind of fear Mohamed might think; he was afraid for the people he knew, for the hundreds of thousands of others, at the prospect of all the killing, the terrible destruction that was being let loose.

And now Nuh. Nuh would have understood instantly how he felt. It was he who had taught Hassan the lines from Salaan Arabey's poem,

> *When warriors die in countless numbers*
> *And the great array of men is utterly destroyed,*
> *People will soon reproach each other.*
> *Oh clansmen, stop the war!*

He ached with longing for Nuh to be safe.

Mohamed was looking around the office, not for anything in particular, just seeing if there were any other papers he could persuade Hassan to take. 'Here, a press release about the regime's scorched earth policy. It's an amazing leak from one of the army's top generals.'

'Thanks.' Hassan took it. 'I'll read it.'

'When?' demanded Mohamed. Hassan felt a rush of affection for his cousin's characteristic impatience. 'Not tonight!' he grinned. 'But I promise I'll read it in a couple of days. And I'll give you a ring when I've done so, if I've got anything new to say to you.'

'That's better!' Mohamed locked up the office. They went out into the night street together and headed back towards the station. Hassan said, 'I can't stop thinking about Nuh.'

Mohamed spat vehemently into the gutter, as if at the people who were after Nuh. 'Filthy hyenas,' he said. Then, 'If he gets out OK he'll be coming to us.'

Hassan asked sharply, 'Abdi said that?'

'No, but it's obvious. You can't stay hidden forever. He'll have to leave the country. He'll be appearing, any day now, maybe here, maybe in Ethiopia.'

So 'us' meant not 'you and me', but 'the SNM'. Hassan said, 'You're crazy.'

Mohamed's voice became louder, more insistent. Storm brewing. 'And why?'

'Nuh wouldn't join a clan-based party!'

'Every Isaaq who leaves is joining,' Mohamed flung back at him. 'The Somalia Nuh believed in is dead. You're out of touch, Hassan.'

Hassan stopped himself from answering. They were passing a boarded-up warehouse, rubbish piled up on the pavement next to it, meaningless graffiti on the walls. Aggressively he kicked a beer can out of his way. He felt angry for Mohamed and the others, people who had grown up with the earth under their feet and all around them the wide savannah plains, the huge arching sky. Space for one's spirit to expand into. There's nothing here for them to do, he thought. No wonder Mohamed gets obsessive about SNM politics.

'You need to get out of here sometimes,' he said. 'And I'd like to see you more often. Come to my place one weekend and we'll go out of town together.'

'Where to?'

'To walk. Somewhere with trees.'

Mohamed grinned but said nothing. Hassan thought, Of course he won't do it, not unless I keep pressing him. He felt rejected, though he knew it was absurd. You want to win me over to your ground, he thought, but you're too bloody independent ever to come over to mine.

They had reached the station. Mohamed put his hand affectionately on Hassan's shoulder to say goodbye. 'So, Hassan, you're going to phone me when you've read that report!'

Hassan's own obstinacy rose involuntarily. 'I told you, only if I've got anything to say that I haven't already said!'

Mohamed was suddenly angry. 'I don't understand you, Hassan Abdillahi Dahir. After what has happened to your father you still feel it is enough to sit in your safe office, behind a desk?'

He had gone too far. Hassan flared at him, furious. 'What do you want me to do? To sit around like you and Aadan, issuing press releases about a war that isn't even happening? A few thousand exiles - do you really think they're going to take on the entire force of Siyad's army? How long do you think they would last if they did? What makes you think it's any different from when your father tried it?'

'It's different because more people have woken up. We should have fought back years ago and it would never have got this bad!'

'You're talking as if we're still in the days of camel raiding feuds, avenging the honour of the clan. It isn't like that any more. It's not two clans against each other, each fighting on the same terms. Those bastards have tanks and aeroplanes, they've been piling them up for years, first from the Russians then from the Americans. And what about all the people of other clans who've been imprisoned, tortured, killed? Where are *their* brothers and uncles? Why aren't you fighting with them?'

'They know we're here. Anyone who wants to fight can come and find us.'

'But I'm Isaaq so it really matters if I'm with you, doesn't it? I owe it to the family, don't I, to the clan? And if you fight on that basis what kind of government do you expect to put in Siyad's place? I want to see his downfall as much as you do but not to install the rule of the Isaaq, dominating over others. You're wasting your time on me.'

Mohamed could go to hell.

All the way home his cousin's words repeated themselves - *You still feel it is enough to sit in your safe office, behind a desk?* At each station the train stopped, the automatic doors slid open, one or two people got on or off. A brief distraction. The moment the doors closed again the words were back to taunt him - *After what has happened to your father?* Down the dark road from the station to his flat, and into his flat, and with him to bed, keeping him awake half the night - *You still feel it is enough?*

And what about Mohamed? Mohamed's own father was dead, and what had he been able to do about it? All that posturing and speech-making, all his papers and secret documents, how the hell was that going to change the fate that had overtaken them all?

Then he would hear his father's voice reciting,

> When misfortune seized me -
> and the Lord's decrees fall immutably upon us -
> why did you not shout until you were hoarse,
> summoning a thousand men to my aid?

The qaat had the expected effect. It was well after four o'clock before he got to sleep. Even then he kept waking, feeling hot and tense. He dragged himself through the next day with difficulty. He was irritable with his colleagues and spent hours drafting a report which would normally have taken him a quarter of the time. Then Barbara appeared in his office to say, 'There's been a mess-up about the rest of this afternoon's appointments. Mike had forgotten it was his turn to take new cases. He's got a meeting.'

'He'll have to cancel it then.' Hassan heard his voice, furious. This is the fight I've been looking for, he thought, and was almost glad that it had come.

'He's already gone,' said Barbara.

Hassan stared at her. *'Gone?'*

'It was something to do with the Tamil deportations. I didn't feel it was my place to -'

'And what the hell does he think is going to happen to his appointments then?'

'He said since they were all new cases I should spread them around among the rest of you and he'll take tomorrow's new ones instead.' She paused. Then, 'He said he was sorry.'

'He's sorry!' Hassan was beside himself now. 'That's charming.' He saw Barbara's face, full of anxiety. Hold it. Save it for Mike tomorrow. There's no reason to load it on Barbara. 'Send them in,' he said. He began to gather up the papers on his desk in one great, unsorted, angry heap. 'This lot will just have to wait.'

Barbara escaped. Two minutes later someone knocked at his door. He hated people knocking, it reminded him of his mother's flat. Couldn't they see the door was open? Why knock, for God's sake? 'Come in,' he barked, and glanced up to see a white woman standing at the door, hesitating as if he were some bloody dignitary whom she was afraid to disturb. Well, let her wait. He changed his mind about the papers and began sorting them.

'Are you Hassan Abdillahi?'

He didn't bother to answer or to look up. 'Sit down,' he said shortly. 'I'll be with you in a minute.' He felt alarmed that he was so out of control. Just calm down. Whatever's going on inside me is nothing to do with this woman. He made himself put the papers to one side. In what he hoped was a normal voice he said, 'What can I do for you?'

'My name's Rachel Sinclair. I've come about a friend.'

8

The ACRAS offices had turned out to be a dingy collection of rooms in an unmodernised Victorian building, with a lift like a cage. Ben would love this, she thought, I'll have to bring him one day. On the fourth floor landing there was nothing but a series of closed doors. She found the one marked ACRAS. It was locked. She rang the bell. The door clicked open a fraction and buzzed. She pushed and went in, to a corridor and another set of doors, these ones covered with posters, and notices - Please Make Sure You Shut The Door Securely Behind You. What on earth is all this security about? she thought, and tried to imagine a newly arrived refugee being confronted with this anonymous, intimidating method of reaching the people who were supposed to be there to help them.

She found a door marked RECEPTION, knocked, got no answer, and went in anyway. The room was like a doctor's waiting room in a poor area of town, with upright chairs arranged formally around the walls, a magazine rack in the middle, a threadbare carpet. The woman behind the desk was on the phone with one ear while trying to deal with an enquiry from an irate middle-eastern looking man with the other. She kept saying, 'Just hold on a minute,' alternately to the person on the phone and the man who wouldn't stop talking. Two others leant over the counter determined not to lose their place. Rachel took a seat. Next to her was a Chinese woman, or maybe Vietnamese? Thin and anxious. Opposite, a burly middle-aged African, bulging out of his anorak. His face had the tired patience peculiar to those who are used to sitting in queues. Next to him was a young man whom she guessed was South Indian, with sleek black hair and intense eyes, ostensibly reading a large textbook. From time to time he underlined something, but his eyes kept wandering back to the desk or staring out of the window, from which the only view was the back of another building. Drainpipes and dirty windows.

It was twenty minutes before Rachel's turn came. 'It's Mike Fraser I'm to see?' she checked, reading out the name she had been given over the phone. The receptionist apologised. 'I'm afraid he was urgently called away. But Hassan Abdillahi will see you. Down the corridor, first turning on the right, then through the swing doors. He's the second door on the left.'

The door stood ajar but there was no name on it. She knocked, and as she did so suddenly wondered whether the receptionist had said 'second door' or 'second turning'. A voice told her to come in. She obeyed his rather abrupt instruction to sit down. While he finished what he was busy with she observed him interestedly. A mass of soft brown curly hair covered his bent head. The name sounded Islamic. Algeria, maybe? Morocco? She had expected someone more official looking, a middle-aged lawyer type in a suit. This man was young, wearing jeans and a casual sweater. There was an air of unconscious confidence, arrogance, almost, in the way he continued to make notes as if she were not in the room. He looked up. He was Somali! She was sure of it, as sure as she had been about the man in the library. The same long face, high cheekbones, the same unmistakeable pride in the way he held his head.

'What can I do for you?' he asked.

'My name's Rachel Sinclair,' she began. 'I've come about a friend.' She watched his face as she said, 'She's a Somali refugee,' but he didn't react. That unnerved her momentarily. When she had told him briefly about Haleemo's problem and still he said nothing, she began to feel that the silence was hostile. Maybe he wasn't a Somali. Should she explain in more detail what was happening in Hargeisa? Or was he thinking, What's this white woman doing here? Why doesn't she let the Somali woman speak for herself?

He asked, his voice giving away nothing, 'When did she arrive?'

'Her little boy joined my son's class a couple of weeks before Christmas. November, I think.'

'When you say she's a refugee do you mean she has refugee status?'

'I don't know. What does that involve?'

He stared at her for a moment and then said, 'I think you'd better tell her to come in herself.'

'That's what I said to her but she didn't want to.' Rachel stopped, feeling she was sounding defensive. What Haleemo had actually said was, 'My English not good enough.' Rachel had said, 'That's nonsense, you've explained to me.' Haleemo was adamant. 'People in offices, different,' she said.

Rachel tried again. 'Maybe you could tell me what the options are?'

'There aren't options,' he said curtly, 'there are only rules. If she has been given formal refugee status she's entitled to apply to bring her children in. If she hasn't, she can't.'

He had thrown the information at her, aggressively. She realised suddenly, This is the man I spoke to on the phone. She looked at him curiously. There was a different quality to his anger today - uncomfortable, reined-in. She asked, 'What do you need to do to get refugee status?'

'You don't have to do anything. According to an international convention, which Britain among many other states has signed, asylum should be granted to people who have a well-founded fear of persecution were they to be returned to their own countries.'

'She's got that, all right!'

He said coldly, 'I'm sure you're right. Unfortunately it is not on your say-so or mine that a decision will be made, but by an official in the Home Office.'

'On what basis?'

'A statement she made on arrival.'

'How long does it take to get a decision?'

'Many months, sometimes over a year. And until then she's here on what's called Temporary Admission which means she has no legal right to be here, let alone bring anyone else in to join her.'

'What happens if they say no?' she asked. 'Surely they can't send her back? It's like a war there, the army is out of control!'

He said, harshly again, 'There are Somalis being refused asylum every month. She's no different from the others.'

Rachel stared at him. Now she was sure that some at least of his anger was directed at her for being so naive. She made herself push on, regardless. 'If they let her stay? Then she can bring the children in?'

'It depends. Even those who are allowed to stay aren't necessarily given full refugee status. They may get what is called Exceptional Leave to Remain, usually for a year. That carries no right to bring anyone in to join her.'

'What happens after the year?'

'She can apply for an extension. After she's been here four years she'll be able to apply for a review of the case.'

'They can let her stay here *four years* and still not let her bring her children in?'

'Yes.'

'But that's unbelievable!'

'Yes.'

She felt defeated. Then she remembered something he had said. 'Refugee Status. Tell me about that.'

'It means that the government accepts you as a refugee in terms of the international convention and is then obliged to accord you the same treatment it would to its own citizens. Which includes, in principle, the right to bring in a spouse or dependent children. It's called a Family Reunion.'

'In principle? There's a catch, isn't there?'

'Many. The arrangements are done via the U.N. High Commission for Refugees, which negotiates between the two governments. But governments remain sovereign. It may not be easy to get the children out, even if the British government has agreed to let them in.'

'Still, it's possible.' She was beginning to get excited.

'Yes. And I should tell you that last year only about one in five of the Somalis who applied were given refugee status.'

He said it with such finality that Rachel was momentarily stunned. She stared at him. What on earth was going on here? Throughout this entire conversation she had felt that he did not wish to be speaking to her, that he considered her questions a waste of his time. What cause did he have to be so arrogant? She didn't care if he thought she wasn't the person he ought to have been speaking to, she was here, and it was his job to tell her.

She bent to pick up her shoulderbag. She was going. Then an awful thought occurred to her. Maybe he was from the other side, a supporter of the Somali government? How naive of her to assume that he would be sympathetic just because he was from the same country. She felt out of her depth. She got up, starting to say something formal about thanking him for his time - and as she did so she suddenly saw in his face the reason for his tension. He looked exhausted, drained of all spirit. He does care, she thought, he's bowed down by it. How stupid of me not to have seen it. That hardness in his voice is a protection, not to have to get close to it; like I do with Alistair. She sat down again and said, 'Look, I know it's no use talking to me, but if my friend comes, can you see if there's anything that can be done to get her refugee status? She's distraught about her children.'

He said, his voice tired now and quiet, 'Send her by all means. But please don't raise any false hopes.'

*

71

Hassan stared blankly at the door for several minutes after she had left. He didn't know what had come over him. He had been so brusque with the woman, and now that she was gone he felt...

He did not know what he felt. There was something unusual about her. The fact that she was here, for a start; white, not bringing any problems of her own, just concerned about a friend. He couldn't think when it had happened before, in all his four years at ACRAS. Friends from the same country, fellow refugees, that was different. But this woman... For the first few moments he had thought, here we have it, western feminist championing the rights of third world women, from a position of profound ignorance. But there was nothing about her manner or the questions she asked to suggest a political activist. There was a quality about her that... He could not pinpoint it. Something about the directness of her response. A woman she scarcely knew was separated from her children. She knew nothing more, it seemed, neither about the forces in Somalia that had driven the woman from her home, nor about the British laws that prevented her from bringing her children to join her. She knew only that it was wrong. She had listened intently when he had tried to explain, but he had the impression that she was listening only to find the answer to that one simple question: Could the woman get her children out?

That quality of hers was around him still, permeating his office, reducing the pieces of paper on his desk to insignificance. He was left feeling - regretful, he supposed; that such straightforward, direct, warmth should be so unusual; that she had gone, taking it with her; and most of all regretful that he had not responded better. He had sent her away without even trying to find out more about her.

It was several hours before he tumbled to what had really been going on. He had arranged to meet his mother after work for a meal and a concert. He arrived early; normally he would have read as he waited but this evening he simply sat in the foyer and watched the people come in and out through the swing doors. Outside in the cold the homeless people would be settling for the night in their shacks of cardboard under the South Bank's concrete arches. He wondered where Nuh was sleeping.

He saw his mother walking towards him, and stood up to give her a hug. She was looking older, with strands of grey hair escaping from the twist into which she always pinned it. He felt a rush of affection.

The hug seemed easy, natural, just as he had always known things ought to be between them. 'Nuh's disappeared,' he said, abandoning his usual careful monitoring of what he told her. 'Mohamed spoke to someone in Mogadishu. There's a possibility he might be coming here.'

He didn't know what he had expected her to say. She said, 'Oh lord, it never stops, does it?' and 'I do hope he gets out safely,' and he knew she meant it. But he knew also that she was making an effort. The naturalness of their greeting had already gone. He moved sideways to safer topics, her work and his, the television film her friend Penny was making, the holiday she was planning with two of her friends for the summer. Throughout the meal she didn't return to the subject of Nuh or anything else to do with Somalia, and nor did he. The conversation was comfortable enough; it was, after all, what they were both used to. But today Hassan had needed more, and he had thought for a moment that they were going to achieve it.

The violin concerto for which they had come was in the second half of the programme. The first half consisted of a long Ravel piece, shapeless and overstated, and something incomprehensible by a contemporary composer neither of them had ever heard of. At the end he joined in the applause halfheartedly and turned to say, 'Not my kind of music!' at precisely the same time that she said, 'I think he was having us on!' They laughed at the pleasure of being momentarily wholly together. They followed the trail of people out onto the landing and stood looking down through the plate-glass wall onto the river below; at Waterloo Bridge with the lit-up buses moving slowly over it, and beyond to the myriad lights of nighttime London. Neither of them needed to say anything to know that they were each absorbed in the magic contrast of those lightly dancing lights and the sluggish, heavy movement of the dark water. Our place, Hassan thought, my mother's and mine; the familiar routes we travel to work, or to meet friends, to go with them to a meeting, a concert, to go walking, and then back again to our single flats. She had taught him by example how to make a life in this city that held within it both the boarded-up warehouses and decaying buildings in which Mohamed spent his days, and the beauty they were experiencing now. He would never have known how to enjoy the things that he loved about London if he had arrived as Mohamed had, or as Nuh might be about to, to be plunged without preparation into an alien culture, having to live in the poorest parts of town on DHSS handouts, the amounts carefully calculated to sustain life but with nothing over to enable you to make it worth sustaining. And if Nuh got here what would he do, cut off from his involvement in Somali affairs, from the people closest to him? From Amina, his wife - 'What's she like?' he had asked Mohamed. 'Foreign educated,' Mohamed had said, making it clear this was not a compliment. 'America. She'll be taking all his money and doing the spending herself. We all thought Nuh was never going to marry, then suddenly he became this woman's inseparable companion. The way he talks about her, I tell you, it's embarrassing!'

The bell was sounding the end of the interval. His mother was offering him a cup of coffee and saying, 'You've just got time, if you swallow fast!'

The violinist walked on stage, a young slim woman with blond hair that hung down her back exactly as Farida's black hair had done. The unexpected reminder took hold of him, weaving its way into the sounds in which he was immersed, filling him with a sense of loss, though it was more than three years since she had left him. The music became Farida's voice, pleading, *You don't understand, Hassan* - Farida talking to him from halfway across the room, not letting him come nearer, her suitcase already half packed. Farida gone, leaving behind her total silence, not one single word -

You are the risen sun and the early rays of dawn.
Will I ever find your like,
you who have been shown to me only once?

Now it was his aunt Khadra's voice, chanting a woman's poem -

You are the sky which gives no rain
while mist shrouds the world,
the moon that shines no more,
the risen sun extinguished,
the dates on their way from Basra
cut off by the seas.

Cut off - as his mother was, so close yet unable to give the one thing he needed of her. Cut off by the seas, and by so much more than the seas, as he was from his father, as Nuh was about to be from Amina, as Rachel Sinclair's friend from her children.

He saw again her face when she had said, 'But that's unbelievable!' And she seemed to be answering all those other voices, the indignation

74

in her eyes finding a way to fight back. Hers was one of those faces about which you knew that whatever you saw on it was what she was thinking; clear, open brow, short hair, shaped simply around her face, alert eyes, her expression immediate. Nothing put on, nothing held back, the whole warm, indignant, responsive person there in her face. Like his father, in fact...

Subhan Allah! Of course, that was it! That was what had made him react so strangely to her presence! That directness of hers was extraordinarily like his father's. The same immediate warmth about people, even the touch of naivete, that inability to face up to the existence of evil, so that when its forces intervened to ruin your life or someone's close to you, you were taken by surprise, outraged. 'He did it just because he was angry,' uncle Ali had said, unable to credit such lack of calculation. 'Any child could have told him it was pointless. But you know what your father is like.' Yes, that was what he was like. Two minutes of showing his real, unconquerable self and they had had him behind bars till the end of time. As Hassan had listened to uncle Ali he had felt an overwhelming love for that quality in his father which nothing had been able to repress. For months he had locked that feeling inside himself, never considering sharing it with anyone, not with Mohamed, not with Jeyam, least of all with his mother. And here today a strange woman had walked into his office, and something in her face had told him, unmistakably, that she had exactly that quality of his father's, however different were the circumstances. He had been unnerved. No, more than that, he had felt invaded. Without knowing what he was doing he had pushed her away in case she intruded any further.

He wanted to see her. He wanted to see that face again, to check whether she was really as he remembered her.

PART TWO

In Transit

... And I am forever a poet.
When I am weary, and want no friend but peace
And say to you, 'This night my songs are done',
Your clamorous voices still would force from me
One ballad more to warm the dwindling fire.

Something was being unearthed, something she would much rather have left dormant. No longer was there one oppressive dream, taking over in the silent hours when everyone else was asleep, then thrust firmly out of sight as she went to meet the day. That dream had gone, she realised with some surprise, but gone also was the ability to keep her anxieties shut away in some region of her unconscious. Haleemo's need had come crashing in, exposing fragments of her own.

There were so many things left unfinished, that was it. People she had never said goodbye to. Arguments she had never finished. Friends with whom she had talked and laughed and watched children play, yet never said the one thing that really mattered, and now it was irrelevant. Places she had not allowed herself to remember.

What point was there in suddenly thinking about them all again? She had found a way to survive without them, and it worked. She was busy and happy, she had her job, her children, her friends, what more did she want, for heaven's sake? The past could add nothing. No, more than that, if she let it loose it could drag her down. It connected with nothing in her daily life, it could only stir up restless feelings that she did not understand and did not want to have to deal with. Leave it alone, you were fine before Anab and Haleemo arrived.

But it would not leave her alone.

'We have to take ten pounds on Monday if we want to go,' Kate was saying. Rachel jerked her attention back from the pictures of the people in the ACRAS waiting room, stranded like flotsam on an unhopeful shore. 'The school journey, Mom,' Kate said. And then, 'Can I go?' so differently from the way Simon or Ben would have asked, wanting so much to go but also not wanting Rachel to have to worry about money.

'Of course you can go,' Rachel said firmly, hoping that her voice didn't give away the sudden flaring anger at Alistair. There had been no letters from him for nearly two months. Kate, who missed nothing, would know that meant his money hadn't come. Rachel tried to imagine Alistair through Kate's eyes - her Daddy, someone adored and waited for. Momentarily she could do it, but immediately the Alistair she knew came thrusting back, the self-concerned Alistair who had abdicated from their joint life. His refusal to sort out a regular maintenance payment was a way of getting at her, of saying, 'You told me to go, now manage on your own and see how you like it.'

Pictures of her own father came into her mind. Almost her earliest memory - playing on the pavement under the pepper tree, watching him set off for work, turning to wave to her every few yards. Taking chairs out into the sunny sheltered corner beneath her bedroom window, his favourite place for reading, and she feeling so grown-up sitting there with him, reading in the thin winter sun. Going with him to the market on the first Saturday of each month, where fruit was auctioned in crates - pineapples, peaches - her own children would scarcely believe that there had been a time and a place where people used to buy fruit on that scale. She used to stand next to Dad, her view hidden by the large men's bodies, then he would lift her up on his shoulders so that she could see the auctioneer. She was rivetted by his patter. Dad would tell her to sit very still, not to move her arms at all, otherwise the auctioneer might assume she was making a bid. And the smells of the place! Fruit smells of every kind, the men's clothes full of dust and sweat, bits of vegetable fallen off crates, trodden underfoot, mixing with the smell of straw from the packing boxes...

That night after Kate was in bed Rachel took the unheard-of step of phoning Alistair in New York. If he didn't answer her letters about money, what other choice did she have? But her whole body was tense as she looked up the dialling code, and worked out the time difference, and slowly dialled the long number. A woman answered. An American voice, sounding half asleep. Rachel was unnerved by the image of the owner of that voice in Alistair's bed. Alistair wasn't there, the voice said, slow and sensual. He was in East Africa. Did she want to leave a message? No she did not, Rachel said curtly and slammed down the receiver. She wasn't going to leave any part of herself, not even her name, as a hostage to that unknown woman.

For several minutes she sat still, waiting for the turbulence to subside. How was it possible that she should be jealous? She did not want Alistair back, of that she was clear. But still the picture of him making love with someone else was profoundly disturbing, stirring up restless feelings about her own funadmental loneliness, the barrenness of never being touched except by the children, whose warm bodies comforted her but also highlighted her need for adult intimacy.

Why had things gone so wrong between them? There was a time, before the children - Was it that Alistair had been unable to accept that he was no longer the centre of attention? But it was more complicated than that. With Kate he had shared the fun and the pride of having a child even if he hadn't shared the work. But once Simon came - Simon had cried so much as a baby, nothing seemed to make him contented, and Alistair gave up so easily, as if the only point of trying to comfort a child was for the good feeling it gave you when you succeeded. If you couldn't succeed you rejected the child. Could he only love where he was flattered and admired? And what if one day she too needed comfort from him, would he be as incapable of giving it? Then she began to let herself see the other things about him that she found difficult, so difficult that she had tried to hide from facing up to them. The way he dismissed the people who had been closest to her before he arrived, her cousins Sannie and Daniel, her mother and father, Auntie. All of Lourensrus, in fact, the life that he would not share with her, as she could not fully share his.

Her father's death. That, more than anything, had forced her to see how little she and Alistair were able to help each other when help was really needed. Her father had become seriously ill when she was eight months pregnant. 'Don't come yet,' her mother had said. 'Wait till after the baby is born. The doctor says it'll be several months still.' Be sensible. She had listened to them, to her mother, Alistair, her own doctor. But she knew at the time that the sensible thing was not the right thing and she was miserable all those last weeks of waiting for Ben to arrive. She had tried to talk to Alistair, needing him to see her misery. He had backed off, refusing to engage. And then only one day after Ben was born her father died, and she had missed forever the chance to be with him again. She had left him alone when simply by being there she could perhaps have helped him deal with death. She had failed him, and had failed her mother who had needed her support. She had been failing them both for years by staying away from Lourensrus too long between visits, because each time she went she had to confront once again the thing that separated her and Alistair. She had been afraid to lose what she and Alistair had, to put any strain on an already diminishing intimacy; and in her fear had lost not only that, which would probably have gone anyway, but also something more fundamental.

There was a letter from her mother. She didn't try to read it until she had settled Simon and Ben in bed. Tonight Ben was inexplicably unable to brush his teeth, and Simon, who for over a year had considered himself too old for bedtime stories said, 'I don't know why you never read to me anymore.' So she read to him, a book he chose, that would have been more suitable for a six year old.

When she came downstairs Kate had spread her homework over the table in the living room. 'That's very conscientious,' Rachel said. 'What's going on?'

'We've got to give in our history project tomorrow. Sir said anyone who's late gets a detention.'

'How much have you still got to do?'

'I've just started it.' Her shoulders said, 'And don't make any comment.' Rachel went in to the kitchen to put the kettle on. The dishes had not been washed. 'It was Simon's turn to help you,' said Kate, so quickly that it was clear she had been waiting for this moment. 'You forgot to make him do it before bed. And I'm not doing it.'

'Oh, stop it. You make me tired, you two. Did I ask you to do it?'

'No, but if I hadn't said that, you might have. Or said you were tired, so that I'd have felt I had to.' Rachel didn't answer. Teabag in mug, pour on boiling water. '*Are* you tired?' Kate asked.

'Yes.' Rachel came in with her tea, and sat down on the sofa to read her mother's letter.

Kate said, 'I hate it when you don't speak to me.'

'I'm not not speaking to you. I'm reading Ouma's letter.'

Kate came and sat next to her. 'I'll do the dishes if you promise to make Simon do my turn tomorrow. He's always getting off.'

Rachel gave her a hug. 'Forget the dishes and get your history book and sit here with me while I read.'

She made herself write to her mother as soon as she had finished reading the letter. She couldn't understand why she kept letting it slip.

She meant to write every fortnight and somehow - *Dear mom,* she began, and with an effort lifted herself from the here-and-now of a March night in London, to imagine her mother in Lourensrus nursing Auntie, who at over eighty had broken her leg. 'They had to operate at once,' her mother had written. 'The doctors said she probably wouldn't come through, and it's almost worse that she did. She's so weak she can't do anything for herself. And the weight she is, even turning her in the bed takes two people. Aunt Anna says I should get a day and a night nurse, but I don't much like the idea.'

'What does Ouma say?' Kate asked.

'Read it,' she said, and handed the letter over. *Dear Mom,* she wrote, *I was so sorry to hear about Auntie.* Then she stopped, not knowing how to go on. There was too little to say, or too much.

In her mother's letter the most significant things were those that were not mentioned. She did not say, Auntie is not expected to recover, but Rachel knew that must be so, for there was no other circumstance in which her mother would have considered hiring nurses. She did not say, nursing Auntie is a terrible strain, though it could not have been otherwise. Auntie, who had spent her life doing things for other people hated anyone doing anything for her. Now she needed someone to feed her and wash her and move her to prevent bedsores, and she would be fighting the indignity at every point.

There were other things never referred to. No mention of the fact that South Africa seemed to be blowing up, with more reports every day of violent clashes in the black townships. It probably had not yet affected Lourensrus, but surely her mother read the newspapers? Or maybe they aren't reporting most of it in South Africa. People make cocoons around themselves, Rachel thought, construct their own reality. There's Alistair, who can scarcely exist without stirring events in which he can feel that he's playing a crucial part, and Mom, who avoids thinking about anything that might make her insecure. Like Alistair, their separation - her mother had never once referred to it in her letters. Instead she wrote admiringly of how well Rachel coped in Alistair's absence, as if only the demands of his job kept him away. She had tried so hard for Rachel's sake to like Alistair and not to mind his politics. Now it seemed she didn't know how to put that process in reverse. The last time she had seen them was when Alistair had just been released from prison, when Rachel's loyalty had been at its most powerful. If her mother found it impossible to move on from that picture, well, that was up to her.

'Will Auntie die?' asked Kate.

'I think so, poppet.' She felt painfully disconnected, sitting here in her living room in Battersea. There ought to be something she could do, some appropriate action.

'Will you be sad?'

Rachel hugged her. 'She's very old. I wouldn't want her to keep living if she can't do any of the things she wants to do.'

Kate was silent a moment, thinking. Then she said, 'Why does everyone always call her Auntie and not Aunt Sara? Like Aunt Anna?'

Rachel smiled. 'I've no idea. Families are like that. All sorts of odd things happen that everyone takes for granted.' Then, 'Actually, everyone used to call her that, not just us. Everyone in Lourensrus knew her, and Afrikaans children are taught to say *Tannie* and *Oom* - Auntie and Uncle - to any older person. She never married, so she never became anyone's wife or mum but she was everyone's Auntie, not just ours.'

Dear Mom, I was so sorry to hear about Auntie...

*

She had hoped to get into the garden that weekend. There were signs of life stirring. Specks of pink on the dark branches of the prunus tree, the green spears of the daffodils rising tall, buds forming, preparing to burst. But all day Saturday it rained. Ben got noiser and more underfoot as she tried to get the household chores done. Simon moped around, unable to find anything he felt like doing. Kate had gone up to the King's Road with her friend Becky. 'What do you *do* all day, wandering up and down a stupid street with shops?' Simon had asked. 'You're too young to know,' Kate had said, and left. Simon's sulk deepened, and he and Ben started scrapping.

'What about going to the ice rink?' Rachel suggested.

They stopped at Haleemo's to see if Ahmed and Asha wanted to come. Anab's child, Sado, was there. Haleemo said, 'Anab went to see someone in East London and Sado didn't want to go.' So Sado came too. For an hour Rachel was beguiled by the delight of watching Ahmed hurtling into the middle of the rink to follow Ben and Simon, appearing not to mind how often he fell, and Asha and Sado, wide-eyed and shrieking excitedly as she cajoled them away from the rails, to slide and almost fall and clutch onto her to save themselves.

But as soon as she had dropped the other children off at home and was alone in the car with Sado, taking her home, Rachel was caught again - this time by Sado chattering innocently about the big boys on the estate where she and her mum lived, and how stupid they were, knocking on other people's doors and then running away; and how her own brother was much better than the ones around here. 'I didn't know you had a brother,' Rachel said, thinking, *I don't believe this, not again.* 'Why didn't he come with you?'

'He wouldn't,' Sado said. 'He wants to stay and fight the government. My mom says he's eighteen so it's up to him to decide. Anyway, he was in Hargeisa when we left and we were in Mogadishu. My mom had to go there to get a job, when my dad went to prison. She says it's good for girls to get an education then if something happens at least they can look after themselves and get a job or something.'

'Is your dad still in prison?'

'No, he died,' she said, with no particular emotion. 'When I was little.' Then, as if conscious that she might be misunderstood, 'He never did anything wrong, they just put him in prison like that, for nothing.'

'I know. Simon's dad was in prison too, and he also didn't do anything wrong.' She drove slowly in at the entrance to the estate, weaving her way over the tarmac between the blocks of flats to the one Sado pointed her to. 'Are you coming to see our flat?' Sado asked brightly as she got out. 'Of course,' said Rachel, and followed her up a stairwell liberally decorated with graffiti. One National Front slogan, surrounded by more generalised verbal abuse, undirected, just a statement of disillusion. The stairs smelt of urine. The idea of Anab in her flowing garments carrying herself with her back perfectly erect up these stairs each time she came home, seemed bizarre. On the fourth floor Sado ran ahead, along the open corridor to the door at the end, and rang the bell. By the time Rachel got there the door had been opened and Anab was inviting her in.

The flat was neat but oddly anonymous. The furniture had as little to do with Anab's own style as the block of flats itself; a cheap sofa and arm chairs covered in synthetic fabric, nothing personal about any of the items in the room. A borrowed life, not her own.

Rachel followed Anab into the kitchen while she made tea. 'Tell me about your son,' she asked. Anab had her back to her, busy with the kettle. She turned her head to look at Rachel. 'What did Sado say?'

'Just that he didn't want to leave.'

'No. And it's bad for young men now in the north, especially the people of our clan. But he says what's the use of being a refugee and having no country of your own?'

The words jolted her, back to Johannesburg of five years ago and her friend Mphande saying, 'I'm not leaving,' when each day they heard of another friend detained, this one banned, that one tortured in prison. Mphande, her colleague, a man who had had to work by day as a messenger and study by night for eight years to get a degree and then to qualify as a librarian. Though she liked and admired him, she had no idea of the other work he did, for the banned African National Congress, but even his public activities were enough to make his friends afraid for him. There was an offer of a scholarship to study in America, but 'This is my country,' he said emphatically, 'no one's going to drive me out of it.' Two weeks later he was detained; under torture he signed a confession incriminating his friends and landing them with long prison sentences, while he, as state witness, walked out free. Then he finally left, no longer able to hold up his head in his country, from which he had said no one could drive him...

'You're a refugee too, aren't you?' Anab asked.

Am I? thought Rachel, momentarily disoriented, whipped too rapidly from London to Hargeisa to Johannesburg. She had never used the word for herself, but she couldn't think why. 'Not really. We were forced to leave, but there wasn't any trouble about getting in. My husband had a New Zealand passport.' And even if he hadn't, she thought, he was white, English-speaking, had contacts.

Anab said, 'Things are changing in your country. I saw on TV, even the children are in the streets, fighting the police!'

'It's been happening for decades. They're unbelievably brave, but I can't see how things are ever going to be any different. The bravest people just get shot or put in jail.'

'It *has* to change,' said Anab, as if that decided the matter. She brought the mugs of tea to the table, and sat down opposite Rachel.

They drank for a moment in silence. 'What made you leave?' Rachel asked.

Anab looked at her curiously. Something's changing between us, Rachel thought. We've never wanted to get into any of this before. Maybe she still doesn't. But Anab seemed to have become ready too. 'I worked in a government office,' she said. 'We used to hear things about the National Security Service, this man is going to be in trouble, they have talked about this one in the meeting, that one is next. If I knew the person, I would send a message to be careful. Then someone told me that they were beginning to suspect me.' She paused, then said, vehemently, 'They had killed my husband already. I didn't want Sado to have no one.' Then, her voice matter-of-fact again, 'So I thought I should get ready, in case I had to leave suddenly.'

'How did you do that?'

Anab laughed. 'You want the whole story?'

'I want to know how people get out. Haleemo's children -'

Anab looked at her oddly again. Then she said, 'No one can get on a plane without a passport and a visa. A friend of my sister is a doctor. She knew a man who worked in the British Embassy, a Somali man. His daughter was in prison, and she used to make sure the daughter got the medicines she needed. So she went to his house at night and said, 'My friend needs a visa. Now!"

'And a passport? '

'I managed,' Anab said, with a lift of her head that clearly prohibited further questions.

And then a phone call from Hymie and Lillian, the South African friends who had taken them in when they had first arrived. 'It's ages since we've seen you, Rachel,' which meant, since you told Alistair to go. Even before, it had always been he who arranged it. Why? She liked them, she admired them, they did everything possible to make her feel welcome. But - Memories of spending Sundays dragging the children to Golders Green on buses, when they would much rather have stayed home, for what was there for them to do in a house full of adults talking? 'Come and eat with us,' Lillian said. 'It's Hymie's birthday on Friday. We've got a couple of people coming.'

'The children -' Rachel said.

'Bring the children, we'd love to see them.'

I really should go, she thought, they've been so kind. But even when she had fixed a babysitter she realised she was still reluctant. She knew what 'a couple of people' would be. Ten, fifteen South African exiles, all vigorously analysing the latest political developments, about which she knew almost nothing, swopping news about other South Africans, last seen years ago. Did they not notice where they were living? Had nothing that had happened to them since they had left made any impact on their consciousness compared to this one obsessive concern? And then - *Why am I not as involved as they are?* - being revisited by that insidious white liberal guilt that she thought she had shed years ago, of which she had been so glad to be free.

She remembered Pat breaking through her unspoken defences in the first few weeks they had worked together in the library, to ask, 'What's your accent, Rachel?' and Rachel had been aware of a pause just too long to be natural before she told her.

'I thought so,' said Pat, 'but I wasn't sure. I didn't think -'

'That I seemed a typical white South African?'

Pat looked surprised. 'Have I offended you?'

'No,' said Rachel. 'It's just me being defensive. I'm glad you asked.' And then, 'When I first came to Britain I had this naive idea that here at least I could slip into the background and just be a person, not part of a category. In South Africa you can't escape it. Whatever you feel as an individual your colour is like a brand. You're typed before you ever open your mouth.'

Pat said, with a firmness that made her want to hug her, 'Anyone who typed you would be crazy.'

But Pat was Pat. Strangers were different, especially the politically conscious. Like Hassan Abdillahi. That odd, almost aggressive way in which he had pushed her away when she had, after all, gone with what must have been to him a perfectly ordinary query. Maybe it was her accent - 'Why do I have to deal with this white South African woman?'

The night after Hymie's birthday meal she was troubled by an endless series of dreams about Lourensrus, from which she would wake, remembering, and then drift off again... To find herself this time in Aunt Anna's house, at some kind of family gathering. At first she thought they were all together, the whole clan. Then she realised that neither of the uncles were there, and of the cousins only Daniel and Sannie. She could not work out why the others had not been invited, especially Stefan and Willem who were after all Aunt Anna's children. It did not occur to her to ask anyone about it. They wouldn't tell me, she thought, I've been away too long. I'm not one of them any more.

Aunt Anna was trying to get everyone to sit down at the table and eat. Rachel's father had disappeared again. He hated it when Aunt Anna was so loud and organising. Rachel went to look for him, but he had gone. He was not there at all, not anywhere in the house nor in the garden. 'I wanted to talk to him,' she told her mother urgently. 'Why did he go without even saying goodbye? There were lots of things I wanted to talk to him about.'

She woke, and lay for a moment letting the dream seep away. And in its place crept the sadness that she had not yet allowed herself to properly feel. Auntie was dying. So far, so very far away.

2

He glanced at his watch and was amazed to see that it was already almost ten thirty and he was about to be late for the meeting with the director. He started grabbing his papers - he was damned if he was going to give those stuffed shirts the chance to make jokes about African time. He ran down the corridor, skidding to a halt at reception to tell Barbara when he would be back. She was trying to explain to a persistent Somali that it was impossible for him to see Hassan Abdillahi today. Behind the exasperated man stood a silent woman, automatically adjusting her headscarf as he arrived. 'Nabad,' Hassan greeted them. The man said 'Nabad ina adeer' - greeting him as 'cousin' to establish familiarity - and then, in the knowledge that no one else would understand while they spoke Somali, 'This stupid woman didn't want to see sense!'

Hassan said, 'She's only doing what I asked her to do. I'm on my way to a meeting. I'm sure one of the others can help you.'

'It's you I must see,' the man insisted. 'I am Yusuf Ali Burale. My sister-in-law's friend, an English woman, she came to see you.'

'Ah! I didn't realise!' Hassan switched back to English and turned to Barbara. 'It's a case I've already started. I'll take it. Do me a favour, phone Martin, tell him I've been unavoidably held up. Be there in a few minutes!'

Back in the corridor Yusuf started in on the inevitable succession of clan questions. 'You are Isaaq?' Hassan cut him short, laughing and refusing to say more than, 'I'm Somali!' He turned to the woman. 'And your name?' Before she could reply Yusuf said, 'Haleemo Nur Warsame.' Hassan thought, this bloke thinks I'm going to let him take over. Once they were in his office he addressed all his questions directly to Haleemo, preventing Yusuf from answering for her, and was amused at how pleased he felt with himself for winning that one. But it was all very brief. All he had time to do was photocopy her documents, and promise to phone her as soon as he'd found out what was happening to her application. Yusuf wrote down a number for him. 'Mine,' he said. 'Haleemo doesn't have a phone.'

'What about your English friend?' Hassan asked. But Haleemo did not know the number; Yusuf, it appeared, had not even met her.

He was only ten minutes late for the meeting, but they had waited for him and it was obvious that Martin was critical, in that controlled, English way. He felt as alien from Martin's style as he had a few minutes earlier from Yusuf's. If Martin had a complaint, why didn't he make it? Straight out, like any sensible human being. Instead there was this implication that Hassan and his lapses were being kindly tolerated, which immediately evoked what Farida used to call his camel look; nose in the air, don't think you can patronise me.

When he got back from the meeting he dialled the Home Office. Not the number members of the public were given, which as far as he could tell was never answered, but the number that got him through to James Freeman. He was lucky to find him in. 'James? Hassan Adbillahi here, from ACRAS. I have an enquiry about a Mrs. Haleemo Nur Wasame from Somalia; entered at Heathrow on November 3rd last year. I wondered if you could find out for me what stage her application has reached?'

'I'll have a go. Give me the details.' Hassan gave them, then lodged the receiver between his shoulder and his ear, to open the day's mail while he waited. James' voice returned. 'Hassan? Look, I'll have to call you back later today. Can't trace the file for the moment.'

Too risky to leave it up to James, he might never get round to it. Aloud Hassan said, 'I'll ring you. End of the morning, say?'

'OK. Do my best.'

What a start! Lost her bloody file. Maybe someone ought to tell them about alphabetical order.

Just after twelve he phoned again, and kept ringing at ten minute intervals. Mr Freeman was busy. Or on the other line. Dealing with an enquiry. Out of the room for a few minutes. Please ring back. Sorry, we're a bit busy, can't deal with your problem now. Try again next week. There's a big backlog... Meanwhile back in Hargeisa, or Jafna, or Baghdad, time was running out.

One thirty. If he didn't get James Freeman now the man would go out for the afternoon, and by tomorrow they'd be saying he was off somewhere for a week's conference. He dialled again. *Al hamdu lillah!* Praise be to God, he was in. 'Ah, Hassan. Yes. Sorry. I gather you've tried before. Rather a lot going on here.'

'That's OK,' Hassan said. 'Did you find anything?'

'Yes, yes, I have the file. Everything seems to be OK. She's been granted exceptional leave to remain. The letter should be going out to her in a day or so.'

'That's not OK. She needs refugee status.'

James coughed. 'So does everyone, in a sense, don't they?'

'James, I need you to help me with this case. She has two young children in northern Somalia, in acute danger. She needs permission to bring them here to join her. Now. If that letter gets sent to her now, she can't reapply for a year, and God knows what will have happened by then.'

'Ah. Yes.' There was a pause. Hassan waited to see what it would produce. 'Tricky,' was all James said.

'Exactly. Can you have a look at the statement they took off her at the airport? Any mention of the children?'

'I'm just looking. Two children, Asha, born 1980, Ahmed, born 1983.'

'Those are the ones she has with her. You're looking for Nafisa and Abokor.'

'No, nothing I can see.'

'Right, so there's additional information she needs to submit before a decision is made. You know what it's like with those airport statements. People don't say half the relevant things because they've been trained to be terrified of officials. Can you stop that letter being sent to her, James? Give me time to get an additional statement in to you?'

James hedged. 'Of course you do realise, don't you, the protocol in these matters? Difficult for me to interfere laterally. Decision by an officer in a different section, not someone who reports to me.'

'I understand all that. But it's an emergency. Those children are in the midst of an explosive situation. I wouldn't like to feel we're putting their lives at risk out of too great a sensitivity for protocol.'

James hummed and hawed a bit further, but Hassan could hear that he was moving. He let James continue talking, waiting for him to work himself round to the point of agreeing. Finally he was rewarded. 'Well perhaps,' James said. 'Leave it with me for a few days. I'll see if I can make a few tactful enquiries. Come back to you on it.'

'Thanks!' Hassan didn't bother to keep the triumph out of his voice. 'That's just what I was hoping you'd say!' And as he put the phone down he felt energy pulsing through him. Amazing, he thought, I feel alive, ready to shout. Just from that one tenuous victory! Fighting suited him, there was no doubt about it, even if it wasn't the kind of fighting Mohamed would have recognised.

He woke on Saturday morning to the sound of rain, and an odd sense that something was about to happen. Was he supposed to be doing something that he had forgotten about? A bit of shopping, clothes to the laundrette. Before Monday he would have to finish that report on appeals. Apart from that, nothing he could think of. He pulled the duvet almost over his head, hoping to go back to sleep for another half hour at least.

But the premonition refused to go away. It wasn't unpleasant, a tinge of tension, but offering possibilities. *Aabahay* - his father! Maybe something was happening to him, this minute, and across all those thousands of miles the telepathy between them had woken him!

Now there was no point in pretending he would sleep again. He got up to make himself some coffee, staring vaguely through the window at the rain as he drank it. It was sheeting down, nothing like the usual boring English drizzle. He thought of going out to get a newspaper but it seemed scarcely worth getting so wet. He liked this kind of rain. Not quite as dramatic as a Somali thunderstorm, but getting on that way. He remembered Farida's excitement once when it had rained like this. 'We used to run out into it when we were children,' she had said, 'with all our clothes on; and get soaked! Did you do that?' 'Yes,' he had said, 'exactly like that! Mohamed and me. My mother could never get used to the idea that it didn't matter getting wet, because it was so warm.'

Why was he thinking of Farida again, after all these years? There was definitely something odd going on inside him. That strange waking feeling had not gone away. Something significant was happening to someone he cared about, someone he was separated from. How he could possibly be aware of it he did not know, but he felt increasingly sure that something was being required of him and he needed to know what it was.

He phoned Mohamed's number. Mohamed himself answered, his voice lumpy, half asleep. Hassan said, 'Have you heard anything?'

'About what?'

'Anything. Aabahay?' And then a new thought. 'Nuh?'

'No,' said Mohamed, awake now. 'What's happened?'

'I don't know. Sorry I woke you. Listen, if you hear anything, phone me right away.'

'What's come over you? You think I wouldn't tell you?'

Hassan laughed. 'OK, forget it. I don't know what's happened to me either. I just woke with this odd feeling. Restless, like waiting for something important to happen.'

'Probably indigestion,' Mohamed grunted. 'I'm going back to sleep.'

Hassan put the phone down. The rain seemed to be letting up. He would go for a walk. The moment he was outside the magic of a world washed clean by rain started working on him, calming his restlessness. The blades of grass held drops of water, nestling in cracks, wobbling like mercury. The air smelt sweet. A bird ruffed its feathers to shake off the wet. In Regent's Park the forsythia greeted him with so sensual a display of yellow that he stood for a few minutes before it, marvelling. Then, without notice, the rain came sheeting down again as if a trapdoor had opened above his head. People scattered to take shelter under trees or run to their cars. He began sprinting towards home, then thought, what's the point? and slowed down to a walk. He was already as wet as if he had been swimming; his shoes were squelching. Extraordinary rain, coming straight down, hard, smooth, unremitting. Enjoy it, he thought, go with it; his and Farida's kind of rain.

And now each thing he passed seemed to evoke Farida, and a time when he had not been alone. He passed Sombhai Patel's shop where they used to get milk and a newspaper, wandering down together as an idle Sunday morning ritual. She and Mr. Patel used to chat in Gujarati, and exchange reminiscences about Malawi, of which she had only a child's memories. Hassan would listen, trying to pick out the odd phrase he had learnt from Farida, but mostly just watching the way her long black hair shifted on her shoulders as she gestured. Once they were out of the shop she said, 'I'm sure he thinks I'm immoral, walking in there with an African! If it was his own daughter, he'd disown her!' They had laughed, but it was a brush with the reality Farida did not want to encounter - her own family. Hundreds of miles away in Lancashire, but waiting for her to return every university holiday, waiting only until her degree was over to arrange her marriage.

'You could tell them about my English mother,' Hassan had said. And they had laughed at that too as they lay together, too delighted with the discovery of each other to be able to take this long-distant future seriously. Farida said, 'The only good thing about you from their point of view would be that you're a Muslim. It's not going to help that you've got a Christian mother who allowed you to grow up in Godless ways!'

'She's not a Christian,' Hassan had said, 'Anyway, in Islam parents are expressly instructed to take their children's preferences into account.'

'I can tell you,' Farida said, 'they haven't heard of that in Blackburn!'

Inside the door of his flat he took off his outer clothes and, dripping over the floor rugs, took giant steps to the bathroom. He turned on the hot tap. Steam filled the small room, caressing him as he stripped. *'My heart is single and cannot be divided,'* he sang, a Somali song he had learnt from his father and then heard again in an East End cafe,

> *My heart is single and cannot be divided*
> *And it is fastened on a single hope,*
> *O you who might be the moon.*

The words were nonsense, he decided. People don't fasten their hearts on one beloved for life, regardless of how distant she keeps herself. But he had to admit he had felt like that for the first desperate months after

Farida had left - so suddenly in the end, as if she couldn't find another way; leaving him with all those unfinished, hurt, angry feelings.

He turned off the hot tap and ran in some cold, as little as possible, testing it constantly. Perfect. He climbed in, giving himself up to the water's scalding embrace. She must have been married three years now, he calculated. Had she simply exchanged her parents for her parents-in-law, still having to look over her shoulder while they monitored everything she did? He did not bother to imagine her husband. The man seemed irrelevant, as much a pawn in the process as Farida herself. He plunged his head under water, wanting the pleasurable shock to surround this last bit of him. He surfaced, shook his head to get the water out of his ears, and gave himself a perfunctory soap and rinse. 'I couldn't tell them,' she had said, each time she came back from Blackburn, 'not with my uncle's family having just arrived from Malawi. I couldn't disgrace my parents in front of all those relatives.' But by the next holiday her brother had just lost his job, so then, too, it had been impossible to add to her parents' anxieties. And the holiday after that her younger sister's marriage was being arranged. 'Zubeida *wants* them to do it. She's had to wait two years because they said it was my turn first and I keep refusing the people they find for me. If I told them now, the boy's family would probably pull out. I couldn't do that to Zubeida. Or to my mom.'

'And what are you doing to yourself?' Hassan demanded. 'Do you owe yourself nothing?'

'In my family's eyes I do nothing but think about my own needs.'

'Well they're wrong, and you know it. If that man they've found for her is so narrowminded, she's better off without him. Write to them, write to them now!'

'Hassan, please,' she begged, as if it would all go away if he would only stop nagging her. 'You don't understand -'

'I understand only too well,' he had said, raging. 'I've seen what a family like yours did to my mother, and you're not going to let them do it to you.'

But she had.

He climbed out, and started towelling himself. The phone rang. He was only half dry and by now wrapped in his aloneness, not wanting to have to connect with anyone else. He let it ring. Then the pressure of that insistent tone became too much for him and he went through to the living room, the towel around his waist. 'Hello.' There was a short pause before anyone responded, the kind, he realised with a shock, that comes on long distance lines, as if the sound of his 'Hello' had taken several seconds to reach the listener. Then a voice said, 'Hassan?'

For a moment he could not speak.

'Hassan? Can you hear?'

'Nuh! Where the hell are you? We've been worried sick.'

'It's OK, I'm out. I'm phoning from Nairobi.' Hassan was gripping the receiver as if it were physically linked to Nuh. His voice seemed unbelievably close. 'I'm coming to London,' Nuh said. 'There may be some problem at the airport. Can you meet me?'

'Of course. When?'

'I don't know yet. Still got some things to fix up.'

'Listen,' Hassan felt the urgency pounding through him, 'whatever you do, don't leave the airport at Nairobi. Stay in transit. It's crucial to your being allowed in here.'

'I'm not at the airport. I came by truck.'

'If you've got any papers to show you were officially let in, throw them away as soon as you're on the plane. Down the toilet, if necessary. Otherwise they might try and send you back there the moment you arrive.'

'Thanks. I knew you'd be useful. Anything else?'

'If you can't let me know the flight, phone from the airport. If they say they're not going to let you in, I'll have only forty eight hours to challenge it, so you have to get hold of me fast. What's happening about Amina and the baby?'

'They're OK for the moment, but I'm going to need your help with them too.'

If I can give it, thought Hassan, but he said nothing. Now was not the time.

'I have to go,' Nuh said.

'Nabad gelyo,' Hassan said - go in peace; and as he stood there, half-naked, with the silent receiver still in his hand, he could hear his father's voice reciting for Nuh their private leave-taking poem -

> Yet may God place a shield of coolest air
> Between your body and the assailant sun,
> And in a random scorching flame of wind
> That parches the painful throat, and sears the flesh,
> May God, in His compassion, let you find
> The great-boughed tree that will protect and shade.

Please God, whispered Hassan, knowing there was no God to hear. Just this once.

*

Outside the common room window the rain mizzled on without commitment. 'The photocopier,' Hassan said. 'Your item, Barbara.' Barbara began explaining why it was time they had a new one. Problems with the toner, the paper constantly getting jammed. No one disagreed. 'Right,' said Hassan; on to the next item. 'Juan, recordkeeping.'

They plodded through the small practical decisions. No one seemed to have the energy to argue about anything. 'Mike, you wanted to say something about the Tamil deportations.'

Mike altered his slouching position marginally and said, 'I assume you all know about the demonstration?'

What a typical Mike introduction, thought Hassan, ensuring that anyone who doesn't happen to be as involved as Mike is made to feel ignorant. He glanced over at Juan. Yes, he was stretching his arms behind his head, his invariable gesture when irritated. 'No,' Juan said, 'I don't know.' I bet he did, thought Hassan. He's being deliberately provocative. Mike said, 'We're protesting against the enforced deportation of the Tamil asylum seekers. Two weeks' time, Sunday the nineteenth, starting at ten, Trafalgar Square.' Silence. Then, 'Well, is everyone going?'

'I'll be there,' Hassan said, though Mike already knew that. Jenny said, 'I'm afraid I won't. I did know about it, but my sister's getting married that weekend, in Bristol.' The others said nothing. Mike blurted out, 'What the hell do we think we're on about, sitting here and talking about photocopiers, and we're not even sure if we're all going to this demo? Hundreds of Tamil refugees are being denied recognition. The government has already sent five of them back to Sri Lanka, and they'll be sending back more. And we can still sit here and wonder whether it's worth the effort of demonstrating!'

Hassan was now fully alert, watching the others. Jenny was staring at Mike, adjusting to the unusual force behind his shambling appearance. Barbara's face had gone a blotchy pink and white. She's offended, thought Hassan - the reference to the photocopier. Juan, his hands held behind his head, rocked slightly in his chair, a detached look in his eye. He appeared to be considering some unrelated topic. Gita spoke, the first thing she had said all meeting. 'You're right. I hadn't thought of it like that. I'll come.' Mike nodded acknowledgement. 'And the rest of you?'

'Hold on.' Juan brought his arms down and leaned aggressively across the table. 'Let's just take this slowly. Is this some kind of politburo, checking up on our political line? I thought this was a job I did, not a party I belonged to.'

'And why do you do the job?' asked Mike. 'I've often wondered.'

Hassan moved in. 'Come on, let's not get personal. What exactly are you proposing, Mike?'

'That we ought to be going together, with an ACRAS banner.'

'An ACRAS banner?' Hassan demanded, incredulous. 'And what do you suppose that will do for our image with the Home Office?'

Mike said aggressively, 'I thought we were supposed to be representing our clients, not the interests of the Home Office.'

'We are. But the word represent is crucial. That's all we can do, and it's the Home Office who decides, in every case. The moment they classify us as part of the loony left we lose any chance of being listened to.'

'The issue,' Mike flung back at him, 'is whether we're serious about trying to change things, or whether we're just going to plod along administering their bloody system for them. And it's clear what your view is.'

'I didn't intend to be unclear. We lose our credentials for getting individual cases sorted out if ACRAS is seen as being constantly on the streets.' He saw Mike was about to reply, and pushed on. 'None of us likes it, but it's how the job is constructed. You knew that when you took it on.'

Barbara suddenly spoke. 'I agree.' Hassan saw Mike's eyebrows lift, as if to say, does she have a vote? She's only the receptionist. Just you try saying that, Hassan thought, I'll make mincemeat of you. Mike glared at him, and said nothing. Hassan turned to Jenny. 'You haven't said anything. You've been here longer than any of us. What do you think?'

'I don't know. To me it's more a problem of time than of principle. If we really took seriously what Mike's suggesting, we could be busy every weekend and three nights a week. Before I came here I spent a year of my life working to defend the right to abortions. It was worth it, but I couldn't do it now, not with two children and a full time job! Not unless we said it's part of the job and we take off time in lieu from normal work time. But then what happens to our casework? We're pushed enough as it is.'

Mike said, 'If this campaign succeeds in getting the policy towards Tamils changed, a huge chunk of our casework would fall away!'

'Yes,' said Jenny, 'but what would you rate your chances of success?'

'It depends on how many people help.'

'Listen,' Hassan cut across, 'we're going round in circles. Let's give it a couple of weeks. We'll come back to it when everyone's had a chance to think about it. Meanwhile things continue as they have been.'

'Are you saying you're deciding, then?' asked Mike.

'That's right,' Hassan said, refusing to rise. 'For the moment I'm deciding. We're already ten minutes over time. There are clients waiting. Any other urgent business?'

He phoned Jeyam that evening, feeling in need of companionship. 'Where the hell have you been,' Jeyam said, 'you're never in when I phone.'

'I'm coming over,' Hassan said. 'Get busy on the fatted calf!'

'Don't be obscene, you're speaking to a lapsed Hindu.'

Over fish and chips Jeyam said, 'We need help on the Tamil campaign. We're running up fantastic legal costs, challenging the deportations. How about running a jumble sale? Or a sponsored walk?'

'No thanks,' grinned Hassan. 'My talents lie elsewhere.'

'Mine too. And here I am spending my days shaking a tin up and down at people on campus. It's amazing what you get dragged into!' His voice was light and cynical, full of the undergraduate energy he had never lost. It was extraordinary, thought Hassan, that someone like Jeyam should have become politically active. Flippant, irreverent, privileged child of wealthy parents; a brilliant maths student with every possibility of finding a comfortable well-paid job, the last person one would expect to find making rousing speeches at meetings. Simply being a Sri Lankan Tamil had pushed him into it. He had been trapped, when he had finished his degree, by the impossibility of going back to Sri Lanka. He had stayed on to do a second degree - 'Give things at home a chance to cool down,' he had said; and when instead they had hotted up he had registered for a Ph.D. Each year he applied to the Home Office for an extension of his student visa, and sent another appeal for money to his father and uncles, who would have paid anything to keep him out of reach of the Sri Lankan armed forces. But what was he going to do when he ran out of degrees?

'We had a dispute about your demonstration at work,' Hassan said. 'Mike suggested we come as an ACRAS contingent. I told him it wasn't on.'

'Why the hell not?'

'Because next time I'm on the phone to someone in the Home Office I want to be able to argue as a respectable caseworker, not be dismissed as a street campaigner!'

'That's all balls. They don't listen to anything except pressure. That job has got to your soul, Hassan Abdillahi. You'll be talking about a house in the country and your pension next.'

'Don't be a fool,' Hassan said. 'My job isn't going to stop me coming to your demonstration. I just won't be wearing an ACRAS label!' But the moment he had left, the protection of their bantering style deserted him, and he knew Jeyam was right. How much do I ever achieve by arguing as a respectable caseworker? A succession of tedious phone calls and form filling, files and reports and meetings; head down, don't stop to think, you might discover you're powerless.

Everyone else had gone home. He had been out at a meeting all afternoon, and come into his office simply to collect his things before going home. A message on his desk, Barbara's writing. 'James Freeman phoned, from the Home Office. He's very sorry, but Mrs. Warsame's letter has already been sent.'

Damn, damn, damn. He stared out of the window, seeing Haleemo's withdrawn face and Rachel Sinclair's urgent one. He felt heavy limbed, and threatened by depression. 'What do you do there all day, anyway?' Mohamed had asked him once. 'I fight cases,' he had replied. And what was so special about this case, that losing it should cast him into despair? 'You have to learn not to waste energy on the ones you've already lost,' he had told Gita in her first week. 'Save it for the ones you've got a chance of winning.' It felt a long time since he'd won anything.

He locked up, and set off down the corridor. 'They don't listen to anything but pressure,' Jeyam had said. He saw Rachel Sinclair's eyes widening as she said, 'They can let her stay four years and still not let her bring her children in? But that's unbelievable!' And then Mike, saying, 'If this campaign succeeds, a huge chunk of our casework would fall away!' Mohamed's voice, 'You still feel it is enough to sit in your safe office, behind a desk?' *No!* It was not enough! If these were his battles, then he should fight them to win. They don't listen to anything but pressure - right then, pressure was what they would get.

He turned back to his office, unlocked, dumped his briefcase on the desk, looked through his files for the number he had been given by Yusuf Ali Burale, and reached for the telephone. Then he put the receiver down again, and for a long time sat thinking. Eventually he picked it up again and dialled. Yusuf was not in. 'Ask him to phone Hassan Abdillahi, as soon as possible,' he said. 'It's urgent.' And he left his home number, a thing he would not normally have contemplated doing.

Out on the pavement he ran towards the station, the rhythm of his feet pounding through his body,

If you, O Aynabo, my fleet and fiery horse -

slowing down as he neared the entrance, halting momentarily at the ticket barrier to show his season ticket, and then thump, thump again, down the escalator,

Do not grow battle-worn, and slow of foot, and weak -

The pounding in his body had become a voice reciting, deep, steady, chanting the rhythmic syllables of a battle pledge; facing up to the challenge that could no longer be evaded.

And if your shining flanks and finely arching neck
Do not grow gaunt and thin as the branch on the dry grey thorn;
And if your frenzied hooves do not flail through the dead,
The bodies piled as high as ever grew the grass;
And if the sky in future does not its colour change,
Filled with the dust of death, reflecting the flare of the fray -
And if a man among us can draw the name of peace
Forth from the deepest well where I have flung it down...

This was his battle. There was one possible way to get Haleemo Nur Warsame's children out of Hargeisa safely, and he would try it; he and Rachel Sinclair, *Insha' Allah*. God willing.

3

The washing machine was running and she had just started hoovering when Simon came and stood in front of her, signalling through the noise of both machines that there was someone at the door. 'You go,' she yelled, still hoovering. 'It's probably one of your friends.'

'It's not,' he mimed, and settled the matter by going upstairs. She turned off the hoover and went to the door. She knew as soon as she saw the man standing there that this must be something to do with Haleemo. His name, he said, was Yusuf Ali Burale, Haleemo's brother-in-law, and he hoped he wasn't disturbing her. 'No, no,' she said, 'please come in. Has something happened?' But no, there was no news of the children. She offered him tea and then waited while he got past the polite introductory noises to hear what he had come for. This took some time, involving a detour via the political situation in Somalia. He fired off phrases like 'the crimes of the fascist dictatorship of Siyad Barre' and 'gross violations of human rights' in guttural but fluent English, without pausing to see if she was following, in just the way she had been used to hearing them from Alistair. She amused herself by imagining them together, both at home with the abstract concepts that made so much less impact on her than Haleemo's personal story had done. Yusuf's rhetoric was peppered with Somali words that he didn't stop to explain but which she eventually guessed must be clan names. 'Marehan,' he pronounced with distaste, and seeing the incomprehension on her face, 'Siyad Barre is Marehan.' Then, appearing to despair of her capacity to understand, he abruptly changed the subject. 'I saw that man, Hassan Abdillahi. It is very good that you are helping my sister-in-law.'

'I only wish there was something I could do,' Rachel said.

'Definitely,' Yusuf said. 'Your influence is very important. Hassan Abdillahi began to be helpful as soon as he heard Haleemo was your friend.'

Rachel stared, and then started laughing at the absurdity of it. 'No, no,' she said, 'it wasn't at all like that. I don't have any influence!'

'Definitely,' Yusuf insisted. 'Only when he heard she was your friend, then he was ready to help me. Before that he was telling me, 'Come back next week!' Anyway, he is Somali. We need some

English people to take up this case. The Home Office people will not listen to a Somali.'

'Honestly, I don't know a single person in the Home Office. I wish I did! I'm a foreigner myself, didn't Haleemo tell you?' But even when she explained, he disregarded it. After all, I'm white, she thought, he's convinced that's all that matters to the officials. And maybe he wasn't far wrong. She had travelled six thousand miles, and still she was shadowed by that unasked-for privilege.

At that point there was a shriek from Ben, not a demanding-child noise, a real crisis. She was upstairs before she realised she had moved, to find Ben with the contents of an entire bookcase on top of him. He was uninjured, miraculously, just a few bruises. Only after she and Simon had got the bookcase back upright, and all the books back in it, and she had cuddled Ben and told both the boys about the time her cousin Daniel had fallen off the garage roof, did she remember she had left Yusuf downstairs, with no one to listen to him. She dashed down again. He was standing at the door, ready to go. He said, as she came breathless and apologetic towards him, 'Hassan Abdillahi said, please will you phone him. As soon as possible.'

'Rachel Sinclair? Thank you for phoning.' His voice had none of the abruptness that had made her feel attacked when she had met him, yet there was something that connected with that, a pent-up energy needing release. 'Would you be able to come in sometime? There's something I thought we might try.' The words were firm and purposeful, as if something involving her had already been decided. Instinctively she baulked. 'Can you give me some idea what it is?'

'It isn't something we could easily discuss by phone.'

What's wrong with this man? she thought. Why is there always a hidden agenda? She pulled herself up. He must think her silence odd. As she was about to say, 'OK, I'll come,' he spoke again, his voice now edgy, 'If it's too difficult -'

'No, I'll come. When?'

'As soon as you can manage. I'm free tomorrow afternoon, if that's any good.'

Tomorrow turned out to be the first day of her period, and everything felt an effort. She had decided not to ask anyone else to collect the children, but to go to ACRAS between finishing work at one and school-collecting time. 'If anything happens and I'm late,' she said, 'you're to walk home together. And Ben, you have to hold Simon's hand across the road.' They had done it once before and all had been well, but today they niggled at each other all through breakfast, and she began to feel guilty in advance, as if some accident had already happened and she was explaining to some outraged authority - herself - why she had been so negligent.

It was cold and blowy as she waited for the bus. Empty crisp packets and cigarette cartons whirled across the road and were blown into little piles up against walls and lamp-posts. People huddled into themselves as they hurried along the pavements, resisting the wind. She realised her body was doing the same, tensing up against the prospect of meeting Hassan Abdillahi again, at the thought of his unpredictable manner, alternately friendly and abrupt. Who was to say which it would be today? And why had he not been willing to tell her what he had in mind? It was like being back in South Africa, having to be careful what you said on the phone.

But when she got there his eyes were smiling, not tired and cut off as they had been last time. 'I'm glad you've come,' he said. She began to relax; and the moment he started telling her what had happened to Haleemo's case she forgot about her own tension.

He was watching her face as he told her, and he was not disappointed. She said, immediately, 'Surely there must be something that can be done?'

'There are various possibilities. Technically she can apply to change her status in a year's time.'

'That's too long!'

'Exactly. We'll do an immediate application anyway, on the grounds that the full facts weren't before the officials when the decision was made; but I can tell you now what the answer will be.'

'It doesn't make sense. If they think she's got enough of a case to let her stay, why would they say no to her children?'

'There are things you need to understand about the context in which these decisions are made. Britain is a signatory to the UN Convention on Refugees; the government would be reluctant to openly flout an international agreement by sending her back. But they're not obliged to take anyone who isn't already on their doorstep, and they go out of their way to make it difficult for people to get here. You know about the Sri Lankan Tamils?'

'A bit,' said Rachel. 'I know that lots of them tried to come in as refugees.'

'Since 1985 there have been a thousand, two thousand Tamils applying for asylum each year. Almost none of them have been given full refugee status. The British government has, in effect, refused to recognise their situation as one which causes them to be refugees, even though the facts of how they are persecuted are public knowledge. They are being described as 'economic migrants', people whose only reason for coming here is that they think they can earn more money in Britain. It's a way of closing the door to what is seen as a new flood of black immigrants. The bigger the numbers of people trying to come in, the harder it is to get full refugee rights for any one of them. You won't get government officials to admit it, but if you look at the figures, it shows.' It was time to get to the point. 'I wondered how well you know Haleemo?'

She looked surprised. 'I'm just a friend. I told you, one of her children is in the same class as my youngest son. He and his sister come over to play quite often. That's about it, really.' He was about to speak when she said, 'We've got another friend whose son is also in Hargeisa. He's eighteen. I suppose that's too old to be considered a dependant?' Then she suddenly burst out, just as his father would have done, 'They killed her husband. In prison. Tortured him till he collapsed. He was a doctor; all he had done was help set up a community project in the hospital. They gave him twenty years and didn't even let him live one.'

He felt moved by her vehemence. 'It's happening all the time,' he said, and for a moment neither of them spoke. Then he started, allowing himself now to feel excited, knowing that he could trust her to react as he needed her to. 'These women you know, the thing that's unusual about their situation is that they have some friends who aren't Somalis. Most new refugees live in a closed world. A lot of them are men, without their families; a handful get work after they've been here six months, some never manage to find anything. They spend their time visiting each other, talking obsessively about what's happening in their own country. What's different about your friends is that they've managed to bring young children with them, so the school gives them a point of contact.'

He's asking me to do something, Rachel thought, and despite the easy way they had been talking, she felt a certain wariness return. 'Once or twice in recent years,' he was saying, 'there have been campaigns organised by local people on behalf of someone who's in trouble with the immigration laws. You may have heard of Afia Begum, who went into hiding with her baby to avoid being deported? Or the Hasbudaks? They had children in a school in Hackney, and the school turned out in force - teachers, parents, children - to try to prevent them being deported.'

When he used the word 'campaign' Rachel felt something closing in on her. She wanted to say, 'And did they win?' but the words would not come.

'Most of them were unsuccessful,' he said, as if in answer to her unspoken question. 'Both Afia Begum and the Hasbudaks were deported. But occasionally a campaign succeeds. There was a Pakistani woman, Rashida Abedi, totally deaf. She had no legal right to stay in Britain - her brother had brought her in and wanted to care for her, but brothers, even if they're British citizens, aren't entitled to bring their sisters to live with them. Yet in the end she was allowed to stay, only because a lot of people heard about her case and made a fuss.'

Her hands felt clammy. To get out into the open, she said, 'You're suggesting there should be a campaign about Haleemo?'

'It's worth a try. As far as I know there has never been one on just this issue before. Almost all of them have been to stop deportations. This is something more positive, if you like, the right to have your children with you. It might arouse quite widespread sympathy.'

With an effort she managed to say, 'Does Haleemo know what you're suggesting?'

'No.' He paused. 'I got the impression she isn't coping very well. I didn't see any point in raising the question with her until I'd seen you. But her brother-in-law thinks it's a good idea.' And then, as if he could see her clutching at this straw, 'He's in no position to start anything himself. Apart from anything else, he works for the Somali National Movement. All the people he knows are separated from their families; he couldn't undertake a public campaign that would single his sister-in-law out for special concessions.'

'And what do you think about that? You're Somali, aren't you?'

He looked startled, but said, 'Yes.'

'So what do you think? About making a special case for one person?'

'Listen.' His tone had become suddenly sharp. 'I don't know Haleemo. She is just one of the hundreds of clients I deal with every week. I'm scarcely likely to be suggesting a campaign on her behalf if she's the only person to benefit, am I?' He seemed to catch hold of himself; more quietly he said, 'If someone is prepared to undertake the task of organising it, a campaign for any one Somali seeking refugee status would highlight the need of all.' He spoke so differently from the way Alistair would have, with no element of self-importance; almost in the voice of a boy, sensitive and vulnerable like Simon, longing for life to be simple. She wanted to be able to respond to that warmth in him, but she could not. He was talking again, as if to help her on. 'In a campaign like this there is always some effect. Whether or not you succeeded in this one case, you would raise public awareness of what's going on, and that would make the Home Office more wary in how they deal with Somali refugees generally.'

He had said 'you'. It was all around her now, there was no way of getting out. 'You're suggesting I do it, aren't you?'

He shrugged. 'I don't know enough about your circumstances, or how deeply involved you feel. I just thought, since you had interested yourself in Haleemo's problems, I should mention the possibility to you.'

'I'll have to think about it. I've never done anything like it.' She could hear the panic in her voice, and she hated it. She could think of nothing more to say. Lamely she added, 'I wouldn't know where to start.'

The silence between them was uncomfortably long. When he spoke again he was businesslike, remote. 'Well, thank you for coming in. I'm sorry to have caused you an unnecessary journey.' And he stood up, to show her to the door.

He had seen the moment he started talking about a campaign that his instinct about her had been misplaced. She had stared at him with the eyes of a dik-dik, that smallest and most nervous of Somali antelope, caught on the road at night by the lights of an approaching truck, about to leap to safety. He was crazy to have asked her back. He had needed to find a way to act, and he couldn't do it alone; but how could he have beeen so foolish as to suggest to a woman about whom he knew nothing an undertaking of that magnitude? Yet rational argument could not stop him feeling let down. He was convinced that she had shown things about herself which had given him grounds to expect more of her. She had offered something, and then stared at him in terror when he had come to collect it. Once he had seen that look on her face he had stopped talking, wanting this to end, wanting her to go. She hovered, as if going would have admitted her inadequacy. His irritation mounted, uncontrollably. For a moment he saw himself in her face as he must appear to Mohamed, saying 'It's terrible, we can't let things go on like this,' and then not being able to cope with the thought of actual fighting. The woman's continued presence in his office had become an oppression. He stood up and went to the door. Get out, his body said. Just get out, quick.

The moment Rachel was outside the building she experienced profound relief, as if she had escaped from something that was dragging her down, back into - Into what? South Africa, again; visions of meetings, demonstrations, leaflets, petitions, speeches, police, prison - an intense fear, bound up with her complicated love and resentment of Alistair and her own inability to follow him. This is Britain, she told herself, not South Africa. They don't arrest people for going on demonstrations here. And then another voice said, they do! For just the other day there had been people arrested outside the South African embassy, in some scuffle with the police. But it wasn't the same, she knew perfectly well it wasn't. Her panic at being asked once again to become involved in political campaigning had been out of all proportion, a carry-over from a life now dead. Hassan Abdillahi must have thought her extraordinary.

And now she felt furious with him for putting her in this position, for dragging up her past and confronting her with it, for causing her to fail yet again. If he thought a campaign was so important, why didn't he organise it himself? He knew about all those other campaigns, he would know what to do, who to pressure. Why ask her ? How would her voice, her petition, her presence in a demonstration make any difference to the officials who decided Haleemo's fate?

She had walked right past the bus stop. She turned and walked back to join the queue, becoming aware as if for the first time of the people around her. She needed to talk to someone, to free herself from the burden that had been loaded onto her. She thought of Evelyn, Sophie, mothers of her children's friends. How could she? She had never talked to any of them about her South African experiences. Not that she had deliberately avoided doing so, but none of them had ever asked, and it seemed easier to meet on the level of what they had in common here. Anab, now she was different. But how could she say to Anab, who herself had risked so much, he suggested a way I could help Haleemo, and I was too afraid?

The bus had arrived. She climbed up to the top deck and stared out, seeing before her immigration officers, police, the officials who have the power to intervene in ordinary people's lives, to stamp a document and destroy the security that has been painstakingly reconstructed. She did not want to be noticed challenging the way the Home Office made decisions. She herself needed to be allowed to stay, so that her children could grow up in one place, knowing where they belonged, as she had done in Lourensrus, not be shifted off somewhere else to start all over again. If she could at least give them that rootedness, they could cope with whatever happened afterwards.

But why just her children? What about Haleemo's?

The bus was approaching the stop near the library. Pat! Of course, why hadn't she thought of it? She still had time before she had to get the children. She began making her way down the stairs. She could talk to Pat about anything, Pat never seemed to judge. The bus stopped. The door opened, but something prevented her getting off. She let the other passengers pass her, and then sat down on the nearest available seat, avoiding everyone's eyes. She wasn't ready. Pat wouldn't judge, but she wouldn't understand either; she had probably been involved in all sorts of campaigns herself. Rachel didn't want anyone telling her she could do it. It would be too difficult to explain why she couldn't.

She knew now that she would tell no one; especially not Haleemo. She did not know how she would face Haleemo this afternoon, knowing she had not been prepared to back up her friendship with action, knowing also that Haleemo was bound to hear from Yusuf. The sensible thing, the only sensible thing, would be to tell her first. But she knew she could not do it.

4

He had shut himself in his office. The door that was almost never closed for once announced to anyone who might have considered talking to him that he was not available. He worked with an angry efficiency, almost as if he were proving something to someone. He filed away all the case papers that he had had out on his desk, slamming the metal filing cabinet draw to shut them out of sight. In record time he cleared his in-tray of the host of minor, irritating pieces of paper that normally hung around for days. Invitations to conferences he was not going to attend. Advertising blurbs for new reference books no advice agency should be without. Viciously he scrunched each item into a ball and hurled it across the room to the waste paper basket, missing at least half the time.

A scrappily produced leaflet in Somali that Mohamed had sent him, handwritten and badly photocopied, not even straight on the page - notice of a demonstration to be held outside the Somali embassy, in protest against a new spate of killings. It would be the usual ghetto-ised affair, of course; no one outside the Somali community would even know it was happening. Of course he would go, he couldn't not go. But he wished to God that Mohamed and his friends would lift their heads a little, and make some effort to communicate with people other than Somalis. A campaign to stop British and American aid, for instance, that would pinch. Siyad's administration virtually subsisted on the aid revenue; if the west stopped supporting him, the whole oppressive apparatus might start to collapse. If they could get local people involved...

Damn Rachel Sinclair, he thought, screwing up Mohamed's leaflet and hurling it, accurately this time, across the room. Damn, damn, damn.

Why couldn't he do it anyway? Why did he need her? But before he had even framed the thought, he knew it was impossible. It would be one thing for him to support, in his spare time, a campaign that started in the world of ordinary people out there; inconceivable for him to initiate it. He couldn't do it, just as Yusuf couldn't. It needed someone who was not a Somali, not a professional refugee worker, someone who could reach beyond, to make others see and care.

The door opened and Yusuf came in, without an appointment of course, to find out if he had got any further with the plans for a campaign. Hassan snapped, 'There isn't going to be one,' and then, realising how curt he had been, 'Sit down, let me explain.' Yusuf seemed not to have expected any better. 'That English woman is no use,' he said. 'It needs someone in your position to intervene.' And he then immediately began to talk about Mohamed, whom he of course knew through SNM, but had only just discovered was Hassan's cousin. And since one of Yusuf's brothers was married to someone in Mohamed's mother's family, that meant that Hassan was virtually Haleemo's cousin, and so - Hassan became once again defensive. 'There's really nothing more I can do,' he said, and had to be almost rude in order to get rid of the man. But once Yusuf had gone the irritation went with him. How should Yusuf understand that the ties of family which had served him all his life were now useless, and that he would have to learn a new means of getting what he needed from officials? And what exactly was the new way? Where there is no nepotism, everyone waits in the queue for their turn, everyone has an equal chance - at what? At arousing the Home Secretary's compassion? You must be joking, Hassan Abdillahi Dahir.

The next morning over breakfast coffee he saw the headline, page two of The Independent, SUICIDE OF KURDISH REFUGEE. Gita's client! No, no - Awaiting deportation. Attempted suicide at Heathrow. Admitted to hospital. Transferred to Pentonville. Claimed he would be subject to torture if returned. No possibility of appeal. On Saturday found dead, hanging in his cell.

He stared at the printed words, seeing other things...

Hargeisa Prison. There was a place he had seen as a child. He was tagging behind uncle Ali, with Mohamed and Nuh, on a cold morning in the brief winter season. They came to the place near the market, where the lone acacia tree stood outside Madar Rashid's teashop, and uncle Ali got talking to the group of men gathered under the tree, talking and talking, till the boys were tired of playing in the sand and waiting for him to finish. Nuh led them off to where, he assured them, he had found a snake longer than uncle Musa's spear. The place was not where he remembered it, if they went just a little further he would find it - until Hassan thought they were lost. And then they had come suddenly upon a high wall, so high they could not see over, with bits of broken glass stuck into the mortar all along the top. 'It's the prison,' Nuh whispered, 'we'd better get away before they see us.' They had run all the way back, Hassan's heart pounding as he pushed himself to keep up with Nuh, who was so much older and could run so much faster, back to where the white flatroofed buildings of Hargeisa huddled together. 'It wasn't the prison,' panted Mohamed. 'If it was the prison, why weren't there any guards?' Nuh said, with complete conviction, 'There were, I saw them coming.' Coming, coming...

Hargeisa Prison. A photograph in an Amnesty report. Detainees sweeping out the prison. The medical director of Hargeisa hospital and nineteen others - doctors, teachers, civil servants - all serving sentences of between 15 years and life for starting a community self-help group. Men, women, school children, arrested for harbouring SNM supporters, for throwing stones at official cars, for being out after the curfew - now in prison, indefinitely. 'Torture of political prisoners is routine,' says the Amnesty report...

His father's deep voice, from another time, way, way back; reciting Raage Ugaas' poem of despair -

> *When men closed their doors*
> *before the awful darkness of the night,*
> *I arose.*
> *There emerged from the depths*
> *of my tormented being a deep groan*
> *like the rumbling thunder of a gloomy rain*
> *or the jarring sound of a thousand exploding guns*
> *or the obscene roar of a prowling, hungry lion.*
> *Only Allah knows the acute hurt of my scarred soul.*

He left his flat early, to get away from the voice. Barbara was in before him. 'Have you seen the paper?' she asked. He nodded, and gave her a hug, not being able to think of anything to say. In his office he began mechanically sorting out papers for the morning's team meeting. Gita appeared. Her slight, normally graceful body was rigid, like that of a frightened child. 'I saw,' he said. They stood silently together, mourning the death and their failure to avert it. He wished he could comfort her, and himself, as he had done with Barbara; but he did not risk it.

'Come,' he said eventually. 'The others will be waiting.'

The sense of gloom did not lift for days, and he saw that he was not the only one so affected. The death of a refugee - simply because his claim to be a refugee had not been listened to - struck at the heart of their work and felt like a personal defeat for each of them. Going to and from work each day he felt unusually oppressed by the people streaming into the underground station, down the escalator, crowding onto the airless platform, pushing into the train the moment the doors opened, standing crushed one against the other yet sealed off from each other, nothing human about their closeness; then pouring out of the doors again, surging along the platform, up the escalator, out into the street. Like the lines of ants he used to watch in his childhood, mindlessly following one after the other, programmed to go where they were going and return again each evening, no thought required, no independent action possible. Work, home. Home, work. Staying late to finish reports. Meetings after work, work-related commitments at the weekends. All the people he spent time with doing the same kind of work, involved in the same issues, in work time and out. This wasn't the way he wanted to live. And what was the point of it? Mike and Jeyam were right, it was not this scurrying activity but policy decisions at the top that decided whether lives would be saved or lost, a great boot stepping on the line of ants, or deciding to walk the other way. The only real hope was to influence where that boot fell.

The telephone rang. Barbara said, 'I've got London Weekend Television on the line. They're doing a two minute slot on the deportation of asylum seekers, a follow-up to the suicide. They want to know if you can put them in touch with someone who's about to be deported.'
'Tell them to go to hell,' he said, and put the phone down. His office felt like a prison, he had to get out. He walked through to reception, with no idea what he was going to do when he got there. 'I'm going to get some fresh air,' he said to Barbara, surprising himself as much as her. She looked at him thoughtfully, then said, 'It's already four. Why don't you just go home?' Conflicting thoughts flashed through his mind; he couldn't sort out which were important, which were not. How could he leave early, after having made an issue when Mike had done the same thing? But the desire to escape had become overwhelming. 'Yes,' he said suddenly, 'I'll do that. Thanks.' He went back to his room to get his things. Where would he go? Not back to the flat, another set of rooms, alone. He dialled Jeyam's number. No

answer. He felt abandoned. What's the matter with me? he thought. Does the guy have to sit at home waiting for me to call? He started piling papers into his briefcase, then stopped. You're crazy, he told himself, carrying papers to and fro like this. You're afraid to be alone, without even your work. He picked up the almost empty briefcase and walked out. He said to Barbara, 'If Juan wants to know where I've gone, tell him I've resigned.' Juan was always threatening to resign, never over major issues, but over things like unwashed coffee cups. Hassan thought, why do I bother to keep up that kind of banter when I'm feeling like this? We hide from each other the whole time.

But he wasn't hiding from Barbara. He wouldn't be leaving now if she hadn't seen. Maybe he was hiding from himself, trying not to face up to whatever was going wrong inside himself.

He took a bus to Regent's Park. He walked through the formal gardens without stopping, along the avenue of tall bare branched trees, past the cafeteria, and out into an area of open grass. He found a spot far from the nearest people, lay down on his back and stared at the sky; for about half an hour, he supposed. Then he rolled over onto his stomach and began to notice where he was. The shape of the bank next to which he was lying, the way the grass sprouted in tufts in some places, and was short and cropped in others. A stump of a tree, recently cut down. Presumably one of the casualties of the great storm. A group of Arab women and children went by. He caught a few Arabic phrases, and watched the way the women's long black garments swirled around their feet as they walked sedately, while the children darted around them, in bright blues and reds and greens, calling excitedly.

He felt somewhat better. Still fragile, but better enough to be glad he was nearly home now, and would have the evening quietly to himself. He had to take his life in hand and stop letting himself get so sucked down by his work. He would spend the weekend just being quiet. He would come here and lie under the trees, and watch the children, and remember that there was a life without crisis and war and prisons and damaged people. He would listen to music, read, sleep a lot, until he stopped feeling so tired, deep inside himself.

*

'We're going to the cinema,' Kate announced, and after her friends had gone spent the next hour in the bathroom, emerging smelling all dressed-up, as Ben said. She tried on five different combinations of clothes and finally set off in her oldest jeans and shapeless black jumper, to meet her friends at the busstop.

'Let me take you,' Rachel had said.

Kate said, 'Everyone goes by bus, Mom!' and Rachel had her first intimation of what might lie ahead for her and this unknown creature who spent hours in the bathroom. She said, 'Well you're not coming back on the bus. It'll be dark. I'll fetch you all,' having no idea whether Kate would regard this as a dire embarrassment or a useful service. It turned out, luckily, to be the latter. 'Ten fifteen, outside the Odeon, Streatham High Street,' Kate said as she swung out of the door.

But now it was only nine-thirty and the phone was ringing. Had something happened? Visions of Kate in trouble, of her friends, more streetwise, having taken her somewhere other than the cinema. Kate out of her depth.

It was Alistair, phoning from Frankfurt. 'On my way back to New York.' His voice was relaxed, as if they had spoken to each other only last week. Her chest tightened in instant defence. 'Are you coming via London?' she asked.

'I'd hoped to, but the flights didn't work out that way, and I have to be back earlier than I'd expected. I just thought I'd say hello.' The blood was thumping against her temples. Before she could stop herself she said, 'You know you forgot Simon's birthday?'

'Oh Christ, I'm sorry. It's been a hectic month. Look, tell them there's a parcel on the way to them all, I posted it in Nairobi. Tell me about them. How are they?' With an effort she made herself talk about each of the children in turn, fighting back the thought, 'If you took the trouble to stop over and see them more often I wouldn't have to be telling you all this.' Stop it, she told herself. He's asking, and you need him to know, so just tell him.

Gradually the very act of sharing her concerns, to however inadequate a partner, brought its own temporary comfort. When she had finished she was able to say, with genuine interest, 'Tell me where you've been.'

'Eritrea, mainly.' He began describing how he had been taken round the liberated zones. For once his knowledge did not have the effect of making her feel ignorant. She asked, 'Did you hear any talk about what's happening to the Isaaq in Somalia?' He said, 'It's appalling. I was saying to Gavin only yesterday - you know Gavin, the editor of

Africa Now? - someone really ought to do a feature on the Siyad Barre regime. It's one of the continent's great scandals, and the media are ignoring it. They won't let journalists in anymore, so no one's printing anything.' Then, suddenly registering, 'How do you know about it?' For a moment she was tempted to tell him about Haleemo, but instantly the embarrassing memory of how she had fled from Hassan Abdillahi's office intervened. She must be crazy to even think of letting Alistair, of all people, near such dangerous territory. Better keep to neutral topics. Then she remembered the far from neutral topic of money, which she had no choice but to raise now that she had him on the phone. Immediately his voice became cold and self protective. 'We've been through all this before, Rachel. No, I cannot make the payments any more regular, because my earnings aren't regular. If we'd still been living together our income would have been just as irregular, and you'd have had to learn to cope just the same. You have a regular salary, don't you? And you don't have to support two households.' At the mention of his other household Rachel's control snapped. 'And do you keep her short of money?' she yelled. 'Does she have to sit at home wondering whether there'll be enough to pay the bills?'

'It's no bloody business of yours!'

'It is my business when Kate comes to me and says can she go on a school journey with all the others, and I don't know whether there'll be enough money or not.'

There was silence. Then Alistair said, in a carefully controlled voice, 'Tell me what's needed.' Her anger collapsed and she was left feeling miserable from her own messy emotions. Why had she yelled like that? Why did she have to be so defensive? 'I'm sorry,' she said, to herself as much as to him. 'Not for asking about the money, but for shouting about your new -' (woman? lover? friend?) 'your new partner.' Even finding a word seemed a dangerous act. Yet the moment she had done so it was easier to accept the fact. Aloud she said, 'You're right, it's no business of mine, and I hope it works out well for you. But we do have to fix up some better arrangement about money for the children.'

'OK,' he said, and she could hear that he too was trying. 'I'll see what I can do.'

After she had put down the phone she sat for a long time, thinking. It was extraordinary how powerful had been the effect of overcoming that one small hurdle. There was something in her own feelings that was limiting her, she saw that now and was amazed she had not understood it before. Simply making herself apologise had been liberating. She had never before felt she had anything to apologise to Alistair for, and of course there must have been - for a start, the way she couldn't stop herself pointing out what an inadequate parent he was. Well, he was, but maybe her attitude had made it hard for him to change. She had to free herself, all of them, from that trap. What had or had not happened in her past life with Alistair was now ancient history, and she could not go on letting it determine how she responded to things in her new life here.

Like her panic-stricken reaction in the ACRAS office, that too. Of course she should have told Hassan Abdillahi that running a campaign was not for her; she had neither the time nor any concept of what he thought a person like her could do. But her inability to say that simple thing, her fear, they were hangovers from the Alistair years. Perhaps she should phone him, and explain? But what would she say? She could hardly start telling him her entire personal history. She would have to leave it; just try not to think of it anymore.

But in her dreams that night she was pursued by the dark accusing eyes of a man with a long face, saying 'And what do you think will become of those children if we leave them there?' Then his face began to change as he spoke, becoming rounder and softer, until it was old and full of lines, and she realised it wasn't him at all, but Auntie. Auntie was showing her how to bottle apricots; Rachel filled her jar too full and the rich syrup dripped stickily over the edge, onto her fingers, her hands, the kitchen table, down onto her legs. Auntie said, crossly, 'If you'd done it the way I told you, you would never have got into such a mess.'

*

On Monday morning Barbara greeted Hassan with, 'You look a bit better today!'

'You were a help on Friday,' he said. 'Thanks.'

'You looked terrible. Were you not well?'

'No; but it was temporary. I hope!'

'Someone's been trying to get you. I said I wasn't sure if you'd be in.'

'I'm not sure I'm officially in, either. It would be wonderful to have a day without interruptions, to try and clear the backlog a little.'

'You do that,' said Barbara. 'I shouldn't think it was anything important. Just that woman with the Somali friend. You know, Rachel Sinclair.'

Hassan stared. 'Rachel Sinclair phoned?'

'Yes.'

'Did she say what she wanted?' Hope was rising, rising despite himself. Stop it, Hassan, just stop; it's probably something unimportant.

'She wouldn't leave a message. She said she had to talk to you.'

Now he did not bother to control his excitement. 'Give me the number,' he said.

It was Anab who had made her go to the phone, without knowing that she was doing so. Anab - and Auntie, working inside her, refusing to be ignored.

Haleemo and the children had come for the afternoon on Sunday. The weather had turned warm. Ben was pleading with her to get out the paddling pool, and she was trying to remember where she had packed it away for the winter. She looked in the cupboard under the stairs, under Simon's bed, in the high kitchen cupboards, everywhere she could think of; and everywhere Haleemo followed her, pouring out a confusing flow of details about what was happening to people she knew in Hargeisa, to which Rachel was trying not to listen. Then she caught the word Anab. 'What did you say about Anab?' she asked.

'Anab's boy,' said Haleemo. 'He is gone.'

'What do you mean, gone?'

'He run away. But they think the army kill him. Yusuf, he tell me. The army, they come to Anab's mother, her house. He run away. Some people say he is gone to SNM, to Ethiopia. But Yusuf say no one in SNM know where is he. Maybe the army kill him.'

It never ends... Rachel saw Anab vividly before her, magnified, bizarre, as in a dream, the beautiful outlines of her features, her dark, shiny skin, her self-contained, sure dignity. This should not have happened to her. She had had enough.

There was no sign when Anab opened the door that she was glad Rachel had come. Her voice was devoid of energy. They sat down.

Sado appeared briefly in the doorway, then went off to the bedroom again. Rachel said, 'Haleemo told me about your son. I'm so sorry.'

'Yes,' said Anab. There didn't seem any more to say, so they sat in silence; but it was a shared silence, and Rachel was glad she had come. After a few minutes Anab said, 'I knew it would happen. He was so angry, so angry about his father, about his cousin.'

'His cousin?'

'They killed him, in his own house, because he tried to stop them raping his sister. My son was there, he was watching. After that he was so angry, he wanted only to fight them. I told him, we all want to fight them, but you cannot fight guns with bare hands. You stay quiet, and when you have finished school we will find a way to get you out, to study in college in Egypt or somewhere. But he was so angry, he couldn't wait.'

'How far is it, to the Ethiopian border?'

'In miles? I don't know. It would take a day and a night, walking. He knows that place. My husband's brother used to send him there, to help with the camels.' Her voice had lifted, her attention momentarily focussed on helping Rachel see it. 'They have to walk for miles in dry country, looking for grazing. They take nothing; when they sleep, they just make a fence of branches from the thorn bushes to keep wild animals off. They drink only camel's milk, for weeks, until they bring the camels back to the watering places. It is a hard life, and it makes boys strong. But now -' She did not need to go on. Now it is different; without other people, without camels for milk; crossing territory controlled by a hostile army.

Rachel said, quietly, 'I should be going. I promised Kate I wouldn't be long.'

Anab said, 'No, wait. I'll make tea. Phone Kate and tell her you're staying a bit longer.'

With the tea was a plate of something that looked like a pancake crushed into flaky pastry. 'Sabaayad,' said Anab.

'It looks lovely. But I've just had supper!'

'Eat some more.'

As soon as she started to eat she realised she was hungry after all. She had been so concerned to get everyone fed and Ben to bed quickly that she'd eaten too little and too hurriedly herself. She had come to support Anab, but subtly something had changed; now Anab was taking care of her.

Anab said, 'I hear you went to see someone about Haleemo's children?' The sense of comfort disappeared, the panic she had felt in Hassan Abdillahi's office flooded back. She knew she would not ultimately be able to hide from Anab as she had hidden from Haleemo. Just take it slowly, she told herself, and she felt Auntie very close to her, saying, 'You do whatever you can do, that's all.' Carefully keeping her voice neutral, she began, 'I hope Haleemo isn't letting herself get too hopeful.'

'We have to hope,' said Anab. Rachel knew she was talking about her own son; and thinking about him again, her panic became irrelevant. She realised, also, that she no longer felt ashamed. Anab had included her, made her feel part of what she was going through. There was no question of passing judgements, no need for guilt about what each of them could or could not do. They stood together facing a monumental disaster, a crime against humanity, the destruction of a people. Her own small crisis belonged to a previous age.

'Your son -' Rachel began. She wanted Anab to talk about him, wanted to help her hold on to him, here in this alien place where there was no one who had known him, no one to fully share her agonising fear of loss. Quiety she asked, 'What is his name?'

'Ibrahim Samatar Abdi.' The moment he had a name Rachel could see him. It was the name of a tall, thin young man, high forehead, laughing eyes; eyes that should have been allowed to live. 'Ibrahim Samatar Abdi,' she repeated slowly. She went over to Anab and put her arms around her; and in the quietness between them she knew that tomorrow she would be phoning Hassan Abdillahi after all. Not to apologise or explain, but to say that she was ready to do whatever was needed.

5

After that things moved extremely fast; out of control, in fact. As if she had decided, carefully, with much difficulty, to step out into a dangerous road, only to find that she had put her foot on a skateboard.

'Use the centre for whatever you need,' he said. 'There's a telephone in reception, but we try to keep that free for incoming calls, so use mine if you need to phone around. Barbara will show you the photocopier, and you can put things through our mail on a modest scale until you get some funds to cover campaign costs. I'll introduce you to the others in a minute. One or two of them have worked in a few campaigns. I'm sure they'll have ideas.'

No, she thought, Not yet, please. I wouldn't know what to ask them. And where do I get funds? And I haven't a clue what I would want to photocopy, or who I am expected to phone, or why you can't phone them yourself, or what this is all supposed to achieve. I have to get out of this. 'Wait!' she said, then paused, and found to her surprise that he had waited. 'I'm sorry, but you're going too fast for me.'

'Yes,' he said, 'I can see that.' He grinned, a boyish grin that brought the whole thing down to size. He was laughing at her panic, yet not laughing at her.

Now that she was sitting there in front of him, her expression open to the world, showing instantly whatever she was thinking, now it was easy to accept that he would have to go slowly. All he had to do was hold on to her, help her walk past whatever it was she was afraid of. Not let her run away again. 'I got carried away,' he said. 'I was excited, about your having come back. I knew I wasn't wrong about you.'

'I think you may have been. Not about what I feel, but whether there's anything useful I can do.'

'No one expects you to do it alone. The whole point is to get other people involved!'

'That's what I mean. I don't know how to.'

'Don't worry. I'm in this too. I wouldn't have asked you to help if it hadn't been something I cared about. But we'll need to make time to work together. When could you manage?'

She hesitated. 'I work in a library, every morning, and two afternoons. The other three afternoons I'm with my children after school.'

'What about evenings?'

'Babysitting's a bit of a problem. I'm separated. I had hoped there would be things I could do from home.'

'There are bound to be. But you'll get on better if you have people around you who've had a bit more experience, just till you feel more sure of where things are going. That's why I was talking about your using the centre as a base.'

She thought for a moment. 'If I could come in one afternoon a week, would you have the time to show me what to do?'

'I'd make the time. When can you start?'

'Just hold it!' And it was she who was smiling at him now. 'There's someone I have to talk to first. I'll phone you as soon as I know if it's possible.'

He knew it was now just a question of waiting, being sensible, not taking anything for granted. While inside his excitement rose

> *Like people journeying while moving camp,*
> *or like a well which has broken its sides*
> *or a river which has overflowed its banks,*
> *or like the poor, dividing the scraps for their frugal meal,*
> *or like the bees entering their hive,*
> *or food crackling in the frying...*

Hold it, Hassan, he told himself. Just take it slowly.

Telling people was the first hurdle. Saying, 'I, Rachel, am doing this thing.' Like changing your style of clothes, deciding to adopt a new persona. She started with Pat, before the children even. She could practise safely on Pat. They had taken their lunch sandwiches to the common and were walking as they ate. 'I've been to that advice centre again,' Rachel began, tentatively. 'The man there suggested I get involved in a campaign.'

'Campaigning for what?'

'For Haleemo to be allowed to bring her children here to join her. The idea is that if we win that one, it would be a precedent for other refugees in the same position.'

'Sounds good,' said Pat. 'How long has it been going?'

'It hasn't.' She took a mouthful of cheese sandwich to fortify herself before she said, 'He's suggesting I start it.' Pat stared at her. Rachel said, 'I think I'm crazy.' Pat let out a whoop of delight that caused a woman walking her dog to startle, and move further away. 'He asked me days ago, but I backed off, I was so scared.'

'Scared?' asked Pat. 'What of?'

Rachel began to laugh. 'I knew you'd say that.' She felt for words. 'He's got completely unrealistic ideas of what's possible.'

'Rachel, are you sure you want to do this?'

'No. Yes. I mean, yes, I'm sure I want to do something to help Haleemo, and no, I don't want to feel I'm responsible for something so big, so impossible.'

'What's impossible about it?' Pat asked, and then caught hold of Rachel's free hand. 'I think it's brilliant! And I'll help!'

Still no call from Rachel. It was those damn children. Three afternoons a week, she had said, three afternoons they could have been using to get started. Once a week was going to be no bloody good. He was crazy to pretend anything could come of this. Who can run a campaign on one afternoon a week? If she didn't phone him today he would phone her.

Don't push her, he told himself. She needs to take her own time, sort out whatever it is that's making her panic. Just wait. Another day won't kill you.

Wednesday. Thursday. Come on Rachel, phone! What on earth is it that's taking all this time?

Asking Evelyn. 'How would you feel about having Ben and Simon another afternoon a week? Just for a couple of months.'

'I wouldn't mind. To be honest, I could do with the money. Ken's union is talking about an overtime ban.'

'What about Fridays?'

'Should be OK. What's happening?'

This'll be easier, second time round, Rachel thought; but even now she backed away from saying it straight, and talked of 'helping' with a campaign. She could see the picture Evelyn had - a busy room, lots of people talking, calling out to each other, telephones ringing; Rachel joining the group of volunteers - addressing envelopes, making the tea. She made herself say, 'There isn't anyone there with the time to start it. They want me to.' Now she rushed on. 'I haven't a clue what to do.'

'I'm sure they'll tell you,' Evelyn said calmly, as if it were a matter of exchanging recipes; and then, giggling at the absurdity of it, 'But rather you than me! OK, it's a deal. And I'm not taking any money for Fridays.'

'Oh, come on, Evelyn! You know I didn't mean that!'

'I know, but that's the way I'm doing it.'

'Well I'm not doing it if you won't treat it like a proper child-minding arrangement.'

'Don't do it then. Those are my terms.' And then, 'It's not your job to decide whether I'm going to help Haleemo's campaign, you know!'

And now there was no avoiding speaking to Haleemo. This afternoon, after school.

Haleemo looked blank. She clearly did not understand what Rachel was offering to do. Nor do I, thought Rachel. 'All I need to know,' Rachel said, 'is whether you'll be happy if I and other people try to make the government change its mind about your children.'

Haleemo stared at her in incomprehension. Was she thinking, Why would I not be happy? Or was it, How can anyone make a government change its mind?

Rachel tried again. 'There may be things in the newspapers about it. I don't know if there will be,' she added hastily, 'but if there were, that would be OK?'

'Who put it in newspaper?' Haleemo asked, even more incredulous. 'You?'

'I could try. But it may be hard to get anyone to print it.'

Now Haleemo was on secure ground. 'In Somalia,' she agreed, 'newspaper never write things against the government.'

Anab, thought Rachel. We need Anab.

A man Rachel had never seen before answered the door to Anab's flat. He spoke to Haleemo in Somali and motioned to them to come in. Rachel tagged on after Haleemo and the children. The man said nothing to her, so she presumed he spoke no English.

In the living room was a young woman in her early twenties, but no sign of Anab. Haleemo dispatched Asha and Ahmed upstairs and sat down to talk to the young woman in Somali. Rachel sat opposite them, and waited. The man stared at her, saying nothing.

After a while Haleemo got up and went upstairs. When she didn't reappear Rachel began to think, This is absurd. Tentatively she said to the young woman, hoping she would understand, 'Is Anab here?'

'No,' the young woman said. Sado came in, picked up some school books from the table, smiled at Rachel and said, '*Nabad*.'

'*Nabad*,' said Rachel. Sado went upstairs. The young woman laughed, and called out to the man to notice. 'You speak Somali?' she asked.

'Just that one word. Sado taught me. Are you a relative of Anab's?'

124

'No,' and she laughed again.'I never saw her till I came here.'

'She is my cousin,' said the man suddenly, in perfect English. 'She came from Somalia only two months ago. Anab saw her walking in the street, and said 'Are you Somali?' That's how we are here.' Then Haleemo reappeared, and simultaneously the front door opened and Anab came in. Everyone started talking at once, a chaos of loud, vigorous speech flying around the room that until Anab's entry had been as draggy as a hot afternoon. Anab despatched the young woman to the kitchen to make tea, then ending her Somali conversations as abruptly as they had started, turned to Rachel and said, 'Haleemo says you've got something important to talk to us about.'

She listened to Rachel's tentative proposal, and then relayed it to Haleemo in a Somali version which took three times as long, and was delivered with such conviction that Rachel herself began to feel, 'Maybe it's not so impossible.'

Anab turned to Rachel and said, 'She says it's a good idea.'

'Anab,' Rachel was laughing, 'she said a lot more than that! Tell me!'

'She only wanted to know that her children wouldn't get into trouble in Somalia if the people there hear about it.'

'My God, I hadn't even thought of that.'

'I told her,' said Anab calmly, 'if she leaves her children there, for sure they will be in trouble. She has to choose. If she wants to see them again, we have to do it.'

Monday morning, and finally a call from Rachel. 'It's OK,' she said. 'How would Fridays suit you?'

'Couldn't be better.'

'And I could manage an hour after work today, if you're free. The children are going to a birthday party.'

'I'm free as a bird,' he lied shamelessly. 'Come.'

He had opened the window. The air drifted in, got in among his papers so that he had to weight them down to prevent them blowing. He looked up to see Rachel already there, in his office. 'Reporting for duty,' she said, and they both laughed. 'I know it's taken me a while,' she said, so directly that it cancelled all his restlessless at the delay. 'But I'm ready now!' He wanted to say, 'Tell me what was so hard about it!' But he wasn't prepared to risk it; not yet.

She was saying, 'I need you to tell me where to start.'

'Right,' he felt the energy begin pumping through him. 'Produce a leaflet, something you can put in people's hands to explain what it's all about. About her children, but also about asylum applications - why she can't bring them here. And what you want people to do about it.'

'What can people do?'

'Nothing, basically, except say they think it's incredible. Like you did. But the aim is to get thousands of people saying it, so that it makes an impact on the politicians, and hopefully through them on the officials.' The disbelief in her eyes was so undisguised that it made him want to laugh. 'It's not as impossible as it sounds,' he said. 'No one can guarantee people will feel moved to do something, but they certainly can't unless you tell them what's going on.'

'There's so much to say. It needs a book, not a leaflet.'

'They don't need it all at once. You walked in here before you understood the first thing about the laws that affect refugees.'

'I still don't understand a lot! Maybe you should write that bit.'

'Nope!' he grinned. 'I've put a few papers together for you to read; get your Somali friends to tell you anything else you need to know. But you draft it. You know better than any of us the people you're writing for.'

'I do? Who am I writing it for?'

'Other people like you,' he grinned. 'And let's hope there are some!'

She stared at him. 'Actually,' she said, 'there are. At least two!' And he listened while she told him about her friend in the library and her childminder. But more than to her words, he was listening to her face, that extraordinarily expressive face that was telling him that now, for the first time, she could see what he had been seeing all the time he had been waiting for her to become ready.

'Let me introduce you to the others,' he said.

First Barbara, whom she felt she knew already; then down the corridor to Juan, a slightly shambling man with a warm, slow smile, in an office smelling of cigarette smoke and old jumpers. Chilean posters on the walls, colourful collages of resistance made by children in some community project. Then Gita, a neat, precise person with a reserved look; her office almost clinical - law books on the window ledge, no clutter of any kind. Jenny - busy but friendly, photographs of her children and friends pinned around the edges of her noticeboard and blu-tacked to the side of her filing cabinet. Then the common room - armchairs, empty for now. 'A desk you can use,' Hassan said. 'Coffee machine, etcetera. I should have offered you something. Do you want one?'

'I wouldn't mind,' she said. 'I meant to tell you, one of my Somali friends knows you!'

'What's her name?'

'Anab. Anab Abdi.'

He thought for a moment. 'There was an Anab who was a friend of my cousin Sabah at university. She may have been Anab Abdi, but I don't remember for sure. What's she like?'

'Tall, carries herself beautifully, dramatic gestures when she talks. Definite ideas. She's not the kind of person you'd forget.' She took the coffee he was handing her. 'She's the one I told you about whose husband was killed in prison. Now her son has gone missing from Hargeisa. It's amazing how she copes. She knows the chances are he's been killed, but because it's not certain she acts as if he's there, fighting with SNM - almost that she's proud he's there, because one day they'll win and drive out the military government and they'll all get their homes back.' She paused, then said, 'She's got a little girl called Sado, about ten. I like watching them together, they laugh a lot.'

As she was speaking he had a picture of himself as a small child in aunt Khadra's kitchen, watching with his cousin Jama while she made *sabaayad*, and filching them off the plate the moment they were cool enough to touch... He came back to Rachel, watching him interestedly. 'My aunt,' he explained, as if she had been seeing the picture too. 'The way you describe your friend, she sounds just like my aunt Khadra. Her husband was in jail for sixteen years and she brought up her family alone all that time. She was tough and hardheaded when she needed to be, but always warm and laughing with us children.'

'That's it,' said Rachel. Then, 'Anab says your father helped her find a job when her husband went to prison.'

'My father helped more people than I could possibly keep track of. And I was only there six weeks in the year. You know my mother's English?'

'Yes. Anab told me.'

He grinned. 'It's the first thing any Somali will tell you about me. Having an English mother means I've got no *Rer Abti* - mother's kin - only half the number of Somali relatives I ought to have!'

She laughed, but there was clearly something else she wanted to say. 'She told me about your father being in prison. I'm so sorry.'

He flinched as she said it. He's afraid even to hear it said out loud, she thought, and knew in the same moment that he was in urgent need of help. She could almost see the barrier that he was instinctively trying to erect against any possible pain her words might bring him. It seemed vitally important that she did not let him succeed. She said, quietly, 'You're close to him, aren't you?' He glared at her with such hostility that she thought for a moment he was going to tell her to get out, in that cold, hard voice that he had switched on in their earlier meetings. Then something in his eyes seemed to give way and he said, simply, 'Yes.'

His first, furious instinct had been to ask her what the hell it had to do with her. Who did she think she was, to expect that he would be willing to talk to her about his feelings for his father? But she had continued to look at him so directly, with those clear, unembarrassed eyes, as if she did not see that he was pushing her away but saw only the fear that lay behind that. Gradually the panic ebbed away. 'Yes,' he heard himself say, and now it felt safe to be saying it. 'Yes, I'm close to him.' But immediately the self-protective instinct returned. That's enough, more than enough.

When he spoke again his voice was firm and confident, as he was used to hearing it. 'You haven't met everyone yet. There's still Mike.'

6

Mike was busy with a client, so it was not until she came again on Friday afternoon that he could introduce Rachel to him. 'Maybe you can tell her how your group got the Tamil campaign going,' Hassan said. 'Show her some of your publicity leaflets, petitions, that sort of thing.'

'Sure,' said Mike.

'In a purely personal capacity, of course,' Hassan risked, and was rewarded by a reluctant grin. To Rachel he said, 'I'll be in my office. When you're finished talking to people, come and find me and we can work out what needs to happen next.'

As he left her he encountered Barbara, looking for him. 'Hassan, your cousin's on the phone. He says it's urgent.' He didn't stop even to say, 'Thanks', but just hurtled down the corridor to his office. He skidded to a stop at his desk, and grabbed the phone. 'Nuh?' But it was Mohamed, phoning from a call-box at Heathrow. 'Nuh's arrived,' he said. 'They're giving him trouble. We need you.'

'I'm coming,' Hassan said. 'Why didn't he phone me straight away?'

'He tried but there was no answer from your home, and your work phone was engaged. So he got me. But these bastards are making trouble. They say they're putting him on the next plane back to Kenya.'

'Tell him I'm on my way. It'll take me at least an hour to get there so just hang on.' As he spoke he hunched his shoulder to keep the receiver in place while he reached into a drawer for a list of phone numbers. 'What terminal?'

'Four.'

'Flight number?'

'I don't know. Do you want me to find out and phone you back?'

'Forget it. Just tell me what time he got in, roughly.'

'Early this morning. They kept him waiting four hours before they even started on him. This place they've got him in, Hassan, it's like a prison. Security guards everywhere.'

'Just calm down,' Hassan said. 'we'll get him out.' He was walking across the room, receiver still propped to his ear, cord trailing him while he reached for his briefcase and jacket, the ones he kept in his office for when he needed to look official. 'And Mohamed, for God's sake don't start shouting. They don't like it! '

Within five minutes he had made three phone calls and was in reception telling Barbara, 'It's a real emergency. If I've got any appointments for the afternoon you'll have to cancel them.' He was out on the pavement and running towards the station before he remembered Rachel, who would be coming back to his room to find him, so that they could plan together what needed doing.

All the time he was arguing with the immigration official Hassan was aware of Nuh standing next to him; aware of every aspect of his physical presence - the body warmth close to him, the smell of his sweat from being cooped up in an aeroplane and then in a series of small rooms, waiting tensely, waiting and sweating. The height of him, several inches taller even than Hassan himself, the way he shifted on his feet when the immigration officer said something Nuh took exception to. But whatever reply Nuh might have been considering, he suppressed it. He had said, in Somali, the moment Hassan had arrived, 'I'm leaving it to you now, brother. They're trying to trap me into saying things they can hold against me.' And from then on he had said nothing to the immigration officer unless expressly commanded to do so.

Nuh's pride - of that, too, Hassan was intensely aware all the time he was arguing, as if it were something one could feel on one's skin, filling the atmosphere around them; Nuh's refusal to be treated like an underling, his contempt for this man who was trying to do so. 'Kenya is a signatory of the U.N. Convention on Refugees,' the officer was saying. 'There is no reason for him not to be returned there. We are under no obligation to accept asylum seekers who have arrived from a country other than the one they are fleeing from.'

'Only provided you can be sure they will not be returned by that country to their own,' said Hassan. 'There is a Somali minority in Kenya and the Kenyan government's attitude is that they have enough of them already. There is every chance he would be sent back to Somalia.'

'From the statement he's given I see no reason why he shouldn't go back,' the officer said. 'He hasn't been imprisoned or tortured, or even openly threatened with either. If he wants to come to Britain just because his cousins are here, that's another matter; he can go back and apply for a visa in the normal way.'

'It's nothing to do with his cousins being here.' Don't shout, he had told Mohamed, and here he was beginning to shout himself. 'This man has presented himself before you as an applicant for asylum, and you are obliged by international convention not to send him back until his application has been considered.'

The man turned back to his desk. He pulled out a form and with his back to Hassan started writing. He took his time over it, deliberately. Hassan forced himself to wait quietly. There was a chance the man had capitulated and was issuing a Temporary Admission document; if that was the case, he didn't want to say or do anything to make him change his mind and tear it up. But it could equally be a Refusal of Leave to Enter form. Hassan's mind raced ahead, working out what his next step would be. It was four thirty on a Friday afternoon, too late to get hold of anyone in the Home Office. There would be absolutely nothing he could do except fax a statement to the Home Office challenging the decision. He would go straight back to the office. Allah, everyone else might have gone by the time he got back. Did he have his keys? He checked his briefcase. Yes, thank God.

The officer had finished writing. His face full of disdain, he thrust a copy of the form into Hassan's hands as if to say, take the bloody thing then, I've lost interest. Hassan looked at the paper. It was not a Refusal of Leave to Enter, but the momentary relief gave way to renewed anger when he saw that it was also not a Temporary Admission document. It was an instruction for the detention of Nuh Ali Dahir, pursuant to further examination of his case.

Hassan looked up to see that the immigration officer had his back to him once more, busy with his papers. With an immense effort Hassan made himself speak calmly. 'Why not Temporary Admission?' he asked. 'There are two of us here waiting to give him a place to stay. There's no need for him to be kept in the detention centre at the state's expense!'

'I'm busy,' said the immigration officer. 'There's a queue of people waiting for me to interview them. If you've got representations to make, I presume you know the proper channels.'

'What's going on?' Nuh asked in Somali.

'They're not sending you back,' Hassan said, 'but they're not letting you in either. They're putting you in detention.'

'For how long?'

'Until I can get on to this bastard's senior officers. That means Monday at the earliest.'

Nuh stared at him, his nostrils moving, his eyes furious. Mohamed was cursing; the immigration officer was looking restless at this flow of Somali. Hassan judged it time to switch back into English. 'There is absolutely no justification for keeping him in detention,' he said, allowing himself the relief of sounding as angry as he felt; he had lost this round anyway. 'I'll be taking this up with the Home Office.' The immigration officer's eyes looked much as Nuh's did - full of contempt for this man who was trying to order him around. The difference was that Nuh was powerless to act upon his contempt.

He spent the weekend at Mohamed's place, needing to be with his own people. There were six men living in two small bedrooms, separated by a hardboard partition. For a kitchen there was a cooker and a sink in one corner of the living room; the bathroom was shared with the Bengali family on the landing below. Hassan joined Mohamed on the living room floor, remembering how as children he and Mohamed and his other Mogadishu cousins used to sleep in rows on the floor when they went to stay with Nuh's family in Hargeisa.

In the middle of the night he heard Mohamed shift and grunt, and realised that he too was awake. Hassan said quietly in the dark, 'I keep remembering a poem Nuh taught me.'

> *My brother is there*
> *and he cannot come to me...*

It must have been the year of the Somali-Ethiopian war, when suddenly it had become impossible to take camels south to graze when the spring rains came and the grass grew tall, and then move north again to the wells when the pastures dried up. No one had paid any attention to artificial boundaries drawn by imperial powers on maps - until the war had forced them to, dividing them, brother from brother.

> *My brother is there.*
> *I can hear the bells of his camels*
> *when they graze down in the valley,*
> *and the leaves of the bushes near my place.*
> *For the rain which makes them grow*
> *comes from the same sky.*
> *When I pray, he prays,*
> *and my Allah is his Allah.*
> *My brother is there*
> *and he cannot come to me.*

Most of the weekend they sat around doing little. There was desultory conversation, people came, others went. The television was on. Hassan felt he ought to get out, go and walk, do anything except stay here; but he couldn't summon up the energy. He wanted to phone Rachel to explain why he had left so suddenly on Friday, but he didn't have her phone number with him. He started to look up Sinclair in the

132

telephone directory but realised he didn't know her address. There were three columns of Sinclairs.

On Sunday afternoon the others all went off together to go and see someone. They tried to persuade Hassan to come too, but he wouldn't. Mohamed stayed with him. When they were alone Hassan said, 'The place you and Aadan were in before was better than this. Why did you move?'

'Couldn't pay the rent. £50 a week for one room. The Housing Department people say, we won't pay more than £40. The landlord says, it's £50, take it or leave it. So you take it, because you have to have a place to sleep. The other £10 you pay out of your benefits.' He laughed, a short bitter laugh. 'When I first came here and people told me, the government is going to give you money, I said I've never taken money from anyone except my family and I'm not starting now. They laughed at me.'

'I told you,' Hassan said angrily, 'I told you to come to me if ever you needed anything.'

'I can't build my life on asking you.'

'I'm your cousin, for Allah's sake!'

'You've got enough to look after already. You're sending money for your father, aren't you?'

Hassan did not answer. Deliberately changing the subject he said, 'What happened to the other bloke you and Aadan were sharing with? Osman?'

'He left.'

'Where to?'

'There was a fight. He started insulting Aadan's sister. In the middle of the fight he bashed his hand against the corner of the cooker, and cut it open. Had to go to hospital to get it stitched up. After that he wouldn't come back. He's in another place now, with Yassin and that lot.'

'What's Aadan's sister got to do with it?'

'She's married to Osman's cousin, on his mother's side. They're Gadabursi. They said she poisoned her father-in-law. Everyone knew he was old and going to die anyway. But his family told the army she did it, and they arrested her and put her in prison for life, just to cause trouble between the clans.'

'And they succeeded, apparently,' said Hassan, his voice cold.

'It was quite a fight,' grinned Mohamed.

'You all ganged up on Osman, and beat him up. Is that it?'

Mohamed became angry. 'Cut it out, Hassan. You don't know what he's like. He's a worm. We're better off without him.'

Later Mohamed asked, 'How do you get your money to Hargeisa, anyway?'

Hassan wanted to say it's nothing to do with you. But that was ridiculous, why shouldn't Mohamed ask? 'I send each month to Ismail in Djibuti. Uncle Ali said he'd find ways to get it in.'

'Do you know how he does it?' Mohamed asked.

'No. Uncle Ali's business deals have always been a mystery to me.'

'I'll tell you,' Mohamed said. 'He had a system going before I left, with the men who worked in Jeddah and Kuwait. Uncle Ali used to support their relatives back home with Somali money, and in return they gave Arab money to uncle Ali's buyers so he could by-pass the foreign exchange regulations and keep importing goods to sell, at a nice profit. Bribing the customs officials on the way, of course.' He looked curiously at Hassan. 'How does all that strike you?'

Hassan shrugged. Mohamed was testing him, and he did not feel like rising. 'If that's how he does it, that's how he does it,' Hassan said.

'There was a time when you would have had high moral principles about being part of it.'

'There's another principle that overrides all others for the moment. I want Aabahay out.'

7

'On TV?' Ben said, staring. 'Ahmed's going to be on TV?'

'No one's asked him to yet,' said Kate, 'what Mom means is that maybe later they might, if those people in the advice centre can make enough fuss about it.'

'Only they say they can't do it themselves,' Rachel said.

'So who's going to?' asked Simon.

'They want us to,' she said.

'Us? On TV?' asked Ben, excitement rising.

'Ben, the TV comes at the end,' Kate explained. 'The TV people will only take any notice of us if we first make a huge fuss. That's what happened at Greenwood school when that English teacher gave them CND poems to read, and the newspapers said it was political.'

'What's political?' asked Ben.

'It's people saying what they think,' said Kate. 'And some people don't like you to do that.'

'I say what I think,' said Ben.

'OK,' said Kate, 'so are you going to tell people at school that Ahmed and Asha's brother and sister ought to be allowed to come here?'

'Only if Ahmed wants it.'

'Of course he'll want it, you stupid,' said Simon.

'How do you know?' demanded Ben. 'He says his brother used to boss him around!'

Rachel said. 'Listen, Ben - all of you - I want you to talk to your friends, and see if anyone has some good ideas about how we can make people know about it.'

Simon said, 'You mean like when that man came to school to tell us all about the lifeboats, and then we did a sponsored run round the common to raise money?'

'Could be,' said Rachel.

'A sponsored run, for Ahmed's brother?' Ben asked, incredulous. And then, in dawning delight, 'Ahmed and I could make a banner, to put up at the place people start!' Rachel and Kate started laughing. Rachel gave Ben a hug.

'With pictures of bomber planes,' said Ben, really getting into it. 'So they'll know it's a war!'

Alone that night in the small pool of light from her bedside lamp, she read the cuttings and duplicated pages Hassan had given her... Military plan to lay waste the entire region along the border between Somalia and Ethiopia. Wholesale destruction of villages, poisoning of water supplies. All Isaaq to be regarded automatically as supporters of the SNM...

'Tell them,' said Hassan that night in her troubled sleep, his face looming up to her and then retreating, alarmingly far away, leaving her standing on her own in the school playground while all the other mothers walked past her without seeing her, without noticing that she was trying to tell them something really important. 'Tell them. Tell them so that they understand.'

Sado opened the door to Rachel's knock, and then ran upstairs. From the living room came the sound of lots of people talking - she seemed to have walked into the middle of a party. Haleemo was there with the children, and two young Somali men, one of whom had a smile that reminded her of Hassan's. Anab was cooking; neither she nor anyone else seemed to expect that there would be a reason why Rachel had come, other than simply to come. People wandered in and out of the kitchen to see how the food was getting on, and to walk off with each new sabaayad the moment Anab had lifted it out of the pan and crushed it with a deft movement of her right hand into a pile of flaky pieces. From the television a flow of inane chatter competed, unsuccessfully, with the equally continuous flow of Somali talk. Rachel abandoned any idea of getting time alone with Anab to look at the leaflet, and simply joined the people in the kitchen, accepting the cup of spicy tea that Anab put in her hands, and settling in to enjoy herself. What she enjoyed most was the sight of Haleemo, a Haleemo she had never seen before, relaxed and vigorous, talking Somali, laughing and calling out to people across the room. She had a vision of Haleemo as she might have been in Somalia before all this happened. Haleemo surrounded by her own people, shielded from loss.

The by now familiar sounds of Somali flowed over her, hovering on the edges of her brain as if she could almost imagine that she understood them...

And she was once again in Martha's room in the Lourensrus of her childhood, surrounded by voices talking in a language she did not understand. She sat on a corner of Martha's bed, scarcely noticed - Martha's appendage, the child she had to look after - while Martha and her friends talked, their voices loud in indignation, or high in humour, or *tse-tse-tse*-ing in sympathy. She could see the room still - the whitewash peeling off the walls, the lopsided old cupboard whose door hung at an angle and had to be held closed with pieces of folded cardboard; one small window, with a curtain fixed into position with tacks so that it could not be drawn and she had to lift it to peer out. The view from the window - the washing line, the loquat tree, the path leading to the kitchen, where the grass was worn away by Martha's constant coming and going... Martha's friends would sit on the bed or the trunk, their bodies filling the cramped space, turning the small gathering into a party by the way they talked and laughed and threw back their heads, with their bodies relaxed, their legs, swollen with too much standing, stretched out in front of them; spreading themselves in a way which Rachel found riveting, for it was quite unlike the way her mother and her friends sat when they talked together. And Rachel would wait hopefully for Lena, who worked next door, to tell about Mrs. Strydom's latest outburst. She could always tell when it began, for Lena's voice became louder and more excited, and soon she would switch into a shrill falsetto imitation of Mrs Strydom, recognisable to anyone who had ever heard Mrs Strydom when she was angry. Lena's face screwed up, she waved her arms violently, and in the midst of the flow of Tswana speech came extracts from Mrs. Strydom's Afrikaans, the constantly repeated, *Wat het ek vir jou gese? Domkop!* - What did I tell you? Idiot! - till they were all rolling about in laughter, and Rachel felt she might burst with the daring of sitting there laughing with them. Martha would turn to her and shake her finger and say in Tswana, *Klaghabetsawena!* - I'll beat you! - in a voice that pretended to be fierce and only had the effect of making Rachel feel warm and safe, included...

'Rachel!' Anab was saying. 'Let's begin.' And then over her shoulder, 'Haleemo-*oy*,' summoning her imperiously to come and sit with them on the sofa and look at the draft leaflet.

'What do you think?' asked Rachel, when they had finished.

'Very good,' said Haleemo. 'Is very good. Everyone going to listen about my children.' Haleemo and Anab had started off in Somali again. She heard the name 'Hassan Abdillahi'. When there was a pause she said, 'I told him you knew him.' Anab and Haleemo looked at each other oddly. 'You told him my name?' Anab asked, and they were both laughing now, at some joke they seemed to think overwhelmingly funny. 'What did you say my name was?' Anab asked. Rachel stared at them. What on earth was going on? 'Anab Abdi,' she said. 'Why, is that wrong?' They were holding on to each other, trying to stop laughing enough to speak. Haleemo managed, 'Her name not Abdi.'

'But - That's what people at school always call you!'

Anab used a corner of the long sleeve of her gown to wipe her eyes. 'Because Sado's name is Sado Samatar Abdi,' she said, 'so they think I must be Mrs Abdi. It doesn't work like that in Somalia. Samatar Abdi was her father's name.'

'And you?'

'I have my own name! From my father. Saeed Barud. We don't throw away our names when we marry, like English women!'

'Anab Saeed Barud,' Rachel tried it out. 'But why don't you tell people? You can't just let them give you the wrong name!'

'What does it matter?' Anab said, with that familiar lift of her head. 'Let them call me what they want to.'

*

A child answered the phone, a boy's voice. 'Can I speak to your mother?' he asked, and felt odd describing her that way. Waiting for her to come to the phone - noises off, children calling, that life of hers of which he knew nothing - he realised that for the first time in their brief acquaintance he wasn't totally confident. He wished profoundly that she should understand that he hadn't meant to leave her on her own in so apparently cavalier a fashion. 'It's Hassan,' he said, 'I'm really sorry about Friday.'

He sounded so like a little boy who has unintentionally broken something that Rachel wanted to laugh. 'It was fine,' she said. 'Jenny was extremely helpful.' Simon was at her side, urgently needing something. 'Just hold on a minute,' she said into the phone. 'Where's the sellotape?' Simon asked, voice injured, as if no one paid any attention to his needs. He's been like that for days, she registered. He doesn't like me being busy. 'I have to have it for my project,' Simon worked up the scale a few notes, 'and Kate won't lend me hers.'

'Top lefthand drawer in the kitchen,' she said, 'if whoever borrowed it last put it back.' Then to Hassan, 'Sorry, usual after school chaos here. I phoned this morning. Barbara said you were busy so I spoke to Jenny. I've arranged to bring in the draft leaflet tomorrow after work. I don't suppose you'll be free to look at it, will you?'

'It's unlikely. Rachel, I'm in the middle of a crisis - that's why I rushed off on Friday. My cousin's just arrived from Somalia, and they're keeping him in detention. I may have to be out tomorrow trying to deal with it.'

'In detention? They put newly-arrived refugees in detention?'

'He was unlucky. Normally they let them in while they're deciding their case. But it's entirely at the discretion of an immigration officer.

If he doesn't like the look of your face he can stick you in there, along with all the people waiting to be deported.'

So it's happening here, she thought, as she put the phone down. South Africa, Somalia, now here; and remembered her cousin Daniel visiting her and Alistair in Johannesburg and saying, 'All the people you know seem to be in political trouble.' Meaning, be careful, Rachel, you're getting to know the wrong people.

Barbara was packing up as Rachel arrived in the ACRAS office the next day. 'Hassan's expecting you.' Rachel walked down the corridor, remembering how long and anonymous it had seemed the first time. And there he was, the same mop of curly hair, the same eyes. 'What's the news of your cousin?' she asked.

'None. I could kill the bastard who put him there. It's so ruddy pointless, him sitting there when he could be with us.'

'You can scarcely believe it, can you?' she said. 'Someone escapes from one country where they're about to put him in jail, and when he arrives in another to seek refuge they promptly do the same!' And then, remembering her conversation with Yusuf, 'Are there any white people in there?'

'In detention centres? Precious few. Some Latin Americans. It's a real third world experience, visiting one of those places. Middle East, Africa, Asia. People stuck there for months, caught in a limbo between countries, between lives, each with a threat hanging over them. It's one of the most depressing places I know. And Nuh, of all people.' He stopped, staring past her at nothing. He was right there facing her. He did not move but she had the clear sensation that he had gone away, somewhere inside himself, cut off from her. She stood very still. After a few moments she could feel him coming back, though again nothing moved, not his face, nor any part of his body. She was sure he wanted to say something, and that he would only say it if she did nothing to break the safety of the silence.

When he eventually looked up there was none of the usual buoyancy in his eyes. 'I'm glad you're here,' he said. 'And now we'd better start looking at the leaflet. I imagine you've got to get back to the children soon.'

'It needs a bit of tightening up,' he said. 'You want to make clearer the focus of the campaign. What do you want to achieve?'

'For Haleemo to get her children here.'

'Exactly. And what's stopping her?'

'The government won't let her bring them in.'

'OK. But the way you've written it here it sounds as if they're refusing because she's a refugee. It's the opposite of that - it's because she *hasn't* been accepted as a one that she can't bring them in.' He stopped. 'Are you with me?'

'Yes,' she said. 'You make it very clear. Give it back to me and I'll have another go. The legal bits are still too new for me. When I tried to write it I couldn't work out how to say it simply.'

He smiled. 'Stop being so humble. I had assumed this was all going to take ages on a once a week basis, and here you are with a leaflet drafted before I've had time to draw breath.'

'It's Anab. She knew just what to say. Oh, by the way, I got her name wrong. She's really Anab Saeed Barud. '

'Saeed Barud. Sounds familiar, but I can't put a face to it. I'm hopeless about names. It's one of the many ways in which I'm not a proper Somali. None of my uncles or cousins would forget a name.'

'Why? What's specially Somali about being good at remembering names?'

'It's a crucial survival tool; tells you who you're related to.'

'Surely you know that anyway?'

'Not related as in immediate family. I mean, even when you meet a stranger. A Somali's name is like a genealogical table.' Her eyes were curious, waiting to be told more. 'I'm Hassan Abdillahi Dahir. Hassan is my own name, Abdillahi is my father, Dahir, my grandfather. You add another one for each generation back. Hassan Abdillahi Dahir Farah Yunis. Etcetera.'

'How far back can you go?'

'Twenty three generations.'

'Twenty three! And you say you're no good at remembering names!'

'That's my own ancestory, that's taken for granted! My aunt Khadra made me learn it when I was about six. It's supposed to be a mother's job, but my mother opted out of that one! She couldn't remember all the names herself.'

'But why make a child of six learn all that?'

'Listen.' He was laughing now, enjoying her amazement. 'I'm in a teashop in Mogadishu. I start chatting to the guy next to me. We can hear from each other's voices we're both from the north. The first thing he says is, 'What's your clan?' and when I say, 'Isaaq,' he begins asking questions to see how closely we're related. He says, 'After Isaaq, what then?' And I say, 'Habar Awal.' He says, 'And after that?' I say, 'Sa'ad Musa', going on through all the names of my ancestors. The moment I say a name that isn't in his own lineage, we know that's where our ancestors diverge. The more names we share, the closer cousins we are.'

'How far back do you still call each other cousins?'

'As far as you want to! If I'm politically influential it's to your advantage to stress the relationship. 'I'm your cousin!' you say, and you can expect to be able to stay in my house, and ask me to find you a job, and settle your debts. I tell you, it's a beautiful system. And that's why I don't know everyone my father has helped!'

Rachel laughed, 'And imagine the shock of landing up here, where no one knows anything about you, and then they even get your name wrong!'

'Somalis are survivors. She'll find a way of managing without relatives.'

'She has,' Rachel said. 'She picks people up on the street and adopts them. I meet three new Somalis every time I go to her flat.'

He grinned. 'Welcome to the clan,' he said.

Welcome to the clan. She kept hearing his voice, thinking about what he had said. Welcome to the clan. Which clan? An honorary Somali, being absorbed by Anab and Haleemo into their world? Or the clan of the dispossessed? A clan united by no single language or culture, people who, having lost their real relatives, pick up new ones on the street - or in her case in the school playground.

Her own people - what were they all doing now, Daniel and all her other cousins? Mr. Kaplan at Lourensrus General Store, who used to feed stray cats out at the back, and let her do it with him on Saturday mornings. Old Mrs. Loubsher, to whom her mother used to take home-made milk tart every Friday, because her teeth didn't fit and she couldn't chew, though she would never admit it. Her cousin Sannie, who would never visit her in Johannesburg after the time Alistair had been so pointedly rude to Sannie's husband, Piet. There was something even about Piet's body that she knew had evoked Alistair's instinctive hostility, before they had started on politics. Piet had mechanic's hands, large and tough. His thighs filled his trousers, which looked as if they would burst when he sat down. His head seemed to shade off into his shoulders without bothering about a neck. On top of this huge body he had a simple, boyish face that Rachel found quite appealling, what they used to call *lekker lelik* - nicely ugly, someone whose niceness is obvious despite less than promising features. He was an affectionate father of their two little boys, and obviously proud of Sannie; though he kept interrupting her to make absurdly pompous statements, he did it as if he thought that was what was expected of him as a husband, and didn't appear to mind when Sannie contradicted him in her usual blunt way - *'Wat se jy, man?'* - what on earth are you saying? And that was another thing, Rachel realised afterwards, that had made Alistair flip - since he wouldn't come to Lourensrus he scarcely ever saw her with her relatives, speaking Afrikaans. Of course she and Sannie and Piet switched to English when Alistair joined them, but it was so automatic for her to use Afrikaans with Sannie that they kept slipping back into it when they were speaking directly to each other. Meanwhile Piet did his best to engage Alistair in conversation, man to man. What did Alistair think about the performance of the New Zealand rugby team? Not getting very far with that, Piet turned to the obvious follow-up topic for foreigners, Why did the rest of the world (for which read, Britain, New Zealand, Australia) boycott South African teams, and still play against all those African countries which everyone knew had the worst dictatorships in the world?

'Stop it, you two,' said Sannie, in the same tone of voice she had used when her sons had come running in with mud all over their feet. 'I've come to see my cousin, not to listen to arguments about politics.'

'I'll leave you to it then,' said Alistair coldly, and walked out of the house. A few minutes later they heard the car starting. Piet blustered, and told Sannie it was time they got the boys cleaned up, they had a long drive ahead of them. Sannie raised her eyebrows at Rachel, and said, 'Do you want us to stay or go?' Rachel was grateful for her directness; she couldn't have borne it if Sannie had tried to cover over the explosion with small talk and half lies, the way Piet was doing. 'Stay,' she said; and they stayed another half hour.

When Alistair eventually returned, he was unpenitent. 'I hope you had a nice time,' he said, imitating Piet's accent, hamming it, making it guttural and unattractive. She was cold with fury. 'That's my language,' she said. 'And the next time you're planning to leave the house when my cousins come maybe it would be better if you just stayed away altogether.'

'My language, my people. Christ, Rachel, two minutes in their company and you slip back into talking like the rest of them!'

He was looking at her almost as he had looked at Piet, and now she was afraid. 'Alistair,' she said, and she realised she was pleading with him to understand, 'of course I hate the things he says as much as you do. But I thought you cared about political change. How do you change people if you refuse to have anything to do with them?'

'I've only got half the number of Somali relatives I ought to have.' She could see Hassan's grin as he said it, relaxed with the knowledge that he only half belonged. 'It's the first thing any Somali will tell you about me!' Accepting it, laughing about it, and getting on with life. She would like to have been able to do that, to acknowledge who she was, all the parts of her, and not to have bothered what other people thought, neither Alistair, nor the Lourensrus people who said, 'Rachel's got mixed up with such a crowd of communists,' nor the politically pure whom she had met occasionally in London, whose eyes took on a remote look when they heard her accent. And maybe, after all, she had grown past all that. Anab and Haleemo had helped her free herself by their unquestioning acceptance of her, and Hassan by his inexplicable confidence. He hadn't needed to know anything about her other than what he could tell from a couple of brief meetings. He didn't need her to be anything other than what she was. And the extraordinary thing was that each time she was in his presence she knew that he was right - being herself was enough.

8

The detention centre was crowded. Fifty to sixty detainees, long termers probably, awaiting the outcome of their appeal against a deportation order. Amidst the babble of different languages in the visitors' room, a couple of solicitors were attempting to take statements. He and Nuh made a corner for themselves, and started talking in Somali. 'The food is terrible,' Nuh said. 'It's reject airline food, the stuff that's burnt and not fit to serve to passengers. One man said he wouldn't give food like that to an animal. The guards said if you don't like it here you can go to proper prison, and they took him away in handcuffs. Handcuffs, like a criminal, for objecting to the food!' Then he lapsed into depressed silence.

'Tell me about why you had to leave,' Hassan said.

'There was a group of us, trying to work out a way of getting regular information to someone outside Somalia. Hardly a foreign journalist comes near the place now, and those who do are afraid to move out of Mogadishu, so they learn almost nothing. And that means there's nothing in the world's press.'

'You don't have to tell me. I've kept cuttings of everything I've seen for the past two years, and it doesn't fill a small notebook.'

'We'd only just got going when someone blew on me. We were as careful as it is possible to be, but the moment you try to work with even one other person you run a risk. There is almost no one you can be a hundred per cent certain you can trust. It makes even the simplest organisation virtually impossible.'

'Do you know who put them on to you?'

'I have an idea. Amina thinks she's sure.' There was a new tension in his eyes. 'She was very angry about my having to leave. I'm afraid she might do something rash, and draw attention to herself.'

Hassan said, 'If she does, it'll probably be no more than you would be doing in her place.'

'Allah will punish him. There's no need for Amina to arrange it.' Then, 'You've never met her, have you?'

'No. I've heard about her, though.'

'From Mohamed?'

Hassan nodded and was pleased to see Nuh smile. 'Don't believe a word he tells you,' Nuh said. 'She could easily have stayed in the States and made a comfortable career for herself - she's a bio-chemist. But she came back. She's much more of a fighter than I am, really.' And then, bitterly, 'I wanted to ask you to help me get her and the baby out. But what's the point, if this is where they'll land?'

'Listen,' said Hassan, 'when you've been here seven days we're entitled to apply for bail.'

'Does that mean Friday?'

'Technically, yes. But you were only put in this place on Friday evening, and everything closes for the weekend. So Monday, in effect.'

'Five more days!'

'Then we have to wait for them to give us a date for a hearing. That could be another week; more, if we're unlucky. But I shall push like hell to get an early date.'

Nuh stared gloomily around the room at the other trapped people, and then back to Hassan. 'I'm going to need your help with something else. The work we were doing - it has to be done, and this is where the foreign press is, after all, that we were trying to reach.'

'It'll be hard,' Hassan said. 'Hard in a different way from trying to work inside Somalia. You can say what you like here, but you can't get anyone to listen.'

'We have to,' said Nuh.

'We have to try,' said Hassan. 'It's not quite the same thing.'

'No chance,' the voice on the phone told him, when he pressed for an early date for a bail hearing. 'Not with Easter coming up. Two short weeks. The lists are already full.

'The week after?' Hassan asked.

'Thursday would be the earliest. No, sorry, Thursday's full. I can do you the Monday after.'

'This is absurd!' Hassan exploded. 'What kind of a legal system is this?'

'Monday, three o'clock if you want it. Up to you.'

Another three weeks! Damn, damn, damn.

*

Rachel bent to give Simon a goodnight cuddle. He turned his head away, refusing to accept it. What's this? she thought, and for a moment wasn't sure what to do. Then she sat down on his bed and waited to see whether any further communication might be forthcoming. He turned his head back, though still not looking at her face, and taking hold of one of her hands began arranging her fingers to make shadow patterns on the wall. 'Look, a rabbit!' he said. Two fingers up for ears, wiggling absurdly. She asked, 'Did anything special happen at school today?' Now it was a wolf - thumb and two middle fingers together to make a long snout, the other two bent over for pricked-up ears. He said, 'Mrs. Donally says you've got to go and see her tomorrow.'

145

'What about?' she asked. He didn't answer. 'Didn't she tell you?' she asked. He turned her hands into wings, flapping them gently. 'A dove?' she tried.

'It's not a dove,' he said scornfully. 'It's a flying goose. Can't you see? Like the ones that come down on the pond at the common.'

'Simon, tell me what Mrs Donally said.'

A crocodile mouth moved towards her face menacingly and attacked her nose. 'It's Ben,' he said. 'Him and his stupid banner.'

The post arrived just as she and the boys were leaving the house. An airletter from her mother - she put it in her bag to read later - and a large brown envelope with her name in a scrawly handwriting she didn't recognise; inside, a collection of printed leaflets and a hurried note on an ACRAS compliments slip - 'Thought you might find it helpful to look at some publicity material from other campaigns. See you Friday.'

'Hold on a minute,' she said to the boys. 'I have to make a quick phone call.'

'Mo-om, we're going to be late,' complained Simon. 'You've got to see Mrs. Donally.'

'We can run,' she was dialling already. 'Honest, I'm not going to talk, just making an arrangement.' Anab had answered. Rachel said, 'Can I come by after work for half an hour?'

Ben said, as she put the phone down 'You're always going somewhere after work.'

They made it in time. Simon left her side as they entered the playground, to avoid the embarrassment of being associated with a mother who had to go and see the Head. Rachel took Ben to his class and then went up the stairs to Mrs. Donally's office. The door was open and Mrs Donally looked up as Rachel was about to knock. There was an edge to her voice as she said, 'Come in, Mrs Sinclair.' And when Rachel had done so and sat down, 'What's this I've been hearing about the Somali children? Something about a campaign?'

'It's a bit of a surprise to me too,' Rachel said. 'It's all happened rather suddenly.'

'Ben's teacher tells me you're organising a big march, and that everyone in the school is going to take part?'

146

Rachel began to laugh. 'It's not quite like that;' but then felt obliged to add, 'Though it seems it might involve quite a lot of people at the school.'

'In which case I do rather need to know, don't I?' Mrs Donally said. Hell, thought Rachel, I've made a real mess of this. Why on earth didn't I think of coming to talk to her first? Now I'm going to sound on the defensive. 'You're right,' she said. 'I owe you an apology.' The only thing to do now was to help her really understand about the children, to hear it the way she, Rachel, had heard it. 'It's a long story,' she said. 'Do you have time?'

'I've got fifteen minutes before assembly.'

Rachel thought briefly about what the librarian was going to say, and decided it would simply have to be faced. She said, 'Could I just use your phone to let work know I'll be a little late?' And then she began.

'She came round fine,' Rachel told Evelyn that evening when she collected the children. 'She ended up telling me about her mother, who had to leave Ireland at fifteen to come to England to look for work.'

'We're all immigrants, when you scratch a little,' said Evelyn. 'Did you know Ken's dad was Polish?'

'What, with a surname like Alexander?'

'They just left off the -owicz bit!'

'Mrs Donally suggested the PTA get a letter out to parents soon, to make sure they hear about it from us before someone starts spreading the wrong story. You wouldn't like to help me draft it, would you?'

'We'll have to be quick, next week's the last PTA meeting before Easter. I'll talk to Sophie. Maybe we can come over to your place tomorrow night?'

Friday. Rachel hadn't realised until she saw him again how she had built her week around the fact of coming back here, of seeing his eyes, expectant, watching hers. 'A lot's happened,' she said.

'Yes,' he said, and she knew that he too had been working towards today.

'You start,' she said. 'What's the news of your cousin?'

Her face as he told her was just as he had remembered it. Every time she reappeared it was the same, but each time it was a surprise to him that this should be so. He heard his voice explaining the technical details of the bail application, the way he would have talked to Mike or Juan, protectionist legal talk, not getting near his feelings. This is not what I want to say to her, he thought. He wanted to tell her what Nuh meant to him, how when he was a schoolboy of fifteen Nuh, then a university student, had taken him to a village a hundred miles inland, to take part in the literacy campaign that had swept the country that year; how Nuh had stood out against the rest of the family in his defence of the government's reforms, and then when events made him change his mind, had become as unshakeable in his opposition, hiding people who were in trouble with the regime, quietly talking to students in ones and twos when he could no longer teach openly about things that mattered... Instead, Hassan heard his voice plodding on, detached and impersonal. He felt trapped, bound to continue talking the way he had begun.

She said, 'Your cousin, what kind of a person is he?'

He was freed. 'He's a man who thinks,' he said, 'all the time. A born teacher.' And having begun, it was easy. 'I feel desperate about his being in detention,' he said. 'Almost as if it's my fault.'

'Your fault?'

'I know it's irrational. But this is where I live, my place. He came to me and I couldn't get him in, even though my job is dealing with cases precisely like his.'

Rachel said, 'And your father?'

He was startled, defensive again. 'What do you mean?'

'Do you feel guilty about him, too?'

He said, slowly, 'I hadn't expressed it like that to myself, but yes, I suppose I do. I feel guilty about being free when he's not.' But the moment it was said he retreated. 'About the campaign,' he said.

His voice had switched, in that sudden way she was now used to. She recognised the signs from all the years of living with Simon and knew that there would be no point in saying more. The thought flashed into her mind, if only Simon turns out to be as whole as this man, I'll be happy.

He was saying, 'Tell me about the grass roots.'

'What's that?'

'You! Didn't you know? Working at the level politicians are always saying is important, and never actually reach. The people out there who don't pay any attention to politics.'

'The grass is doing OK, thank you, in my little patch. In fact it's growing too fast. I'm not sure I can keep up!'

'Go on,' he grinned, 'tell me.'

'There's going to be a meeting at the school. It wasn't my idea, it was Sophie's. She's a friend of mine, on the PTA. They'll organise it, if we provide the leaflets and posters and things. And then there's Pat's band.'

'Pat's band?'

'My friend at the library. She plays the saxophone in an all-women band. She's persuaded them to give a benefit concert - funds for the campaign!' He stared at her, and then started laughing. 'Well, you said we'd need funds,' she said.

'True, I did. What else did I say?'

'That we need to get lots of people involved, and that's what I still can't see. It's just me and my friends, and I can't see how it'll ever be any different.'

'Listen, Rachel, you've been going exactly two weeks! It's phenomenal what you've done already. And that concert will give you access to people who aren't just you and your friends. What you want to make sure is that you don't just let them come to the concert and go away again. It's not mainly their money we want; we want them to do something.'

'Like what?'

'Like collect other people! At this stage it's a numbers game. Signatures on a petition. With addresses. Then when you get the petition forms back, you've also got an address list of sympathetic people. You can use that when the next stage becomes clear.'

'People collecting people collecting people. It's like that suffragette slogan, Hammers producing hammers producing hammers, and never a nail driven home.'

'You'll drive this one home,' he said, 'if anyone can.'

Gita appeared at the door. Rachel's eyes announced that she was about to take flight. 'I have to get started,' she said, and she was moving off already.

*

149

It was difficult, now, to remember what had made her days seem busy before. A new level of energy had been mysteriously released to fuel her. Chores that would once have loomed large now somehow got done between times or were simply left undone, and no one seemed to suffer.

Late one night as she was looking for her cheque book to pay a bill she found in her bag a letter that had arrived from her mother days before - still unopened. That brought her up short. The letter was full of foreboding. There had been floods all over South Africa, her mother wrote, terrible floods, thousands of homes washed away. 'It's too late in the year for such heavy rain. I don't know what's happening to the world, nothing is the way it used to be, not even the weather.' Apart from the floods, the letter was entirely about Auntie. Nursing her had taken over her mother's life, it seemed. There was nothing else to report.

She must write. Tomorrow. And then she saw what tomorrow evening would be like - to Evelyn's, to get Ben and Simon; home, to cook supper; then the PTA meeting, leaving Kate to babysit. And after she got back she really had to do her tax return. She kept putting it off, it was so complicated, what with Alistair's money that never came regularly. She still hadn't had the letter he had promised about maintenance arrangements. Maybe she had better write again.

And her mother? She saw her mother's face, saw her standing at Auntie's bedside, trying to get her to eat... Be realistic, Rachel, she told herself, you can't do everything. She would write to her mother the next day. But that would be Friday, her ACRAS afternoon, and she didn't like harrying the children to bed on Friday nights, there was enough rushing all week.

The weekend. She would write to her mother over the weekend, come what may.

9

'Nuh was disappointed you didn't come today,' Mohamed said.

'He knows I've got a job to do,' Hassan said tersely, warding off feeling. 'I've got behindhand with all my other cases.'

'You work too hard, Hassan.' Mohamed sounded really edgy about it, ready for a fight. 'What's eating you?'

'My clients are other people like Nuh,' Hassan barked. 'And they don't have cousins who are lawyers.' Stop it, he told himself. I'm angry with the bastards out there, not with Mohamed. Less sharply he said, 'I can't come tomorrow either; but make sure he knows I'm busy here for him. I've got the bail application ready.'

'He wants to know how you're going to raise the money. Other people in detention have told him you need two people each to put up £2000. Have you got that kind of money?'

'No. But I can borrow it. I'm getting an increased mortgage on the flat.'

'What about the other person?'

'I'll find someone.'

'Your mother?'

'I'd rather not ask her. It might seem like the tip of an iceberg to her. And it might be.'

Mohamed stared at him, uncomprehending. 'It's for Nuh, and you don't want to ask her?'

'I'll find someone,' Hassan repeated, refusing to answer directly, and heard his voice hard again despite himself, keeping Mohamed out. He felt like crying with the longing for things to be different.

Only as Mohamed was leaving did he feel relaxed enough again to say, lightly, 'Tell Nuh I'm not giving up till I've had my one ballad more.'

'What's that supposed to mean?'

'It's an old joke between Nuh and me. A line from one of Ilmi Bowndheri's poems. He'll know.'

'You and Nuh and your poems,' Mohamed said, but he was laughing again too.

'It's one ballad more, is it?' Nuh used to say in mock complaint when each summer Hassan plagued him to teach him the songs he and his university friends were singing -

... And I am forever a poet.
When I am weary, and want no friend but peace
And say to you, 'This night my songs are done',
Your clamorous voices still would force from me
One ballad more to warm the dwindling fire.

But Nuh, too, would have saved up things to tackle him on, some issue he had heard discussed on the BBC Somali Service, something about British politics, an English book he had managed to borrow off a friend. Always thinking, learning, working things out.

'Tell him,' Hassan said, his longing turned now to a determination that Nuh should be once again free to live in that way, 'it's been far too long since I learnt any new poetry.'

*

Rachel said hello to Hassan briefly, then went to settle herself at the desk in the common room to go through the petition forms Mike had given her. A protest about the Tamils who had been expelled. A Zairean who had been kept in immigration detention centres for seventeen months while his case was being considered. Seventeen months! All these petitions, just about refugees, and presumably we're all chasing the same people for their signatures, each for our own particular little campaign.

Well, there was no point sitting here thinking defeatist thoughts. She had only a couple of hours, she'd better start writing.

We, the undersigned, request the Home Secretary to take account
of the army repression being directed against the people of northern
Somalia, and to give sympathetic consideration to -

Hopeless. Far too longwinded. No one she showed it to would understand what they were being asked to sign. And she didn't know whether she should phrase it in those general terms, or whether she should keep it to Haleemo's case. She would have to ask Hassan.

She walked into his room without knocking, as she had been expressly instructed to do; and he was standing there with his hands on Gita's shoulders, talking to her in an extremely personal way. Neither of them saw her. She disappeared back into the corridor, and went to ask Jenny instead.

Rachel had been gone for over an hour and had not come back to him. He made himself get on with other things for a while, and then went to find her. Not in the common room. He stood for a moment, puzzled, then went to reception. 'Seen Rachel?' he asked Barbara. 'Through there,' she pointed to her small office, leading off the reception area.

She was typing. 'Can I see?' he asked, looking over her shoulder. A petition. She was just finishing the last line. She pulled it out and gave it to him to read.

'Jenny's work, not mine,' she said. 'I've discovered the secret of this job - asking other people to do things you can't do yourself!'

'I've kept the rest of the afternoon free. Tell me what you want me to do.'

'You can show me how to use the photocopier. Barbara says it's temperamental.'

'It's out of the ark,' he said. 'We're thinking of giving it to the Science Museum when we get our new one. But I'll be happy to initiate you.'

'I'd like to take copies of this home today, then we can send them out to the parents before school closes for the Easter holidays.'

'Don't you think you'd better wait till you've got the leaflet ready to go with it?'

'I forgot to tell you,' she said. 'We're getting it printed.'

'Printed!'

She grinned, pleased with herself. 'The husband of one of the women at school runs a printshop. He's doing it free. And it's got a photograph!'

'Of Haleemo ?'

'With Asha and Ahmed, against a background of the school playground - mums meeting their kids after school!'

'Does another of your friends have a husband who's a professional photographer?'

'Don't make sexist assumptions,' she said. 'She's one herself!'

'I protest, that was a trap!' He put the petition into the copier. 'How many copies do you want?'

'For the school, about two hundred.' She set the counter, and pressed the green button to start. They watched for a moment to see that all was well. 'I was thinking about MPs,' she said. 'How many are there?'

'About 630.'

'Would you have a list? Names and addresses?'

'I've got a list of names, yes. You don't need addresses. You can send things to any of them at the House of Commons.' He looked curious. 'What are you planning to send, at this stage?'

'The leaflets, and the petitions.'

'Blank petition forms?'

'Yes.'

'You're going to ask MPs to collect signatures?'

'Yes. It came to me when I was looking at all those petitions Mike showed me. They must be bombarded with petitions people have signed, about every cause under the sun. I was trying to think how we could present ours so that they didn't just think, oh God, another set of signatures. Then I thought, I feel much more involved in something when I'm given a job of work to do. If we ask them to actually collect signatures -' He was doubled up with laughter, the way Anab and Haleemo had been when she'd got Anab's name wrong. 'I know most of them will just throw them in the dustbin,' she said, 'but if just two or three respond to the challenge, it'll have been worth it, won't it?'

'Yes,' he gasped through his laughter, 'yes, yes, yes.'

'So what's so funny then?'

'I'm laughing at the idea that it's me who has to teach you how to run a campaign!'

Barbara was at the door. Extraordinary, he had forgotten they were in Barbara's office, forgotten there were other people around. 'Hassan, call for you. It's the director.'

He went back to his office to take it. Martin, wanting to discuss next year's budget. And the moment he had put the phone down it rang again - the secretary of his local Amnesty branch, postponing the next meeting. When he went back to find Rachel, she was in the common room looking for something in the reference files and talking to Jenny. He had been about to say, do you need me for anything? But it was clear that she did not. It was absurd, but he felt disappointed.

They finished stacking the petition forms on the floor next to the filing cabinet. The centre was quiet. Almost everyone had gone, and it was time she did. 'Before I go,' she said, and looking up saw that he was not back sitting at his desk as she had expected, but perched against the edge of it, as if waiting. 'The meeting the PTA is organising,' she went on. 'Will you speak at it?'

'Who else is speaking?'

'We wanted Haleemo to, but she won't. She says her English isn't good enough. Anab will talk about the situation in Somalia. But we need someone to talk about the campaign, what people can do. I wondered if you would.'

'When's the meeting?'

'Not for four weeks. It's about to be Easter holidays, and then we'll need a couple of weeks after the beginning of term to remind people. But they've asked me to fix speakers now; we're doing a letter for the children to take home before the holidays, with the petitions.'

'And you don't think that in four week's time you'll be wanting to do it yourself?'

'What, speak at a meeting? No way!'

'I don't know, the rate you're going you might be picketing the Home Office by then!'

'I wish you'd stop saying things like that. It makes it worse.'

'Makes what worse?'

'Me feeling a fraud. I feel like one of the tailors in The Emperor's New Clothes. Going around saying, Sign the petition, Join the campaign. But the campaign doesn't yet exist, there's nothing there to join. And it won't exist until people join it.'

'That's right,' he said calmly. 'It's a con trick. A necessary one. And in case that Puritan conscience of yours is getting at you, it's an entirely moral one.'

'I've never doubted the rightness of it, I just feel so foolish! All it would take is one sane child to say, look, they're naked! For years I've been one of the people who said, what good will it do if I sign a petition? Now I'm asking other people to sign ours, but I still feel that. What good *will* it do?'

For a moment he didn't answer. He was looking at her but almost, she felt, past her. Then with a sudden restless movement he was at the window and was staring out at the rooftops. With his back to her he said, 'I feel the same about trying to get Nuh out of detention. There's this vast paraphernalia of the law that's supposed to protect us, and none of it is any bloody help.' When he turned again she had the impression that he was pulling himself back with difficulty. She wanted to say, forget it, I know you've got more pressing things on your mind. But he had started talking again before she could say it. 'It's like trying to wear away a solid mound of earth with something as insubstantial as your own breath,' he said - and she saw immediately, and with extreme clarity, the boulders on Duiwelskop. Midday. That still, inescapable heat, and all around the boulders - massive, black, unyielding... Then Hassan's voice again, joining her there in the heat and the stillness. 'All we can hope to do is move the air a little, to create the smallest wind. We don't know how solid the mound is. We don't know how long we'll have to keep going, or whether there will be any rain to help us. The people who say it's pointless can always show you plenty of rocks that are still standing. We just know that sometimes it works, and air's the only tool we've got.'

She was comforted, as she always was, by his continual use of 'we'. 'What makes you keep propping me up?' she asked. 'If I were in your position I'd hardly think it worth the effort.'

'It's worth it, all right.' He made another of his impulsive movements, to perch again against the edge of the desk nearest to her. 'Rachel there's something I've been wanting to tell you. The week before you came back I was almost immobilised by depression. A lot of things seemed to be going wrong all at once. One of our clients committed suicide - they were about to send him back to almost certain imprisonment and torture. You may have seen it in the papers, the inquest's just started. If you feel helpless about whether the world out there will care about our petition, just try to imagine what it feels like in this job, where you're dealing with people's destroyed lives day in, day out.'

He paused, and once again she had an extraordinarily clear awareness that it was vital that she say nothing, do nothing, but just continue to be there, to make it possible for him to come back. 'There's also my father,' he said.

It was the first time he had spoken of it without any prompting, giving words to that private pain that kept cutting him off. 'When you first came in here, the day I was so offhand with you, it was because I was out of my mind with worry about my father. You simply can't imagine what the conditions are like. They detain people, but they don't feed them. My aunt cooks for him, and has to hand the food over to the prison guard. If she doesn't include a bribe, she knows it will never reach him. Often it doesn't reach him anyway. Most of the time I try not to think about what's happening to him, it simply paralyses me. Then every now and then it sweeps over me, and I feel desperate. It was like that that day. I felt as you feel about the petition, but at the most personal level possible, alone with the knowledge of what was happening to him. And out there was the uncaring world that went on with its daily business, paying no attention, allowing a man like my father and thousands, hundreds of thousands like him, to rot in prison. Then you walked in, just one of those people out there getting on with your life, but you had stopped long enough to see what was happening to someone else, and to be angry.'

Angry - 'I've sometimes felt I don't know how to be angry,' she said. 'That it never lasts long enough.'

'There are people in whom it lasts so long it devours them. Don't ask for it to last. What you're doing is better, transforming it into action.'

'You make it sound much bigger than it is.'

His grin told her he was back to his normal buoyant self. 'That's only because I can see slightly better than you where it might lead!'

'I'm late for the children,' she said. 'I'd better go.'

She was standing at the door, ready to leave, her bag slung over her shoulder, her arms folding a pile of petitions to her chest. Don't go, he wanted to say, not to Rachel, fellow campaign worker, but to Rachel, the woman who had made it possible for him to talk about Nuh, about his father, about his own depression. 'When will you be back?' he asked, knowing she would say, 'Next Friday,' and thinking, It's far too long to wait.

'Not next Friday,' she said. 'That'll be the Easter weekend. The Friday after that.' She must have seen his disappointment but not understood it, for she smiled and said, 'Don't worry, I'll keep working at the campaign. I've got a lot to get on with meanwhile.'

All he said was, 'Phone me anytime, if there's anything you want me to do.'

10

A long weekend. At least that meant he'd have time to visit Nuh. In every other way the prospect was unappealing. Time stretching ahead, time alone.

This campaign that he had so foolishly set in motion - He had imagined them working together, and he himself finding at last an opportunity to act. But in his eagerness to prove to her that she could do things she did not believe herself capable of, he had created a situation in which he now had almost no role. She had built up her own group of people who together would decide what needed doing. He knew none of them, and anyway, how could he muscle in now? They would see an outsider, male, claiming to be an expert, trying to take over. All he was left with was waiting for Rachel to come in to the office once a week, to tell him what was happening. And *was* there any point? Was it conceivable that a group of women with no political experience could influence a Home Office decision? When he was with Rachel he knew that whether they had a chance or not they had to act as if they did, but that was an effect she herself had on him, nothing to do with a sober assessment of the odds.

'The demonstration,' Mohamed said, arriving in his office just as he was leaving. 'It's on Sunday. Did you remember?'

'Of course I did. What do you take me for? Go and look in reception, I've put leaflets there for all our clients to see.'

Mohamed grinned. 'Calm down. I only thought you might have forgotten, what with Nuh and everything. You're coming with us?' But 'us' meant the Somali National Movement contingent, and Hassan knew that if he said yes, Mohamed would think he had begun to win him over, and the pressure to join would be resumed with increased determination. 'No,' Hassan said. 'A couple of people I work with here might be coming. I'll go with them.' Mohamed made a dissatisfied noise. 'Mohamed,' Hassan said, 'do you want non-Somalis to support this demonstration or not?'

'OK, OK.' Mohamed conceded defeat; this round.

As it turned out, he went alone. Mike had an emergency meeting of the Tamil Support Group, and Gita cried off at the last minute -

relatives had arrived unexpectedly from Leicester. Shades of Farida, he thought, and felt glad to be shot of all that. He walked through Regents' Park, heading for the embassy in Portland Place; past multicoloured beds of polyanthus and pansies, indulging in a fantasy of sharing the glory of the colours with Rachel as he told her all the things about his father that for months had been trapped inside him. Don't be ridiculous, he told himself, you hardly know the woman; and then realised with some surprise that this was literally true. He felt known by her, but that was not the same thing.

At the southern end of the park was a row of parked coaches, empty, with 'Cardiff' and 'Liverpool' signs on them. A group of Somalis was coming out from the underground entrance as he past. One of them waved, a comradely greeting, going to the same place. Nearer the embassy the groups of three and four had become parties of fifteen, twenty, till the people walking towards the crowd had become a crowd themselves, overflowing the pavements and straddling the wide road that once had been intended for the carriages of the aristocracy - and now for the Mercedes of the embassy staff. Hassan climbed up onto the railing nearest him, to look over the multitude of black heads that stretched endlessly ahead. It was a long time since he had been surrounded by so many Somalis. Several thousand people, at least. One or two white faces. Journalists? He doubted it. This probably won't even make tonight's news, he thought, and felt a flash of fierce anger. How many people does a regime have to slaughter before the media will pay any attention? But he knew the answer; it wasn't numbers that mattered, but who it was being killed.

There was the usual line of policemen forming a cordon round the embassy. Their faces were blank, unreadable. That means they're tense, he thought, as if such a large number of black people in itself constitutes a threat to the peace. But they did nothing except link arms to make a barrier, and look out at the crowd from under their helmets. The embassy windows were closed. Would there be anyone there, he wondered? They must have known about the demonstration, surely they would have moved out for the day? As if in answer to his question the man next to him said, 'They're in there, all right. We saw the police let someone in.' Hassan felt excitement rising. Something was going to happen, and it seemed now as if he had been waiting for this for weeks. He caught sight of Mohamed, on the far side of the embassy. He jumped down off the railing and started pushing his way towards him. From somewhere to the left he heard himself being hailed, 'Hassan Abdillahi Dahir!' ringing out over the melee of voices around him. His eyes searched, and found, to his amazement, Madar, one of his more distant Hargeisa cousins. He hadn't even known Madar was in England. He waved and yelled back. He knew he couldn't reach him but felt excited that he was there, one of his people, claiming him.

'Look,' said a man next to him, 'that window on the third floor, someone's opening it.' Hassan stared. Yes, one window, just wide enough to point a camera through. Taking photographs of the crowd. Then a head appeared. He's crazy, Hassan thought, and waited for the stones to start raining in on him. 'We've got your photographs,' yelled the man from his window. 'We're sending them back to Mogadishu.' The crowd, already vociferous, had only been waiting for some provocation. All around Hassan people were shouting back, pushing, shoving, as if they had to get near to get their hands on him. Something whizzed over the heads of the policmen towards the building, too small and light to do any damage but enough to create an atmosphere of potential violence. The police cordon tightened; they started shoving back against the crowd. The man at the window was still shouting, spurred on by the crowd's aggression. 'You'd better go home if you want your relatives to be safe.' A tall woman a few yards in front of Hassan yelled back, 'You have killed most of them anyway! What have we got to fear?' Something about her voice electrified him. He tried to manoeuvre himself into a position where he could see more of her than the back of her head, covered in a head scarf. But by the time he got a few feet forward he could no longer identify which head it had been. There was no one nearby whom he recognised.

Suddenly he saw her - Hibo! Yes, it definitely was! *'Hibo!'* he yelled, gesticulating furiously. He saw her turn her head for a moment to see where the call was coming from, but she did not see him, and in a few moments she was lost again in the sea of black heads, bobbing up and down as the waves of movement heaved and surged.

Hibo, here in London! One after another the people from his other life were being returned to him, reappearing half way across the world in this strange new guise of refugees. In his last summer in Mogadishu she had been staying in aunt Khadra's house, some sort of relative of uncle Hirsi's, as he remembered. Her husband had just been put away by a military court and aunt Khadra had, typically, taken her and her young child in. Hassan was aware all that summer of her physical presence - unattainable, of course, and perhaps for that reason all the more powerful. He would sit and play silly games with the little girl while Hibo and aunt Khadra worked, joining in their banter until they would shoo him out of the kitchen, telling him he was in the way, there was work to be done...

Mohamed again. He pushed with renewed energy, calling out to him. At least three heads nearby turned, all Mohameds. He tried again, 'Mohamed Omar Dahir!' but his voice was lost in the general noise. He urgently wanted to be with someone who belonged to him, through whom he could properly become one of this crowd, not a half-outsider. But his own movement had now become swallowed up in the surging pressure of bodies, taking him further away from Mohamed. He gave himself up to the inevitability of the current. Then he realised this was not the crowd's own movement, it was the police, pushing people back. There seemed to be a tussle going on. Desperate to see, he hauled himself up onto the base of an equestrian statue that stood in the middle of the wide road. It was already overloaded with people but he managed to cling on, and it gave him just that foot of extra height he needed to see what was happening to Mohamed. Four huge policemen appeared to be trying to separate a group of fighting men. Hassan called out, 'Mohamed, stay away!' - panic memories of Mohamed as a boy, unable to resist getting in on a fight. But this was something different from a fight in the dust outside their house in Mogadishu, surely Mohamed must know better than to get embroiled in it! Hassan abandoned his foothold on the base of the statue, and with an immense physical effort launched himself forward, pushing against the pressure of bodies to get near Mohamed, to stop him before it was too late.

But it was already too late. Something strange was happening. The dinning noise of thousands of people shouting seemed to have given way to a single eery drone, and everything had gone into slow motion. The heaving of the crowd. The arms moving up in the air to fling pebbles. The bodies of the policemen closing in on Mohamed. He knew now that nothing could stop what was going to happen. He watched, impotent, through the painfully long few seconds that it took for the two burly men to grab hold of Mohamed, one from each side, and a third to raise his truncheon-bearing hand to the sky and bring it down on Mohamed's head; and then for Mohamed to wrench one arm free and with all the power of hatred thrust his clenched fist into the man's face.

Mohamed was gone.

That was all he could take in for a few seconds. He had lost yet another. His father, Nuh, now Mohamed. Mohamed, taken from him, taken by the police, his fiercely resisting body dragged and kicked and shoved and heaved into the police van; doors slammed. Mohamed, Mohamed, he moaned, Mohamed... *No!* The adrenalin started working again, pumping furiously through his body, urging him forwards through the crowd till he emerged right next to the van. It was surrounded by policemen, a tight, hostile human barrier. 'Where are you taking them?' he demanded, raising his voice above the clamour. None of the anonymous faces in uniform answered. 'I said where are you taking them?' he yelled, the anger now burning through him, uncontrollable.

'Just stay away, you coloured bastard,' one of them said, scarcely looking at him. 'Unless you want to join them.' Now that there was an individual face to direct his voice at, he could control it somewhat. 'I want to know where you're taking them,' he repeated, staring straight at the man who had spoken.

'It's nothing to do with you. Just clear off, blackie, I've warned you already.'

'It is something to do with me. My cousin's in there, and I'm a solicitor. I want to know where you're taking them.' He began memorising the man's number, and made it obvious that he was doing so. 'Paddington Green Station,' the policeman said abruptly. 'Now clear off.'

Hassan lay awake a long time that night, too exhausted and in too much of a turmoil to sleep. He had managed to see Mohamed for half an hour before one of the policemen had come in to the small, bare room they had been allowed to use, and informed him that he was under instructions to remove the prisoner, back to his cell, Sir. They had Sir-ed him all over the place once he got to the police station. Someone had clearly tipped off the senior officer and the word had got around, Coloured solicitor trying to make trouble, give him the Gentleman treatment.

The word had not been in time to save Mohamed. They had roughed him up in the van, he said. Nothing obvious to show for it, but he had a terrible headache and ached all over, and had been violently sick in his cell. Hassan looked at his exhausted face, distorted with anger, and felt a compassion so deep that for a few moments it cancelled out all other sensation. He did not try to put his arms around Mohamed's shoulders, as he would once so easily have done. What had happened to Mohamed in the brief hour since he had been set upon by those three large bodies had taken him across some intangible boundary of the spirit, to regions where Hassan could not follow.

Finally Mohamed spoke. 'Those fuckers, did you see them?'

'I did. I was yelling to you to stay away.'

'They were getting Aadan. I went in to help him.'

So simple. 'You're crazy,' Hassan said.

'No more than you,' Mohamed said, and there was a flicker of a smile on his painful, angry face. 'Look where you are now.'

'OK, but it's different. I'm not punching a policeman in the nose for your sake. And I wouldn't either.' Then all desire to smile was gone, replaced by the heaviness of what lay before them. 'I wonder if you have any idea what trouble you're in?' he said, almost more to himself than to Mohamed. Assaulting a policeman. Maybe he could get them to drop that charge. If they knew he had witnessed what had happened it was just possible that they might decide it would be politic to avoid any possibility of formal complaints about racist behaviour. Possible, but unlikely. But that wasn't the real problem. The first thing they would be doing once Hassan had left would be demanding to see Mohamed's papers; his Temporary Admission document, which began, 'You are a person liable to be detained.' And then they would be contacting an Immigration Officer. We've got one of your people here, they would say, Mohamed Omar Dahir, in for assaulting a policeman. He's applied for asylum. How does his case stand?

He did not want to have to explain all that to Mohamed, not now with his face so raw with pain and anger, but he had to know what he was up against. Watching his face closely he began, 'I'll go now and see if I can persuade them to let you out for tonight. But it's unlikely. Tomorrow they'll bring you before the magistrate. I'll be there, and I'll apply for bail.' Yet another bail application.

'What will I get?' Mohamed asked.

'Allah knows. Depends on what kind of magistrate you land. With any luck, only a fine.'

'And what about the fact that they laid into me?'

'We'll tell the magistrate, and then it will be up to us if we want to make a formal complaint.'

'So we'll complain!'

'Yes, if you think it's worth the effort. It's the Police Commission that will hear it. Policemen, hearing complaints against other policemen. You can imagine how well that system works.' Mohamed spat. Hassan continued. 'It's not really the courts or the police that are the problem now. It's immigration. Have you got your Temporary Admission paper on you?'

'No. It's at Aadan's place.'

'Did you tell immigration that you'd moved from your last address?'

Mohamed glared at him. 'No,' he said. 'If you followed all the regulations those people put on you you'd never have a soul to call your own.' Then, slightly more conciliatory, 'I was going to. I just hadn't got round to it. We were so busy organising the demonstration.' Hassan just looked at him, saying nothing. Mohamed said, 'Come on then, tell me.'

'Your piece of paper, Temporary Admission - it doesn't mean you have any legal right to be here. They've just let you in instead of keeping you in detention while they decide your case. And as far as they're concerned the most essential condition is that you don't try and disappear once you're in. They get worked up if people change addresses without telling them.' He paused again, the compassion returning. 'I don't like having to tell you this, but there is a chance they might decide to take away your Temporary Admission.'

'That means?'

'You land up where Nuh is. And no question of bail. Since you've already moved once without telling them, you'll be regarded as a security risk, however much we explain.'

Nothing changed in Mohamed's face. 'Let them do what they want with my case,' he said. 'I've had enough of this place. I'm going back to fight.' Hassan raised his eyebrows, but said nothing. 'I've been thinking about it for days,' Mohamed said, and there was a trace of the old Mohamed in his voice, enthusiasm rising. 'Things are beginning to move at last, Hassan. We've heard there's going to be an agreement between the Somali and Ethiopian governments, not to allow each others' liberation groups on their territory. We reckon we'll be given a couple of weeks, and then SNM will have to be off Ethiopian soil. Back into Somalia, where we should have been months ago.' He laughed, a hard, angry laugh. 'It takes a treaty between two dictatorships to make the so-called leaders of SNM get off their arses and start doing something!' Hassan did not want to hear. There was something in Mohamed's eyes that made him wary. Mohamed said, 'And I'm going in with them.'

I don't believe it, thought Hassan. He's talking big, to keep himself from being afraid of what's happening to him here. Aloud he asked, 'How do you propose to get there?'

'Fly to Djibuti,' Mohamed said. 'Remember? I've got a Djibuti passport. I told you I might need it again.'

Hassan felt overwhelmed with exhaustion. 'I'm going,' he said. 'I'm going to see if I can persuade them not to charge you, and let you out of here. If I can't, I'll see you tomorrow, when they bring you before the magistrates.' And he got up to go, just as the policeman came in to inform him that he was under instructions to remove the prisoner back to his cell. Sir.

They dropped the charge. Extraordinary. He used his best professional manner - solicitor representing client, scrupulously polite as they had been with him, no mention of what they all knew he had seen at the demonstration. He had no hope of success, and to his astonishment they were sweet reasonableness itself. 'We will of course have to inform the immigration officials that he has been involved in an Incident,' said the police officer. 'How they choose to proceed is, of course, entirely their affair.'

Entirely, as always. Entirely at their discretion.

He tried to get Mohamed to come home with him. He felt convinced that Mohamed was still in terrible danger, no longer from the police and not, for the moment, from the immigration officials, though that would come; but from himself. He wanted to save him from it. He could not have said what exactly the danger was, except that he had been aware of it from that moment he had been brought into the small, bare room and had seen Mohamed's face - hard, distorted with anger - and felt such terrible compassion. He did not know how keeping

Mohamed with him could change anything, but he knew it was what he had to do.

Mohamed refused to come. Not just refused, turned violently aggressive, as if all the anger that had not yet found an object demanded to be let loose. 'What are you trying to do to me, Hassan? Become my prison warder? You afraid I'll find another policeman to punch, and then you'll have to come and get me out again? I'm going to my place, I tell you, and I'm getting myself ready to go back - home!'

Home. What home did Mohamed have, to go back to? Mogadishu was out. Hargeisa? Mohamed could not go near the place except as part of a conquering army, and what chance was there of that? Djibuti, that was the nearest he could get - the hottest, most barren stretch of lava deposit on God's earth. Who would want to go back to Djibuti and call it home? Or to try to walk across into Ethiopia to find an army about to be thrown out, equipped only with what weapons they had managed to capture...

I have no forts, no houses,
I have no cultivated fields, no silver or gold for you to take.
You have gained no benefit by killing my men
and my country is of no good to you.
The country is barren.
If you want wood and stone, you can get them in plenty.
There are also many ant-heaps.
The sun is very hot.
All you can get from me is war.

11

From Box Hill Station they walked past a row of houses, shepherded the children across a road that seemed small and rural until cars came whizzing round the corner at lethal speed, and then over a stile into a meadow, in which the river wound in a lazy arc round towards a patch of forest. On the other side of the river towered the hill, just waiting to be climbed.

The first time Rachel opened up the Ordnance Survey map to see where the footpath went Asha was at her side, staring silently. The other children had gone tearing across the meadow, and Haleemo and Anab were walking sedately after them. 'We want to find one of these red dotted lines,' Rachel explained to Asha. 'That's a public footpath, where we're allowed to walk.' Asha continued to stare silently, in the way Rachel had learnt was a demand for further explanation. 'See, that blue one's the river,' she said, pointing to the lines on the map. 'And these orange ones all together show you that the land gets higher, so that's the hill. So if we stand this way -' she turned herself and the map, and Asha dutifully followed, 'Now, can you see where the path goes?'

'There!' Asha pointed triumphant. 'Next to the river!' And she ran off to instruct Ahmed that he was to walk only next to the river because they weren't allowed anywhere else. Ahmed wriggled out from her grasp and went haring after Ben across the field. Asha came back anxiously to Rachel. 'It's OK,' Rachel smiled. 'They're not doing any harm in this field. It's when there's a crop growing that you have to be careful otherwise the farmers get mad at you.' She could see that she had done nothing to allay Asha's fears, rather the reverse. She put out her hand to take Asha's and said, 'Come, let's catch up with the others.'

Asha took her hand. 'They have guns?' she asked.

'The farmers? No! Well, maybe for shooting birds or rabbits, but not people!'

Asha looked disbelieving. A gun is a gun, and her experience had taught her that the behaviour of men with guns cannot be predicted. 'I want to go home,' she said, miserably.

Looking out from the top of Box Hill, over colours and shapes so different from the yellow-grey veld of her childhood that had stretched flat to the horizon, she had been caught by surprise to feel brought home again to the same sense of opening out, of oneness with all that lay spread out beneath. Fields and hedgerows and folding hills, patches of dark forest and a light green dusting of spring shoots on the nearest trees - the English poetry her father used to read to her, now lifted off the page and made real.

In the train on the way back Haleemo said, 'In Somalia there are big mountains, bigger than this.'

'Tell me,' Rachel said.

'There is a place in the mountains called Sheikh, very beautiful. I went there for my auntie's wedding.' Then she started trying to tell Rachel and Kate about something called a *fijaan* - something made by the women in the bride's family, but more than that Rachel could not gather. 'Anab-ey,' Haleemo summoned Anab from the seat behind them, 'help!' And between Haleemo's Somali and Anab's English and both of their hand gestures the fijaan was made to appear before them. A large basket, curved like a woman's body - 'A special basket,' Haleemo said, covered with leather and decorated with beads that came from Saudi Arabia; and in it a bowl filled with *muqmad* - 'Special Somali food,' Haleemo said, and Anab laughed and explained, 'It's small pieces of meat, stored in ghee, like the men take when they go for a long time with the camels.' Then Anab described how the women would cover the meat with dates or a special type of sweet, and then with another basket, and tie it all closed with a cord wound round and round, the end hidden so that no one would find it. Then they would dress the fijaan in a white garment, like a bride, and at the wedding a girl from the bride's side would call a young man from the bridegroom's side to come and unveil it. If he could not find the end of the cord he would have to sing a song or do something silly that would make everyone laugh at him; and then it would be the turn of some other young man to try. 'Yes,' said Haleemo at each new detail Anab described, 'yes, yes,' getting more and more excited, and it was her excitement as much as Anab's telling that made the scene so vivid. 'My mother,' Haleemo said, 'she make already fijaans for all granddaughters for when they are marry, one for Asha, one for Nafisa -'

She stopped. When she went on her voice was despondent. 'She put them in the house, safe, with all our other things. Now everyone is run away. Maybe the soldiers have taken them. All gone. All gone now.' And she seemed to need to keep saying it, to make herself take in the unbelievable fact. All gone; so many things, all gone.

*

He walked into the common room looking for Jenny - to find Rachel. On a Wednesday!

'What are you doing here?' he demanded, 'and why didn't you come and tell me instantly?'

'It's school holidays,' she said. 'I've taken leave, to do things with the children.'

'Like sitting here at a typewriter!' He grinned, and swung himself onto the neighbouring desk, sitting there with his legs dangling like a schoolboy.

She said, as if defending herself, 'I've been extremly child-oriented all week, and until lunch-time today. Simon and Sado and I have been making gingerbread men. Gingerbread people, actually. Sado wanted to make some with long skirts.'

'Simon likes to cook, does he?'

'Simon likes to do anything with his hands, and anything with an adult companion.'

'I'd like to meet him.'

'Come sometime then. In fact, come on Sunday. We're having an envelope-stuffing party.'

'What, all the petitions to MP's?'

'That's it,' she laughed. 'And to about a hundred organisations. Jenny's given me a list. The envelope party was Kate's idea. She's disappointed that we haven't had any meetings yet!'

'So what makes it a party rather than a meeting?'

'That's me,' Rachel said. 'I'm allergic to meetings. And it's spring, so I thought it was time we did something frivolous. The party is in the daytime so the children can come too. They can help us till they get bored, then be outside if the weather's OK; and Pat's bringing her saxophone, which Kate is dying to learn. And Anab and Haleemo are going to cook for us, Somali food.'

'I'm coming!' he said. He got down from the desk and reluctantly prepared to return to his office. 'Is anyone going to have time to stuff envelopes?'

Five thirty. He looked up to see her in the doorway. 'You busy?' she asked.

'No more than usual. Come on in. I had a feeling you were going to disappear without telling anyone.'

'I do have to be going,' she smiled, 'but I just wanted to ask if there's any news of your cousin?'

'Only that we've got a date for a bail hearing.'

'Will he be given it?'

'Nothing's ever sure, but I can't see that they have any conceivable grounds to oppose it. So by next Thursday he should be out and staying with me, a free man. In a manner of speaking.'

'Meaning?'

'That the euphoria of not being in detention won't last forever. At some point he'll begin to take it for granted, as he should do, and look around him and realise he's stuck in a pretty hopeless situation. Not unlike Haleemo's, actually. His wife and child are in Mogadishu, and there isn't much chance of their getting out. The usual problems - no travel documents, no visas, not a lot of money. Nuh got himself across the border at night, walking through the bush, hiding by day to avoid the soldiers. It would be difficult for Amina to do anything like that, with the baby. And then there's work. He was a university teacher in Mogadishu. He's a bright guy, and he needs to be doing something with his life, not just hang around feeling useless.'

'If he's got those kinds of qualifications, can't he get a job?'

Hassan looked at her without speaking for a moment. 'I thought you knew,' he said. 'Asylum seekers aren't allowed to work for the first six months.' And her reaction came, exactly as he had known it would.

'Not allowed to work? But that's crazy! I just assumed most of them couldn't find work. Surely the government would prefer them to work than to have to live off benefits?'

'You would have thought so,' he said. 'It's all to do with maintaining the fiction that people like Nuh aren't really here until they've been officially recognised as refugees. Which may of course be never. According to British law he hasn't actually 'entered' Britain yet; he's 'arrived', but that's not the same thing. Arriving is a physical fact the Home Office can do nothing about, but you have only 'entered' when they give you a piece of paper that says you have.'

'It's all make-believe!'

He said, 'The emperor's new clothes, in fact.' She laughed. He felt wonderful every time he made her laugh.

'Well, enjoy his company anyway,' she was saying. 'I'm sure it will be lovely for you to have one of your family with you.'

She was going, he could see it in her eyes. He wanted to hold on to her, to stop her from constantly going away from him. As if in answer she said, 'Hassan, I have to go. Anab's with my children, and she'll be wanting to get back home.'

'Just tell me quickly first, anything new in the campaign?'

'Bits and pieces. One of the teachers has a friend who is a journalist on a local paper. She said she could ask him to write something.'

'Don't let him. Write it yourself.'

'How can we?' she asked, surprised. 'They won't print what we write, surely?'

'On the contrary, they're much more likely to print something if you give it to them ready written. It saves them the effort of having to think. And that way you make sure they say the right things. If some ignorant journalist waltzes in and hears what you have to say, and then goes away to write a piece on it, he's bound to get all sorts of things wrong. And he's very unlikely to emphasise the things you think are important.'

'I wouldn't have a clue how to write a newspaper article.'

'Yes you would. Just go and buy a few copies of the local papers, and spend an hour reading them. There's a standard formula, easy to copy. But make sure you tie it to some event. They won't consider it news unless something has happened, and things happening thousands of miles away don't count. You can't just write a Poor Haleemo kind of article, they'll throw it in the dustbin.'

'But what event is there to tie it to?'

'You might have to manufacture one.'

'Like what?'

'I wait to hear, Rachel. I fully expect that on Friday you will walk in here and tell me. And you'll say, it was Kate's idea, really. Or Pat's. Or Evelyn's!' She was laughing again, and today she didn't say, I wish you wouldn't say things like that. He felt like leaping up and dancing in celebration. 'I'm going too,' he said. 'Give me a minute to pack up and I'll walk down with you.'

Going down the stairs she asked, 'Where did you learn all this?'

'What, about refugees and the law?'

'No, about campaigning.'

He thought for a moment. 'I don't know. I've never thought about it. I suppose most of the people I know are in some way or another having to fight the system in order to survive.'

'But you're different. Mike, for instance, you told me he had a lot of experience but when he talks it's like listening to a foreign language. You always manage to make it connect for me, with the other things in my life.'

171

'Maybe it's because I've seen a lot of lousy campaigning,' he said; 'people who're on lots of committees and use jargon no one else understands and are constantly expecting the masses to follow them. There was a lot of that about when I was a student. Mike's the same kind, really.'

'I'm the opposite,' she laughed. 'I never expect anyone to follow me.'

'A very useful quality,' he said firmly. 'It's what keeps you thinking. You just overdo it a bit.'

He watched her run towards the bus stop, disappearing into the crowd of people emerging from the offices and shops. The air was soft and caressing, all bite gone out of it. He decided he was not going home on the underground. He took the bus and stared out of the window all the way. A couple of stops before his own he got out, to walk the rest of the way. He needed exercise. His body felt underused, full of untapped energy. It was madness sitting in an office all day, especially in weather like this. He strode out, enjoying feeling the movement in his calves and thighs, then he began to run. He ran till he was breathless, then walked again, feeling more at peace with his body. He began noticing the people around him; a brisk, efficient-looking woman in high heels and tailored clothes, clicking her way along the pavement towards him, her breasts pushing forward, filling her blouse; a couple of school girls eating icecreams, talking and laughing as they crossed the road with scant regard for the traffic, every movement flaunting their newly-discovered sexuality. A young black woman in tight jeans came out of a shop just in front of him, her bottom swaying enticingly with each step, evoking a sudden flash of desire.

He stopped walking suddenly, as if the fact had come to stand before him, naked and unashamed, demanding to be attended to. He needed a lover. He had known it for weeks, if not months. But there had been so much happening, so many urgent demands on his energies that it had been pushed aside, something known but to be dealt with later, when all this was over. But of course it never would be over. He might get Nuh out, but there would be others, always others. They would keep arriving, these people from his previous life, and half of them would land up in his office with crises for him to sort out. Hibo - maybe seeing her again so unexpectedly had stirred up the awareness of desire; and then Rachel, in and out of his office with that extraordinarily expressive face of hers, standing within touching distance, making him feel alive and on a high of energy whenever she was in the room, waking up this part of him that had lain dormant far too long. Rachel, so near yet unreachable, tied to a life so demanding that to carve out even three hours a week away from her family had seemed to her a major revolution.

What he needed was someone single, unattached, and immediately available. A woman without a husband in prison, or relatives like Farida's, or children, someone with plenty of time and no other emotional demands taking her constantly away from him. But it would also have to be someone like Rachel, someone with depth to her, who made him feel safe, so that opening up to talk about what he was feeling seemed the only natural response. And someone he could laugh with.

Not someone. Rachel. He needed Rachel.

*

That evening Rachel's mother phoned. It had never happened before. It would not have occurred to either of them that it was possible to communicate across continents in this way, and Rachel assumed that only a death could have occasioned this. But Auntie had not died. 'She won't,' said her mother, her voice raw with misery. 'It just goes on and on. It's too terrible.'

Her mother talked non-stop, and she could talk only about Auntie. Rachel listened and made sympathetic noises, and all the time a hard knot of tension and guilt was forming in her stomach - I ought to be there, helping her. Finally her mother said, 'We'd better stop, *skat*,' - darling - 'this is costing a fortune.'

Dear Mom, she wrote, It was lovely hearing your voice tonight, even though the reason for phoning was a sad one...

She tried not to think about how long it was since she had last written, but in fact she was appalled at herself. Her mother's voice had been a more vivid reminder than any number of letters could have been. She had not complained, had not even said, 'It would be lovely if you wrote more often, skat.' But the need in her voice had been obvious and she, Rachel, was the only person who could fulfil that need. There was Matthew, of course, her brother. He was nearby. Well, not that near, actually, the better part of a day's car journey away, but at least he was in the same country and could have arranged to see their mother in an occasional weekend. But when she had asked her mother whether Matthew had been, the reply had been vague. 'He's terribly busy, you know. His practice is doing so well. And he's off to the United States in a couple of weeks time. A Research Conference.' Which meant that Matthew had not been. And she, she had been too busy responding to the voices all around her even to write regularly...

I think sometimes, she wrote, about how it would be if I had never moved away, or perhaps only as far as Bloemfontein. I picture myself driving out with the children on a Sunday. I can just see them, running down to the river the way Daniel and I used to do, and coming to you to have their scratches and cuts treated with Dettol and plasters. I hope you still keep the Dettol in the kitchen, not the bathroom, so it's always handy! And in my fantasy you and I are sitting in the garden and talking, and we don't have to rely on letters which take so long and feel so inadequate.

Tonight when you phoned I understood, maybe for the first time, just how much you have needed support while you've been nursing Auntie, and I know that I have let you down by not writing more often. I have thought about you a great deal all this time, and I myself don't understand what has stopped me putting those thoughts onto paper more often and sending them to you. Maybe being so far away made me feel helpless, for all the things that would have come naturally to me to do at a time like this would only have been possible if I were there. I seem to have suffered from a sort of paralysis, not knowing how to join up the Lourensrus and the London bits of my life. I think that's changing, at last. I'm only sorry it took your phone call to jolt me into realising that I don't have to accept the distance as inevitable.

*

She dreamt that night that she was going back to Lourensrus. Auntie was with her, not Auntie in her eighties, bedridden, but the Auntie of her childhood, a woman in her fifties with a pear-shaped body and a small head, her hair cut short and straight like a child's, held firmly off her face by one long hairslide. They were travelling together in an overnight train, and Rachel was lying ready for sleep on the top bunk and looking down at Auntie, who was standing in the narrow space between the bunks, changing into her pyjamas. From this angle Auntie seemed even more pearshaped than usual - narrow shoulders, flat chest, blouse drooping limply where a bosom should have been, then swelling as it reached what in anyone else might have been a waist. Her tweed skirt, many sizes bigger than her blouse, stretched firmly over her huge, solid hips and thighs. She took off her blouse, appearing not at all bothered by Rachel's staring eyes. Under her hand-knitted cotton vest her breasts hung like empty cloth bags close to her body. When she took off her skirt Rachel half expected to see that she was padded around the hips, but it was all her, that wide, bony spread.

Then they were not alone in the compartment, for there were two other women with them, who oddly seemed to have been there all the time. They were younger than Auntie but still old to Rachel, and their preparations for bed involved an astonishing array of creams and lotions which they smeared on only to wipe off a few minutes later. One of them turned to Auntie and said '*Tannie*' - auntie, everyone's aunt - '*Tannie* never uses anything on her skin, does she?' 'No,' said Auntie, her tone blunt and tactless as always, 'I've never used any of those stupid creams.' The two women nodded in acceptance of her judgement, and continued to plaster their faces. 'That's probably why Tannie's skin is still so good,' one said. Rachel looked at Auntie's face, brown and wrinkled and leathery from more than fifty years of sun and wind, unprotected except by her wide-brimmed felt church hat on Sundays. It is a good skin, Rachel thought. It's her skin, nothing else.

And then they were no longer in a train, but in Auntie's house, in the room with the pictures of Jesus on the wall, looking pale and sad in long white garments with hair that hung to his shoulders like a girl's; the room which Auntie had given up sleeping in because it was too full of things that needed sorting out. Daniel was there with them, and he and Rachel had opened the bottom drawer of Auntie's huge darkwood chest and found, among her clothes, a collection box for the Sudan United Mission Society, a cardboard box of sealing rings for the jars of stewed fruit that lined Auntie's pantry shelves, and a bag full of wool scraps. Rachel's mother was there in the room, saying 'Leave Auntie's things alone, you should ask people before you go nosing around their things.' She and Daniel paid no attention but went on lifting up clothes to see what they would find, knowing that Auntie took for granted their right of access to her cupboards, as to her love. And then it was not Daniel there with her, but Sannie; and then Jill, and then Stefan, and then all of them, one after the other, all Auntie's nieces and nephews, each replacing the one before, each one younger than the last. Rachel turned and saw that Auntie was there in the bed after all, and that her mother was standing at her side saying, 'Sara, you have to eat, the doctor says so.' Auntie turned her head away to the wall, and all she would say was, 'They all keep going away.'

PART THREE

Departures

*For of course that life is sweet I grant you
and where terror dwells are not all men the same?*

Each morning she luxuriated in being able to wake in her own time without the alarm, knowing it wasn't just the weekend but ten whole days of glorious leave, and for the children no school, no childminders, no holiday playcentres. Ben climbed into bed with her each morning, his sleepy little body snuggling warm into hers, no corners anywhere. Then Simon, saying 'Move over, Ben, I want to get in too!' Kate would come bouncing into the room, up onto the bed, sitting cross legged, slipping her hands under the blankets to tickle Rachel's feet, threatening to pull the bedclothes off them. No need to chase anyone to get ready. A slow, leisurely breakfast, sitting in her dressing gown drinking coffee and reading yesterday's newspaper while Ben built a house around her with the sofa cushions, and Kate curled up like a cat in the armchair reading, and Simon sat at the table amidst the uncleared dishes, pouring water into the glasses and tapping them with a fork to make a musical instrument. And outside, the sun glinting on the daffodils in the windowbox.

All week there was a lightness in the air. When she opened the door to bring in the milk, a woman across the road was standing in her open doorway wrapped in her dresssing gown, chatting to her neighbour while her cat watched lazily from the window ledge. On the common, when she took Ben and Simon with their bikes, she was greeted by the early flowering trees in full blossom, a profusion of pink. When she popped out one evening to get some bread from the Gujarati shop that stayed open late, there was a man out washing his car, not as people wash cars in winter, quickly with cold hands, wanting to get back inside, but making it last; enjoying being out.

Pat stopped by on her way to a band practice one evening, to talk about arrangements for the benefit concert. The children had not met her before, and she made an instant hit by taking her saxophone out of its case and letting them have a go at playing it. If we'd been in Johannesburg, Rachel thought, working together as we do here and me liking her so much, I'd have brought her home before I'd known her two weeks. Yet here it took Haleemo's campaign to bounce me into suggesting it! Of course Pat had a full life of her own, a whole circle of friends her own age, but it was clear she enjoyed the children and liked being in a noisy, busy home. She would have come long ago if Rachel had suggested it. 'I don't know what I've been doing with my life,' Rachel said.

'You've had one or two things to deal with,' Pat said mildly.

'Well, I've decided I've finished dealing with them. I'm entering a new era.'

'I had noticed!'

Kate was riveted by Pat. Not only by the saxophone, Rachel realised, but by Pat's style, her feminist-fashion clothes, purple-pink track suit and spring green shoes, lace-ups with good soles, the kind of shoes you could walk for miles in. Sensible shoes, Auntie used to call them, in the days when no girl Rachel knew could be persuaded to wear them. Kate's face was alive with concentration as she watched the way Pat moved her hands when she spoke, or listened to the way she teased Rachel for being over-cautious. Pat was clearly aware of the admiration - it would have been difficult not to be. Rachel thought she handled it perfectly, not drawing any attention to it but including Kate in their conversation in the most natural way. 'Here we sit,' Rachel thought, 'thirty-four, twenty-four and thirteen years old, and we're planning this concert together.' She felt light-hearted, almost heady, more full of energy than she could remember having felt for years.

*

'Where's Mohamed? ' Nuh asked. 'He hasn't come for days.'

Hassan told him. 'He hasn't been near me either. Not a phone call, not a visit.' And, he thought, I'm damned if I'm going to phone him first. This time it's up to him. 'I don't believe he'll really try and go back,' he told Nuh. He had heard it too many times before, that holding on to an impossible belief. He had seen it in the eyes of people from every corner of the earth, wasting their lives away here in the miserable safety of exile, while a war waited to be fought thousands of miles away, and the voice that never slept kept whispering, the others are suffering, why should you be exempt? Anyway, he thought, where would Mohamed get the money for the ticket? He's not stupid enough to ask me for it.

But he was anxious nevertheless. Mohamed wouldn't have been in Britain now if he hadn't a capacity for rash, impulsive action.

'Maybe he'll be better off going back,' Nuh said. 'Fighting is what Mohamed does best, isn't it? '

Hassan smiled reluctantly. 'Not disciplined fighting, which is the only kind that would be any use in the present situation. That's one of the problems with an army that starts as a breakaway from another army. The principle is there from the beginning - if you don't like the decision, split, form a rival group. Did you know Mohamed and his mates have been organising against the present SNM leadership?'

'No. But it doesn't surprise me. '

'So what kind of a basis is that for turning into a loyal fighter? Going back would be a disaster for him, in every possible way.'

'And staying here?' Nuh's nostrils lifted again in disdain, as they had done that first day in the presence of the immigration officer. 'It doesn't seem to me this place offers a glorious future to people like him.'

'It offers the possibility of survival. I'd like him to survive.'

Nuh recited,

> 'Everyone will receive what has been prescribed for him,
> even though he runs fast
> or sets out early in the morning
> or climbs a high hill,
> no one will gain more than his allotted portion.'

Hassan asked, 'You really believe that?'

'Of course. And so should you. It's the only way anything makes sense.'

'So God also willed Siyad Barre on Somalia? God planned the rape of the north? The people brutally assaulted? Shot in cold blood? Wells poisoned? God decreed that Aabahay should be in prison?'

'Ultimately, yes.'

'What does that mean - ultimately?'

'We can know that it has to be God's will even though we find it impossible to understand why.'

'That's meaningless.'

'No it's not,' said Nuh. 'It's an apparent contradiction, but human experience is made up of contradictions.' He looked at Hassan silently for a moment, then said with sudden force, 'To despair of God's mercy is a sin. I'm sorry that living here has caused you to lose your faith, Hassan.'

Perhaps, despite himself, he was jolted by what Nuh had said about faith and despair. Or it may simply have been that each time he saw Nuh he was reminded that there was an issue he could not indefinitely avoid. Whatever the reason he phoned his mother that night. 'Just to say hello,' he said, 'I haven't seen you for a while.' They chatted pleasantly about nothing in particular, and all the time he was trying to say, 'Mom, I need your help. Nuh's in trouble.' He couldn't.

He stared at the dead phone, as if waiting for it to come to life of itself. Eventually he picked up the receiver again and dialled Jenny's home number. 'I want to ask you a favour.'

'Go ahead.'

'It's nothing to do with work.'

'I said go ahead. What are you waiting for?'

'Would you stand surety for my cousin, to get him out on bail?'

'If I've got the money, yes. How much?'

'£2000.' Silence; then, 'I haven't,' she said. He had known it, of course. Where would she get that kind of money, on the kind of salaries we get? With two children, and supporting a husband through his medical training? But she was saying, 'Jeff's dad's got money. I'll get Jeff to ask him to lend us some. Does it have to be in my account at the time you apply?' He tried to say, 'I don't know, but I'll find out,' but the words wouldn't come. He felt choked up. She was talking, to fill the space till he had recovered. 'It must be awful, trying to be a caseworker for your own cousin.' Her voice pattered on, to save him from having to speak. 'When the children are ill Jeff refuses to treat them himself. He says his stomach gets all tight, seeing them like that, and he's bound to make a wrong diagnosis.' His own voice had returned. 'Thanks,' he said. 'You're a real friend. I'll let you know what to do about the account.'

All Friday afternoon Hassan was in a meeting. She didn't see him until she was about to leave. He came into the common room, harried. 'They sprung the meeting on me at the last minute,' he said. 'This whole Friday arrangment is becoming a farce. Find something more definite for me to do.'

'I thought you were coming to help us on Sunday.'

'Rachel, I'm perfectly happy to address envelopes, but I had envisaged taking a slightly more active role!'

'I've a hundred things I'd like your help with, but you're always so busy. I don't feel -'

'Stop it. Just tell me, and I'll do it.'

'OK, our benefit concert. We need help publicising it. We want to use it to reach a new set of people, not just the school, and not just the politically active types we'll be sending petitions to.'

'Stay for half an hour, and we'll put together a list of organisations right now.'

'I can't, Hassan.'

'Rachel, for God's sake -' He stopped himself. 'OK, correction, it's me who wasn't available when you made time today. Give me Pat's phone number, and I'll work it out directly with her.'

Rachel laughed. 'You'll see her on Sunday, do it then.' She picked up an armful of petitions. 'I must go,' she said. She looked at the remaining pile of petitions. 'We're going to need all those on Sunday, plus that load of cover letters.'

'I'll bring what you can't manage,' he said.

'Do you have a car?'

'No, but it's no problem. I've been training for this moment by carrying heavy legal documents for the past six years!'

I love this man, she thought, simply. I love his energy, his bounce.

He said, 'Rachel, why did you come back? You never explained. You just said you'd changed your mind.'

The question was so unexpected, and his eyes so serious, that for a moment she was non-plussed. Eventually she said, 'I was glad you didn't ask that day. I couldn't have told you.'

'It didn't occur to me then. I just knew I'd been right about you after all, and that made me so glad I didn't think further.'

'It was lots of things. Things going on in my life that all seemed to come together. Most of them had nothing to do with Haleemo.'

'Like what?'

She hesitated, sorting out where to begin. 'I suppose, first, Alistair. My husband. He phoned, just when I was trying to hide from the fact that I'd run away. He was in Europe and could have made time to see the children, and didn't. I only talked to him for about five minutes, but it was enough to stir me up totally. Feelings I'd thought I'd got past - every time he comes back into my life I discover they're still alive, and in control. What I do or don't do, what I'm afraid of, it's still in reaction to Alistair. I knew I had to get out of that, or I'd rot.' She realised she was not explaining herself clearly. 'It's campaigns,' she said. 'Alistair's life revolved around campaigns when we were together.'

'Where was that?'

'In South Africa. I'd assumed you knew, from my accent.'

'I suppose there is something not quite British about it. I'd never given it any thought.'

'Alistair was from New Zealand. My family used to say I'd begun to talk like him. Maybe I've been doing a chameleon act here too without realising it - defence against being stereotyped. White South African isn't the best of labels.'

'No label's worth anything,' he said. 'I'm glad to know you're South African - it makes sense of things that didn't before.'

'What do you mean?'

'That you're not really new to all this.'

'No. When Haleemo started talking about the army rolling in, beating people up, people in prison when they'd done nothing wrong, it felt as if something was following me, catching up with me. I never found a way of doing anything in South Africa. I have an aunt -' She stopped. What was she doing telling him about Auntie?

'Go on,' he said.

'She's dying,' Rachel said simply. 'She's been dying since soon after I got involved with Haleemo, but her body won't die.' She stopped again. Her chest was tight, her breathing difficult. She felt as if she were doing something dangerous, crossing open veld alone at night. Not even in her letters to her mother had she risked telling about how Auntie had been growing inside her all these weeks, reviving memories, appearing in her dreams. It was not something anyone else could understand. Yet Hassan's eyes, looking steadily on her face, waiting for her to go on but not pushing her, made her know it would be safe. 'She was eccentric,' she said. 'The rest of the family used to laugh at her - affectionately, but they would say, 'It's Auntie, what can you expect?'' She was awkward and outspoken and tactless, but she had the most extraordinary capacity for love. She never married; maybe because she didn't have her own children, she loved other people's, really loved them. All of us, her nieces and nephews, she was the one who linked us all. But much wider than that, she had a special feeling for children in need. She used to work in the black township near us - social work, I suppose, but it wasn't a job, she just knew people who worked in the school and the clinic, and she worked with them. The poverty is terrible. There are hardly any jobs for the people in the township, and they don't own any land.'

'Your aunt?' he reminded gently. 'You were going to tell me how your aunt connected with where you are now.'

'Yes. I don't really know how to say it. She was there all my childhood, just part of the environment I grew up in. I never thought about her particularly - you know what it's like when you're a child, everything that you happen to be born into is natural. Only later you look back and things strike you. Since I left home I've hardly thought about Auntie, never written her more than a card on her birthday and at Christmas. I knew she got news fom my mom, so it didn't occur to me to write separately. But since I've known she was dying she seems to be here the whole time.'

'Talking to you?'

'Yes.' And there was now nothing surprising in his being able to put it into words so simply. 'I never saw her show any sign of caring what other people thought of her. She just did what she thought needing doing. You know what you said about being angry? I suddenly remembered - something that happened when I was a child. About ten, maybe less. Auntie had a garage that she never used for her car; she piled things in it, things she collected from the white people of Lourensrus to give to people at the school or the clinic in the black township, who always knew someone who needed them. My cousin and I used to play in that garage. It was a fantastic place for children, and Auntie never said the things other grown-ups did, about not touching things. One day when we were in there a lorry drove up, and these men delivered cartons and cartons of babyfoods, which they stacked in the garage. Auntie said they had come from a wholesalers, a kind man had donated them for the clinic. After they'd gone my cousin and I started playing shop with them. When we'd arranged them all we called Auntie to admire, and she saw that the lids of many of the jars had bulges in them. The vaccuum-sealing process must have been faulty. We had seen it, but not understood.

I can still see Auntie's face. It went all blotchy-red, and her mouth twitched, and then suddenly she let loose this torrent of distress. That there could be men so evil that they would sit calmly in their offices and off-load onto her this food, which they knew they could not sell because it was contaminated! Knowing that they were sending it to innocent children. I had never seen anyone so angry. And then Auntie walked back into the house, and she said it all over again to my dad, and then when my mom came, to her as well. The anger just kept coming out, and couldn't be soothed away.

The next day I was with her when she went out to the township. There was a man at the clinic, a social worker whom she liked a lot, and there weren't many men she tolerated. I was standing there next to her when she told him all about it. He was sitting behind his desk. He was late middleaged, his hair begining to go white - tight little curls around the shape of his head, and all sprinkled with white, as if someone had spilt the salt. He sat there listening to Auntie, and when she had finished he simply put his head in his hands and stayed like that, not saying anything, for a long time. I could see that his silence calmed her, as nothing my dad or mom had said had been able to do. When he lifted his head he said, 'Miss Faure, there are people like that in the world; and there is also you.'

For a few moments neither of them spoke. Then he said, quietly, 'Rachel, do you know what the time is?' She looked at her watch in instant panic. 'My God, quarter to seven, and it's going to take me half an hour to get home. I have to phone Kate.'

He put his hand on the phone to stop her lifting it, and with the other hand touched her arm. 'Just hold on. Two minutes isn't going to make any difference. Don't tell her you're coming, ask her if she's OK to look after the others for another hour and a half. Then we can go and eat together.'

'Hassan, she's only just thirteen.'

'I thought you told me she was grown-up for her age?'

'She is, but -'

'So, let her decide. If we go and eat straight away, you can still be home by nine.' She wavered. 'You want to come, don't you?' he said.

'Yes. But it feels like doing my own thing at their expense.'

He kept his hand on her arm, increasing the pressure slightly. As if forcing herself over a major hurdle she said, 'All right, I'll ask her.' He let go of her arm and stood leaning up against the wall, listening. Her voice as she spoke to her daughter was indefinably different from the one she used with him. There was a warm, easy intimacy about it that made him feel on the outside, looking in, but content to be so. That's how mothers ought to sound with their children, he thought, and felt sad about all the things that stopped his own mother being like that with him. 'OK,' she was saying. 'No later than quarter past nine, I promise. And you know what to do if anything happens, phone Evelyn.' When she put the phone down she was laughing. 'She and Simon are in the middle of a television programme,' she said. 'They think it's wonderful I'm not coming back yet because they can go on watching it. And Ben's in bed already.'

'*Al hamdu lillah!*' he said, and leapt off the desk. 'Come on, you with your strictly rationed time, let's get moving!'

2

It was an Italian restaurant, small, warm, and not at all crowded because it was still so early. Rachel ordered aubergine that came baked in its own individual dish, with melted cheese bubbling over the top. She felt as if she were on holiday.

'Do you want some wine?' he asked.

'Why not? What do you fancy?'

'Get what you like. I don't drink alcohol.'

'I forgot,' she said. 'You're a Muslim.'

'Not a practising one anymore, but some of the habits stick. You have some, go on. It would give me great pleasure to see you regard this as a party.'

'I do already. Do you know, this is the first time I've been out for a meal without the children?'

'The first time?' Hassan repeated, incredulous. 'In thirteen years?'

She laughed. 'No, I mean the first time since Alistair.'

'Since Alistair. It sounds like the name of an era. Before Christ. Since Alistair.' She giggled, and he felt delighted. 'How many years is it Since Alistair?'

'Almost two, I suppose,' she said, 'But he was gone so much before that, it's really been longer.'

'And you haven't been out for a meal without the children in all that time?'

'No. Does that seem extraordinary to you? Maybe if I were single it would to me too.'

'You are single.'

'No, I mean alone, without the children. It's different!'

He grinned, 'I'm beginning to see that.' He paused slightly before saying, 'Rachel, you can't structure your entire personal life around the children.'

'You sound like my friend Pat. She keeps telling me that.'

'Tell Pat I'm on her side.'

'I'm not sure she'd have you. She's lesbian.'

'If Pat's got anything about her she'll know it's a basic campaigning strategy to ally with anyone who supports you on the Major Issue, whatever your other differences!' Her eyes laughed with him. He put his hand out across the table to touch hers. The wine came, and water for him. As they clinked glasses she said, 'Thank you for pushing me,' and then, laughing, 'I don't mean about the wine! About coming here tonight. And before that, about trusting myself to do something useful.'

'Stop it,' he said, fiercely. 'You distort what's happened when you say thank you.'

'Hassan, tell me about your father.'

He stared at her, then he put his glass down and said, 'You're amazing, Rachel. I don't know anyone else who would do that.'

'Do what?'

'Just ask me, outright like that. You keep doing it. All the others in ACRAS have known about my father for over six months. I flew off to Hargeisa after he was arrested, to try to bribe a way out for him. When I came back they had put flowers on my desk, with a card saying they were thinking about me. I know they do, still. But no one ever mentions it.'

'People don't. They're afraid to make it harder for you.'

'So how come you're not afraid?'

'I've been where you are. Alistair was in prison, at a time when I still loved him. You know what you said once, that you felt guilty about Nuh?'

'You felt that about Alistair?'

'I think you can only understand that if you've experienced it. At Simon and Ben's school there's a woman I know whose child died of leukemia. There was nothing anyone could have done to prevent it, but you could tell she was torn apart with guilt that she hadn't been able to keep him alive... Lord, take me instead of him. And if the Lord doesn't listen, it's a judgement that you didn't really love him enough.' She waited for him to say something. He said, 'Don't stop.'

'My marriage with Alistair was in trouble before he was arrested but for a long time afterwards, each time I started to feel resentful it turned into a panicky kind of guilt. When we first came to Britain Alistair used to take me to meet other South African exiles, people like him who had organised and campaigned and been in jail for years, and had left South Africa before I was old enough to have the least idea about politics. Alistair used to brief me about them so that I would know how honoured I was. Like, you're about to meet a hero.' Hassan was laughing. 'No, honestly,' she insisted, 'and in a way he was right, they were people whose trials I'd read about in the papers, I admired them enormously. But being with them simply reinforced my own failure, that I'd never done anything to merit the suffering they had had to bear.'

'What do you do about feelings like that? That you know are irrational but still have the power to paralyse you?'

'I don't know. If I did I wouldn't have stayed paralysed under mine for so long!'

He said slowly, thinking as he spoke, 'For me the guilt is more about where I am than what I have or haven't done. When I was a child I didn't have any choice, but now in a way I feel I abandoned my father by deciding to live here. But even that's irrational. Whenever we talked about it he insisted that there was no future for a lawyer in Somalia. He couldn't have been more right!' He paused. 'It feels all wrong to be free when he is not.'

'You're thinking of yourself. Think of him, what he needs. It'll be easier to accept being away and free if you concentrate on what he would want for you.'

He stared at her, but it was his father's voice he heard, saying *Go back now, and be safe.*

They came out of the restaurant. 'I need a 77 bus,' she said, 'or anything that will take me to Waterloo. I can get a train from there.'

'188,' he said. 'This way.' And he steered her, his arm around her shoulder. He left it there, light and casual, requiring nothing of her in response.

'How do you know where all the bus stops are?'

He laughed, 'I spent half my childhood travelling on buses with my mother. Doing the museum trail. She's a great consumer of London's cultural life, never stopped making up for the lost time in Somalia!'

'She left your father?'

'Yes. Though at first it was on the pretext of bringing me to school here. I don't think my father would have let her take me if she'd said outright she was leaving.' They had come to a corner with traffic lights, and he stopped while he pressed the pedestrian button. Green. 'Come,' he said, buoyant as a child, and took hold of her hand to make her run across. 'By Somali standards,' he went on once they reached the other side, 'my mother was a terrible wife.'

'In what way, terrible?'

'For a start, one child only, after all these years!'

'They said that? People in your family?'

'All the time. Except when my father was around! Especially uncle Musa. He's my father's oldest brother. He has two wives, whom he beats, he nearly pulled out of the family business because my uncle Ali decided to send his daughter to school, and he's an out-and-out tribalist. So you can imagine how well-equipped he was to cope with my father bringing back an educated English wife! In that kind of family everyone is entitled to know what everyone else is doing, and to comment on it. She put up with it for eight years, and then she left.'

They had reached the bus stop. A middle-aged couple was waiting already; a couple of young men leant up against the nearest shop window, detached members of the queue. 'Let's get out of the wind,' he said, and headed for a doorway. It's extraordinary, she thought, having someone telling me where to go, when to run, when to stop, and yet it's not in the least like being ordered around. It's as if he's sharing each new place with me, inviting me in.

He went on. 'And my grandmother! I used to go with my father to visit her, in her village near Hargeisa. My mother hardly ever came, she was never comfortable in the village. My grandmother used to ask my father, when are you going to take another wife?'

Rachel was incensed. 'With you standing there?'

'Oh yes,' he laughed. 'My grandmother herself was one of three wives. She's spent most of her life herding goats and sheep; it's hard work and more wives meant more people to share it. The Somali part of me knew it was a perfectly normal desire on her part that he should have a proper Somali wife who would bear him a reasonable number of children, and look after him as a wife should, not spend most of the year away in England. But there was also the part of me that had to look after my mother.'

'Did you say anything to her?'

'You bet I didn't! Nor to anyone else. But each time we went back I used to have this dread that when we got there we would find the new wife already installed.' He paused. 'He's an unusual man, my father. If you're a real man in Somali society you don't admit to needing women. My father was never like that. Even I knew that he liked women! I knew he would hate my mother being away so many months of the year.'

'Did you blame her, for leaving?'

'Blame? I was miserable, but - Yes, I suppose I did. Up till then my entire experience had been in that kind of family. I didn't have any other standards to judge her by.'

'And now? Does she know that you understand?'

'We never talk about it. We get on fine if we stick to the present. It's like a pact she's exacted from me, not to make her think about that part of her life again. But it doesn't work, because I'm the result of that part of her life, so I feel as if she's cutting me out the whole time.'

Rachel said, 'It's like that for Kate. She's the only one of my children who saw much of Alistair when she was little, and she still misses him a lot. He gives them so little time. It would be easy for him to visit them more often, and I get so mad at him for not bothering that I deal with it by trying to forget all about him. But I'm sure Kate would feel safer if we kept him in our daily life a bit more, by talking about him.'

He nodded. 'I've wondered occasionally whether my father ever made a secret marriage.'

'What do you mean?'

'Well, there's no possibility of casual affairs in Somalia.'

'But a secret marriage? What woman would accept terms like that?'

'Someone whose relatives were too poor to arrange a reasonable marriage. She would at least have got financial security out of it.'

'And a husband who only visited her when it suited him?'

'Somalia is full of wives who hardly ever see their husbands. So many men go off to work in Jeddah or Aden, or as sailors, and are gone two years at a time. Then they'll come back, produce another child, and be off again.'

'But your father - I don't understand, why go to all the trouble of a secret marriage if he could have taken a second wife openly?'

'If he had, my mother would have stopped coming back altogether, a lot earlier than she did.'

'And you think he still wanted her?'

He was silent for a moment, staring at the traffic. Then he said, 'There was a song my father used to sing when I was little. It was just a popular Somali song, lots of people sang it, but I used to think he really meant it and that he was singing it for my mother.'

'Sing it.'

'It's in Somali, you wouldn't understand!'

'Sing it!' she said. 'I want to hear what a Somali song sounds like.'

He sang. Right there on the pavement, with the people walking by. He had never sung in so public a place, nor had he ever sung a Somali song to a non-Somali. The couple at the bus stop turned to stare, then looked away, embarrassed. Rachel listened, her eyes all attention. When he had finished she asked, 'What does it mean?'

'I can give you a proper translation. I found it once in a book -

My heart is single and cannot be divided,
And it is fastened on a single hope;
O you who might be the moon.'

He went straight on, not looking sideways to see how she was reacting. 'There's something about my mother. She's got a self-sufficiency about her that acts like gravity for anyone close to her. Even though she cuts herself off in that maddening way, it doesn't stop you wanting to be allowed in.'

He turned now to see her. She was looking at him in that unselfconscious way, all her attention on the other person. 'I'd like to meet her one day,' she said.

*

192

It was cold, cold.

She lay bunched up under the bedclothes, pulling up her knees and hugging them with her arms to hold on to herself, to make herself safe. Even that was not womb-like enough. She pulled the blankets higher, over her nose. Blocking out air, closing off space, retreating from thought.

There was no retreat. There was no going back on what had begun to happen.

She was back, in her room in Lourensrus. It was winter; cold, cold in the high-ceilinged, never-heated room with its thick white-washed walls. She lay huddled between the uncomforting sheets and stared out of her window, whose curtains she never drew, out at the nakedness of the sky where each star cut sharp and clear through the black cold infinity, with no trace of cloud to serve as a blanket to the earth.

And then it was morning, and she had woken to the knowledge of that cold, her knees already pulled up to keep her feet from touching the once-hot water bottle, now inhospitably cold and rubbery. It was too cold to move, let alone get up. She closed her eyes against the day, feigning sleep when her father put his head round the door to call her - 'Rachel, you'll be late!' She disappeared further under the blankets, until her whole head was under, part of the warm, enclosing dark, blocking out air. Her father's voice - 'I'm not calling you again. If you want to be late it's up to you.' No, no, she wanted to call in panic, don't leave me to do it alone.

She woke, to her bedroom in Battersea. She was cold, but she knew she had no reason to be. The bed was warm, the house was warm, but her body felt bloodless. She got up to renew the hotwater bottle. It lay against her, burning her where it touched but apparently unable to transfer its heat. She cradled herself to make her own warmth, hugging her knees. She rocked herself like a baby, rocking until the bed rocked with her. It'll be OK, she told herself, over and over again. Don't be afraid. It'll be OK. You can't run away, it's happening already. Don't be afraid.

Holding on to herself, rocking, crooning, comforting, until eventually she fell asleep.

Don't rush her, he said to himself, lying still wide awake long after he had gone to bed. Remember what happened last time you rushed her. Don't make her take fright and run away.

When an hour later he was still not asleep he got out of bed, and sat by the window in the living room, looking out at the silent night street below.

*

A row of terraced houses, each with a bay window and a front garden no deeper than four feet. The lintels and frames of the windows painted white or occasionally picked out in red or green or lilac; the rest was brickwork. Rowan trees on the pavement, cars parked in the road, a couple of kids on bikes and skateboards. He found number fourteen. Shifting his load of petitions to one arm he knocked on the door.

From inside came the noise of children calling, mothers instructing, a balloon popping, and then, striding above it all, someone playing a single note on the saxophone. A child answered the door, a girl of about ten. She looked at him for a minute as if not sure how to place him. '*Nabad*,' he greeted, to sort out her dilemma for her. She grinned and started speaking in Somali. 'If you want to see the grown-ups,' she said, 'most of them are in the kitchen. It's us children doing all the work in here.' And she skipped down the hall and through a door, back into the room from which most of the noise was coming.

He made his way to where he imagined the kitchen to be. He opened the door. It was not the kitchen but the saxophone room. Three teenage girls gathered around a young woman in jeans, hair very short, one large dangling earring. 'Sorry, I didn't mean to interrupt,' he said. 'I imagine you're Pat!'

'And you're Hassan. We're obviously both well briefed!'

'Where's the kitchen? I've been told that's where the action is.' One of the girls jumped up. 'I'll show you,' she said, and, when they were back in the hall, 'Jenny's there too. You work with her, don't you?'

'I do,' he said. 'Are you Kate?'

'Yes!' Then, suspiciously, 'What else do you know about me?'

'That you're thirteen, and grown up for your age.'

'That's OK then,' she said, and opened the kitchen door for him. For a moment he stood in the doorway, taking in what he saw. The walls were covered with a profusion of children's drawings and models.

Sitting around the table a group of women, Jenny among them, talked and laughed as they took sheets of paper from three different piles, folded them twice, put them in an envelope, sealed it and then threw it into a large laundrybasket. There was no sign of Rachel. A couple of young children were playing with lego on the floor. A baby was crying and being shushed by a little Somali girl with her hair in plaits around her head. Standing over the cooker with their backs to him were two Somali women, one of them unusually tall, and the room was filled with the smell of basmati rice and cinnamon and cardamom. He was assailed by familiarity - the smell, the noise, the women all talking together as they worked, the child crooning in Somali over the baby that would not be shushed - and by the knowledge that this was Rachel's house, that she was here somewhere, her warmth and directness having made all this possible.

Jenny saw him and lifted a hand briefly to wave and say 'Hi!' At the same moment the tall woman at the cooker turned her head to call to the child - and her voice was the voice he had heard and her head the head he had seen at the demonstration. 'Hibo!' he said beneath his breath, and stepped over the lego to reach her. Both of them started talking at once in Somali - 'I saw you at the demonstration!' - 'It was you! I heard someone, but I couldn't see who!' - 'And since when do you call yourself Anab?' - laughing and exclaiming, with Haleemo joining in now, the three of them together creating such a stir that the women at the table stopped in their work and turned to stare. 'Pay no attention,' he heard Jenny say lightly. 'He behaves like that every time a Somali comes into our office. They all claim to be each others' cousins!' He turned round briefly to make a face at her, then back to Hibo and said, in Somali, 'No wonder I didn't recognise your name!'

'You didn't know my sister?' she asked.

'Your sister?'

'She was at university with your cousin Sabah - Anab Saeed Barud. I thought you would remember her name!'

'I do, vaguely. But Rachel said - And what's your sister's name got to do with it?'

'It's the name in my passport,' she said, and waited for him to take it in. 'I had to leave in a big hurry.'

'Allah,' he said slowly.

'My sister gave me her passport so I could get away. Once I got here it seemed simpler to leave my name the way it was in the passport.'

'And Rachel? She's in and out of your place - hasn't she heard Somali friends call you Hibo?'

'All the time!' She and Haleemo were doubled up with laughter again. 'I think she doesn't hear, it's just another Somali word to her! When she started talking about you I knew that as soon as we met again she would find out. But before that I thought, there's no point telling her. It's safer to stay Anab for everyone at the school, even Rachel. There are plenty of racist parents there who might want to tell the Home Office, this black woman cheated. And now, with all this going on,' she swept her arm in a wide gesture to include the women at the table, the house-full of activity, 'there may be journalists coming.'

'Tell the Home Office yourself,' he said vehemently, 'before someone else does.'

'Why would I go and look for trouble?'

'They won't blame you for having had to use a false passport to get out. But keeping up the deception here is a completely different matter. All they have to go on when they let you in is that you say you're in political trouble. If they discover later that they can't trust what you've told them, it casts doubt on everything you've said. You have to prevent that by showing them you're being honest, explain how it happened. But do it soon. How long have you been here?'

'About a year and a half.'

'I wish you'd got proper advice in the first place!'

'I didn't know you were there!'

He grinned. 'I've been wanting to meet you again for years. If it has to be to sort out your immigration papers, it's a price I'm prepared to pay!'

'You haven't changed,' she laughed. 'And you still spend too much time hanging around the kitchen with the women! Why don't you go and get some work done?'

Beneath everything else that was going on Rachel was waiting, waiting for him to come. Each time the doorbell rang and Sado ran to open it she listened to see if it would be him. When she heard his voice saying *Nabad* her whole body was glad, and she waited for him to come into the room. But Sado came back in alone, and Rachel heard his footsteps go down the hall, towards the kitchen. She wanted to get up and follow him, but she made herself stay where she was, to stay calm and keep working.

'Mom, we're running out of petitions,' Simon called from the other side of the room.

'There'll be more in the kitchen,' she said.

'I can't go,' he said urgently. 'Me and James are having a race.'

And now Hassan was in the room, carrying a pile of petitions and saying, 'Anyone got a use for these?' And in no time at all he had joined Simon and James as they raced each other to fill envelopes, and was laughing with them as if he were a boy himself. She went on collecting the envelopes the children had finished and checking her lists, but all the time now she was aware that he was there, in the same room and she felt like singing.

'Productivity seems to be extremely high,' he said. 'I don't think I'd last long if this was my permanent job!'

'Beware,' she said. 'They're obsessed with speed, but quality control's another matter. I've found several envelopes with no cover letter in them!'

'How do you get them to work like this?'

'Incentives. A chocolate bar for every fifty envelopes completed.' She was about to say, it was Kate's idea, when she saw the glint in his eye, and began to laugh.

'Don't tell me,' he said. 'Kate's idea!'

Once that afternoon, for the space of about two minutes, they were alone. The call came from the kitchen that food was ready, and the children emptied out of the front room. He began to tell her about Anab - who was not Anab - and then Kate arrived to summon them to eat, and they were swirled up again into the general activity. After the meal she lost track of where Hassan had got to. She was in the front room, clearing up with Haleemo. Then people started leaving, and she stood chatting to each in turn on the doorstep. Then Ben had a nosebleed and she took him upstairs to calm him.

She finally saw him again when she went down to the kitchen, to see what state it was in. They were standing over the cooker, Anab - who was not Anab - and Hassan. All she could see of Hassan was his back, his head bent in concentration as he practised rolling out the dough for sabaayad. Anab was standing next to him watching, her smile tolerant and amused. Simon was sitting on the kitchen unit next to the cooker, his legs dangling over the side, with no trace of his usual shyness with strangers. There was no one else in the kitchen. None of them had noticed her. She stood still, as if her entry would disturb something of infinite value. Behind her in another room she could hear the rising-falling of voices - Kate talking to her friend Becky, who had decided to stay the night, Sado teaching Asha the words of an inane playground song -

> When Lucy was a baby
> a baby Lucy was...

the thumping sounds of Ben, apparently recovered, and Ahmed racing each other up the stairs. Hassan had finished frying his sabaayad. He lifted it out, crushed it onto the plate with his right hand so that it turned from being a single pancake into a pile of flaky pieces. Then he raised his head and turned to share his triumph with Simon, laughing with the pleasure of it. His eyes laughed, his wide mouth, his whole face, his entire body laughed, and Anab and Simon were laughing with him. And in that laughter everything came together for her - the longing they all shared for the simple familiar things from the life that had been lost, and that could never be recaptured; a vision of Simon, free from tension, of Anab, the sadness vanished from her eyes; the sound of the other children, there in the background, safe, but not needing anything of her; the past, the present, an impossible future, all reconciled, extraordinarily, in that one lithe beautiful honey-brown man, standing in her kitchen cooking, and filling the world with his laughter.

3

She was walking down to the river bed. Daniel was with her, but she was hardly conscious of him, for she was concentrating on picking her way through the low thornbushes and avoiding the sharper stones. An awkward wind kept dying down and starting again, blowing dust into her eyes. She was barefoot, and placed her feet carefully on the hard-baked earth, stopping every now and then to lift a foot and brush off the red ants before they bit. Then she and Daniel reached the point where the thornbushes ended and the sand began, and without needing to say anything to each other they began to run, running down to the dry gravelly river bed that now had a small trickle of water winding its way along the lowest point, but that during the summer rains would become again an awe inspiring torrent. They ran and ran, the wind in their hair, laughing, until they came to the boulder that jutted out into the river bed like a sentinel. And then they threw themselves down on to the sand and lay there laughing and touching; and she saw it was not Daniel, but Hassan. From somewhere behind her Daniel's voice said, 'He's not our kind of person, Rachel.'

The moment she woke she needed to speak to him. She waited, what seemed like hours, while the children finished breakfast and she found Ben's socks with the aeroplanes on them, and equipped Simon with Pritt stick and a stapler - 'Honestly, Simon, it's time you started keeping track of your own things!' - and Kate got into the bath, immersing herself in Strawberry Body Shampoo, the result of Saturday's expedition with Becky to the Body Shop; and all the time Rachel was wondering why none of them seemed to notice the need that ticked away inside her, ready to blow up at any moment. Finally when they were all out of the way she picked up the phone. She tried not to think what she would say, but already her heart was pounding as if she were about to make a public speech. She dialled the ACRAS number. There was no answer. She looked at her watch. Only 8.20. She felt completely thrown. All her spiritual energy had been concentrated on getting herself into a position where she could speak to him; it had not occurred to her that he might not be there to be spoken to.

She was there before him.
   All yesterday in her house he had needed to talk to her alone. Once everyone else has gone, he had thought, once the children are in bed. But Hibo had stayed too, and they had all three sat up till well after eleven, talking about Hibo's documents and all the problems arising from that. When Hibo had finally got up to go she had said, 'Come Hassan, walk back with me. Then I can give you my papers now.' She must have seen him hesitate, for she said, 'It's just opposite the station so it's on your way.' And he had had no choice but to go. Her papers

could have waited another couple of days, but it was hard to say that to her, having raised her fears by insisting she needed to tackle the problem. Besides, she might also be nervous of walking back at night, a black woman alone with a little girl after pub-closing time. And so he had left, without even being able to say to Rachel, 'When will I see you again?'

He wanted to phone before he left for work, to say, when are you coming in again? To make sure he could keep the time free. But something stopped him. Would she want him to phone? Perhaps because he had now seen her on her own ground, and could picture her so clearly in the kitchen that overflowed with the signs of that other life of hers that had been there before he ever appeared, that would be there whatever space he might manage to stake out for himself, that would continue to claim, forever, her primary allegiance. In the bustle and warmth of last night that other, vivid, life of hers had seemed something to celebrate, not a barrier. All boundaries had merged. There had been no classification of his people or her people, everyone belonged equally to one another. This morning he seemed once again separated from her by vast distance - she there, part of a Monday morning breakfast with her children, he here alone in his own flat.

He left the house without phoning her. And when he arrived, on his desk was a note from Barbara, 'Rachel coming in about 12 to photocopy more petitions.'

At ten to twelve he looked up to see her standing in the doorway, hesitating. Almost as if she were not sure it would be safe, he thought, but that could not be possible! She must know, of course she knew, she would not be here at all if she didn't know. Yet in that momentary hesitation they were back to the first time she had stood there nearly two months ago, and had looked as if she did not know whether to come in.

He moved without knowing he had done so. He was standing right next to her, and everything had gone quiet. Making no move to touch her he said, lightly, 'I'm expecting you to tell me that your name's Rachel Sinclair, and you've come about a friend.'

She felt as if she were outside herself, noting with detachment everything that happened between them. She could hear footsteps going away down the corridor, towards the common room. His arms were held at his sides, not moving but poised as if about to. He had his shirt sleeves rolled up a couple of inches so that part of his forearm was showing. Smooth brown skin, almost hairless. Infinitely desirable. 'It's the last day of the holidays,' she said, as if he were waiting for an explanation of her presence. 'I go back tomorrow, when the children start school.' She paused. Don't be afraid, she told herself. It's happened already. It's going to be OK.

'Rachel,' he said, slowly, 'There were piles of petitions left over yesterday.'

'I know. It was just a code I used for Barbara. But I think she's cracked it.' She watched as the grin spread across his face, and felt the same delight bursting inside her. 'Fridays are not enough,' she said. 'We need time together.'

'I've been thinking that for a long time. Let's abscond.'

She registered, I was right, it is OK, and then went on quietly, calmly, as if they were discussing something perfectly ordinary. 'What about lunch hour? I bet you don't even take one.'

'Depends. If you could get here, I would.'

'I can't,' she said. 'There isn't time. But Battersea Park's half way for both of us. I worked it out in the night. I could get there from the library in ten minutes, ten minutes back, that leaves forty minutes for us. For you it would be longer, twenty minutes each way. You'd be away from here an hour and twenty minutes. I'm sure you could make that up by staying on later in the evening, when I have to be with the children.'

'Rachel,' he said, staring, 'I can't believe this is you. Something's happened.' There were more footsteps behind them. The longing to touch his arms almost overwhelmed her. Why don't we go into the room and close the door? she thought. But still she did not move. 'I feel,' she said quietly, 'as if I'm being blown open.'

He did not remember how it had happened, but a few minutes later they were standing on the pavement outside the ACRAS building, and they were alone, alone with only London's anonymous crowds walking past, and who cared what they thought? He took her hand and said, 'Let's run!' And they ran like children, laughing with the wind in their faces. 'Where are we going?' she called. 'I've no idea,' he called back. They stopped and turned to face each other, holding hands and laughing. 'I've remembered,' he said. 'Lunch. There's a place I was going to take you - but it's in the opposite direction!' She said, 'Forget lunch. Let's get to the river.' And they were off again, running, dodging through the people on the pavements, pausing breathless at street corners then seizing the first gap in the stream of traffic to dart into the middle of the road - pause, wait for another gap, then dart across again. The wind in their hair, the strength of feeling her hand in his, the freedom as they ran, ran,

> *as swift as if hurled from a sling*
> *down a steep escarpment,*

everything speeding up, bursting with energy like the excitement that had been released in each of them -

> *like roads, much pierced by spears of rain,*
> *which run towards a well,*
> *like a dry valley turned into a river in spate...*

And then they were at Waterloo Bridge, and going two at a time down the steps to the Embankment, and across the road and finally at the river, panting, laughing, leaning over the railings to look at the sun glinting on the water. 'There's a poem,' he said, 'when we were running -' He broke off.

She said, 'Go on.'

He burst out, 'I wish you knew Somali! I can't possibly translate it.'

She put out her hand to touch his arm, stretched out tensely as he held on to the railing. He stood absolutely still as she trailed her fingers up his arm and then down again to his hand, his fingers,

> *like the dawn when the sun touches with its rays*
> *the thin high clouds,*
> *as beautiful as the sky spread out to dry after rain,*
> *with all its stains removed...*

And then, how much later he had no idea, she had slipped her arms lightly around his waist as if she were about to draw him into a dance and he was hugging her and looking down at her laughing face and feeling exhilarated that this should be happening after all the waiting. And he knew she was laughing at him for caring so much that he couldn't share the poem, laughing because of course it made no difference to anything.

*

On the bus going home she sat on the top deck, right at the front looking down. The cars, the lorries, the buses, the people on the pavement all seemed far away, slightly unreal, as if she were watching them on a screen. At one set of traffic lights a solitary and scruffy man in his late fifties shambled into the road just as the lights were about to turn green. In a detached way she wondered why he hadn't noticed the two lanes of traffic that were about to mow him down. She felt oddly that she knew him, and then realised that he looked almost exactly like Mr. Kaplan who ran the Lourensrus General Store, and who used to let her help him feed all the stray cats that gathered outside his back door. She hadn't seen him since Kate and Simon were small children, and here he was just below her, walking out in front of the traffic in the same vague way that the real Mr Kaplan would have done. He got safely to the middle of the road, thank goodness. The lines of traffic started up on either side of him. Stay there, she willed him, stay there and be safe. And then for the rest of the journey home she found she was talking to Mr Kaplan - without her mouth moving, but she was definitely sitting there in his dark living room as she used to sit on Saturday mornings after they had fed the cats, with the curtains drawn because the sun gave him a headache, making a dark private place where she could tell him anything she liked and no one else would ever know. And she was saying to him, this extraordinary thing is happening to me, Mr. Kaplan. There's this man, his name's Hassan, and he is unlike anyone I have ever known; and when I am with him there is no time, no anxiety, no limit of any kind. There is just him and me and an amazing sense of being free. And he has beautiful arms.

*

Everything seemed to move at once. Inside him, the world blown open by Rachel, and at home that evening, Mohamed - arriving without any reference to Paddington Green Police Station or why he had stayed away for over a week. He was simply there, and they started again. His face was alive and vigorous just as before, with none of that terrible distorting anger. Hassan put his arms around him and laughed with pleasure and relief and said, 'Why the hell haven't you been to see Nuh?'

'I have,' Mohamed said casually. 'I've just come from there now. I'm hungry. What are we going to eat?'

And then, Nuh's bail hearing. After all their waiting and agonising the event itself seemed incongruously simple. Mohamed went with him. When it was over they emerged from the court building, blinking in the spring sunlight, unable to take it in. Then he grabbed hold of Mohamed's hand and shouted, 'Come on! What are we wasting time for here? Let's go and get him!'

All evening people kept arriving. Mohamed had gone back to get a group of his friends - Madar, the cousin who had hailed Hassan at the demonstration, Aadan and the others who shared Mohamed's flat, someone who had been a fellow lecturer with Nuh in Mogadishu, someone else who was a cousin of Amina, Nuh's wife. Hassan left Nuh to hold court in the living room while he spent the first few hours in the kitchen, providing food and relays of tea, and sharing in the talk which overflowed into the kitchen from the living room, which simply could not contain all the bodies. Madar chaffed him about playing the role of a woman. 'Someone has to,' he said. 'I'll teach you if you like!' At which Madar roared with laughter and went back into the living room to tell everyone the joke. Towards midnight the numbers began to thin down. Then someone arrived with a supply of qaat, and Hassan knew they would now go on all night. At about two he finally took himself off to his bedroom, leaving them his sleeping bag and a pile of blankets.

Next morning he picked his way across the sleeping bodies on the living room floor, and through to the kitchen. Nuh was there already. 'You're up early,' Hassan said, closing the kitchen door not to wake the others.

'I haven't been to sleep,' Nuh said, pouring out some tea and handing it to Hassan. 'What happened to you? You didn't take any qaat?'

'It doesn't suit me, staying awake all night. I just think about what's happening to Aabahay.'

Nuh looked at him for a moment before saying, 'Your father's ill, Hassan.'

Hassan stared, blanking out with fear. Please God, no more. He's had enough. 'What kind of ill?' he asked.

'We don't know exactly. Some kind of skin disease. They wouldn't let my father see him. But Sabah says whatever the original disease, in prison conditions there's almost bound to be secondary infection by now. She's sent some antibiotics she managed to get from the hospital.' He paused. 'She says it's probably also malnutrition.'

I'm not listening, Hassan thought. I'm not hearing this. It's someone else. He heard his voice, unemotional, practical, asking, 'What would you say are the chances of the medicines reaching him?'

Nuh didn't answer. He said instead, 'I don't know why, but I couldn't tell you while I was in detention.'

Hassan nodded and put his hand out to rest on Nuh's shoulder. 'Thank God we've got one of you out at least.'

'*Allahu akbar*,' Nuh said. God is great.

Allahu akbar, Allahu akbar... In his childhood in Mogadishu there had been a beggar, a madman who wandered the streets, his hair dishevelled, his clothes ragged, his eyes wild, calling, Allahu akbar, Allahu akbar. Hassan and Mohamed had joined the trail of small boys who tagged after him, laughing and commenting at his strangeness, till one day Hassan's father had seen them at it and ordered them straight home, where he had said in a voice Hassan scarcely recognised, 'I don't want to ever see you doing that again. That man may be closer to Allah than you'll ever be.'

Allahu akbar. Allah, if you exist, be close to him.

Moving, at such speed, from the Mogadishu of his childhood - Nuh's larger than life presence in his flat - the knowledge of his father's painful skin - rush hour on the underground - a morning of new cases - And then whipped clear of it all to lunch hour in Battersea Park and the still unbelievable, exhilarating closeness of Rachel. Aware of her body, warm and responsive, next to his as they climbed the stone steps of the Peace Pagoda, to stand in front of the gold statues of Buddha staring out over the Thames, watching the boats go by. Walking along the avenue of cherry trees, on a luxurious carpet of fallen blossom that lifted in little swirls of pink and white around their feet. Watching the joggers in their shorts, bodies glistening with sweat, the mothers bending over children in pushchairs to wipe up ice cream spills, a couple of boys on bikes, vying with each other as they wheeled in intricate circular patterns up and down the gravel roadway.

They lay together on the grass, turning onto their sides to look at each other, laughing for no other reason than the joy of being able to be there, then each at the same moment rolling over onto their backs to lie with their bodies still touching, and stare up together through the leaves of the horsechestnuts, already in full blossom, proud white candle flowers, while the plane trees next to them still held bare mottled branches to the sky, with only a rumour of green from the tips of buds about to burst. 'It always amazes me,' she said, 'the way they never get defeated by the winter.' He rolled over and propped himself on his elbows to look down at her face. Slightly defensively she said, 'It's takes courage, being prepared to start all over again.'

'Are you telling me you're afraid?'

'Not when I'm with you. But at night, when I'm alone.'

He lay down next to her again, and lay holding her, rocking her gently. After a while he said, simply, as if telling a story to a child, 'The last woman I loved suffered from what you've described, but in an extreme form. She was called Farida. She was Indian, from East Africa, originally. They were Muslims, like my family, but all the years they were in Africa they'd made sure their daughters had no contact with the Africans who surrounded them. We were together two and a half years and in all that time she never got herself to the point of telling her family about me. When she was with me she knew that loving me was the only thing that made sense for us both. When she was back with her family, she was afraid. The fear won.' He took her face between his hands and, holding her with his eyes said, almost violently, 'Don't be afraid!'

'It's not that kind of fear,' she said quietly. 'There's nobody telling me who I can love. But I'm afraid of opening up something that I might then have to learn to live without, all over again.'

*

'Has Hassan said anything?' Hibo asked. 'About my papers?' She knows I'll have seen him, Rachel thought. Is it so obvious? And again she felt as if she were carrying a bomb that might go off at any minute. Why do I need to be secretive about it? she thought. What is it I'm afraid of? Trying to keep her voice neutral, she said, 'I meant to tell you. He's sent off a letter to the Home Office, but he says just try not to think about it. It'll probably be months before there's a reply.'

Hibo. She must get used to thinking of her as Hibo. It was unnerving the way her name kept changing, a name was so intimately part of the person. Discovering that she had been using the wrong name for her made her feel as if everything she had known about Anab - Hibo - might now be up for question, that there was nothing one could rely on.

'Hassan Abdillahi Dahir,' Hibo was saying, thoughtfully, as if she were surveying what she knew of him and assessing his character. 'You know it was his cousin Sabah who helped me get a visa? The one I told you about, the doctor.'

'Did you know him well?'

'I lived in his aunt's house for a few months. He was there for some of that time.' Hibo laughed, a slightly dismissive laugh, Rachel thought. 'He likes talking and joking with women, Hassan Abdillahi Dahir. Like his father!' The insecurity came flooding back.

This time she was in the middle of a landscape that was unknown to her, though in another way it was familiar, as if someone had described it to her in great detail. A lone umbrella tree stood craggy, outlined against the sky. The ground was hard and parched, as the veld around Lourensrus became in the winter, but here it was not winter but baking-dry heat, and there were no small thorn bushes nor the remnants of the summer grass, just the barren earth, stretching endlessly. She longed for the air to move, and knew that until it did she would have to keep standing here, alone. Then she realised that she was not alone. Hassan was standing near her, not next to her but a few paces off, and she could not understand why she had not realised before that he had been there all the time. His eyes were laughing and his hair rose bouyantly off his forehead. She longed to touch it, to feel it springy beneath her fingers. She knew that now that he was there everything would be all right, it would not matter that the air was so still and oppressive. She took a step towards him, stretching out her hand to his hair. 'There's something I've got to tell you,' he said, before she got there. 'My name's not Hassan.' She woke, feeling icy cold.

*

He left Nuh to his friends and retreated to his bedroom, taking with him the telephone which he plugged into the socket next to his bed. Then he lay on the bed, reading. Waiting.

He had no idea how many people were now actually living in his flat. There were sleeping bodies wrapped up in blankets on the living room floor when he left for work in the morning, and young men sitting in chairs watching television and talking when he came back in the evening. The kitchen showed signs of having provided an endless series of scratch meals. The only thing to do was to regard himself as one of the collective. He ignored everyone else's unwashed dishes - they had all tomorrow to deal with them, after all - got himself something to eat, and sat down to join them. He knew he had small hope of talking to Nuh alone, not at any rate for the first few weeks that he was here. After that, maybe. By then someone new would have arrived, with fresher news from Mogadishu, from Hargeisa. Though perhaps Nuh was not the only magnet. Most of these men probably lived in the kind of place Mohamed had, two or three to a room, lousy bed-and-breakfast places or short-term rented rooms, with paper peeling from the walls and damp patches everywhere. Now that they had discovered the comfort of his flat they would certainly keep coming. How bizarre, he thought, that I am finally to be reintegrated here in my own London flat into a Somali world, where people talk in Somali and laugh and argue just as they always did in Aabahay's house. Only his bedroom he kept to himself, against the incomprehension of the others - just as his mother had once done. Keeping a private space, inviolable, in which to speak to Rachel when she phoned.

Kate took longer getting to bed each night, as if she knew and was keeping guard. Of course she must know. Kate saw everything. With difficulty Rachel stopped herself from saying, 'Isn't it time you got some sleep?'

Kate did not want this to happen. Without anything being said between them, Rachel knew it. She remembered Hassan talking about his fear that his father would take a second wife. 'Don't be afraid,' she wanted to tell Kate, '*Don't be afraid!*'

Rachel's voice, so near, so real. He said, 'I want to see you tonight. 'I'll come to you.' Silence. What was going on? Then her voice again, cautious, 'Hassan, the children -' No, not that. He heard himself sounding cold in response, 'You said the children were asleep.'

'We can't, Hassan. Not here. Not yet.'

It was Farida's voice, *Hassan, you don't understand...* He ended the call abruptly, and was miserably alone all night, knowing nothing would ever be simple.

In Battersea Park the next day he said, 'You're still afraid.'

'No!'

'Last night on the phone -'

'I told you, it's different when I'm not with you!'

Quietly, but with a definite note of challenge he said, 'There's a Somali concert on Saturday night. Get a babysitter and come. Nuh's almost certain to go back to Whitechapel afterwards, and we can be alone in my flat.'

Yes, she said, yes, yes, yes, the same Rachel who had run down to the river with the wind in her hair, unafraid.

There must have been four hundred people already in the hall when they arrived, and three hundred and ninety eight of them Somalis. There was no sign that anything was about to happen. The stage curtains were closed. Young men went in and out between the hall and the foyer and the gallery upstairs, buying cans of coke, greeting friends, cat-calling the man with the microphone who put his head through the curtains every so often to test the as yet un-functioning sound system. Across the aisle from her a couple of older men shared out and began to chew something that looked like leaves. A group of small children ran up and down the aisles, while their mothers talked to friends they had just rediscovered. The women kissed each other on both cheeks, and then stood holding hands and smiling as they talked. There were young women in jeans and women in long dresses like the ones Anab - Hibo - wore; a handful with headscarves, the rest with their hair piled up in a variety of styles, including one with henna-red hair in an enormous beehive. People who were clearly used to dressing up, to being seen; well-off city people. And I suppose they must be, she thought, Haleemo and Hibo too. No one else would have had the money to acquire passports and air tickets, to bribe their way out of the mess their country is in. These are the ones who got away.

She looked up to find his eyes laughing at her. 'I feel incredibly wide awake,' she said.

'I notice!'

'I've got an odd feeling I've been here before. You know? Exactly here, with you, surrounded by these people. It feels as if we've been doing things like this together for years.'

'We have, in a manner of speaking. Look, do you see that tall guy who's just come in, the one with his hand on the other man's shoulder? That's Nuh. Come and meet him.'

He watched as she gave to Nuh the complete attention she turned on each new person she encountered, saying, 'I've been hearing about you ever since you arrived, I'm so happy you're out!' so obviously the literal truth that it disarmed Nuh, who had had no similar preparation for meeting her. 'You work with Hassan?' Nuh asked. She laughed. 'No!' she said, and Hassan said 'Yes!' simultaneously. She said, 'He's been helping one of my friends with her asylum application. And educating me about Somalia!' Nuh said, 'Don't let him start on poetry, he'll never stop!'

But once they sat down Nuh and his friends talked in Somali the whole time and made no attempt to include Rachel. Was it deliberate? From Nuh, surely not, but he could imagine the others thinking, so Hassan's got a white woman! And afterwards they would make snide remarks about the loose morals of western women. They can go to hell, he thought, trying to resist being invaded by the old familiar tension - his mother, all over again. Rachel seemed unaware of the exclusion. She was absorbed in watching the group of singers, who had dragged onto the stage and were now holding up between them a large banner in the SNM colours, red, white and green. The drummer got going, then the electric guitar, then the lute, the whole works, traditional and modern, and the chorus launched into an energetic political song. The boys in the gallery went wild with enthusiasm, throwing down SNM pennants onto the stage. Rachel was staring up at them, her face like a mirror reflecting their excitement. She ought to have been an actress, he thought, I've never seen anyone with a face like hers. He bent over to tell her, before she needed to ask, 'It's a song that was composed for the independence celebrations in 1960.' He moved his mouth close to her ear so that she could hear above the drumming and dancing and singing. 'They've changed the words. It used to tell the British to get out, now it's telling Siyad Barre to get out!'

'What was that man doing, moving his hand over the singer's head like that?'

'It's Somali body language. It means, I like what you're saying!'

Her face lit up with pleasure. 'I like that!'

'So this is how you should tell me!' he said, and made his fingers dance above her head. She reached up to catch them and he whipped his hand away, only to bring it back again to hold hers. The group had started up another song, lively and vigorous, accompanied by dancing. When it was finished she said, 'It sounded like the same few lines over and over again.'

'It was! A love song. They're often like that.'

'What did it say?' He thought for a moment how to translate it. 'It's a man pleading with the woman he loves. The religious elders teach that it would be immoral for her to give in to him. He says don't listen to them. One day you're going to die, so love now while you have the chance!' He stopped, assailed by the inadequacy of his words and the power of the original -

> *Since, when you die, delight*
> *by earth's silence will be stilled*
> *Then let not now the preacher*
> *turn you from your song...*

'I hate doing such banal translations,' he said.

Her eyes said, don't worry, I believe it's beautiful, even if I can't hear it. Her eyes, whose delight nothing could silence.

The music was over. People were streaming noisily out past them. Hassan and Nuh talked vigorously in Somali for a few minutes. She watched, loving watching him switch so effortlessly from one self to the other. He turned to interpret for her. 'Everyone's coming back to my flat,' he said. 'Nuh and a whole group of his friends.' His eyes were saying, 'I'm sorry. There's nothing I can do.' Aloud he said, 'Do you want to come?'

'I'd love to, but I'll need to phone Pat. The concert went on longer than I'd thought it would.'

'I'm sure Pat's used to late nights,' he said, but he took her to the public phone in the foyer. It was out of order. 'Phone from my place,' he said. 'It'll be OK.'

211

They came back to Nuh who said, 'We're waiting for Aadan. He's busy with the people backstage. You go ahead, we'll see you at the flat.'

As they walked to the underground Hassan said, his arm fiercely around her shoulder, 'I can't bear this. Your house is always full of your children, and mine with Nuh and his mates.'

She said, 'If sometime it was just Nuh?'

He laughed and his arm relaxed slightly. 'Could we shut ourselves in the bedroom and leave him to look after himself? No, I'm afraid that wouldn't go down too well! He's a strict Muslim.'

'I thought they all were, but it didn't stop them being enthusiastic about that love song.'

'Ah, but that's poetry! Poetry lets people live in fantasy the thing that's forbidden in real life! And aside from morality, in Somali households people aren't expected to need privacy.'

'How do they ever produce children?'

'Late at night, I imagine, when everyone else is asleep. But Nuh and his friends will outlast your time-limit, by many hours.' They had arrived at the underground station. They got their tickets and went through to the escalator. He got on first, and stood on the step below her, turning round to face her so that their eyes were for once on the same level. He said, 'That other white woman, the one in the gallery, I saw you looking at her. What were you thinking?'

Rachel laughed. 'That her face looked underdone compared to all the glowing brown faces around her! And that I suppose I look like that. If she hadn't been there I'd have forgotten how different I must look from everyone else.'

'Did you see she had a child with her? Half Somali. It made me feel, I don't know how to say it - a pain for my mother. She must have sat like that on so many occasions, bound by her child to keep trying to be part of a group of people that would never completely admit her. And then I looked at you and thought, she doesn't look in the least out of place.'

'I grew up surrounded by black people. Your mother didn't. I loved it tonight - there's a warmth that comes over me in that kind of crowd that's bigger than any feeling that I don't belong.' They were on the platform; now getting into the train. There were single seats but not two together. Without discussing it they both positioned themselves in the standing section near the door, their bodies close together, his head bent down to hers. She went on talking, as if they were alone. 'I'm not sure I know what belonging is, anyway. There were lots of ways in which I felt I didn't belong in white South Africa, right from when I was a child. The black people I knew -' She stopped.

'Go on. Tell me about them.'

'It's hard to explain what it's like. Even if you hate the way things are, it's impossible to find ways past all those barriers. Everything's structured to stop you meeting each other on equal terms. A few friends at university, some political mates of Alistair's. That's about it. And a man I worked with in a library, he was the closest, I suppose. But even then - Everything's loaded, you can never just be yourself. Mphande used to talk about being courted by white liberals so that they could boast of having black friends. He wouldn't have told me that if he'd thought I was one of them, but you live with a double-think all the time, trying to work out how other people will react, everyone judging everyone else's motives. I liked Mphande a lot, if we'd been free of all that I might have fancied him, but I never let myself get near it. Not because of the law or the social taboo, I'd rejected all that, but I'd have hated him to think I was using him to prove to myself that I wasn't racist.' She broke off. 'I hate talking about it. It's like a nightmare, thinking about all that again.'

He said, quietly but firmly, 'Tell me about when you were a child.'

'That was different. Not so self-conscious, but in another way even more limited. The only black people any white child meets are servants. Usually not even their families. It was a bit different for me because of Auntie taking me into the township, and knowing the people she worked with, at the clinic, the school.' The train stopped. Doors opened. Onto the platform, into the lift. She carried on, oblivious. 'There was this retired doctor, he was amazing. He had a reputation for being able to cure people whom ordinary doctors couldn't help. A faith healer, I suppose. I went with Auntie once when she took someone to see him, a white woman who was scared of lung trouble but just couldn't give up smoking. It wasn't at all like going to see a doctor, it was like being received by a guru. He had immense presence. I was riveted by the sight of this white woman sitting there so humbly, asking him for help. He spoke as I used to imagine the prophets speaking, slowly, making a pronouncement that you have to pay attention to. He said to her, your body is God's temple, you have no right to abuse it. She never smoked again! '

The lift juddered to a halt. Out, through the ticket barrier, out onto the night street. It seemed as busy as by day - cars, buses, street lights, streams of people emerging from the underground. 'Tell me more,' he said. She laughed, remembering how he had sat, silent, while she had told him about Auntie. 'You like being told stories, don't you?'

'Depends on the story. I want all of yours!'

She said nothing for a moment, her senses beguiled by the movement of their hips touching as they walked, body against body. 'I'll tell you about Ellen,' she said... A memory of cuddling into Ellen's lap, body into body, of Ellen's hands working at her hair, brushing, pulling. The brush kept catching in the tangles and hurt. She would lean into each brush stroke to outwit it, but still it pulled, and Ellen went on brushing, relentless. She caught sight of the child in the mirror, having her hair brushed at just the same time, stroke for stroke. 'Look at that little girl,' Ellen said. '*She* doesn't cry when it pulls!' Rachel had laughed, and so Ellen said it again next time, and after that if she ever forgot, Rachel would remind her, 'Tell me about the little girl in the mirror!'

To Hassan she said, 'Ellen used to take care of me when my mom had to go back to work. Then one day my parents told me she wasn't coming back. At first I didn't believe them. How could she possibly have gone without even saying goodbye? Maybe she had got fed up with me, but that wouldn't have made her leave, she would just have scolded me and it would have been over. Then my mother started talking about how Ellen had stolen things, small things, a cup, a tea pot, a few spoons, and I began to realise she hadn't decided to go, she had been sent. But it still made no sense. If Ellen took cups and spoons from our kitchen, it must mean she didn't have enough. We had plenty, why couldn't we let her have some? Ellen was my friend, I couldn't understand how they could have sent her away.'

His arm was tight around her again, pulling her body close to his as they walked. 'Did you ever tell them?' he asked. 'What you felt?'

'I don't remember. I suppose they must have known, because I remember how they explained it to me, gently; and I remember feeling beside myself with fury.'

'So you knew how to be angry, even then!'

She stopped and stared at him. 'That's extraordinary. It's true, but I'd forgotten.'

When he had closed the door of his flat he stood for a moment to savour the experience of watching her face as she took it all in. Her eyes lit up in delight at the African textiles on the walls, the books everywhere. Then he latched the door, and led her by the hand to the sofa; but she moved down to the carpet, saying, 'The floor's simpler!' And then he was lying with her, on their sides facing each other, their bodies still afraid to press against each other, their hands moving to touch eyes, hair, cheeks, lips, touching as if to assure themselves they were finally here, alone.

It was he who became anxious about Nuh arriving, not she. Eventually he said, 'Nuh has a key. When he finds the door latched -' She lay holding on to him a moment longer. Then she suddenly let go and sat up, and her desire was as evident in that jerky movement detaching herself as it had been in the holding on. He felt exultant, the joy ready to burst. When he came back to her after unlatching the door she had got up off the floor and had settled herself in a chair and started leafing through one of the books that were lying on the low table.

'I love this flat,' she said. 'If I had nobody to think about but myself I'd live in a place exactly like this.'

'Stay,' he said, vehmently. And the moment he had said it he saw in her eyes that he had triggered off her fear again. I know what it is! he realised, it's a fear of letting herself admit she wants it, and then not being able to have it. 'Rachel,' he began.

The phone rang. 'My God,' she said, stricken. 'I forgot to phone Pat!'

He answered, speaking in Somali for a few minutes. When he put it down he said slowly, 'That was Nuh. They're staying at Aadan's place. You are witnessing a typical Somali event. Flexible planning is what it's called.'

She knew he was waiting for her to speak. His eyes were full of a kind of pleading that she had never seen in them before. Why? He did not need to plead, he knew that. Very quietly he said, 'Stay the night.'

She sat absolutely still and waited for something to move inside her again. Eventually she heard herself say, 'I want to. But I don't know how to make it possible.'

'Tell Pat you're staying,' he said, still quietly. 'Ask her to sleep there tonight.'

'Hassan -'

'Rachel, please, please listen to me. You will not hurt your children by being one night away from them. They are asleep, and there is someone there with them. But if you are afraid and turn up the chance now that it is here, you will be doing terrible damage to both of us.'

Yes, yes, yes, she said, but she could not say it aloud.

'Phone Pat.' His voice was normal now, and confident. 'Just find out what's going on there.' And he put the receiver into her hand, and dialled for her. Then he came and sat right next to her, and put his arm around her shoulders and held on to her firmly, not like a lover now but like an older brother, holding her so that she would not be afraid.

Pat's voice. She heard it as if it were somewhere extremely distant, part of another life which she had left hours, days, weeks ago, could still remember clearly, and knew that one day she would have to return to. Pat telling her that she and Simon had played five games of carpet rummy, and three of a game called Spit, at which he had beaten her every time; that Kate had had a sax lesson and been terribly pleased with herself; that all three of them had been asleep for a long time.

Rachel said, 'Pat, how would it be if you slept there and I came back early tomorrow morning? Before the children wake up?'

'I was wondering when you were going to get round to that. Go right ahead. See you at breakfast.'

They stood facing each other, silent and awed, looking at each other's naked bodies. He felt the nakedness all the way through him, as if he were exposing himself, making himself vulnerable at some level far deeper than the body. Her breasts were rounded and neat against her body, not full breasts as Farida's had been, but reflecting in their gentle shape the openness and simplicity of her person. For a moment neither of them moved. What is she thinking? he wondered, and the vulnerability increased because he did not know.

He was beautiful, more beautiful even than she had imagined, with nothing to interrupt the lovely lithe line of his body, his smooth brown skin, his long limbs. She did not know why they were standing there so still, when she wanted so much to touch him.

'Are you afraid?' he asked quietly.

'No. It's just -'

'Just what?'

She did not know how to say it even to herself. 'It's been a long time,' she said - the excitement awakening again in her body, building up, about to burst yet momentarily held still in wonder. Her hand moved to his chest. She felt a tremor go through him, as if it were a shock being touched. 'Come,' she said, and she took his hand and led him to the bed, and they lay facing one another, their eyes fixed on each other's. And then whatever it was that had been holding him back disappeared, and he pulled her towards him.

Long after she had drifted off to sleep he lay awake, his arms around her, his legs twined around hers, feeling the smoothness of her naked body down all the length of his front. Then he too must have slept for a while, for he was woken by her calling out, as if she were in the middle of a nightmare. He tightened his hold around her and with one hand smoothed her hair like a child's, calming her from the fears that he could not even imagine. He did not understand how it was that someone so brave and full of love could be afraid of so many things; but he did not need to understand, not all at once, anyway. He needed only to be allowed to be near her, part of her life, so that he could cure her of her fears, one by one, until she was freed to be the full, joyous, complete human being that he had known from the beginning she was.

After a while he drifted off, and was woken again by Rachel. But this time she was fully awake and calm, sitting up on the bed right next to him with her legs tucked under her, her head inclined as she looked down at him in quiet concentration and moved her hands softly over his chest, his arms, slowly and thoughtfully, learning each part of him with her fingers. She saw that he had opened his eyes and was watching her. She smiled but said nothing and just went on touching him. His stomach, his balls, his thighs, his calves, his feet, and then back up again, to trail her fingers over his rising penis and then up again to his chest, his neck, his face, his eyes. He said, 'I can't believe how lovely you are.'

'I have to leave in an hour's time,' she said. 'And I want to make love again before I go.'

4

The street was deserted. Sunday morning, ten to six. Walking back
from the station she passed a milkman, a boy delivering newspapers,
and the neighbour's cat. Otherwise everything was quiet. Light -
daylight - awake like her body to the delight of the day, and just as
silent in its joy.

She let herself quietly in at the front door. No sound. Everyone still
asleep. She stood just inside the door for a moment, taking in the
small signs of the children's lives as if she were seeing them for the
first time, from the outside. She could feel the warmth and familiarity
sidling up to her, folding around her. She did not want it. She wanted
only to be left alone, not to have to do anything or speak to anyone,
but just to be still and feel what was happening inside her.

All that day she was aware of her body as if it were a new discovery, a
silent partner that had been there all along but whose presence she had
for some inexplicable reason not noticed. Now it walked with her at
every moment. She bent to pick up Ben's pyjamas from the bathroom
floor, and sensed as she did so the weight of her breasts pulling
forward, as they had done when she had knelt next to Hassan on the
bed and looked down on his long, relaxed, sleeping body, and leant
over him to touch every part of it. She stood in the kitchen grating
cheese for lunch, and felt a heaviness in her thighs as she stood there.
Go and lie down, her legs said to her; which she did - and that in itself
was extraordinary, letting herself lie down in the middle of the day for
no other reason than that her body told her to. And then the moment
she lay down she felt again Hassan's body lying close to hers, and then
the weight of him as he came on top of her, pressing down on her
belly but raising himself on his elbows so that he did not squash her.

And then Simon was in her room saying, 'When's lunch? I'm
starving.'

She got through the afternoon somehow or other, though she could
not have said afterwards what any of them had done. At about four
o'clock she decided to bath. 'You're going to bath?' Kate asked,
incredulous. 'In the afternoon?'

'Yes,' she said calmly. 'I feel like it.' And she lay for a long time in
the steaming water, with the door firmly locked; and when Ben

hammered on the door and said, 'I want to show you something, when are you getting out?' she called, 'Show Kate, I'll be a few more minutes.' Then she went on lying in the bath as if she had all the time in the world, looking down at her breasts that had become beautiful because Hassan had thought them so. What on earth have I been doing for all these years? she thought. How was it possible to live month after month, and not know that I had all this inside me?

*

After Rachel had left he had slept again. He woke mid morning to a quiet flat and sunlight streaming in at the window, and lay for a long time, not wanting to leave the bed that she had shared. Then he got up, quite suddenly, and realised that he was full of energy, that there was nothing he could not have tackled today. He spent an hour cleaning up the kitchen, which for a week had never been empty enough for him to get to. Restoring it to its usual organised state gave him immense satisfaction. Then he sat in the chair Rachel had sat in before she had phoned Pat. On the low table was the book she had picked up to look at, African textile design, a large format book with full-colour illustrations. She had been holding it when she said, 'If I had nobody to think about but myself I'd live in a place exactly like this.' Stay, he said to the book. Stay, to each thing she had looked at and delighted in, to the smell of her hair still on his body, to her presence everywhere. Stay. Stay. Stay.

Nuh did not return for a couple of days. There was no one with him when he came. Hassan said, 'I'm going to have the privilege of a conversation alone with you! I can scarcely believe it.' Nuh laughed. Hassan went on, 'And it's about time I cooked a proper meal. What shall we eat?'

Nuh looked at him oddly. 'It's light still. I'm not eating yet.'

It was a moment before Hassan registered. 'I completely forgot, Ramadan's started.'

'Today.' Nuh paused, and then said, with real amazement, 'It shouldn't surprise me that you don't keep the fast anymore, but that you didn't even know!'

Somewhat defensively he said, 'There are a lot of things going on at the moment.'

219

'Yes,' Nuh said drily, 'I noticed the other night.' Hassan tensed, waiting for further comment. Nuh said only, 'Well, you go ahead and eat, since you're not fasting.'

'Don't be silly. I'll wait and we'll eat together later.'

Nuh was coming to the end of his evening prayers, alternately standing and kneeling, head to the ground and arms stretched out in front of him, all the time reciting the Arabic words that Hassan had not used for years. Hassan moved quietly past him to the kitchen, closing the door so as not to disturb him. He peered into the fridge to see what he would cook.

About ten minutes later the door opened and Nuh came in, holding a copy of Rachel's campaign leaflet. Hassan sensed the familiar challenge in the way Nuh stood, watching silently as he got the rice started. Hassan said, 'You're about to ask me a question.'

'This campaign of yours,' Nuh began, and waved the leaflet. 'I found this on the table. Why is it all about one woman and her children? She's not the only one in that position.'

So that's what's getting at him, Hassan thought, adding the washed rice to the frying onions. It sizzled, sending off steam. Ever since Nuh had been released from detention he had been trying to reach Amina by phone. Sabah's line appeared to have been cut off. Other relatives or friends Nuh managed to speak to would say only, 'Amina's all right, don't worry.' Nuh would say, 'If you see her, give her this number. Ask her to ring.' There had been no call.

Nuh was saying, 'Why not campaign for refugee status for all Somalis?'

'It's a question of strategy.' Hassan measured out the water. 'If we did that, we'd only raise fears of a flood of black immigration. It's no use asking for blanket concessions, you have to demand something it's possible for them to give.'

'So all that effort, just for permission for one person?'

'This place works on precedent. If we win and they accept her case, it'll be harder for them to turn down the next one that looks exactly the same. Nothing's guaranteed, it's still all at their discretion. But it is just possible we can create a slightly more positive climate in which that discretion gets exercised.' He turned the gas flame to low and put on the lid. Then he turned to look directly at Nuh. 'From the very beginning of the campaign I've had Amina and your child vividly in mind.' Nuh looked slightly mollified. Hassan pressed his advantage, 'There's a meeting next week, at the school Haleemo's children go to. It would be good if there were some more Somalis there. Maybe you can bring a few people?'

'You're never going to get other Somalis involved, not the way you're going about it. Who's going to go to a meeting on an evening in Ramadan?'

'I didn't choose the date,' Hassan said, 'but even if I'd been fasting, I'd be going. It'll be over by nine.'

'It's not just that. People aren't going to have any patience with all these British subtleties. They'll want plainer speaking than that.'

'Then it'll be your job to try and convince them. *Proudly posturing in the assembly place* isn't enough. Politics has to be about what it's possible to achieve. That's no different here from in Somalia. The accepted forms are different, that's all. People may not like them but they have to learn to use them if they want to get anywhere.'

It was almost midnight when they had finished eating. He left Nuh and got ready for bed, intending to read. Their bed, his and Rachel's. Amazing, extraordinary, fact. For what seemed a long time he lay without reading, without doing anything. In the space a thought began to form, gradually at first, then coming suddenly into sharp focus. Now it was Ramadan there would be special prayers at the Whitechapel Mosque every Friday, and Nuh was certain to want to be there.

*

'Nuh's going to be out,' he had said. 'Give the campaign a miss for once and I'll take half a day's leave.' Then on Friday, just as she was about to set off from the library, a phone call - 'Rachel, I can't make it. I have to go out. I don't know when I'll be back.' His voice was strained. He clearly did not want to be asked questions. 'Come to ACRAS, I'll get back as soon as I can. There may still be time.'

She felt cold. She said nothing except, 'OK.'

'Rachel -'

'Tell me later, Hassan.' Her legs were trembling, she needed to put the phone down before the trembling took over.

The afternoon at ACRAS was long and unproductive. There was plenty she could have done but she could not concentrate, nor did she want to talk to any of the others. When four o'clock passed and Hassan had still not returned, she knew that even if he arrived now there would be only just time to get to his flat and have to set off home again half an hour later. Five o'clock, still no word. Five thirty. She knew she should just give up and go home, but she couldn't. She phoned Evelyn and Kate to say she would be late. 'There's a huge pile of work to get through here,' she lied, and felt miserable doing so.

She finally left at six thirty, narrowly missing a bus and having to wait another fifteen minutes for the next. When Simon opened Evelyn's door to her she heard Evelyn's voice, yelling at her son Mark. 'Pick those fucking bricks up, and if you do that *once more* I'm going to -' She stopped in mid-sentence as Rachel walked in, to a living room liberally scattered with the signs of five-year old activity. There was a smell of burning from the kitchen. 'I'm really sorry, Evelyn, the bus -' But Evelyn didn't let her finish. 'Forget it,' she said. 'Just take them home. I've had enough for today.' And then, recovering slightly now that help was at hand, 'You can take Mark too if you like!'

'You go and look at what's burning,' Rachel said. 'I'll get this lot cleared up.' When Evelyn returned to the now relatively tidy room she said, 'I didn't mean to bawl you out, Rachel. It's not just you. Ken's just phoned. He's not coming back tonight, he's gone with his mates for a drink. And I'd bloody put myself out for once making something nice.' Rachel gave her a hug and said, 'I feel awful being so late. I'm really sorry.' But the hug was not enough to cancel out the guilt and tension in her stomach that went with her all the way home, while Simon sulked and Ben whined at every corner shop they passed, 'Why can't I have an ice cream?' Finally she capitulated and bought a carton, 'For everyone to have for afters. But *not* before supper.'

There was no let-up once they got home. Simon immediately began to squabble with Kate about which television channel to watch. Kate appealed to Rachel for justice. 'Sort it out yourselves,' she snapped, applying to them the firmness she had failed to exercise on Ben, 'I'm getting supper.' Kate marched off to her room and slammed the door. Rachel removed the ice cream carton forcibly from Ben, who started howling. Simon turned the television volume up, sitting right in front of it as if to establish property rights. 'Turn it down!' Rachel yelled. Simon adjusted it infintesimally. They're punishing me, she thought, near to tears. Not just for being late, for wanting something for myself.

Ben was at her side again saying, 'Mom, *why* can't I -'

'Because you can't and that's it!' she yelled. 'You've put everyone in a bad mood, you and your ice cream. I wish I'd never bought it.' Ben looked surprised at her out-of-control voice. 'But you promised us we could have it today,' he said. 'Don't you remember? Yesterday, when we passed the shop and there wasn't time.' She had forgotten. She felt instantly remorseful, and absurdly grateful to Ben for being unperturbed by her sudden outburst. She gave him a hug and went to find Kate. Grudgingly Kate allowed her into her room. Rachel sat on the bed and said, 'Poppet, I'm sorry I shouted at you for nothing. And I'm too tired to cook. Why don't we take the boys out and have a pizza for once?'

Kate took only a minute or two to come round. The boys were by now horsing around in the living room. At the suggestion of a pizza they rushed for the door and out onto the pavement, racing each other to the corner. She and Kate walked staidly behind them, the older generation, and with each step Rachel was more vividly aware of the pleasure of Kate's companionship. For the first time for hours she felt normal. It's OK, she rejoiced. Everything's OK. Whatever it was that kept him, it'll be OK.

Even Kate had been in bed over an hour by the time the doorbell rang. She opened the door to find Hassan standing there, and saw instantly that he was in trouble. Without speaking she took his hand and drew him in. 'I've come straight from Heathrow,' he said. 'It's my cousin Mohamed.' She closed the living room door quietly behind them and led him to sit with her on the sofa. He said, 'He's left, to join the SNM in Ethiopia.'

'You're afraid,' she said.

'He's my brother,' he said simply. 'We were companions all through my childhood. His own father was killed fighting for the SNM, five years ago.' She said nothing but held onto his hand, hard, and waited for him to say more. 'I've known for nearly three weeks that he was planning to go, but I didn't want to believe it would happen. We had a big argument about it. That's nothing new, we argue all the time. But since then - I couldn't let that argument be the last real conversation we ever had.'

'So you went with him to the airport.'

'I don't know why I couldn't tell you on the phone. I -'

'Don't worry. I'm glad you went with him.'

'I was trying to hold on to him until the last minute. It was awful. There were so many people, there was no way - You know what it's like at airports, you hang around for hours, and you talk about inane things. No one says what they're really feeling.'

'You're shivering. I'm going to make you a hot drink.'

'Don't go.' He kept hold of her hand to stop her. 'I should have known, once he's decided something you can't reach him with arguments. But I knew he didn't have money for a ticket. I'd forgotten about the SNM. They bought it for him and got him waitlisted on a couple of flights to Djibuti. Late this morning he arrived in my office to say he had a seat, he was going.'

The door opened. Kate, in her nightdress, half asleep. Rachel let go of Hassan's hand, too quickly. 'I heard you talking to someone,' Kate said, and went on standing in the doorway, looking lost and unwanted. Hassan got up and went to sit in an armchair. 'Come, poppet,' said Rachel, stretching out her arm. Kate came and cuddled up next to her on the sofa, lying with her head in Rachel's lap, eyes closed. Hassan looked from her to Rachel, non-plussed, as if all further communication were now impossible. Rachel said quietly, 'Go on.'

He hesitated, then lurched into it. 'There's something else. My father. He's ill.' Through the awareness of his pain as he told her, was another kind of awareness, more profound - the knowledge that in some way she herself did not yet understand, she would be able to help him. Not knowing what she would say she heard herself ask, 'Have you told your mother?' Immediately it was obvious that she had strayed onto dangerous ground. 'She's entitled to know,' Rachel said, gently, but refusing to retreat.

'I'll think about it. But it's difficult.'

'It's only difficult if you're expecting some kind of helpful response from her which she may not be capable of giving. You'd be telling her for her sake, not for yours. If Alistair were really in trouble I would want to know.'

At the mention of Alistair, Kate's eyes flew open. She stared at Hassan as if he were a total stranger, then gradually her lids drifted slowly closed. They waited until her hand relaxed its grip on Rachel's. Then he started again, speaking softly but urgently, a lifetime of thinking and feeling to be shared. 'Mohamed's almost certainly going to be killed. They've got most of the population of that area on their side, which is enough to keep the conflict lingering on, but they don't have a fraction of the military force the government has. The Ethiopian government won't give them shelter any more, so they're being forced into direct confrontation before they're militarily prepared for it. At least that's what I think. Mohamed says the longer they wait the harder it'll get. Maybe that's true. I don't know. I don't know anything any more. I only know I don't want him to die.'

'I don't want you to die,' he had said to Mohamed, in those terrible few minutes alone in his office before they had been overtaken by all the others. 'Nor do I,' said Mohamed. 'Nor does anyone. But we have to, sometime.'

'You don't have to go back.'

'*There is a time -*' Mohamed had replied, and waited for Hassan to complete the quotation. But for once Hassan refused, so Mohamed completed it for him.

> *There is a time when to die*
> *Is better than to live,*
> *A time when life and prosperity*
> *Are forbidden to an honourable man.*

*

And now the meeting at the school was only three days away. The slow buildup of the weeks before gave way to an acceleration of final phone calls and arrangements and practical tasks, merging into the crescendo of heightened emotion on which everything now seemed to be carried forward. Ben and Ahmed's banner was spread over the living room floor, last minute touches added, protected from the carelessness of siblings by a notice that read BEWAR - WET PANT. In the school playground Sophie and others from the PTA handed out leaflets. Haleemo seemed always to be in conversation with someone, having now not the slightest difficulty in focussing despite the fact that she was fasting from dawn to dusk. Hibo took to stopping by to see Rachel on her way home from college, tired from a long day with nothing to eat or drink, and, Rachel privately thought, not yet ready to face her flat, where the latest in the succession of new arrivals to whom she had given shelter would be waiting for her to direct the preparation of the meal with which they would break their fast once it was dark.

'Who's it this time?' Rachel asked.

'Two girls, seventeen and nineteen.'

'Relatives?'

Hibo laughed. 'They're not even the same tribe. The people at the airport had my address because I was there last week to fetch my cousin. They phoned me at midnight and said, there are some Somalis here and they don't know anyone in London, will you take them? What could I say?'

'So tomorrow it's the DHSS and all that lot again?'

Hibo gave a tired smile. 'That woman in the Housing Department, she's tired of seeing my face. She thinks I call them all from Somalia on purpose, to cause trouble for her.'

'And your exams?'

'Three weeks.'

'I hope your tutors know why you keep missing classes?' Hibo shrugged, an eloquent shrug that said, let them think what they like. Rachel said, impatient, 'You take pride to extremes. You should tell them. They're not officials, you know!'

'No, but they're not interested either.'

'Try them,' Rachel said. And then, a sudden inspiration, 'I know, invite them to the meeting!'

'The school meeting?'

'Why not? Aren't there other Somali students at your college?'

'There are about ten of us.'

'OK, so the tutors ought to learn something about what's going on, shouldn't they? Take leaflets and petitions and tell them to come. Tell them you're going to be one of the speakers, that should wake them up.'

The schoolkeeper appeared at the other end of the hall and looked suspiciously at Hassan who was standing on a chair to put up a poster. 'We're for tonight's meeting,' Rachel said. He grunted and left, reappearing a few moments later with a stack of chairs. 'A hundred chairs they want,' he said. 'Waste of bloody time putting them all out. They never get a hundred for a PTA meeting.'

'We hope we will tonight,' Rachel said. 'And there'll be lots of us to help clear up at the end.' He grunted again, and set off to fetch another stack of chairs. Hassan's eyes were laughing. When the schoolkeeper was out of earshot he said, 'He's probably jealous because he can see we're enjoying ourselves. Come on, to work. Let's get this thing up.' They each took hold of one end of Ben and Ahmed's banner, stretching it out between them. Aeroplanes with black blobs dropping from them onto hills and fields remarkably like English ones, except for the addition of a few camels; people standing next to round huts with conical thatched roofs, or running away. 'It's supposed to represent Somalia in a state of civil war,' she said apologetically. He stared down at it, considering. ' I have to say I don't go for the bomber planes,' he said. 'It seems like tempting fate to suggest a form of disaster that isn't actually happening.' He looked up, and the expression on her face made him laugh. 'Your maternal instinct appears to be under some strain!'

'My main instinct at the moment is to put it where it won't be too obvious! But it's their way of making a contribution, and they've got to see it up.'

He held one corner in position while she fixed the other one to the pinboard with extra long drawing pins. 'If you hadn't told me Ahmed had had a part in this, I'd never have believed it. Somali homes aren't anything like that, certainly not in the north where Ahmed comes from.'

'What are they like?'

'Traditional houses, the kind nomads use? Beehive shaped. They're called *aqals*, and they're entirely portable, made of huge semi-circular supports with grass mats laid over them. When you move camp you just take them to pieces and load them onto camels. You being women, of course,' he grinned.

'Talking of women's work, did you know Haleemo has managed to save £80? Towards air tickets for her children.'

'Save? On Income Support?'

'Not on Income Support. You can scarcely feed yourself on it. She's working.' Hassan stared. Rachel said, 'Look out, your corner has dropped.' He adjusted it. 'What's she doing?' he demanded.

'Cleaning. In a bed and breakfast place, the kind that the Homeless Persons Unit puts people in. She and the children were there themselves for their first month, apparently, and she saw that the landlord paid a woman to come in and clean, so she went and asked if she could do it.' Rachel stood back to check whether the banner was straight. 'Up a little more your side, I think.'

'The landlord pays cash, I presume?' Hassan asked.

'Yes, and precious little of it. £1.30 an hour. He knows she can't complain because she'd lose her benefits if he reported her.' She looked at him curiously; his voice had been cold, impersonal. 'You sound very lawyerlike. You're not going to tell me you disapprove, are you?'

'No. But I'd rather you hadn't told me.'

'Why on earth?'

'While I'm handling her case I'm her legal adviser. If I'm told she's breaking the rules it puts me under an obligation to advise her not to.'

'I've never heard you be so pernickety! Would you rather she made no effort?'

'Don't be a fool,' he said sharply. 'I'm not talking about what I think. I'm talking about her legal position. She hasn't been in the country six months yet, and she's expressly forbidden to work. If the DHSS finds out they'll cut her benefits, but that's not the worst. If she's caught breaking the terms on which she's been allowed into the country, the authorities are perfectly entitled to throw her into detention. And don't think they wouldn't do it, because they do, every day. Not so often to mothers of children, it's mostly single men, but it's a real possibility. Tell her from me she's crazy to take the risk.'

Rachel was glaring at him. 'I don't understand you,' she said. 'You know perfectly well why she has to do it. It's no different from Hibo having to use a false passport to save herself from going to prison for the rest of her life.'

'And if you remember I advised Hibo the same, to cease at once doing anything illegal. It's one thing to do it in order to get here. It's quite another to go on ignoring the rules once you've applied for asylum.'

'Haleemo *has* to work to save her children. If the state is stupid enough to make a law telling her she can't, they're just asking for it to be broken.'

'And when they catch her they'll say, you've broken the law, here are the penalties. Maternal instinct is no defence. '

'Then you can sod your precious law,' she said, furious now. 'It's no use to anyone.'

'It's not my law. I merely try and help people get the best possible for themselves out of it.'

She was not listening. 'I want to tell you something about Haleemo,' she said, her voice getting louder. 'Since we started the campaign something has happened to her. She used to sit passively and take whatever came to her. The only thing she could see was her trauma. And apart from that, when I first knew her she would have thought it beneath her to take a job cleaning for someone else. Now she doesn't care. She's seen a chance that she may get her children out, and she's got something to work for. You're asking her to stop trying, to go back to living in fear.'

'We all have to live with fear. It's part of the human condition, and it's a permanent part of the refugee condition.'

'Well tell her yourself then!' she lashed out.

'I will,' he said, equally vehemently. 'She needs to understand what she's up against. There's a Somali proverb, Of the lion that keeps quiet and the lion that roars, the one that roars is better.' He saw that her face had suddenly become panic stricken. 'Rachel - don't worry! There's nothing frightening about us having an argument!' He wanted to hold her, but the damn schoolkeeper had come back in. And now the others were arriving, Haleemo, Yusuf, Evelyn, all the children, arriving together like one great party, all noise and bustle and excitement, cutting him off from Rachel, from any possibility of comforting her. He made himself turn from her, from her face that was so naked with misery he was amazed everyone didn't see and comment. Haleemo adjusted her headscarf and began to tell him excitedly about how so many of the women in the playground had come up to speak to her about her children since getting the leaflet. 'They all want to help Nafisa and Abokor,' she said, as if it were a perpetual source of surprise. He said, lightly, 'That's as it should be. And this evening we begin in earnest. *Bismillah!*'

Bismillah al rahman al rahim. Let us begin in the name of God, the compassionate, the merciful.

All these weeks Rachel had been working towards this meeting, and now that it was here she could hardly concentrate because of the panic that had been unleashed inside her from feeling angry with Hassan. Once again she had the sensation that she was two people, one outside her body, observing with detachment the other self who was going through the motions of welcoming people, responding to the children's excitement, taking up her place behind the table with petitions. Hibo arrived, with a group of women whom Rachel had never seen, an Asian woman, two English, one African. 'From my computer course,' she said. Someone came up to hand over an already completed petition form, thrusting it into her hands, saying 'I told them about it at my church.' And then another who had taken the petition to work and said, 'I'll take some more if you like, the people at the playgroup said they'd pass it around.' All these people had filled their petitions even before waiting to hear what would be said at the meeting. The leaflet had spoken to them, as Hassan had told her it would.

And then at each turn when her thoughts came back to him she was flooded with misery that she should have done anything to cause the least separation between them. Don't worry! she heard his voice comforting her, saw his eyes meeting hers across the heads of the crowd. Don't worry! And of course that detached part of her knew that she was being absurd to worry, that there was too much between them for one argument to make any difference. But the hidden part continued to panic and longed for the meeting to be over and for all these people, whom she had worked so hard to summon, to be gone so that she could speak to him alone, and touch him, and feel his bodily warmth that alone would have the power to reassure the child within her.

'My name's Burrows,' someone was saying, 'I'm from the Wandsworth Weekly News,' and abruptly she jettisoned her anxieties to talk to him, to make sure he had a copy of the leaflet, and then to hand him over to Evelyn. 'Maybe you can take Mr Burrows and introduce him to Haleemo?' Up at the front of the hall someone from the PTA was trying to get people to quieten down so that the meeting could begin. Rachel gathered up the petitions and was about to slip into a seat at the back of the hall when the door opened once more and a couple of Somali men came in, Nuh and one of the men she had seen with him at the concert. 'Hello Rachel,' he said, his deep voice resounding in the now-hushed hall. He looked towards the platform, where Sophie had already started welcoming people and explaining why the PTA had called the meeting. He lowered his voice almost to a whisper and said, 'This is my friend, Aadan. We just wanted to hear what was going on.'

'Great,' she whispered, and together they took their seats.

And now, finally, it was happening - here in this hall where she had sat together with Hibo so many times watching their children perform in Christmas plays and harvest festivals and end of term concerts; surrounded by the familiar faces of the people who for four years had constituted the society of which she had, to her surprise, become a part. She felt a strength emanating from the mere fact of so many people having gathered together out of a common concern. Maybe that's the real point of meetings and demonstrations, she thought, the effect they have on us who take part! And now it seemed so obvious that she wondered why she had never understood this before.

Nafisa and Abokor, what were they doing? It seemed odd that they should not know that thousands of miles away over a hundred people had gathered to hear about them, and to see if they could work out a way of bringing them safely to their mother. If only we're not too late, she thought, and as she heard the words in her mind she could hear Auntie saying, in that awkward way she had, thrusting something real and unwanted in front of people, 'By the time the Lord moves their hearts to pity it will be too late.'

From the platform Hassan had seen Nuh and Aadan arrive and had watched Rachel take the seat next to Nuh's. He saw her lean towards Nuh to comment on something, and Nuh incline his head to hear and nod appreciatively. Watching, Hassan felt a surge of love for them both, and joy that they should be sitting there together. The panic had disappeared from Rachel's face. All she needs when she's like that is someone else to respond to, he thought, then she forgets herself. He left her, as it were, in Nuh's hands, and turned his full attention on the task before him.

He had not addressed a public meeting for a long time, not since his student days in fact, and never about Somalia. He had made light of it when Rachel had first asked him but now that he was here he regretted that he had not given more thought to preparing what he was going to say. He realised how little he knew about the people whose faces were staring up, not yet at him but at Hibo, who was telling them in her accented but forcefully expressed English, and with all her usual poise, about what the army was doing to people in Hargeisa. They were listening attentively but he could not tell from their expressions how much of what she was saying would be new to them. Did they know anything about the position of refugees generally? Were any of them the kind of people who would have been involved in other campaigns? He needed to know if he were to pitch what he was going to say at the right level. Rachel would have been able to guide him, if he had only thought to ask her.

He looked again to the back row. She was no longer whispering to Nuh but was looking straight ahead, listening, and her face was like a mirror in which the emotions behind Hibo's story became visible, her anger and her compassion, her pride and her determination not to be defeated.

He stood up to speak. He began quietly, with what he had prepared. An explanation of the international conventions on refugees. Statistics, how many Britain accepted each year compared to the larger numbers in other European countries and the vast numbers in refugee camps in the third world. The effect of the government's new regulations. 'People who are fleeing from persecution have no choice but to lie and use forged papers,' he said. And while his voice continued explaining - clearly enough, but without any particular inspiration - he was thinking about Rachel's anger as she had said, 'Haleemo *has* to work to save her children.' He wanted to tell her that even if he as a lawyer had to argue against her, he as Hassan felt as she did; and he remembered, as he so often did at moments when he felt a strong impulse to communicate, words that he had once heard his father recite, years ago. He wished he could share them with Rachel - But why just with Rachel, why not with all these people? If she could hear and understand the poetry that moved him, so too might all these other people whom her activity had called together.

'I want to quote for you,' he heard himself saying, 'some lines by one of Somalia's greatest poets.' Then he grinned and said, 'But I need a minute to think how to translate them into English!'

From the back of the hall Nuh's voice called out, 'Recite them in Somali first!'

He did so. There was an appreciative murmur from Hibo sitting next to him on the platform and from Yusuf in the front row. Haleemo's face was stricken. Hassan lent forward to say to her quickly in Somali, 'I'm sorry, but I think they need to hear it.' She nodded. By now the atmosphere of the meeting had entirely changed. There was a buzz of talk, an electric curiosity at what was being said in this private language. People said *shshsh* as they strained forward to make sure they did not miss what he was about to say. He finished scribbling and looked up. 'Right,' he said, 'I've got it, near enough.' He waited until the hall had become still and then he began, reciting as he had so many times heard his father do, slowly and majestically,

> *Three things one does not recover from -*
> *oppression that knows the backing of brute force,*
> *poverty that knows the destitution of one's home,*
> *and being deprived of children.*

In the stillness after he had finished he said, 'There is nothing that those of us here tonight can do to take away the oppression that Haleemo and thousands like her have suffered, or to compensate for the loss of their home, their exile. But there is no reason for her to remain separated from her children. They are alive and can be brought back to her again at the stroke of a pen, by our government giving her the recognition that it has pledged by international convention to give - the recognition that she is a genuine refugee and as such is entitled to live here not on sufferance, subject to special oppressive laws, but as anyone else in this community expects to live. And that includes the right to have her own children with her. It's up to us to make sure that happens.'

*

Hassan came to her as everyone was leaving and said, quietly, 'I just thought I'd let you know, Nuh says he's going back to Aadan's place tonight.' Rachel stared at him. 'I'll see what I can do,' she said slowly. He said, 'If it's impossible, forget it.' But his eyes were saying something different.

As they were clearing up she said quietly to Pat, 'I want to ask you a big favour.' Pat looked at her and said, 'You want to go back to Hassan's tonight.' She wanted to so much that she was afraid to try and read in Pat's eyes what her answer might be. She said, 'If you come back with me, and I get the children to bed before I go?'

'If you think it's worth it, leaving so late.' They both started laughing. Rachel said, 'You're sure you don't mind?'

'Of course I don't! I like your kids. And I don't have a partner at the moment so I don't specially mind where I spend the night.' It was the first time she had said anything direct about her own lovers. 'But you'd better arm me with what to say if one of them wakes in the night and wants you. It's bound to happen sooner or later.'

'I know, I've been thinking about it. You'd have to say I'd missed the last train back and had to stay over. I don't think the boys would be bothered. But Kate -'

'Yes, Kate's too sharp for that. You're going to have to talk to her sometime. It's not a crime, you know, having a lover. If she has to get used to it, she has to.'

'I know. I will. I'll find some way before the next time, promise!'

In the train heading north Hassan said, 'You were in a panic, weren't you, because we argued?'

'Yes.' It was easy now to laugh at herself.

'I'm glad to see you've repented!'

'I told you, I always know I'm safe when we're together.'

'We were together when we were arguing.'

'No we weren't. An argument is like a barrier, like pushing the other person away.'

'And you were afraid I'd take the hint and go?' She laughed, and felt the pressure of their bodies trying to get even closer, and was full of relief and joy. 'You see,' he said, 'how absurd you are!'

They lay together after lovemaking, quiet and close, he on his back, she on her side snuggled up to him. Gradually he stirred again, and rolled over onto his stomach, propping himself up on his elbows to look down at her face. He looked for a long time and then announced, 'You are infinitely desirable, and infinitely satisfying.'

'It's mutual,' she said.

He rolled back again and began to sing, almost a hum, lazy and relaxed. It was like the song they had heard in the concert, a couple of lines repeated over and again. When it had come to an end he asked, 'What was it like when you were with Alistair?'

'Love-making?'

'Mm.'

'Different. Very different.'

'In what way?'

'Difficult to describe. More - mechanical, I suppose. No, that's not right. More, we did what you do when you make love because that's what you do, rather than out of strong desire. At least not on my part, and I don't think on his either. Though it's impossible to tell with

Alistair. Even he doesn't know what he's feeling, so no one else has a clue.'

'I'm not particularly interested in Alistair. It's you I want to know about.' She didn't answer. He lay accepting her silence for a few minutes, then said quietly, 'Don't stop. I want to know!'

'I haven't stopped. But - ' She began running her fingers through his hair thoughtfully. 'Your hair was the first thing I saw of you. You sat there with your head down, not wanting to speak to me. Do you remember?'

'Vividly. But I didn't know you were looking at my hair.'

'I was. I've had a desire to get my hands on it ever since.'

'Don't rewrite history, Rachel.'

'You can never tell, about history. Whether you're rewriting it, I mean. In one way you're right, it was so long since I'd thought of myself as desirable, I'd just learnt to cut it out, not to operate at that level. Now it seems so obvious that I wanted you all along and was afraid to let myself feel it.' She sat up and positioned herself so that she could get both hands working on his hair. 'I love the way the curls spring round my fingers.'

He stretched out his hand to her hair to return the caress. 'Do you realise you are avoiding telling me about how you used to feel with Alistair?'

She stared down at him. 'Am I? Honest, I didn't mean to.'

'You are so experienced a blocker you don't even know you're doing it. But I'm not giving up.'

'I'm trying,' she said. 'It's difficult to remember in any detail. I suppose there wasn't a lot of lovemaking after the first few months. We started having babies so soon. I don't know, Hassan, those early years have been blotted out by what came after.'

'Did you never feel you were in love with him?'

'Oh yes. But even that was a different experience from now. It was a - I don't know how to say it - a one-dimensional kind of being in love. There wasn't anything else I had to think about, no children, no job, no campaign. I was a student in my final year, so I suppose I had to study occasionally. But none of that mattered, I was in love, full-time. And in a funny way that meant it wasn't *me*, it was a longing to disappear into the other person, be absorbed.'

'And now?'

'It's not like that at all. It's me, really me, alive, loving you, us loving each other through our bodies. It's not a closing in at all, everything keeps growing, my friends, the campaign, the children. Even Simon's changed. I'm beginning to think his anxiety was really mine, expressing itself through him.' She paused. 'And you. It's because you're the way you are, not wanting me in a possessive way but really wanting me to be myself. I feel as if I come into being more strongly every day we have together.'

'You've always been there. It's only you who didn't know it.'

'It's not as simple as that.' Her voice had become agitated. 'When you say that it sounds like a sleeping beauty, woman fast asleep until the man who loves her properly kisses her and brings her to life.'

'I deny that!' He sat up indignantly. 'That's your version, not mine. I was saying the exact opposite, that you've always been there!'

She glared at him, then the anger collapsed, a balloon pricked. 'OK, it's my anxious version, the one I don't want to have to believe. I don't ever want to lose myself in someone else again, it's too destructive. And it takes far too long to recover from it.'

'Rachel, you have to stop creating fears where none need to exist! I don't even know what you're talking about.'

'Listen,' she pulled him down to lie next to her again, to bring his face next to hers. She spoke urgently, and now there seemed to be no difficulty in knowing what she wanted to say. 'I'm thirty four. I've spent four years in London and the ten years before that living with Alistair in Johannesburg, and that's my adult life. The part in Johannesburg is gone for good, all those people I was close to and couldn't bear to leave, and will now probably never see again. And even if I do our lives will have become so different we won't have anything to say to each other. Since I met you, I don't know why but I keep remembering things about South Africa, dreaming about them - and it's always my childhood life I go back to. Those early years with Alistair hardly feature, even though they were really important years in many ways, with the children, and all that was happening around us politically. But *I* wasn't there. It's almost as if I obliterated myself to become Alistair's lover, Alistair's wife. Look how I can't even remember what it felt like being me at that time. I don't know what kind of a person I was. That's a really panicky feeling, Hassan, like whatever went wrong is still there and I might slip back into that.'

'You won't. I never saw anyone as real as you. Even if there was something that limited you while you were with Alistair, you've freed yourself from it. It's years ago, what you're talking about.'

'Not that many years. When I first saw Haleemo I could see it in her eyes, *She's me!* I thought, *she's cutting herself off because she can't cope.*'

'You're panicking now, aren't you?'

She nodded. He relaxed his hold to free one hand so that he could stroke her hair, as he had done when she had woken with a nightmare, her hair, and then her neck, her lovely smooth shoulders, her warm breasts. Eventually the tension in her body eased. 'Keep doing that,' she said, 'it's wonderful.' He smiled at her. 'As long as you like.'

'It's gone. The panic. You've stroked it away!'

'There's no need for it,' he insisted. 'You're living on outdated fears. Even if you had to leave this place now -'

'*Don't!*' She was laughing but he saw that she shivered, and her body seemed to be asking to be held tight again. 'I'm never leaving,' she said. 'I couldn't start again another time.' He held her, rocking her. 'No one's asking you to,' he said.

5

In the Somali community word had spread - Hassan Abdillahi Dahir had recited Somali poetry to an audience of over a hundred English people! When Hassan walked in to the Whitechapel centre he was greeted with, 'I hear you're an orator!' - user of rhetoric to confound your enemies. Hassan laughed, thinking of what Uncle Musa would have said. But he was aware of something odd beneath the tribute, an intention to distance him, almost. He didn't bother to think what it signified until he and Nuh were alone and Nuh said, with a definite note of warning, 'People are talking about you, Hassan.' Then he suddenly realised. They can go to hell, he thought.

'So?' he said, unencouragingly.

'You didn't tell me Rachel has children.'

'You didn't ask me. And I'll save you asking the rest. No, she doesn't have a husband. He left her about two years ago.'

'He divorced her?' Nuh asked sharply.

'I've never asked. Either that, or they're separated.'

Nuh stared at him, incredulous. 'You're going with a married woman and you haven't even bothered to find out if she's divorced? What's happened to you, Hassan?'

'It's perfectly simple,' Hassan said, his own tone hardening. 'He has left her and has no intention of coming back. I neither know nor care about the legal formalities. I love her, and I injure no one else in doing so; and if your morality isn't broad enough to accept that, you can lump it.'

Nuh glared at him and made no further comment. Hassan got up to go out of the room.

Much later that evening as they sat down to eat together Nuh suddenly said, 'I don't suppose she's a Muslim?'

Hassan started laughing. 'I thought you hadn't finished with me!'

'Well, you never know, she's got a lot of Somali friends.' He was half-smiling himself, but the tone was totally serious as he said, 'It's a waste, someone like you not being a proper Muslim.'

In the days after the school meeting Rachel became aware that the emperor's new clothes effect had disappeared. It was no longer difficult to believe that the campaign existed when so many people had gathered together to witness its birth, and in doing so had freed her from the last vestiges of awkwardness about her own role. Each morning a few more brown envelopes landed on the mat inside the door, and inside them were petition forms, filled with signatures. Her librarian's instinct seized on these papers to classify. In a large ring binder with coloured cardboard dividers she filed the petitions alphabetically according to the first name on each sheet, assuming this to be the person who had collected the other signatures, and therefore a useful contact for the future. She compiled a list of organisations and people who had sent donations to the campaign fund, and soon had to open a file of Letters Received, including one from a women's group in Norwich which asked the campaign group to send one of their members, preferably Haleemo Nur Warsame herself, to speak at a meeting they were organising on Third World Women. Norwich! How on earth had news of the campaign reached Norwich?

One letter caused great excitement among the children at breakfast, for it was on embossed paper, from a local councillor! He had fond memories, he wrote, of the people of northern Somalia, having worked there shortly after the war, and he was distressed at what was going on. Well, you never knew, maybe his distress would cause him to talk to a few of his colleagues. 'Start a file called Contacts with Politicians!' said Kate. And Rachel did, laughing at herself as she did it.

'Did you know,' Evelyn asked when Rachel collected the boys, 'that our MP used to have a child at our school? Justine. Nice girl. I was just thinking what a pity she's left, otherwise we might have got him to our meeting.'

'Where does she go now?'

'A private school, what else? His son has been going to one since he was five, but Justine's only a girl so the local primary school was good enough for her.'

The next day at the library Rachel asked Pat, 'Do you know anything about our MP?'

'He's a twit. Young, arrogant, conservative, ambitious. What else do you want to know?'

'What was his margin in the election?'

'Very small. This used to be a safe Labour seat until the yuppies moved in. He's been putting up a great show of being a good constituency MP. Opposing the new road schemes.'

'His own Conservative government's plans?'

'Yes, but the entire constituency is threatened by them. No one wants a motorway outside their front door.'

'Still,' said Rachel, 'it shows that for the moment getting back in is more important to him than party loyalty.'

'What plan are you hatching, Rachel?'

'I was wondering if we could persuade him that by taking up Haleemo's case he'd pick up the ethnic minority vote.'

'He wouldn't!'

'He's not going to know that, is he? Particularly if Hibo tells him!'

Hassan, too, was on a high of energy, fuelled by the unaccustomed sensation of power, the simple act of having moved people by what he had said. A hundred plans occured to him, floodgates opening from all the months of impotence. He used a management meeting of the Whitechapel centre to pass round petitions, and asked if they would be willing to host the next public meeting. An American research student who had been pestering him for information on refugee issues reappeared, wanting 'just an hour or two of your time.' Hassan stopped himself from telling him to get lost, thinking, we could use his kind of perseverance! So he gave Cliff Thomson fifteen minutes of his time, long enough to tell him about the campaign and suggest that the only way to learn about refugee politics was to get involved. 'Participant observation, the anthropologists call it.'

'I've found you a press officer,' he reported jubilantly to Rachel that evening. 'A man I'd back against a reluctant newspaper any day!'

Pat's concert was now less than two weeks away. Working with her on publicity, he thought fleetingly of suggesting they invite some Somali musicians to do a guest appearance, 'To show that refugees don't only bring their problems with them,' he said. But then he remembered it would still be Ramadan and reluctantly they postponed the idea.

And after that? It had seemed such a huge thing to get this far, and yet it was nowhere. People collecting people collecting people. 'What are we going to do with them now that they've started arriving?' Rachel asked. How could their compassion be turned into something powerful enough to move the anonymous authorities to put their signatures to the right piece of paper?

'The press,' said Mike. 'They won't pay any attention till they have to, and that only happens once you've been picked up by the media.'

'Specialist journals might pick it up initially,' Jenny said, 'even if the newspapers don't. Women's journals, black community papers.'

'But go for the respectables too,' Hassan said, 'National Children's Association, church magazines, anything that claims to believe in the importance of family life. We've got to get off the margins.'

'There's no reason we can't get in the national press,' said Cliff. 'We just bombard them with a new press release every week, get them so they begin to think something's happening that they're missing out on.'

'We need something colourful,' Hassan said, 'something that looks good in a photograph.'

'You're going to get it,' Rachel said. 'A women and children's demonstration outside the MP's surgery. We're going to get the school mums to turn out straight after school, it will only take us fifteen minutes to march down there. Evelyn says he wouldn't have the nerve to turn us away. Pushcairs and balloons, banners about Divided Families, and Hibo leading it, to present the petitions. You couldn't get anyone more photogenic.'

'What we really need is television cameras,' Hassan said, excited. 'Who do we know who works in television?'

Lack of sleep finally caught up with him. When he got in after work he had thought he would just lie down and read until it was time to start preparing food, and then he woke to find it was already dark. In the kitchen Nuh was staring at the instructions on a Sainsbury's vegetable quiche. 'I can't let you get the food every night,' he said. 'This thing says all you have to do is heat it up, but you'll have to show me how to work the cooker.' Hassan laughed and showed him, but said, 'I'm earning and you're not. Don't go buying things again.'

'I'll do exactly as I think fit,' said Nuh.

Nuh had not again mentioned Rachel, and Hassan offered him no openings. But noticeably fewer of Nuh's friends chose to come to Hassan's flat, and even with Nuh himself there were more frequent flashes of tension. He read the papers compulsively, and when Hassan got home tackled him about what he had read as if Hassan were somehow responsible for the misguided values and misuse of power of all western politicians. All evening the television was on. Nuh sat mesmerised through each documentary and news programme, fuming at the stupidities of those who held the field while he stood helpless at the sidelines, an injured player. Turn the bloody thing off, Hassan wanted to shout, but he didn't because he knew Nuh had nothing to put in its place. He'll rot, living like this, Hassan thought. There must be some better way for him to use all that mental energy.

But there were moments when the Nuh who had been his mentor reappeared, arguing not from frustration but from an urge to understand, and persuade. Once when they were talking about Mohamed and Hassan burst out, 'I wish I could feel more positive about what he's doing,' Nuh looked at him curiously. 'Aadan tells me you don't support the SNM?' he asked. It was not a criticism, he was really interested to know whether this was so, and if so, why. Hassan said, 'That's not quite right. I support them, as I support anyone who opposes the regime. But Mohamed wanted me to get involved as a member and I couldn't see the point. I would celebrate if I thought they had any chance of success. I don't, and I'm surprised if you do.'

241

'You've got to look wider than just at the SNM. There are movements among the Ogadeeni and in the south. There's talk of the leadership of all three movements working out a common strategy. '

'But meanwhile? Doesn't it bother you being so closely associated with a clan-based party?'

'If there were another option I would take it. Anyway, it's not Mohamed who makes policy. SNM was set up to counteract clan oppression, not to perpetuate it.'

'And if they succeed in driving Siyaad's forces out of the north, do you think they'll create a state in which the Gadabursi and the Dulbahante and the Ogadeeni would feel safe?'

'You're jumping way ahead of history. Stick to what we know now. SNM is committed to restoring Somali democratic values and a proper respect for Islam. That's enough for me.'

'Oh come on, Nuh! Islam's no protection against evil.' Nuh stiffened. 'Calm down, that's not an attack. I just can't see how the cycle of violence will ever end. People who've suffered will take it out on others once they get the chance. Listen, a twenty year old came in to see me today, escaped from the army. His friend was caught; they crushed his genitals. I hear stories like that every week. People being taken out of the prison cells in Mogadishu at night to the beach, and kept with their heads under water until they are almost drowned. As soon as they've recovered enough to breathe again, they go back under. Again and again, for hours.'

'Who are you telling? You think I don't know?"

'I'm asking,' Hassan's voice rose, 'when people can do that to their Muslim brothers, how you expect me to believe that an Islamic state would carry some special guarantee of purity?'

He knew he had gone too far. Nuh said, speaking now not like a cousin but an uncle, 'Sometimes I think there's no Somali left in you, Hassan. You know as well as I do that the Prophet explicitly forbade the use of torture. Anyone who does such things is behaving in an unIslamic way.'

Hassan gave up. 'It seems,' he said, 'as if Siyad has been there forever, and there will never be any way to get him out.'

Nuh said vehemently, 'His time is coming, I promise you. *I saw a man who will not live long to enjoy his wealth* - Do you remember? Ismail Mire's poem?'

Hassan took over and Nuh listened, nodding, as Hassan recited the lines that once, in another life, Nuh had taught his young cousin.

> *'He is full, satiated, and has grown fat buttocks like a big ram;*
> *His bags are full of loot taken from men of honour and valour.'*

Then his own voice joined Hassan's for the final line,

> *'Watch silently, Muslims, and see how those who prosper*
> *lose their souls!'*

*

'I'm telling the children I'm going to Hassan's for a meeting after work,' Rachel said, 'and that if I'm late I may stay over.'

Pat's eyebrows lifted. 'I thought you said that wouldn't be good enough for Kate?'

'I'm doing it gradually. It'll be a start.'

Simon was stirring in his sleep when she got in next morning. She was tiptoeing past his room towards her own when she heard him call out, as if in a dream. She stopped and stood perfectly still, waiting until she was sure he had gone off to sleep again. Then she slipped quietly into her room, undressed, got into her nightie, and climbed into bed. Her heart was thumping as if she had narrowly escaped being caught burgling. This is ridiculous, she thought, I have to find another way of handling this.

At breakfast the boys seemed much as normal. Ben had gone bounding in to the living room to jump onto the sofa next to Pat in her sleeping bag, and demand that she get up for breakfast. Simon was moaning about the cornflakes being all powdery at the bottom of the packet. Kate was definitely uncommunicative, snapping at Simon and not responding to anything Rachel said.

Pat was still drinking coffee as Rachel left with Ben and Simon. 'See you at work,' she said. It was tea break before they had a chance to talk. 'Was everything OK last night?' she asked.

'Fine,' said Pat. 'But you made me want to laugh at breakfast. If you think it's invisible, you're wrong!'

Kate had a history project that had to be in the next day. At least that was what she said. Rachel had not heard the project mentioned until supper, after Kate had discovered that Hassan was coming. As soon as he arrived she came in and spread out her books on the living room table, exercising her traditional right to Rachel's company after the boys were in bed. Hassan and Rachel went on talking but it was imposible to be natural in the face of the silent protest of Kate's shoulders hunched over her books. She's waiting to be pushed out, he thought, to have legitimate cause to resent me. Rachel's tension was almost tangible. When ten o'clock came and still Kate had made no move to go Rachel said, 'It's bed-time, poppet.' Kate said nothing. She packed up her books, accepted Rachel's good night hug without returning it, and left.

When he was sure Kate could no longer hear Hassan said, 'I feel like public enemy number one. Maybe I shouldn't have come.'

'Forget it. She'll be all right in the morning.' But the tension in her voice belied her words. He touched her face lightly. Her eyes flashed anxiety. 'Don't worry,' he said. 'I am perfectly aware of the need to be discreet.' He outstared her, willing her to be calm. 'Rachel, I want you to talk to Kate. About us. It's not helpful to anyone, letting things drag on like this, unstated.'

'I know I should. But I don't know how to.' She had her head turned the other way. 'Look at me, Rachel.' When she did he asked, 'What's going on?'

'It's not just tonight.' She's withdrawing from me, and it makes me afraid. Ever since Alistair left - from before, probably - Kate has been the person I've been closest to in the world. She knows that's not true anymore. She is angry and scared, and I understand why. Talking about it may make it worse.'

'If you and Kate are as close as you say, she won't be able to stay withdrawn for long.'

'It happens. Kate's at the age when it often happens between mothers and daughters anyway. I thought she and I were immune, now I see we were more vulnerable than most. It's probably my fault, I needed a partner and because I wasn't ready to find one I used Kate. Now it's as if I've jilted her, for you.'

Something was growing inside him, a feeling that he did not want to recognise. He could hear his voice sounding cold and distant as he said, 'What did all that closeness amount to if you can't find a way to talk to her when there is something real to be said?'

'You don't understand, Hassan. It's not possible to help her see why I need you. She's never had any experience like ours. All she can see is that you're taking me away from her. She's a child and she's afraid, and I want to comfort her and say, 'Don't worry, there's nothing to worry about,' but she's also not a child and she won't let me comfort her that way anymore. You don't underst- '

'Don't tell me I don't understand!'

His voice was hard, angry, full of pain. She stared at him in astonishment. 'What is it?' She put out her hand to touch his cheek. He pushed it away, getting up abruptly as if he needed to distance himself from her. No, she thought, no, this can't be happening. Not to us. He said, 'When you talk that way about Kate, I can already hear you say - tomorrow, next week, next year - I can't do this to Kate, we have to stop seeing each other.'

'You know I'm not capable of that!'

'Who knows what your fear will make you capable of?' He could hear the words continuing in his head, but some stubborn self-protective pride stopped him from saying them aloud. There are things happening to us that are too much like a re-run of history...

Farida's room at the university. She didn't like him being there, it made her anxious. She was packing as they talked and she wouldn't look at him. He said, 'Don't go. It's a device to get you back. Your mother is probably not ill at all.' He tried to touch her but she wouldn't let him near her. Then she sat on her bed, tight and controlled and told him that he was right, her mother was not ill. She was going home to be married. She was sorry she had lied to him, she hadn't been able to find a way. She had meant to write and explain when she got back to Blackburn. She was sorry she was leaving, sorry she had ever loved him because now it meant she had to hurt him so much. She had turned down three potential husbands already and she couldn't go on like that forever. If the man seemed tolerable at all she would take him and try to make the best of it, she was too tired to keep fighting. She didn't know why she had ever bothered to fight at all, why she had struggled to go to university, to do anything. It all seemed pointless. He asked her what she proposed to do about her thesis. She said she would try and finish it at home, before she got married. There wasn't any reason why she couldn't work on it there just as well as here. She had been so tense with indecision for the last few months she had got almost nothing done anyway. He asked her whether she intended to write to him. She said, 'Hassan, you know I can't.'

Rachel had put out her hand to draw him back to sit next to her. He felt the rigidity of his body lessen slightly at her touch. 'I need to talk to you about Farida,' he said. He stopped again. 'I haven't often spoken about this. It's not easy.' She waited, saying nothing. 'The main thing you noticed about Farida was her clarity. She always knew what she thought. The way she talked when she was with friends, confident, humorous, articulate, it was impossible to believe - But her family wasn't there, you see, it was a separate life that none of us saw, and I never understood how much she needed their approval, how afraid she was to break with them. All the time we were together she tried to keep me a secret, even from her closest friends. Not the fact that we were seeing each other, but that she slept at my place sometimes. I thought it was ridiculous to go through that kind of pantomime, I couldn't believe her friends didn't know. And then university holidays, half the bloody year, and each time she was back in Blackburn I couldn't phone or write or contact her in any way.'

'Did she have to go back for holidays or did she want to?'

'Both. That was the problem. If she hadn't loved them she could have fought them. You and Kate.'

'It's not the same, Hassan.'

'Listen, there isn't anything I don't know about divided loyalties, and I know for sure that avoiding the issue makes it worse for everyone. I want you to talk to Kate. And I need to know we're going to have a night together again soon.'

'You know I want to! It's only -'

He did not let her finish. Harshly he said, 'It isn't good enough saying I want to but. I need to know we're making time for each other, regardless, that it's not conditional on other people approving.'

'It's not conditional on anything,' she said.

He stared at her as if weighing what she had said, then suddenly relaxed. 'There's a poem,' he said, laughing at himself, 'and I know it in translation too -

For of course that life is sweet I grant you
and where terror dwells are not all men the same?

Here have I been telling you not to be afraid! Listen, Jeyam's flat - he's said we can use it when we need to. He's got plenty of friends he can go to for an occasional night.'

*

246

She had thought she would feel odd walking into the home of an unknown, absent person, and taking it over as their own. But it didn't take more than a minute, nothing more than the sensation of adjusting her eyes to being inside after the bright light and colours of Regent's Park, which they had walked through on their way here. The last time she had been there was in her first year in London, a Sunday in high summer when Alistair had just come back from one of his journeys; a day of too many tourists and long queues at the ice cream kiosk, while Ben screamed in his pushchair and Rachel and Alistair argued as to whether it would be more sensible to carry him; a day made miserable by Simon's continuous whining, which evoked the usual impatient reaction from Alistair and the equally predictable overprotective counter-reaction from Rachel. Beyond that she could remember little, except that nothing they did succeeded in pleasing all three children simultaneously, and that the longer the day went on the more clearly Alistair conveyed the impression that this was all somehow her fault.

Today the place was radiant, and not only from their own inner radiance. The late afternoon sun had sunk low, touching the trees with a soft light. The flower beds were ablaze, colours undimmed by the dimished sun - tulips, pansies, wallflowers, others whose names Hassan told her and she promptly forgot again. An avenue of trees still laden with blossom. Shrubs in full bloom, a brick red japonica, masses of blazing yellow forsythia.

And then they were in Jeyam's bedroom, and there was no longer even a momentary strangeness as they became once again naked together, simply a joyous return to what seemed now the most natural way to be. Jeyam's things all around them evoked no outsider's presence, only the tactful greeting of an unknown friend. Be free, they said. Here, for these few hours, there is no one requiring anything of you.

Throughout the night they seemed to drift in and out of sleep. One of them would turn and instinctively the other's body would rearrange itself, knees tucked into the other's, arms encircling; warm soft stomach against warm smooth back, edges blurred. Sometimes they would stir long enough to talk a little, to touch and caress and start making love all over again, and then drift back into sleep. Once she became aware of Hassan's voice quietly reciting,

You are like a place with fresh grass after a downpour of rain
On which the sun now shines...

She felt moved by something in his voice that had nothing to do with her. Still half asleep she murmured, 'That's beautiful, Hassan. Did you translate it?'

'I wish I could say yes. Impossible task, translating poetry. You'd have to be a poet yourself.'

'What you need most is to love it. You could do it, if anyone can.'

'I've never had a motive - until now.'

And then she was asleep again.

Another time it was she who woke first and lay listening to his breathing, soft and even next to her. Gently she began to run her fingers through his hair, starting at the base of his neck and working upwards. 'Hassan?' she whispered. He did not move. 'Hassan, I want to ask you something.' There was a pause as the words slowly penetrated. 'That poem you recited tonight, where did you learn it? Not only that one, all the poetry you know.'

'And for this the woman woke me!' he said, and rolled over to face her, his eyes laughing.

'Go on, I want to know.'

'It was all around us. I used to hear them reciting, my uncles, my father's friends, the radio, everyone. Poetry's a national habit.' The disbelief in her face delighted him. 'Honest!'

'Everyone?'

'Well, maybe that's a bit of an exaggeration. But a lot of people. And in my family particularly. My grandfather had a phenomenal memory for poetry and he made sure all his sons took it seriously.'

'And where did he learn it?'

'Like everyone else in those days, sitting around the camp fire with the other camel herders, listening to someone recite.'

She stared. 'Your grandfather herded camels, and wrote poems?'

He was now fully awake. 'No, he didn't write poems. Number one, he couldn't read or write. Number two, Somali poems aren't written, they're composed. In your head. And then you speak them to an audience, and people who're listening memorise them and go and recite them to other people. That's what my grandfather used to do. He was a memoriser, not a poet.'

'What about your generation, people who've grown up in towns?'

'Ah, my father would tell you most of them are ignorant and uncultured. Mohamed, for instance, he only knows the bits everyone quotes.' Mohamed...

Where was Mohamed? Was it possible that he and the others had a chance of succeeding? That they would reclaim the land and the life that had once been theirs, a life in which nomads could gather round a transistor radio and listen to the latest poems being broadcast from Mogadishu? In which people could sit in the teashops of Hargeisa and not be afraid? He wanted so much to believe it, but he could not. All he could see ahead was another terrible time like the one their grandfather had known, when in the devastation after the wars of the Sayyid people had died in tens of thousands of famine and disease, and been driven to eating rats and carrion...

He had gone away again, gone on some private journey in which she could have no part. Moving gently so as not to disturb him, she rolled over onto her back and looked out through the window whose blind he had insisted on leaving up so that he could see her body when they woke in the night. The moon was up, and the sky seemed as light as if it had been early morning. There were wisps of cloud drifting into patterns and out of them again. She looked back at Hassan's face, still withdrawn into itself. She lay quietly next to him, and waited for him to be ready to return.

*

She woke, slowly, woke to the pleasure of his arms warm and brown around her and full daylight coming through the window. It was a minute or two before she worked out that there was something amiss about being able to wake like that. She jerked herself upright and grabbed the clock. Eight fifteen. The alarm pointed to Off. 'Hassan,' she shook him. 'Something happened with the alarm.' She was scrambling frantically into her jeans. 'Phone Pat for me, tell her to say something to the children, I don't know what. I won't get there before it's time for them to leave for school. Ask her if she can take the boys on her way to work.' He was up, kneeling on the bed and putting his arms out to hold her around the hips, firmly. 'Just steady on. You're late anyway, another minute or two won't make any difference.'

6

Kate was still at home when she got in. Rachel did not say, 'What are you doing still here?' She knew.

'I waited for you.' Kate's voice was hard and accusing, unlike any tone Rachel had ever heard her use. She could think of nothing appropriate to say. She wanted to hug her but was afraid to do so, afraid that it would be angrily rejected. Kate said, 'Are you going to do this often?' The girl was close to tears, desperately making herself angry to hold them back. 'Poppet,' Rachel began.

'Don't call me that ridiculous name! I'm not a child and I wish you'd stop treating me as if I was.'

Rachel felt no responding anger, only a misery that this had to be happening between them. 'I don't think of you as a child. But I didn't know if you wanted me to talk about it. I was leaving it to you.'

'Leaving what to me? Leaving me like the boys, with Pat to make excuses for you. I hate it when you stay at Hassan's place, I hate Hassan, I wish you'd never met him, or Asha and Ahmed's mum, or Sado's, or any of them. I hate them all!'

'No you don't. It's just Hassan you're angry about, so don't start telling yourself it's all of them.'

'How do you know what I feel? You know nothing! ' And then the violence of her anger collapsed, and she said, in a petulant little-girl voice, 'And I'm not going to school today, you can say what you like.'

'That's OK. I won't go to work either.'

Kate stared at her. 'You have to.'

'Just as you have to go to school, normally. This isn't a normal day. I'll phone and tell them I can't come in. '

Kate was still staring at her, almost distracted from her anger; but not quite. 'What are we going to do, then?' she demanded, as if she suspected that she was being manipulated.

'Whatever you like. Poppet - Kate - I'm sorry to have upset you. I didn't mean to, honest. And I'd like to give you a hug. Can I?' Kate's mouth quivered, and then she gave in. She hurled herself at Rachel, sobbing, burying her face on Rachel's shoulder, sobbing, sobbing. Rachel held her tight and said nothing, and did not know what she would say when the sobbing stopped. But at least Kate had let her hold her. The worst of the misery had gone.

Kate disengaged herself. 'I haven't had breakfast.'

'I haven't either! When I saw the alarm hadn't gone off, I just pulled my clothes on and ran for the bus. I haven't even been to the loo!'

Kate giggled. 'Go now. You must be popping.'

When Rachel came out of the bathroom Kate said, 'Let's make pancakes!'

Kate cracked the eggs and whisked them while Rachel measured out the flour and stirred in the milk. She passed the bowl to Kate, and got out the frying pan and the margarine. 'Butter,' said Kate, 'let's make them with butter today.' The butter melted, turned a delicious light brown, Hassan's colour. The mixture was smooth and yellowy, rising in bubbles as it cooked. 'You toss,' said Rachel. Kate took the frying pan handle in both hands and stuck her tongue out as she concentrated on catching the pancake that came, plop, right back into position, and they laughed at the illicit delight of having taken the day off, at the healing that was happening and that they both so much needed. They sat down to eat, and their fingers became sticky from honey and lemon juice. Rachel waited for Kate to talk about Hassan again, but she didn't. What would there be to say, anyway? I love him and I need to spend time with him. That does not mean I do not love you, that you are any less safe. We are the same, nothing can change what we have.

It was not strictly true. Something had changed, not in her love, but in Kate's readiness to take it on trust. Neither of them wanted to talk about it.

'Mom,' said Kate, her face stricken. 'I forgot to tell you - there was a phone call from South Africa!'

'A phone call? From Ouma? When?'

'This morning. It wasn't Ouma. It was someone called - I forget. I wrote it down. She couldn't understand why you weren't here, and I didn't know what to say.'

Rachel took the note - Anna de Wet. There could be only one reason for Aunt Anna's phoning. Auntie had died. Mechanically she gave Kate a quick hug to comfort that tight look from her face, got out the phone book to find the international dialling code and began to dial the long number; cautiously, as if expecting it not to work. Amazingly, the ringing tone. Aunt Anna's voice saying, in Afrikaans, *'Ja, wie is dit?'*- Yes, who is it? - A voice from so long ago, not just four years, a life time away. 'Aunt Anna, it's Rachel.' Dimly she was aware of Kate's body next to hers, registering surprise. Of course, she had automatically spoken in Afrikaans. She had not even noticed she was doing so.

'Rachel? I was getting worried. Where were you? I thought I would get you before you went to work.'

'I'm not at work today.' Rachel pressed on, not giving Aunt Anna any chance to enquire further. 'It's Auntie, isn't it?'

'Yes. No, not that, she's still with us. It's your mother.'

'My mother!'

'It's a terrible strain on her, the whole situation. She doesn't want to worry you about it, you're so far away.' It was a criticism, and Aunt Anna made no attempt to hide it. Rachel ought not to have left South Africa, she had no business going so far away from her mother. The position was not logical for Aunt Anna would also have said that it was Rachel's duty to go with her husband wherever he went. The root problem was the husband. If Rachel had not married such a man she would not now have been stuck on the other side of the world far from where she belonged. Alistair was not an excuse but an additional fault. 'Your mother is completely exhausted,' Aunt Anna was saying. 'She never gets a break. The rest of us try to help but she has got so obsessed by the whole thing she hardly lets us.'

'Aunt Anna, I -' But she didn't know how to go on. Could she really say, I didn't know it was as bad as that?

'Look, child,' Aunt Anna said, 'I don't want to interfere but I think you should come. You're the only one who can bully her into taking help. That brother of yours is no use. He's in America, busy with his career.' Some detached part of Rachel's brain registered, Aunt Anna's in good form, character assassination all round. 'Listen, child, your mother needs someone. I told her to ask you herself but she wouldn't. I thought someone ought to.'

The words flowed on. Rachel's mind was by now incapacitated. With an effort she eventually cut across to say, 'I can't think straight. I'm going to put the phone down and work it out, and I'll phone you back. Tonight.' Then, belatedly, trying to behave normally, 'How's everyone else? Sannie? The children?'

'They're all fine. We just wish the Lord would take Auntie now and be done with it.'

She felt as if she were returning to Kate through layers of experience. She had been oblivious of her presence after the first few words, transported by Aunt Anna's vigorous Afrikaans back to Lourensrus, to a previous era, to the shock of discovering that it still existed. Now she noticed dimly that Kate was once again calm and grown up, and was taking charge of her, putting her arm around her and making her sit down next to her on the sofa. 'They want me to go,' Rachel said, blankly, 'to help Ouma with Auntie. I don't know how to do it, Kate. I should go, I don't want to let her down, but I can't see -'

Kate was staring at her. 'What would happen to us?'

'That's the thing, that's what I can't see. And it costs a bomb. I don't even know how much, but - Aunt Anna didn't know Daddy wasn't with us. I think Ouma hasn't told people. Aunt Anna thought I could leave you all with Daddy.'

'Oh.' Kate was silent a moment. Then, scarcely daring, 'Can't Daddy come?'

Rachel watched her face, full of longing yet afraid to show it. Seeing it so, Rachel hated Alistair. 'He's got so many things to do he can't usually stay long. If I go - it's so far and so expensive I couldn't just go for a few days. It wouldn't be much use to Ouma.'

'You want to go, don't you?'

'I don't want to go, but I feel I should. Actually, poppet, I feel panicky even thinking of going. It sounds so silly, but I never imagined I'd go back. I don't want to be all unsettled again.' Kate hugged her. She can't possibly understand, thought Rachel, she's a child of thirteen, but here I am talking to her about these ridiculous, complicated feelings. And thinking of how precious this companionship was to her, her remorse about her neglect of her own mother returned. She had been so preoccupied with - With what? With the children, with Haleemo and Hibo's troubles, with the campaign. With Hassan.

She did not want to go away from him. It was all too new, too important. Already the children's needs made it difficult for her and Hassan to have time together, she could not handle her mother's as well.

'Mom, it's OK, we can stay with friends.' And then, in a much younger voice, 'How long will you have to be gone?'

'I don't know. When I think about you three, I think, as short as possible. When I think about Ouma, I think, as long as possible. I can't work it out. Maybe two weeks?'

'Two weeks!'

'It'll be like when you went to camp, only two camps in a row.' And she realised from the way they were both talking that the decision had already been made.

*

Each time she had spent the night with him he hated her having to go away early in the morning, leaving only the space in the bed where she had been, the smell of her body on his. He had to work at himself not to feel each departure as a premonition of what it would be like if one day she left and did not return. Today it was harder than usual. He could not free himself from the awareness that she was anxious, and that he could not be with her to help her become calm. Mechanically he tidied up Jeyam's bedroom, cleaned up in the kitchen, and left a note on the table - Thanks, mate. He did not feel in the mood to write more and he knew even that wasn't necessary. Thanks, mate, for letting us have, briefly, the illusion of a place of our own.

When he heard that she was to go away, six thousand miles away, he had a moment of blind fury. You can't! he wanted to shout, not you too. Immediately he took control of himself and put his own needs aside to listen, and support. But that moment of insecurity was enough to alert him.

'When?' he asked.

'As soon as I can fix everything up. When my father was dying I waited for a sensible moment to go and I was too late. I'm not doing that again.'

'What are you doing about the children?'

'Kate's going to Becky's, Evelyn's having the boys.' She had never before talked to Evelyn about her family in South Africa but there hadn't seemed any need of explanations. Her aunt was dying, her mother needed her. An international language, instantly intelligible. 'And don't worry about the campaign,' Evelyn had said. 'We'll keep it going.'

Hassan asked, 'And money? How will you pay for the ticket?'

'I'll ask Alistair. I'm just waiting for it to be the right time of day in America before I phone him.'

'You're asking Alistair for the money?'

254

'I don't have a choice. I know he's got plenty, and there's no other way I can raise it.'

'You amaze me, Rachel. I had the impression that the last thing you'd want would be to make yourself beholden to Alistair.'

'It's not for me. It's for my mother, and Auntie.'

'And you reckon Alistair can tell the difference?'

'I don't care what Alistair thinks. It's a big enough difference to make me feel fine about asking.' She laughed, 'Maybe the campaign's made me used to asking other people to give their time and money in a good cause! Anyway, Alistair's quite generous, in a selfish sort of way.'

'What's that supposed to mean?'

'That he likes people to notice, and be grateful. He sends the children lavish presents but he won't arrange for regular maintenance payments. Something dramatic like this will probably appeal to him.'

'You ought to do something about getting maintenance sorted out.'

'I've tried. He doesn't answer my letters.'

'Stop writing to him yourself. Get your solicitor to do it.'

'*My solicitor*,' she mimicked. 'What makes you think I've got one?'

'Allow me to present my compliments. You've got me.'

It had turned into the kind of day Hassan most disliked. There were constant interruptions, none of them minor enough to be dismissed yet none of them major enough to make him feel it had been worth losing concentration. Not that his concentration was much in evidence. He could not detach himself from the fact that Rachel was about to leave at any moment, and that he could not even be sure he would see her alone again before she did. He was irritable with everyone who crossed his path. With Gita, unfairly, when she asked for advice on a point of procedure that he thought she ought by now to have known. With Mike, with considerably more justice, when an application for a student grant Mike was supposed to be handling turned up beneath a pile of newspapers on top of the filing cabinet in the common room. And then Barbara came in for her share, by putting through to him a call she herself could have handled.

'He specifically asked for you,' Barbara said defensively.

'It's for you to decide who he can speak to, not him.' He disliked both his curt voice and Barbara's anxious face. He returned to the papers he had been working on.

255

Within minutes he had given up and dialled Rachel's number. Bloody engaged, yet again.

'He says he's your cousin.' Barbara's voice on the phone was cautious, seeking to avoid another eruption. 'He's been waiting a while already. Shall I send him in?'

'What's his name?'

'Nuh Ali Dahir.'

'I'll come and get him.' He sped to reception thinking, what is it, that couldn't wait till this evening? When he got there Nuh's face looked closed. Hassan said as lightly as he could manage, 'What are you doing, masquerading as one of our clients?'

Once in the corridor Nuh said, 'I hadn't realised what a big man you'd become.'

'Don't,' said Hassan. 'I hate it.'

'Hate what?'

'The fact that being busy gives people that big man impression. It's nothing to do with status, only with the number of people who can't find their way through the morass of regulations that surround them. We never catch up with the work.'

'And I bring you more.'

'Don't be stupid.' They had reached his office. 'In here,' Hassan said.

Nuh pulled an opened brown envelope out of his pocket and handed it to Hassan. 'It arrived this morning. I'm going to Whitechapel tonight and I didn't want to wait until tomorrow before asking you about it.' A Home Office envelope. Hassan knew before he opened it what it would be. He took out the duplicated sheet and scanned it quickly. *You are to report to Heathrow Airport...* He looked up. The tension in Nuh's face moved him, reminding him of how he had looked in detention. 'It's OK,' Hassan reassured him. 'They're only calling you for interview. Standard practice. You get a chance to tell them again why you're applying for asylum.'

'The same immigration officer?' Nuh's nostrils were quivering.

'It's possible. But he has to write down everything you say, and we can rehearse it beforehand to make sure you cover what's required.' Nuh looked unconvinced. 'I'll come with you if you like,' Hassan said, but Nuh lifted his head in that unmistakeable way that said, I fight my own battles. I need no man's help.

All day Rachel's phone was either engaged, or no answer. When finally she phoned she seemed totally preoccupied with her arrangements. She had braved the librarian, she reported, expecting coldness and had been met with quiet consideration. No need to regard it as part of her annual leave, he had said, you'll be needing that for the children's holidays. When Pat had heard she had simply put her arms around Rachel. 'Don't worry about Kate,' she had said. 'It's probably better it came to a head. Give me the address where she's going to stay and I'll fix up a couple of saxophone lessons with her while you're away.' And then, 'Listen, why don't I come and stay with the kids? Then they won't have to be split up.'

'I would never have thought,' Rachel told Hassan, 'that it would be so easy to walk out of my life for two weeks.' He felt a flash of anger again and wanted to shout, and what the hell about me? Steady on, he told himself, you know that isn't what she meant. Instead he said, 'I want to see you. Can I come round tonight?'

'Not tonight, Hassan. I need to be alone with the children.'

And of course he knew that was perfectly reasonable.

*

She knew when she got back from taking the children to school on Friday morning that there was now nothing to stop her from booking her ticket. Speaking to Haleemo had been the last thing, the one she had thought would be the hardest. She had waited for her until ten minutes after the children had gone in to their classes, but Haleemo did not appear. Rachel was filled with foreboding. Something new had happened, something urgent, and here she was abandoning the campaign by going away. She gave up waiting and walked to Haleemo's house, to find that Haleemo had simply overslept. She opened the door to Rachel, adjusting her headscarf over her still dishevelled hair, with eyes not yet fully adjusted to the waking world and her long loose *diri* dress crumpled from sleep. Rachel started laughing, from relief that her fears of a crisis had been unnecessary.

They sat together in Haleemo's kitchen drinking tea as they had done on that first day, and Rachel told her about having to go away. 'Hibo and Evelyn say they'll keep everything going,' she said, and it all seemed simple. She offered to walk back to school with Asha and Ahmed, who had been nervous about getting into trouble for being late. 'I'll explain,' Rachel said, and the children stopped being anxious and skipped along, one on each side of her. It felt good to be doing this one last thing with them, all on her own.

Now she was back in her silent, empty house, and there was nothing to stop her phoning the airline to book the ticket.

'British Airways, Sunday night,' the woman was saying, 'Or South African Airways? There are a couple of seats left on tomorrow night's flight.'

'Not South African Airways,' Rachel said at once. Why? She was going back to the place itself - what did it matter if the moment of return started from Heathrow airport? It was too soon, too soon. She could feel the long forgotten tension settling in her stomach again. What was it that thinking about South Africa did to her? Why did it seem so enormous a psychological barrier to cross, to accept that she would be going back?

'Sunday,' she said.

It was finally, irreversibly done. As she put the phone down she began to tremble, taken over by shivers that would not go away. She made herself a cup of tea, 'Hot, strong, sweet,' she could hear Auntie saying, 'good for shock.' And when that didn't help she filled a hotwater bottle and sat hugging it to herself, with a blanket wrapped around her. She sat that way for a long time, looking around her at the kitchen, at the children's drawings blu-tacked to the walls. Ben's skates just inside the door where people could trip over them. Simon's library books, overdue and still not returned. Kate's walkman and latest cassette of The Cure which she left wherever she had last used it, and then got mad when Simon fiddled with it; and then out of the window at the garden where the apple tree was laden with scores of tight green little knobs, and the climbing rose, which she never pruned and which still rewarded her every year, was producing its first crop of dark red buds. They would open in a matter of days, as soon as she had gone, probably, into an exuberant display of overblown pink roses. This place that had become her home and which she was now afraid to leave.

The children... Kate would be OK. Her going away might even ease things, she thought, give Kate time to get used to the idea of Hassan. Simon and Ben? They were used to being with Pat, but it would be different for two whole weeks, night and day. Last night at supper

Ben's lower lip had trembled and he had climbed onto her lap saying, 'Why do you have to go?' the kind of question to which adult reasoning could provide no answer, for it meant, 'Why do you put someone else's needs before mine?'

'Have you still got a lot to do?' he asked on the phone, willing her to say no.

'Yes,' she said. 'I've got to pack and get the house sorted out. I've been so busy lately it's in a complete mess and I can't possibly leave it that way for Pat to walk in to.'

'Come on, Rachel, Pat's not going to mind!'

'You've no idea what you're talking about. Ben's capable of bringing life to a halt if he can't find the one puzzle he's decided to do, and they're all out of clean clothes. Plus there are lots of things to do with the campaign. People may need to get hold of you if there are any new developments.'

'I'll do whatever I can. And if necessary things can just wait two weeks.'

Immediately she was angry. 'They can't! It took me far too long to get started anyway. I have a terrible premonition that we're running out of time, that something is going to happen to Haleemo's children before we get anywhere.'

'If it does,' he said steadily, refusing to rise to her anger, 'it will not be your fault, so stop working yourself up about it.'

'Hassan,' - in a tone of voice that said, it matters terribly to me that you should understand - 'It feels harder to walk out on the campaign than on my children. It's not that I think it'll come to a halt when I'm not here, it's something more basic than that. Something about my commitment to myself. I need to know I didn't give up on it.'

'You didn't, and haven't, and won't. It would be impossible for you to let anyone down.' And then he let her go, back to tidying her house.

As she dialled the ACRAS number for the third time that morning she pictured them all there - the people waiting in reception, Hassan's desk with its pile of papers that never got smaller however fast he worked. With the constraints of her own routine broken, she had forgotten that he would still be caught up in his. When his voice came on the line she asked, 'Hassan, am I interrupting your work?'

'Rachel, for God's sake try not to be stupid. I am sitting here waiting for the bloody phone to ring. Just hold on a minute, there's someone at the door.' When he returned he said, 'I don't even know if they have telephones in Lourensrus. Will I be able to phone you?'

The question took her by surprise. Her instinctive response was that it would be too confusing to have Hassan trying to be with her while she was trying to be the person her mother needed her to be. She had been saying to the children, to her work, to the campaign, 'Just do without me for a couple of weeks.' She would do a vanishing trick, and then come back again and take up everything exactly where she had left off. Yet the moment Hassan asked the question she understood that of course it could not be like that. Going back would change her - and changing her, would change everything around her. Hassan knew, and was afraid. Carefully she said, 'There are phones; but it costs an awful lot. And my mother -' It was not the answer he needed, but for the moment she could find no other. 'We'll think about it,' she said. 'Hassan, nothing's going to change. And I want to see you alone before I go. When can you manage?'

'Now,' he said. 'Give me half an hour to cancel the day's appointments. Come here, and we'll go to Jeyam's.'

*

There were so many things that he urgently needed to say to her in their precious three hours together, and in the end most of them remained unsaid. On the underground she talked compulsively, and almost entirely about the campaign, ticking off a list of still-to-be-done jobs, most of which could perfectly well have waited till her return. She's behaving as if she may never come back, he thought, and in the insecurity that followed that thought, the things he had wanted to say were pushed one level further down.

Once they got to the flat new barriers presented themselves. Jeyam was in, as he had said he would be. Hassan had forgotten that he and Rachel had never met, and that of course she would not feel relaxed about going straight to love-making, to that most direct form of communication that wiped out temporary misunderstandings and minor resentments, that affirmed as no words could the power of their need for each other. Instead she turned on Jeyam the complete attention she gave to each new person she encountered, listening, looking, her face open to him, making Hassan feel excluded and peripheral and at the same time aware that he was being childish. For was this not the very thing in her that he had first loved, and would he really have wanted her to react to his friend in any other way?

Jeyam seemed much younger than Hassan. He was slightly built, with alert eyes and a lock of hair that he kept shaking out of them, which perhaps contributed to the boyish impression, and he talked from the moment they walked in. It felt strange to be meeting him for the first time in a place that was his but where she already felt at home, and with all three of them knowing that she and Hassan had come only to use his bed. But his directness disarmed her. 'So you're the famous Rachel,' he said. 'The bedroom's all yours. I promise not to listen at the keyhole, and I'll be gone in half an hour.'

'What's famous about me?' she laughed.

'You're the only known force capable of getting this guy to take off work in the middle of the day. A role much to be encouraged.'

'Come,' said Hassan to Rachel. 'If you encourage him he'll go on like that for hours, and we have more important things to do.' When they were alone with the door closed behind them she sat on the bed that had been hers and Hassan's and now was Jeyam's, and made no move to get undressed. 'Are you sure he doesn't mind?' she asked. Hassan came to sit next to her. 'When you come back we'll have to make time for you to get to know my friends. You'd only need another half hour in his company to know that there isn't anything he minds, from a friend. He would be a terrible enemy but luckily I don't ever have to face that prospect. And nor will you.'

Even the love-making was different. Rachel, it seemed, could not detach herself. Jeyam's bed squeaked as they moved on it, something they had laughed about when they had made love here before but which now made her say, 'Take it easy, we're making too much noise!' He slowed down, trained by all the weeks of attuning himself to her pace, to what she was ready for. There was no point in doing anything else, in fact, because if he had tried to brush aside her unnecessary concern he would only have made her doubly tense. But even while he was adapting himself he knew that he was angry at having to do it, angry and hurt that she did not appear to see his need. He wanted to tell her, yet the child in him held back from doing so, demanded that she should prove her love by seeing it for herself.

And then his body took over, saying it for him. He did not care if he overrode her wishes, if she was not ready. He needed her to focus on him and exclusively on him, and he needed it now. With an urgency that he had never before felt he began to make love to her entire body, starting with her shoulders, then her breasts, her belly, turning her over to reach her back, her buttocks, throwing back the covers and moving down on the bed to her thighs, her knees, her calves, her feet, and then back again, this time on top of her, to look down into her face and see, in a burst of joy, that his urgency had broken through to her and done away with her catalogue of minor responsibilities, and that she was there, his Rachel, one hundred and one percent focusing on him. And in the release of that knowledge he too was freed.

For some reason that she herself did not understand she was crying as she came, a sob building up in her chest until there was no longer space to contain it, and then breaking as the climax broke under Hassan's caressing fingers. He held on to her hard, so hard that it crushed not only the sobs but also her chest. She had to push him away to free herself, laughing through her wet face and wiping her tears with her freed hand. 'I don't know what that was all about,' she said, 'I'm happy, really I am.'

'You frightened me. I thought I had done something to hurt you.'

'Never.' She shook her head vehemently. 'You couldn't. It was - I don't know how to say it. Not sad crying, just an overflowing-ness. There was so much feeling inside me, coming wasn't enough to release it. '

'What kind of feeling?'

'Everything. Being able to be like this with you. Knowing I have to go away. Feeling in a panic about it.'

He smiled. 'I've been waiting for that. I've been saying to myself, there's something funny going on. Rachel is faced with a new decision and she does not appear to be in a panic.'

'It's pathetic, isn't it? I'm thirty-four. I keep expecting to grow up, but I never quite get there.'

'We probably never will. But you nearly had me fooled this time.'

'I feel as if this is another of those challenges life keeps presenting me with, and that I always want to run away from. Like when you suggested the campaign.'

'This is different. It's looking after someone you love, the thing you're best at. There's nothing new required of you.'

'Nothing new. Something old, and unfinished. It's not going back to my mother and Auntie that's the problem, it's going back to South Africa. It's such a mixture of feelings, I don't even know how to say it.' He waited. 'One of them is a hangover from the days of Alistair. I'm trying not to pay any attention to it.'

'Come on, let's hear it.'

'That people will expect me to come back full of intelligent comments about what is going on politically in South Africa, and I won't have anything to say.' He started laughing, helplessly. 'What's so funny?'

'Everything. For a start, which people? Me? Hibo? Evelyn? Which of us is going to expect you to be a roving journalist?' He waited for her reluctant acknowledging smile. 'And even more ridiculous is the idea that you won't have anything to say! I expect you not to stop talking for weeks.'

'Yes, but it'll just be things I've seen in Lourensrus, little incidents with the few people I know.'

He rolled over and propped himself up on his elbows, looking down at her face. 'Listen, you thickhead - I've been trying to show you for two months that you responding to the ordinary people in front of you equals a political act. Has the campaign taught you nothing about yourself?'

'What I'm doing here is easy compared to being in South Africa.'

'Why? Because the police aren't on your back?'

'That, but it's not only that. I don't risk cutting myself off from anyone I love.'

'Ah.' He slipped down to lie next to her again, taking her face between his hands and holding it still, studying her expression. 'So that's what it's all about!'

She pulled away from him defensively. 'You don't know what it's like in Lourensrus, how people see the world, the categories they think in. My family, all my mother's relatives, they all live within fifty miles of where they were born. That's the limit of their world. They're straightforward, warm, people but they simply don't know how to absorb difference.'

'Yet they have lived all their lives with people of a different race on their doorsteps?'

'It's like *All things bright and beautiful*, the rich man in his castle and the poor man at the gate. There are people who are not like you and you accept that, but they are not your people. When your own people don't see things as you do, that poses a threat to everyone's security. That's why Auntie was so difficult for them to handle. They could only cope with her by turning her into an eccentric - it's only Auntie, we all know she's a little odd. Auntie wasn't in the least odd, she was the most human person among them, and they damaged her by confining her in that way.'

'Do you feel you're like Auntie? Another outsider?'

'No, I haven't got her courage. She was profoundly uninterested in what other people thought of her. I was never like that. I thought differently from the rest of them but I didn't confront them with it, just as I didn't think of talking to anyone about my sexual feelings. You maintain your place in that kind of world by accepting the limits.'

'What are you saying, Rachel?'

'I can't do that any more, don't you see? I haven't been able to for years. I was cutting myself off from Lourensrus long before I actually had to leave. I only went back once the whole last year I was in South Africa, after my father died. When he was there it was still possible. He was part of the place, but not so much of the people, if you know what I mean. When I was a child he used to take me up this hill behind our house, and introduce me to rocks and lizards and cactuses and cave paintings, the way he introduced me to books. They were like a world of his own that he escaped into when the people around him pressed in on him. I could go back to doing those things with him, and feel I was there, being part of what I had grown up with, however different I had become in other ways.'

'Auntie was different, too.'

'I've told you, I'm not like Auntie.'

'You knew you couldn't stay in those confines forever, so you left. That takes courage too.'

'No, it was the opposite. If I'd had real courage I'd have kept going back, despite Alistair and the kind of life I was getting drawn into.'

264

'There's a Somali proverb, that whenever you win someone for yourself you lose someone else.'

'That's it,' she said, excited. 'It was losing people I was afraid of. I'm sure that's why I never found a way to act, why I stayed away from direct political involvement. Running away again. Anything to avoid open rupture.'

'The proverb is about allies in war or politics, not about love. You don't have to lose people's love because you disagree with them politically.'

'You don't understand, Hassan. In South Africa politics is everything. It's not something you think about once every five years when you vote. It's how you treat ordinary people, every day.'

'It's like that everywhere. In societies in a state of crisis it's more obvious, that's all. Mohamed and I have shared more than I could begin to explain, yet there are things about his politics that I hate. You don't have to be afraid of hating, Rachel, like you don't have to be afraid of being angry. With anyone, even me. Remember how afraid you were when we argued about Haleemo? If we think differently we *have* to fight and it won't diminish our love for each other. You have to stay yourself and I have to stay myself, otherwise there's no one there to love. It's the same with your Lourensrus people. Especially with people you love, you have to be able to fight what you hate in them.'

'It's no good telling me things like that, Hassan. I'm no good at fighting.'

'Fighting doesn't have to mean physical violence, or losing your temper and shouting. Mohamed and I do that and there's nothing wrong with it, but it's a cultural style, that's all. I would never behave that way with my mother. Fighting essentially means knowing what you have to do, and doing it, whatever anyone else thinks. Like Auntie did. Like you do, when you stop panicking.'

All the vehemence had gone out of her. There seemed nothing more to say, just his face to memorise. The small lines of his smile around the corners of his mouth, his nostrils, firm and symetrical, his high cheek bones, the way his hair rose perpendicular from the root.

His eyes were following hers. He said, 'There's something else, isn't there?'

'Yes. But it's so ridiculous I don't want to say it.'

'Come on,' he said gently. 'I promise I won't laugh.'

She said, almost inaudibly, 'I'm afraid of leaving this life, leaving you. I'm afraid something will happen and I will never be able to come back.'

He touched her cheek, caressing it with the backs of his fingers, then down under her chin, and back up to the other cheek, spinning invisible threads to hold, and protect. He said, 'No, it doesn't sound ridiculous to me. That's what happened last time you had to leave somewhere suddenly. You just have to summon your reasoning to tell your feelings, this is different.' His hand moved down to her breasts. 'I would like to start all over again. How much time have we got?'

'Not enough.' She stretched out her hand to pick up her watch from the bedside table. 'Fifteen minutes before I need to get dressed.'

'Fifteen bloody minutes! I can't bear it.' Desire had left him. He sat up, his body preparing itself to accept the inevitable separation. 'There is so much I still want to tell you. About my father. About everything.'

'Start now.'

'There's too little time.'

'There may always be too little time. We'll have to learn to do things anyway, not wait till there's enough time.'

'Let's get dressed and tidy up, then we'll know how much time we have left.' Moving seemed to help him, for the moment they had started to dress he launching into talking about his father. 'There's so much in my life now that he doesn't know about. I'm sure I could make him understand if only we could have time together again.' He broke off, and then lashed out, 'I can't cope with the thought that there may never be a time. You talked about growing up - when I think about what's happening to him I'm like an angry, helpless child. I can't find any way past rage and misery.'

She said quietly, 'Maybe you shouldn't try. It's probably the only appropriate response.'

'You know what you were saying, about something happening to stop you coming back?'

'Don't you start taking it seriously!'

'I used to feel exactly like that each time I had to leave my father. I used to imagine being told one day, we're not going back. Decided by adults, for reasons that no one would explain.'

'And in fact that's what happened, wasn't it?' He looked up sharply. She went on. 'Incomprehensible actions by people who wield power over us and who never have to give reasons - that's what finally made it impossible for you to go back to him. The fear isn't so irrational after all.' They had finished straightening the bed, and stood looking at each other across it. He said, 'There is something about the way you understand me that I find almost unnerving. I love you, Rachel.'

'Yes.'

'Ever since Mohamed went back I've been expecting something to happen in Somalia. Something cataclysmic. I wish you weren't going away.'

'Do you understand why I have to?'

'Totally. It's all part of the same thing. Me and my father, you and your mother and Auntie. I want you to go. I'm glad you can.'

He came all the way back home with her, and would have walked with her to the school to fetch the children but she wouldn't let him. 'Say goodbye now,' she said, 'while we're alone.'

She stood on the doorstep to watch him walk back towards the station. He had gone only another three steps when he turned again and came back. 'I want to tell you one more thing. About my father, and Mohamed.'

'Go on then.'

'Mohamed's father was killed raiding a prison, trying to release political prisoners. Ever since Mohamed went back I've had this - fantasy, I suppose, that I scarcely dare think about but long for all the same, that Mohamed and the others fighting with him will attack Hargeisa prison, and my father will be free.'

She put her arms around him, and held him.

*

Pat loaded Rachel's luggage into the painted van that her band used for touring. Rachel sat in the front and the children sat in the back, distracted by the novelty of perching among music stands and odd shaped boxes.

When they had checked in Rachel's luggage Pat suggested that they should go and explore what the cafeteria had to offer. Ben and Simon started racing along the concourse in excitement. 'Can I have an eclair?' Ben asked Pat as they stood in the queue, turning to Pat rather than to Rachel, and she remembered how Asha had done the same to her that day so many months ago when Haleemo had nearly fainted in the playground.

Kate had stayed with her a few paces behind, and of course she loved that although she sensed there was an underlying anxiety in Kate's affection, as if she were asking, 'You do still love me, don't you, even if I was nasty about Hassan?' Rachel answered the unspoken question with a hug. Kate said, 'It's nice for Ouma that you're going. I'll come and help you one day when you're old!'

'Don't you dare ever go and live six thousand miles away from me! I need to see you far more often than that!'

'Poor Ouma,' said Kate.

Then everything happened quickly. Pat said, 'They're calling your flight.' Kate said, 'Hurry, Mom, you'll miss it!' Ben clung to her and said, 'I want to come too,' having been perfectly happy until one minute ago. Simon became pale around the temples, as he did when he was tired or cross. She gave each of them a hug, and went towards the door marked PASSPORT CONTROL - PASSENGERS ONLY. She turned to wave, and saw Pat had Simon's hand and Kate had Ben's; and then she was through, holding out her South African passport that had not been used since she had first arrived, her body tensing involuntarily against having to submit it, and herself, to the scrutiny of the impassive official behind the desk.

PART FOUR

Return

*Must I from time everlasting
Again and again cry out
'Let's leave each other alone!'
But leave me alone they would not.*

Somewhat to her surprise she enjoyed the flight, grateful to be in limbo. She gave polite but unencouraging answers to the chatty overtures of the woman next to her, and for the half hour after take-off sat staring out of the window, her mind numb, watching the clouds sift endlessly by.

Through the night she dozed off and on, her thoughts drifting into dreams and back again. 'I thought you would never come,' said Auntie. 'There were so many things to think of,' Rachel explained, but felt miserable that she had let the so many things stop her, even so. Another time it was Hassan, touching her face, her eyes, saying,

You are like a place with fresh grass after a downpour of rain
On which the sun now shines.

Don't you dare ever go and live six thousand miles away from me, Rachel.' And she was saying, 'Don't be silly, I'm only going to collect some signatures for the petition.'

The first light slipped over the horizon, edging with pink the wisps of cloud beneath them. She became absorbed in following the shape of the land, like a relief map in a primary school classroom - little bumps for mountain ranges, darkened patches where trees grew close together. She was grateful for the chance to take it in from this safe distance before she would have to descend and be part of it again.

The lights in the cabin went on. The pilot hoped they had had a good night. The air hostesses brought round damp cloths to wipe their faces. Breakfast, then landing forms to fill in. Place of birth, Lourensrus, South Africa. Present place of residence, London, UK. She imagined the immigration official looking at her form and then at her, suspicion in his eyes. She could already hear his cold voice saying, scrupulously polite, 'Would you please step this way. There are one or two questions we want to ask you.'

They had landed. She waited until the entire plane had emptied, then followed the last person down the narrow aisle. Out -

The light hit her with such force that she was completely taken aback. An early winter morning, yet still it dazzled her, sweeping her back in memory to a time when the light had been always like this, day in, day out, as natural as the air she had breathed, meriting no comment. Her inner tension had not diminished but her body responded independently, opening out to receive and be received by the cool early morning air, the light, the incredible sense of space.

Almost before she could register these sudden and unexpected sensations, they were in an airport bus heading towards the terminal building, and then she was part of a queue moving slowly towards the immigration officers' desks. She stood behind a group of middle-aged African women, returning from a church conference, maybe? Something unmistakably churchy about their clothes, the kind her mother and Auntie used to wear. What were these black women feeling as they waited for their turn? From the outside there was nothing about them that suggested the tension she was experiencing. Everything seemed so ordinary, so normal.

Her turn came. The official flipped through the pages of her passport, stamped it and handed it back to her without comment. She took it mechanically and walked through to the baggage collection hall. There had been no questions. Well, of course there wouldn't have been. Who did she think she was that they would bother about her?

She had three hours to wait at Jan Smuts airport before her onward flight. In Johannesburg again, yet not in it. The friends whom she had not seen for almost five years were a half hour's bus ride away. But there had been no time to let anyone know she was coming. Perhaps she should phone? And say what? 'Hello, I'm here again, but there's no time to see you.'

The flight to Bloemfontein was in a smaller plane that flew low enough for her to see clearly roads, rivers, farm houses, small towns, the short yellow winter grass of the Free State veld. She began thinking about what she would do when they landed in Bloemfontein. She no longer knew what time the trains left for Lourensrus. If today's train had gone she would phone one of her cousins, Daniel or Sannie, and stay overnight with them.

They landed. She emerged once again into the crisp air, the light, the space. This time the familiarity wrapped itself quietly around her as she walked to the low airport building. A group of black men in overalls ran out to the plane with trolleys for the luggage, another group pulled a long hose, others were weeding the airport gardens. She had forgotten, this endless supply of black manual labour.

She had only been inside the airport building a few moments when she realised that someone was coming towards her, a heavily built man in a suit, about her age. She realised with a shock just before he reached her - Daniel! She had not seen him since - since, she supposed, that disastrous visit he had made to Johannesburg, when he and Alistair had been so tense with each other. More than ten years ago, and now here he was bearing down on her, reaching out his hands to put them on her shoulders just as his father Uncle Dirkie used to do when she was a little girl, and to greet her with the standard family hug and kiss that had been missing from her life for so long.

'Daniel! How on earth did you know?'

'You've forgotten what the Lourensrus grapevine is like!' Without asking he relieved her of her hand luggage (which was not at all heavy). 'Aunt Anna and your mother and mine have been constantly on the telephone for the last four days. I'm driving you to Lourensrus.'

'Driving me! Have you got time?'

'There's a new road. Doesn't take more than an hour and three quarters now.' He was shepherding her, as if she were slightly disabled, towards the baggage reception point. 'In any case, Sannie says I ought to go soon if I want to be sure of seeing Auntie again. I'll stay overnight and come back early tomorrow morning.'

'That's lovely,' she said. 'It'll give us time to see each other. It's been ages.' She felt a rush of pleasure at being back once again in that magic circle of belonging. Her suitcase came towards them on the conveyor belt. She reached forward to get it. 'That blue one?' asked Daniel, and before she could answer he had lifted it off and was checking the label. 'That's all?' he confirmed. Rachel nodded, bemused, and felt herself being propelled towards the swing doors and out into the car park.

Within a few minutes they were on a vast dual carriageway that circled the city and then headed southwest, dead straight for miles ahead. Extraordinary, she thought. What on earth did they want to build a road like this for? There's nothing out there except a few dusty small towns. Sixty miles later she had her answer when a convoy of army vehicles came towards them as they approached Mogetla, a sprawling dormitory town for black workers, out in the middle of nowhere. Everyone knew there was no work in Mogetla. It was simply a labour reserve, keeping the inconvenient sight of black poverty far from the comfortable homes of Bloemfontein's white residents, and forcing workers to make the long journey in delapidated, overcrowded buses every morning and evening. A road like this would make it easy to move in the troops, if there were unrest in Mogetla.

'It's quite a road, isn't it?' Daniel was saying, and she realised with a shock that he was expecting her to share his uncritical pride. 'It's not a patch on the old one,' she parried, not wanting to get drawn so soon into political conflict and destroy the warm sense of connectedness, barely an hour old. 'Do you remember the time we went on holiday, your dad and mine driving in convoy, and our car radiator boiled before we'd even got past Mogetla?'

Daniel talked most of the way, filling her in with news of all the family. After the initial shock of having a man take over her life again she was in fact grateful to be allowed simply to sit and watch the veld unfold before them. Its clear winter colours seemed almost unbelievably beautiful. The yellow-grey grass, the black boulders, the occasional white flip of a longtailed bird, swooping down onto the telegraph wires, to perch, see-sawing like an insecure trapeze artist. The vegetation became sparser, the farmsteads more widely spaced. At a suitable distance from each was the inevitable collection of African huts, where old women bent over their chores and barefoot children stopped in their play to gawp at the car whizzing past, their skimpy clothes reduced to the colour of dust by constant wearing and washing. No young men or women. All gone away, migrant labour into the towns. The old familiar anger flared again. There was no reason why this land could not sustain whole families. It did for white people, like her farming cousins, Willem and Stefan. You just needed enough of it and these people had none, 'squatters' now on land that had been taken away from their ancestors generations ago. Those children probably didn't even know it ought by rights to have been theirs.

The long-forgotten names slipped by on the roadsigns - Donkervlei, Oumanskraal, Uitsig, each one taking her another step back in time - and ahead simply the road, stretching straight to the blue of the distant horizon. She felt she was being absorbed into that magnitude of space, a more fundamental initiation process than the news Daniel was giving her. By the time they pulled off the main road to drive slowly into Lourensrus nothing surprised her anymore, nothing seemed strange, or even striking in its familiarity. She was home, that was all.

*

Rachel was with him each morning as he woke. The first strand of awareness was the sensation of her body next to his, nestling soft and warm in her sleep, then waking to his touch. He would watch with delight as she slipped, with such simplicity, from the almost childlike state of being cradled in his arms to being sexually awake, her body moving against his. He would lie like that, holding on to her presence while at the same time accustoming himself to the fact that she was not literally there. Then he would get up, and the day would be like any other day before she had come into his life.

But it was not the same, for his whole system seemed keyed up beyond its usual pitch. He dealt with each job briskly, wasting no time on unnecessary indecision. But it was an over-tense kind of efficiency, as if every minute she was away had to be used to maximum effect. Since he was not eating until after sundown when Nuh broke his fast, he worked on late at the office each day. I'm acting, he thought, as if time's running out. Time for what? For whom? He was all antennae, looking out for signs, for significance. Something cataclysmic about to happen, he had said to Rachel.

There were spaces inside him and around him, spaces that had been crammed full for more months than he could remember. Moments of silence into which voices appeared, made their statements and moved on again, leaving the sounds sifting around inside him...
Nuh, singing in the bathroom as Hassan woke one morning,

> I long for you, as one
> Whose dhow in summer winds
> Is blown adrift and lost,
> Longs for land - and finds
> A grey and empty sea.

The bathroom door opened and Nuh walked past to the living room. Hassan called out, 'Nuh-*ow*!' Nuh came in to sit on the edge of his bed and said, 'You want me to teach you that song, don't you?'

They laughed and Nuh promptly sang it for him, then again, this time with Hassan joining in.

'It's Eid next week,' Nuh said. Eid, end of Ramadan, time of rejoicing. 'Aadan's aunt is cooking for Eid. Will you join us?'

'Sure!'

'After that, I reckon we can expect some activity from Mohamed and his friends.'

Hassan said sharply, 'What have you heard?'

'Nothing. There's no hard news since the Ethiopians closed down the Movement's radio. It's just my guess. If I were an SNM army commander, I'd wait till Ramadan was over before undertaking anything dramatic.'

So that's what's coming, Hassan thought. Time's running out, for Mohamed...

Mohamed's voice,

> *Must I from time everlasting*
> *maintain servile politeness,*
> *abstain from evil words,*
> *and observe the peace?*

Nuh again, appearing in his office without notice to say, 'Mohamed phoned! From Dire Dawa in Ethiopia!'

Hassan's heart began pumping madly. 'Is there a number where we can call him?'

'They had just arrived in the town and were about to leave today. It was the first time he'd been near a telephone. He sent his salaams.'

'Did he sound OK?'

Nuh laughed. 'He was talking as if he was about to take Hargeisa singlehanded. You can't tell whether it's just Mohamed, or whether it means anything.'

> *Must I from time everlasting*
> *implore each new morning*
> *for restitution for my men*
> *who've been wantonly slaughtered?*

James Freeman, phoning from the Home Office. 'Hassan? Yes, I had some interesting papers land on my desk today, from the press officer of a campaigning group calling itself *Let the children in*. I gather you know something about it.'

So Cliff's been sending press releases to the Home Office! But of course, why not? He said, 'I imagine you remember the case.'

'Indeed. Very regrettable, sorry there wasn't anything I could do.'

'I'm interested that the papers came to your desk. It wasn't even your case, I thought.'

'We do try to keep informed,' James said mildly. 'That's why I was phoning, actually. I gather the situation in Somalia is rather volatile, and it's not terribly easy to find out what's happening. So if you have access to information you think we ought to know about -'

He almost laughed out loud, remembering when he had said, I want to be able to be argue as a respectable caseworker, not be dismissed as a street campaigner.

'Listen,' he told Nuh excitedly that evening, 'things are moving! This man I know in the Home Office, he actually *asked* me to tell him what's happening in Somalia! I promised him a briefing paper. I billed you as a brilliant university lecturer, detailed knowledge, independent views.'

'Me? I'm going to write it?'

'You wanted to tell people here, didn't you? These people are more important than the press. You could make them understand what they would be sending people back to if they denied them asylum.' He rattled on excitedly. 'Has to be short, they won't read anything more than two pages. And you can't let it sound like an SNM propaganda piece.' He paused. 'Will you do it?'

Nuh shrugged as if he couldn't see the point. It was so unlike him that Hassan felt a stab of fear. It's getting to him, hanging around all day with nothing to do but wait for a decision on his case. 'Listen,' he said, forcefully now, 'I need your help. We need to spread this campaign till Haleemo's name becomes a symbol of the wider issue. That meeting in Whitechapel, you'd be the ideal person to organise it.'

'Everyone's too preoccupied with what's happening back home.'

'The worse things become at home, the more people will be forced to flee, and land up in your and Haleemo's position. You can't separate the issues. Talk to Hibo. She knows plenty of people in East London, and she's a fighter. She'd be a good link person between Rachel's lot and yours.'

Nuh looked at him curiously. 'How come you're so optimistic?'

'Optimistic! What gave you that idea?'

'You've always got an answer. Nothing puts you off.'

Hassan said slowly, 'It's the opposite of optimism. I can't cope with the knowledge that there's nothing I can do. About Aabahay. To help you get Amina out. To keep Mohamed safe. This presented itself to me as something I could do, so I'm doing it, that's all.' With renewed urgency he said, 'You have to connect yourself with where you are now. I saw what happened to Mohamed, he couldn't make the psychological adjustment to being on the margins after being right in the centre of a storm, so he acted as if the only part of Britain that existed was the Somali community. That's fine for short-term survival but you may have to stay a long time.'

'And you? You're at the opposite extreme. You keep yourself so separate.'

'I am separate. That's history, part of who I am. Somalis are a part of the London I inhabit, not the whole of it. And if you're going to have to live here you'll have to try and make it that way for you too. You're too big a person to be confined to a ghetto.'

Nuh said, cautiously, 'I could talk to Aadan.'

'Early June would be a good time,' Hassan said, pressing his advantage. 'SNM will almost certainly be organising something for the 26th like they did last year. Our event could be part of the build up to that.'

'You don't waste time, do you?'

'There may not be time to waste.'

Must I from time everlasting...

He pulled the office door locked behind him and walked out into the street - their street, where they had run in such abandon the day she had come to him to say, 'We need time together.' And now he was assailed by pictures of Rachel. Rachel in Battersea Park, looking up at the trees and saying, 'It always amazes me, the way they never get defeated by winter.' On the phone saying, 'It feels harder to walk out on the campaign than on my children.' Rachel laughing, Rachel crying, Rachel's face full of delight, of anger, Rachel challenging him, listening to him, touching him.

That evening he phoned Pat. Even dialling the number, Rachel's number, was pleasurable. Kate answered, her voice closing off when she heard who it was. To Pat he said, 'I just wondered how you were doing.' She laughed, 'I'm ready for bed when Ben is! I don't know how Rachel does it.' A brass note sounded, very wobbly. Hassan said, 'She probably doesn't aim to give them saxophone lessons before bed! Could you use any help? Babysitting, or whatever?'

'You couldn't do Sunday, could you? There's a band practice I don't want to have to miss.'

'Sure I could, if Kate doesn't object.'

'I'm not going to give her a lot of choice! I have to go, Ben's yelling from the bathroom. Come about twelve.'

The phone was down, that brief, tenuous contact with Rachel's world once again cut off.

And now something began to wake him early each morning - the voices, or the spaces themselves. The first time it happened he assumed it was just a matter of stirring in his sleep. He opened his eyes long enough to look at his watch - four thirty - and lift the blind to see that the light was just up. Then closed his eyes and expected sleep to return. It did not. He was fully awake. He got up and sat by the window looking out at the silent street, as he had done on the night when he had sung a Somali song to Rachel, and had known that if he could only keep from rushing her, she would come to him.

It happened again the next morning, and the next. He came to accept now as he went to sleep that the next thing he would be aware of was the first still light of morning, the silence interrupted only by the repeated chirping of a sparrow. His spirit more than his body was waking him, to claim for itself that quiet time alone before the day would begin.

Time alone. It seemed strange to be welcoming it, inviting in that quietness. Through all these last months he had been fighting time, running from it, demanding more from it than it could give, driven by his urgent need to be with Rachel and before that to escape from thinking of his father. And before that? Had it been like that before too? The continual pressure of his work, the community centre, friends, finding Farida and losing her - perhaps he had been living in this over-intense, grabbing way for longer than he knew. Now he sat alone at the window watching the light gently strengthen, the outlines of the trees clarify and take on colour against the clear May sky, and saw Rachel's beautiful open face and felt the simplicity of her warmth, and he knew that in her going away just as in her presence she was calming him, helping him to learn to be quiet, and to accept.

And then a morning came when he knew it was now time not to sit here any longer but to be outside and walk, to be nearer to the trees, part of that early morning light. Quietly so as not to disturb Nuh he dressed and let himself out, and walked along the silent pavements till he came to the park, only to find the gates still locked. So he walked round the perimeter, slowly, not walking to get anywhere, stopping frequently to look in through the borders of shrubs to the grass and the tall trees, each standing alone and strong and sure of itself. He remembered how he had lain on that grass at the depth of his depression after the suicide of the young Kurdish boy, and had known that he would have to find in himself a way past despair.

By the time he reached the far side of the park the world had begun to wake. A milkfloat went by, and a cat. There were other people on the pavement now, walking purposefully. Cleaners, perhaps, heading for the offices where they would do their two hours and be gone before the office workers arrived. He realised he was now only a couple of streets away from his mother's flat. Without any special thought or tension he changed course and arrived at her front door. No need to wake her, he had a key to her flat on his own key ring, her protection in case of emergency. Quietly he let himself in.

'I thought you might like tea in bed for a change.' He set the tray down on the floor and perched on the edge of her bed. She leant up on one elbow and took the mug, laughing with pleasure. She put out a hand to briefly ruffle his hair, still damp from the morning air. Her own hair was dishevelled, falling around her face and onto her shoulders in a way he seldom saw it these days. 'You're mad, Hassan. Where have you been?'

'Early morning walk.'

'I don't see you for months and then you arrive at dawn. What's going on?'

'Too much,' he said. 'I needed to be quiet, that's all. You know Nuh's been living with me?' There was a quick flicker of appreciation in her eyes that made him know she had understood what that meant to him, both the joy and the constraints. Before she could say anything to spoil it he said, 'Your garden's looking beautiful. I had tea on the patio while I was waiting for a reasonable hour to wake you!'

'I've spent a lot more time in it this year. It's good therapy, I find.'

Therapy - for what ill? For anxiety about his father? He wanted to hear her say it but was afraid to ask in case he got the wrong answer. And then Rachel was with him, saying, 'You'd be telling her for her sake, not for yours.' He wanted to say, Mom, Aabahay's ill and we don't know if the medicines are getting to him... But the moment had gone. She was talking about blackfly, and how she hated the idea of spraying but would maybe have to this year.

When he left she said, 'That was a delightful mug of tea!' and he knew that from this simple, spontaneous act he had made her happier than in all their meals and concerts for several years past. The knowledge was a burden, but he accepted it. It's OK what we have, he thought as he walked back. She isn't capable of more and I only create tensions by wanting it. The only thing to do is accept her as she is, us as we are.

Nuh's face as he greeted him was more alive than Hassan had seen it since his arrival. 'Sabah sends her greetings!'

'You got through!'

'They've just phoned me. I still don't know where they've been. Amina and the baby are leaving for Hargeisa, as soon as they can find a truck driver they can trust.'

'Is there such a thing?'

'She doesn't have a choice, she can't get a visa. There are hardly any Somalis in the embassy now and you know you can't bribe the English.' He caught Hassan's eye, his half-English cousin. They both laughed. 'Once she's in Hargeisa,' Nuh went on, 'my father will get her to Ismail in Djibuti and he'll fix her up with papers.'

He's losing all sense of reality, Hassan thought, he's talking as if it's all going to happen.

'When they get here,' Nuh was saying, 'there isn't going to be room for us all in your flat. Tell me how to start looking for my own place. The places the others live in are terrible, I'm not bringing her to that.'

'Leave it till she gets here,' said Hassan, turning away so that Nuh did not see that his eyes were saying, if she ever does.

> *Must I from time everlasting*
> *coax into false calmness*
> *the husbandless wife*
> *and the fatherless child?*
> *Must I from time everlasting...*

2

'They all keep going away.' Auntie stared past her at the white wall of the room from which she had not moved for the past two months. Her eyes rested on Rachel's face. They stared. Staring seemed to require great effort. Her eyes were set far back in her small head. The skin on her cheeks hung in lifeless brown folds. Rachel wanted to caress it, that skin which had never been touched by those stupid creams. 'They all keep going away,' Auntie said.

At first Rachel thought that though Auntie stared at her she did not see her, or perhaps did not recognise her, but then she began to understand that this was not so. The eyes saw her and knew that it was Rachel, the grown-up Rachel who, like all the others on whom she had spent her love, had gone away. What was there for her to respond to in such a face?

The eyes moved on, as if looking for the others. Beyond the white wall with the pictures of Jesus in long robes and long hair Rachel saw them too, the faces of all Auntie's nieces and nephews. Matthew, who was too busy with his career to spare the time to come to see her. Daniel, who stood here now because Auntie was dying, but how often had he been before that? James with his business in Durban that was always failing, could never be left. Jill who had gone to Cape Town to be a dancer and had never been seen in Lourensrus since. Stefan and Willem who were so bound up with their new methods of irrigation. She, Rachel, who lived six thousand miles away. All those years Auntie had read them stories, and squeezed oranges for them when they were ill, and knitted socks for the boys and dolls' clothes for the girls, and let all of them ruffle endlessly among her drawers and cupboards that were stacked with things that would one day come in useful. And in all the years since they had grown up how many of them had done more than remember her at Christmas and on her birthday? Only Sannie had kept faith, driving down from Bloemfontein almost every Sunday to see her mother, Aunt Anna, and every time making sure that she brought her children to see Auntie also, giving her another generation of nieces and nephews to be an outlet for her love.

Daniel was saying, 'I'll leave you to have some time alone with her.' When he had gone she pulled up a chair and sat close to Auntie's face, and holding her hands began to talk to her. She told her about her children and the things they said and did. She remembered aloud the things Auntie had said to her when she was little, things Auntie had taught her which had stayed with her, always. She talked quietly, with lots of pauses so that she didn't tire her. Watching the watery, staring eyes for signs of a response, she had the clear impression that Auntie was there, the whole person, trapped inside a body that could no longer express to those outside the strength of her awareness. The eyes of an old, suffering body, not of Auntie herself, looked out blankly at Rachel, but inside somewhere was a conscious person who was listening to every word she said.

She stood with her mother in the doorway of the room where she was to sleep, the one she had visited again so recently in her dream, the room that had once been Auntie's own. When it had become too full of all the things she accumulated, Auntie had abandoned it to the piles of cloth and church magazines and overflowing drawers, and had moved, without sentiment, into what had been until then the spare room. She took with her only her nightdresses, underclothes, and the pictures of Jesus. The room remained her room except for sleeping. 'I can't believe it,' Rachel said. 'It's exactly as I remember it!'

'When I first came to live with her I tried to sort it out,' her mother said, 'but she minded so much that I had to stop. I wanted to make it nice for you. I could have done it now, with her lying there not knowing what's going on, but it seemed underhand.'

'This is the way it's nice for me. I shall love sleeping here.'

After they'd had tea Aunt Anna instructed Daniel to take Rachel's mother over to see Mrs. van Niekerk. When they had gone Rachel said, switching automatically to Afrikaans as she always did with Aunt Anna, 'My mother looks ten years older than when I last saw her.'

'It's the last two months that have done it, child. I'm glad you've come.'

'I'm glad you called me. I'm only sorry I didn't see for myself earlier that I should come. I just assumed I was stuck on the other side of the world and there was nothing I could do.'

'You'll have to get that husband of yours to stay home a bit more often, then you can come again. For a proper visit, when all this is over.'

'Aunt Anna, didn't you know Alistair and I were separated?'

Aunt Anna looked sharply at her. 'Your mother never said anything.'

'No, I gathered that when you phoned me. She's known for two years.'

'Things don't change here as fast as for you young people. She probably thought people would be shocked.'

'Are you?'

'I'm sorry for you, that's all. In my day we knew marriage was for life and we just got on with it.' Rachel waited, knowing Aunt Anna wouldn't be able to resist an attack on Alistair. It came. 'Mind you, none of us will miss that man of yours. He did you no good, him and his politics.'

Do I fight, or don't I? thought Rachel, and then decided that if she let the first round go without a struggle, they would be on top of her the whole two weeks. 'He's a good man in many ways,' she said. 'And I admire the work he does. It was personal things that went wrong between us, not politics.'

Aunt Anna glared at her and did not answer directly. 'I hope you know, Rachel, that this is not the time to be having political arguments with your mother.'

Rachel smiled. 'I know. I just thought you should know where I stand.'

'It's pointless,' her mother said. And then, switching to Afrikaans, 'I can't settle to anything. I might as well be with Auntie and let you rest.'

'It's not me who needs rest, Mom, it's you.' She took both her mother's hands. 'Aunt Anna says I'm the only one who can give you orders, but I don't seem to be very successful! Now listen!' She made her voice exaggeratedly firm. 'I'm staying with Auntie every morning, and if you don't want to rest, get out of the house and visit one of your friends. You can be with her as much as you feel you need to in the afternoons. And when you want a break, we'll ask Maria to take over for a bit to give us time together.'

For the next hour she heard her mother moving around in the kitchen, talking to Maria. Then silence. Maria came in. 'Tea, *klein mies*,' she said. *Klein mies*, little madam. Maria had called each of the girls that since their childhood. Too late to change now. Rachel took the cup from the tray. 'Thanks,' she whispered, not to disturb Auntie who had drifted off for a moment. When she woke, the pain would return. Let her sleep. 'Where's my mother?'

Maria said, conspiratorial, 'The *ou mies*, she's sleeping!'

'Good. And what about you? Why don't you go and rest now I'm here?'

'Ee, klein mies,' Maria chuckled quietly, as if Rachel had said something really humorous.

'I'm serious, Maria. You must be as tired as my mother. Go and rest, I can call you when I need help.'

'A-a, klein mies, I am used to it. I don't need rest!' And she went off, still chuckling.

On some mornings she hardly spoke to Auntie at all, except for the little running commentary to coax her through the succession of things that had to be done to her. Rachel heard her own voice instinctively taking on the soothing tone one uses only with the very young or the very elderly, to assure them that all is well when everyone knows that all is not well. It's all right, Auntie, Maria and I are just going to turn you onto your side for a little, just to get the pressure off your back. Come, Auntie, just a tiny bit more water. You've only had two sips. Let's try with the straw this time. Just let me sit you up a little higher. One more sip, there we go.

Occasionally there would be a period, perhaps ten minutes, when Auntie needed nothing and would lie with staring, vacant eyes. Then Rachel would talk softly to her, holding her hand, and she would be still and seem for the moment to be released from the tyranny of her body's discomfort. Rachel kept talking as long as the stillness remained.

There was no clue from Auntie as to what kinds of things she wanted to hear, so Rachel followed her instinct and told her about her children, as if they were here in Lourensrus, playing outside in Auntie's garden as she had done as a child, and might come in at any minute to say that Ben had fallen out of the loquat tree. She described how good Kate was at looking after little ones, 'She's got your gift, Auntie.' How Ben ran off in the playground each morning to join whoever happened to be there, 'Always sure of his welcome, the way you used to tell me Aunt Anna was when she was a little girl.' About Simon, and since there was no one in the family she could think of that he was like, she just let him be Simon, and told Auntie how in the holidays he had learnt to make gingerbread men from her and sibaayad from Hibo. As she was describing this she realised that of all her relatives Auntie was the only one to whom it seemed natural to talk about Hibo and Haleemo and Hassan. So she did that too, describing how they had had to leave their country because of a government that would not let ordinary people live in dignity, and that put good people like Hassan's father and Hibo's husband in jail. She knew that Auntie as she had once been would have understood all that, she, the only one of them who had been prepared to let herself see what was going on around her.

But every morning Rachel began her stories for Auntie in the same way, to be sure that if her body did not allow her to listen for long she would at least hear this one thing. She talked of the time when Auntie used to take her in her car to the township, how she had remembered those journeys all her life, and how they had made possible the things that were strongest in her.

Auntie lay still, and stared. Then she turned her face to the wall and said, 'They all keep going away.'

*

Midday. Maria came to relieve her. Rachel stretched to awaken her limbs, to get ready to live again in the world outside this room. She slipped quietly into the passage and out to the *stoep*, the verandah. After the diminished light of Auntie's room the glare accosted her, wonderfully welcome. She stood looking up at Duiwelskop, then went down the three steps from the stoep to the ground, and round the house to the corner beyond the loquat tree where she and Daniel used to mark out hopscotch squares in the sand. Yes, it was warm there, sheltered from wind by the angle of the walls. She went inside to find her mother, in the kitchen staring into a cupboard. 'Auntie must have about two hundred bottles in here,' her mother said.

'Forget her bottles, Mom. I've found a warm place in the garden. Come and sit with me.'

'It's pointless them taking up room in the cupboards.' And then, 'But I couldn't bear just to throw them away, they came with my mother from Oupa's farm.' And then again, 'But I don't know who would want them. No one does bottling any more these days.'

'Close the door,' Rachel said, doing it for her, and then took her arm. 'Come, we're going outside.'

'It'll be cold. I'll need another jersey.'

'It's warmed up a lot since this morning. But get another jersey if you like.'

Her mother moved towards her room. 'Ask Maria to bring us some tea.'.

'Maria's with Auntie, I'll do the tea.' Ask Maria. Ask Maria to bring me my spectacles, ask Maria if the post has come yet, ask Maria - Ask me! Rachel wanted to shout. Can't you see Maria's as tired as you are? It's absurd for me to get up from the dinner table to walk into the kitchen and say, Maria, please go to my mother's room and fetch her spectacles, when I could just as easily have fetched them myself.

She carried the tray out and saw that her mother was already sitting there. 'I'm glad to see you doing as you're told for once!' she said, and suddenly, perhaps simply because of the tone of banter she had used, she felt Hassan's presence and longed to be with him again.

Her mother talked continuously, a catalogue of minor worries. Rachel let it flow over her, knowing that nothing more was required of her than to receive it and make occasional comments. When there was finally a pause long enough for her to initiate something, she asked, 'What's the news of Martha?'

'I haven't heard anything of her for years. When I sold the house and came to live here with Auntie she went to work for old Mrs. Venter. But I heard she didn't last long there.'

'What happened?'

'Mrs Venter said she was too cheeky.'

'Cheeky? Martha?'

Her mother shrugged. 'You know what old Mrs. Venter is like, she could never keep servants. And Martha was used to working for us, she probably didn't like the way Mrs Venter spoke to her.'

Rachel felt a rush of fury. There were a hundred things she wanted to say, but she suppressed them. She would only make her mother more tense. When she thought she could speak again without sounding angry she said, 'Daniel said he'd come again next week. I've booked him for a climb up Duiwelskop!'

'I can't see why you always want to go up it,' her mother said. 'Your father was just the same. There's nothing up there but rocks and thorns.'

'I like rocks,' Rachel said, and they were on safe ground once again.

She chose her moment carefully. It had been a better than average day. Auntie had not been too restless, and she and her mother had taken a good half hour's walk to see Mrs. van Niekerk's garden. 'There's nothing in it at the moment,' said Mrs. van Niekerk. 'You should come in summer.' But to Rachel it was full of plants she had not seen for years, and even then had not bothered to notice properly because she had not known a time would come when she would not be surrounded by gardens like this one. Mrs. van Niekerk gave them home-made *melktert*, an egg and milk mixture cooked to the proper boer recipe, silky smooth and sprinkled with cinnamon sugar. Rachel could see that it pleased her mother to watch her enjoying all these things again.

So it seemed safe to venture a little further. When they had handed over to the night nurse and were sitting companionably in front of the fire Rachel said, 'I'd like to go and see the township, see how it's changed. Can I borrow your car?'

'No you can't,' barked her mother, so unlike the person she had been all day that Rachel was shocked into silence. Her mother tried to recover a little grace. 'It's very dangerous these days. You have no idea. You've been away a long time, you don't know the things that have been happening. I'm not having you expose yourself to danger.'

In as mild a voice as she could manage Rachel said, 'Mom, I'm not thinking of going at dead of night. I meant tomorrow, after lunch. All I want to do is drive there and walk around a little.' She had made things worse. 'You are under no circumstances to get out of the car,' her mother said fiercely, and illogically since she was refusing to let her use the car at all. 'I tell you, things happen to people there.'

'Who do you know who goes there?'

'No one goes there. It's not safe.'

'So if no one goes there, how do things happen to them?'

'Rachel, you are determined to be obstinate.' She sounded tearful now, unable to cope with disagreement.

'Forget it, Mom, I didn't mean to upset you. How about some Ovaltine before bed?'

The next day she said, 'I thought of going out to get a bit of fresh air.'

'You do that,' said her mother. 'You need it.'

'I'll go and say hello to Mr. Kaplan.' Immediately her mother's tone changed. 'He's become so bad tempered since his arthritis got worse,' she warned. And when that didn't seem enough to deter Rachel, 'And he really doesn't take care of himself properly.' Meaning, Rachel knew, that he didn't shave often enough and had foodstains down his front. 'Never mind,' said Rachel, 'I still want to see him.'

Mr Kaplan was no scruffier than he had always been, and just as pleased to see her. 'Do you still feed the cats?' she asked.

'Come and see.' He took her out to the back. The moment he opened the old gauze door leading from the kitchen into the yard the cats appeared, at least five of them, mangy as Mr Kaplan himself, rubbing up against his legs and miaowing in short, demanding little cries. Rachel went through the ritual of helping him feed them, to the immense satisfaction of both of them. When they were back inside she said, 'Mr Kaplan, will you lend me your car? I want to go to the township and my mother's not happy about me taking hers there.' Mr Kaplan snorted and shook his head, whether at her mother for being over-careful, or at her for being over-rash, she did not know. But he accepted her, as he had always done, on her own terms.

The car was the one he had been driving when she was a schoolgirl and it looked as if it hadn't been serviced since. If the road to the township is anything like it used to be, she thought, this jalopy will fall to pieces before I get there, and then my mother really will freak out. 'Are there any special instructions?' she asked.

'Just drive it. If it breaks down, send a *pikanin* to fetch me.'

She pictured what he was seeing. Catch hold of any child who happens to be passing. Say, hey, *pikanin*, here's ten cents, go and fetch Baas Kaplan. She said, 'Maybe I should just walk!'

'You drive my car,' he said firmly. 'Your mother wouldn't like it if I let you walk there.'

She began to laugh helplessly and he joined her, laughing in conspiracy, two renegades who had never quite belonged. When she had recovered she asked, 'Has there really been violence in the township here? I know there has everywhere else, but Lourensrus looks as if nothing has changed.'

'Just the usual gangs of *tsotsies*. Nothing political.' Because of that shared laugh she risked challenging him a little. 'Wouldn't it be better if it were political? People who burn down police stations are fighting back against something that's oppressed them. Surely that's better than *tsotsies* killing someone just so they can take his pay packet?'

'Girl, take my car and go, I don't want to argue with you. It's all very well for you to have fancy ideas. I have to live in this town.'

Miraculously, the car started first time. It shuddered and made a terrible noise, and had no suspension worth speaking of, it complained about every pothole in the dirt road just as Auntie's car had done, but it worked. She felt odd to be driving herself there, but otherwise everything about the journey was familiar. The children with their bare, skinny legs running to the roadside to watch as the car went by. The dust that billowed up from the untarred road to envelop them, however slowly she drove. The low huddle of buildings appearing as the car rounded the last spur of Duiwelskop. Nearer, and the huddle separated out into hundreds of individual buildings, their corrugated iron roofs still held on with bricks. Nothing had changed, nothing, and the anger rose within her, a fierce anger against all those people she loved who shut themselves inside their safe houses on the other side of Duiwelskop from where the township was hidden from sight, and didn't want to know.

She could not have said before she reached the township which road she would have to take to Martha's house. The car just seemed to get her there. She pulled up. Before she could pick her way over the broken bottles and bits of cardboard that lay between her and the door three children had appeared from nowhere and were staring at her curiously. She asked, in Afrikaans, 'Does Martha Mogoera still live here?' The children continued to stare. Then the oldest one darted in to the house, to reappear with a woman who looked about eighty years old, bent and shrivelled, her skin hanging from her. '*Dumela, meh,*' Rachel said. Good morning, mother. And then, having run out of Tswana, she repeated her question in Afrikaans. The old woman turned to the oldest child and they had a rapid conversation in Tswana. The boy interpreted, 'She live here before. Then she go away.'

'Does your grandmother know where she went?'

Another long conversation. The boy turned again to Rachel and said, 'No.'

'No idea at all?' Surely she must have said something else in all that long exchange.

'She go. Some other place.'

'She used to work in my parents' house when I was a child. I have been away a long time and now I am back I want to see her. Tell your grandmother I will be so glad if she can tell me anything about where she went, so that maybe I can visit her.'

'She sick. She go away some place far. She not know where.'

'OK,' Rachel gave up. She touched the old woman's thin dried up hands. 'Thank you, *meh*. Go well.'

Back in the car she weaved her way between the potholes, avoiding the mangy dog that lay asleep in the middle of the road, easing through the group of children who gathered to inspect the car as it passed. Then past the clinic, the police station, the one run-down shop, and on to the school. She parked in Auntie's spot under the pepper trees and climbed out. This, too, was just as it had been, a long low brick building with a stoep running the length of it, terribly in need of maintenance. Daniel had spoken glibly about all the money that was being spent on schools for blacks. Well it certainly hadn't reached Lourensrus. Aunt Anna had taken her to see the new gymnasium and science block at the white school. No expense spared, donation from an old boy. They always win, Rachel thought. Which old boy from this school is going to have money for a science block?

The afternoon shift children were filing out into the dusty yard. She looked at her watch. Three thirty, assembly time, even the timetable had not changed. She remembered arriving once with Auntie just at this time, and Auntie holding her back to stand unnoticed to one side. Rachel had liked being there, for once not being stared at by the children, free to watch the row upon row of heads with tight black curls. The headmaster had marched ceremoniously out of his office and begun to address them, a harangue about bad behaviour - the tone was instantly recognisable though Rachel understood none of the words. The rows of curly black heads remained impassive, waiting for the lecture to end.

And then the singing began. First the voice of one of the teachers rose into the still, crisp air of early winter. She tried to peer past the taller children to find the owner of that voice, deep and rich, carrying far beyond the school yard as if calling to people they could not see. The sound went over her but also into her, making her alert. Then the voices of three hundred children burst over her in unison, strong and sure, breaking into effortless harmony that gave the music depth and power beyond anything she had ever experienced.

For a few moments she was unaware of anything except the soaring fullness of that sound. Then gradually she began to realise that they were singing a hymn, and though the words were in Tswana the tune was one she knew, *All people that on earth do dwell.* She had sung it many times in her own school assembly, but she was stunned by the contrast, by the miracle of mere children like herself being able to produce sounds of such strength and beauty.

The voices stopped. The air was cold around her bare knees. The pupils were filing back into their classrooms, talking to each other as if nothing special had happened. Auntie had taken her hand and was heading towards the office. Rachel whispered, 'How do they learn to sing like that?'

Auntie was preoccupied. 'That's just the way they sing,' she said. 'I don't think anyone teaches them.'

3

'We agreed no phone calls,' he wrote, 'but you said nothing about letters, and certainly not poems. So I enclose one I've translated for you, as per instructions.'

Then he changed his mind, tore up the note and sealed the envelope with only the anonymous poem inside.

> *He who has lain between her breasts can call his life fulfilled.*
> *Oh God, may I never be denied the well of happiness.*

The Eid party for which Aadan's aunt had cooked was crowded and noisy, the smell and taste of food such as he had not experienced for years, the company just as his father would have liked it. He kept expecting to be caught up in these rare, specific pleasures, but the newfound quietness stayed within him all evening. When eventually he decided it was time to go, Nuh to his surprise and pleasure joined him, taking for granted that they would leave together.

In the train on the way back Nuh asked, 'How long is it since you kept the fast?'

Hassan calculated. 'About twelve years, I suppose. Since I was seventeen or so.'

'But you used to when you were in Mogadishu, surely?'

'That was different. When everyone around you is fasting, you don't ask for meals in the middle of the day.'

'And here? You never kept it in England?'

'When I was at school, for a few years. But you wouldn't have approved of the motive.'

'Go on, try me.'

'It was mainly to defy the teachers. I saw the kind of flak the Pakistani kids got from a couple of the teachers when they were fasting. It's bad for your health, your parents shouldn't let you do it while you're studying - making it sound like concern for their well-being, but going on at them, constant remarks. It made me mad, so the next year I kept the fast along with the Pakistanis. You might say it was my first political act!' Nuh was smiling. Hassan continued. 'I persuaded the others to come with me to talk to the headteacher before Ramadan started. We said we wanted him to make it clear to the staff that religion was a personal matter and it wasn't their business to discourage us.'

'It's not the orthodox reason for fasting,' Nuh laughed, 'but I've known worse.'

'Actually I'm exaggerating. It may have been only defiance at first, but once I'd taken up a position I had to work out what I thought so I could defend it!' The Pakistani boys had fasted because their parents said, you're a Muslim and Muslims fast in Ramadan. No reasons. That didn't seem to him a lot better than the teachers' attitudes. 'It was an English teacher who helped me most, actually. He'd worked in Morocco and got interested in Islam, though he wasn't a Muslim himself. He used to lend me books and we'd discuss them. Then I started going to the mosque with one of his friends. It was an important part of my life for a year or two.'

Nuh was looking at him oddly.

'Go on,' said Hassan. 'What are you thinking?'

'That you have the right instincts but you won't let yourself be guided. It's a kind of intellectual pride with you, to feel that you have to think everything out for yourself.'

'Don't you?'

'Not the ultimate truths. None of us has the power to do that.' The certainty in Nuh's voice transported him momentarily, to early morning in his father's house, waking to the sound of prayers being recited on the radio. And before that, sitting crosslegged on the ground with Mohamed and the other small boys in the Quranic school, chanting the Arabic syllables... He came back to Nuh, sitting opposite him in the train, waiting for him to explain. How could he convey to a man who had lived all his life in that unbroken tradition why the teaching had not stuck with him?

Nuh was asking, 'Was it your mother? Did she try to stop you?'

'What kind of a question is that?' Hassan snapped. 'She married a Muslim!'

'But she left him.'

'That had nothing to do with it.'

'Calm down, Hassan. I'm only trying to understand.'

Hassan smiled an apology. 'OK. It's just - I suppose -' He was thinking, if I understood my mother better myself I probably wouldn't react so defensively. But he didn't feel like saying it, even to Nuh.

'Someone told me,' Nuh said, 'that you once nearly married a Muslim woman?' Hassan looked up. 'Was she a Somali?'

'No, an Indian Muslim. And if you want to know, it was precisely her parents' blinkered concept of their Islamic duty that prevented it!'

Nuh said calmly. 'Everyone has to sort out what is archaic custom and what is true Islam. Submission should only be to the will of Allah, not of man.' He paused. 'A Muslim woman you loved and you didn't marry her. It's a pity.'

'I also thought it a pity,' Hassan said drily. 'But it's extremely unlikely that marrying her would have changed my views, as marrying a non-Muslim wouldn't have changed yours!'

All Sunday afternoon with Rachel's children, Hassan's insecurity flared. Kate had gone to Becky's for the day. 'Boycott?' he asked, and Pat's wry smile told him that he was right. 'She'll get over it,' Pat said, but he thought, the longer she takes, the more anxious Rachel will become. Ben too was a trifle suspicious, but he came round after Simon had suggested Hassan take them on the common with their bikes. The moment they got there the boys took off like dogs let off the lead. Hassan ran after them, till he realised it was useless and slowed down to a walk, waiting for them to circle back to him. Alone in the middle of the common with the wide expanse of grass around him, he watched the parents at the playground end pushing swings and guiding tricycles, and for the first time he tried to assess on what basis he and Rachel could continue being together. Until now he had imagined nothing further than a continuation of the private world they had created for themselves, absconding, as it were, abandoning all other commitments to concentrate entirely on each other. But of course it couldn't go on like that indefinitely. And if he wanted to live with her it would be he who would have to give up his way of life to join hers, not the other way round. Recognising that was a shock, for since the night she had said, 'If I had nobody to think of but myself I'd live in a place exactly like this,' he had without being aware of it envisaged their life together as being on his ground. But now he saw that of course the children would need to stay in their own home, with their schools and friends near by. Was he ready for that? And how would he feel when he came home to her at the end of the day, to find her preoccupied with the children, and he would have to wait hours in a place that was not his own before she had any attention to spare for him?

Then he thought of the other possibility, that Rachel would say, 'It's not fair on Kate, we can't do it.' And they would be back to occasional nights together, each requiring separate negotiation.

No, no, no!

He stayed to help Pat get the children settled for the night. 'I'm into it now, I might as well,' he said, and took Ben up to give him his bath while Pat got their supper ready. When he came down again Pat said, 'The women-and-children's march to the MP - it seems a real shame not to have anyone filming it. You're sure you can't think of anyone we could contact? Cliff's drawn a blank.'

'I'd have told you long ago if I did,' he said - and then suddenly remembered his mother's friend Penny, about whose latest film he had been hearing each time he and his mother met. Pat said, 'You do!' He was about to explain that he couldn't possibly involve his mother in this, when he was caught by another unexpected memory, Rachel saying, 'It was losing people I was afraid of. I'm sure that's why I never found a way to act.' He had been so confident in his answers. Fighting means knowing what you have to do and doing it, he had said. If we think differently we have to fight and it won't diminish our love for each other...

Before he could change his mind he phoned his mother. 'I'm coming round to see you,' he said.

'Now?' she sounded surprised at the urgency.

'Mom, there's a campaign I'm involved in. I need your help.'

His mother answered the door dressed in old dungarees and with hands covered in garden soil. 'Come and see, I've just been putting in some plants I treated myself to.' She took him out through the kitchen to the patio and the small patch of lawn and flowerbeds. 'The clematis, see?' It was up against the furthest wall, bearing one proud flower, waxy whitish-purple, touched by the summer evening light. Hassan gave her a hug. 'You're full of creativity, aren't you?'

'Merely an agent. I've had a clematis up here on the patio for two years. I gave it the largest pot I had, but after the first year it went on strike. They refuse to thrive in pots. Come, let's go inside. I'll wash all this off my hands.'

She asked him if he would like to stay and eat, and began to chat about an exhibition she had been to see, till he almost wondered whether he had said what he thought he had said on the phone. But he had, he knew it, they were just slipping into the old habit of easy openness about all the things that didn't matter and avoiding the things that did. 'Mom,' he interrupted, 'this campaign, it's really important that we get television coverage. I wondered if Penny could help?'

'Tell me about it,' she said.

'There's a Somali woman who can't get permission to bring her children in from Hargeisa,' he said, and then rushed on with the details, not giving her a chance to react. Within minutes the initial tension had faded and he was telling her not only about Haleemo but about Rachel, for there was no other way to describe how the campaign had started - and the release of being able to talk about her was so great that it banished all other considerations. He described how he had instantly loved in her the way she had responded to a need that was not her own, how her unselfconscious face was always alive, concentrating on the other person. 'I'm afraid of losing her, like I lost Farida.' His own voice startled him. He had not known he was going to say that, nor had he even been conscious of the thought. 'I feel alive with her, full of joy in a way that I haven't since Farida left. I'm afraid of losing that again. Her children - her daughter resents me. I don't want Rachel to have to choose between me and the children because I know who would win! There's been too much loss lately. Aabahay, things getting worse all the time in Somalia, Mohamed - I haven't told you, but he's gone back. I couldn't bear to lose Rachel too.'

'Does she know you feel that?'

'I'm saying this all wrong. At one level I know there's no question of her leaving me, she's the kind of person you know you can trust. But she has so many demands on her time and she's not about to drop other people just because she's found a lover. I love that in her, but it means there's terribly little space left for us. And now her going away so suddenly.'

'Perhaps you should phone her.'

'We decided it was too complicated. Her mother hasn't yet accepted that she's separated.'

His mother raised her eyebrows. 'Rachel's not told her? That does sound a bit like Farida!'

'She has told her,' he said defensively. 'Her mother just doesn't want to know.' This is no bloody good, he thought. There's far too much she doesn't understand about Rachel. I was crazy to try. 'Forget it, Mom. Let's talk about something else.' She made no comment. He stood looking out of the kitchen window onto the garden, watching a thrush in the corner by the dwarf rhododendron. An internal voice nagged at him, you can do better than this. It was he who was closing off doors, not she. He knew it yet he seemed unable to stop himself. With an effort he said, 'I'm sorry I was so abrupt.' He turned to face her. 'The moment things go wrong we seem to fall back on the old habits. I want to get past that. There's too much happening. I'm afraid if we don't learn to talk to each other about it we're going to sink into meaningless platitudes forever.'

'It's as much my fault as yours. I also want to try.' Then she stopped, as if she didn't know how to proceed.

'The thing I find hardest is that you will never talk about Aabahay. Rachel once said -'

'Hassan, I've been thinking. About Rachel and Farida.' He tensed, defensive again. She said, 'From what I've gathered, Rachel took a while deciding to let herself love you.'

'I spent weeks waiting for her when I thought it must be as obvious to her as to me what was happening. She was like that about the campaign, too. Her first reaction is, leave me alone, I was fine the way I was. But she's too honest to stay that way. When something's in front of her she makes herself look at it, and when she's worked out what she should do, she does it. One day she just walked into my office and said, we need more time together.'

'There you are, that's very different from Farida, isn't it? If Rachel spent time struggling with her fears beforehand, it's more likely that she can sustain what she's taken on.'

'Yes,' he said, surprised, 'I suppose it is.' She had turned and had started automatically washing a couple of mugs that had been stacked in the sink. He could almost feel her closing herself in, somewhere unreachable. 'You're doing it again,' he said, his voice hard in his urgency. 'There's something else you're thinking and you're deciding not to say it. Why do you keep cutting me out?' She swung round as if stung, and flung back at him, 'I don't want to cut you out!'

'Then don't!'

'It's - Hassan it's hard for you to understand.'

'Then it's your job to tell me more, so I can.' He relaxed, and took a step forward to put an arm around her. 'I'm no longer a child. I haven't been one for many years.'

'That's part of it, I suppose.' She released herself from his hug, gently, but definitely needing to stand separate from him. 'When you were younger I didn't want to land all that adult bitterness on you. And then once you were grown up, you were busy with things of your own. There seemed no point in going over ancient history.'

'It's now no longer ancient history. Not since Aabahay was put in prison. I need to be able to talk to you about him. And I'm sorry if this is hard for you to hear, Mom, but I need to know if you think of him at all, now, in prison, and if so what.' She was staring straight at him, her eyes meeting his, not hiding, but she said nothing. He felt exhausted, as if he had run a long way and achieved nothing. He pulled out a chair from the kitchen table and sat down heavily, his elbows on the table, his head resting in his hands. 'Penny,' he said, not bothering now to look up. 'Would you be prepared to speak to her about the campaign?'

'Of course I will. I'm sure she'll be interested.' She sounded grateful for the let out. He heard another chair being pulled out, his mother coming to sit next to him. Quietly she said, 'Hassan, there was something I wanted to say about Farida. I was very fond of her as you know, but there was something that troubled me about the way she launched into living with you, like I did with your father, refusing to face up to the things in herself that were going to make it difficult for her to stay with you.' Hassan looked up, amazed. She went on, 'You've been brought up so differently, I don't think you can really imagine. There's an intense excitement in breaking a taboo, in discovering that the barriers between people you have been taught to accept, as if they were facts of nature, are man-made and can simply be ignored. Your father was the first black person I ever got to know, the first person in fact who was culturally different from me. He had the most natural charm, a sort of boyish enthusiasm for life, that he communicated effortlessly.' She broke off, then seemed to push herself to go on, 'It's so long since we spoke about those days, I don't know any more what you remember. But it was that same quality in him that made life intolerable for me once we got to Somalia. He needed people to share that energy with, all the time. Endless, endless people. He never got tired of them, never said no to any of them, was always glad to see the next one arrive and settle in to talk. And because he shared so much with them culturally, that left me isolated.'

'I knew about your being left out. I hated it, too, for you. What I didn't know was whether there had ever been a time when it wasn't like that.'

'Oh yes, that there was. And I don't suppose, now, that he meant to exclude me, just that he was incapable of understanding the effect it had on me.' She smiled, self deprecating. 'It's easy to be rational about it now. At the time I was eaten up with resentment. I found it impossible to cope with being demoted from the position of the one person on whom he turned all that charm, to being a marginal extra, useful when no one else was around.' She paused. 'I don't suppose this makes things easier.'

'Just go on. Don't stop now.'

'One of the reasons it's not been easy to talk to you is that for a long time I felt guilty at what I had taken away from you. You were miserable when we first came to England. I don't know if you remember.'

'I do.'

She smiled sadly. 'Yes, I imagine you do.' And then, in a more practical voice, 'But you have your father's gift of buoyancy, thank God. You are so like him, Hassan.'

'Including in the ways you found difficult?'

'Sometimes,' she acknowledged, smiling. 'I do think of him, Hassan. Constantly. I don't understand why it should have been so difficult for me to tell you. I think putting him in prison is the worst thing anyone could have done to him, shutting him away from other people.' He nodded, seeing his father's face, tired and drawn. His mother came and stood next to him. He turned in his chair and leant his head against her gardening dungarees. She stroked his hair, in a way she had not done since he had been a little boy, and said, 'When you rushed off to Djibuti, I was afraid for you and I knew nothing could be achieved, but I was glad you went. It seemed the only thing either of us could do at that point, to let him see you.'

It was a moment before he could speak. With difficulty he said, 'It wasn't like that. He didn't want me there.'

'You must be wrong. He was afraid for you, maybe.'

'But the fear made it hard for him even to talk to me as we used to talk. He just said, *I want you to go back, and be safe.*' Hassan put his arms out to hold on to her, and buried his face in her dungarees, and wept.

*

As he opened the door Nuh was on the phone saying, 'Yes, *Aabo*,' and 'No, *Aabo*,' and 'I'll tell them, *Aabo*.' His father, uncle Ali. Hassan stood still, waiting. It seemed a long time before Nuh put the phone down and said slowly, 'From Djibuti. He's left Hargeisa. He's sent the rest of the family to the interior, to the cousin who looks after his camels.' They stared at each other, stunned. Nuh said, 'He is convinced there's going to be fighting in Hargeisa.'

Hassan's first thought was, 'They can't go away and leave my father alone!' Then he forced himself to try to take in the wider implications. Uncle Ali would not have left if he had felt there was any other choice. He had no source of wealth that would survive the journey to exile. His money would be valueless outside Somalia, and none of the carefully constructed empire of influence could be carried with him to a new place. The family would become again a part of the nomadic life from which they had all started, their only chance of survival if the life of the towns broke down. But uncle Ali's herds had never been intended to support so many people. What would happen when they were exhausted?

'Uncle Musa refused to go,' Nuh was saying. 'My father says he's crazy, I mean literally, the whole situation has affected his mind. He's waiting for the fighting, to see with his own eyes the entrails of the enemies of the Prophet spread out in the streets of Hargeisa.'

'*Subhan Allah!*'

'And grandmother won't budge. She says she's too old to move, and that someone has to stay to take food to your father.'

Hassan sat down abruptly. 'I feel as if the world is coming to an end. Everything we knew is breaking up.'

'If there is fighting in Hargeisa, the SNM may win. It may be the start of a return to life as we once knew it.'

Hassan stared at him. 'I can see it helps to think Allah is on your side. My feeling is he usually backs the wrong people.'

Nuh said angrily, 'It's not the right time to mock.'

'No. You're right.' He remembered something. 'Amina. She was going to try to get to Hargeisa!'

'My father got a message to her not to.' And Nuh turned his back, to stare out of the window.

For the next few days Nuh stayed in, doing little but lie on the sofa next to the telephone. All attempts Hassan made to persuade him to go out with him were useless. Even to Whitechapel Hassan went alone, and found the centre buzzing with rumours. Everyone had some item of news to share, phone calls from Canada, from Sweden, people passing on messages second, third, fifth hand, no way of telling what was reliable.

Hibo was there. He said to her, 'Haleemo ought to get someone to send the children out of Hargeisa, into the countryside.'

'She wants someone to take them to Djibuti, to wait there till we get permission to bring them here. But people are afraid. If you leave your house the army moves in and takes everything.'

'They may lose everything anyway,' he said.

'Whatever we do we're never going to be in time.'

He nodded and knew he didn't need to say to her, but we still have to do it. When he got home Nuh was in the same position as when he had left.

> *Must I from time everlasting*
> *again and again cry out*
> *'Let's leave each other alone!'*
> *But leave me alone they would not.*

4

I need to talk to you, she wrote, sitting up in bed, wrapped in a dressing gown.

Coming back has been a clarifying experience, in more ways than I could have imagined. There is so much that is familiar, and so much that has become unfamiliar because I have changed. The thing I expected to find most strange was being without the children, yet it feels perfectly natural, not to say luxurious! I think of them often, and I am helped not to miss them by being able to talk about them, for everyone here regards them as part of the family and wants to know what they are like. I find that comforting, a confirmation of the fact that the children are, after all, part of a continuous line of humanity. Aunt Anna is collecting photographs for me to take back, of all their cousins.

People here can't understand why I don't return, now that I am separated from Alistair. 'It was only because of him that you went, wasn't it?' Aunt Anna asks. Yes it was, but it wasn't only because of him that I stayed. When I tried to explain the political reasons she said, 'And are you going to tell me everyone's equal in Britain?' I had a picture of the detention centre at Heathrow, filled with people from Africa and Asia, and none from Europe or North America, or of the policemen calling you a coloured bastard until they discovered you were a solicitor and then calling you Sir. Aunt Anna's response was, 'And then they criticise South Africa?' When I suggested that if she thought such things were wrong she ought to be at least equally shocked by the far worse things that happen here, she took defence in the usual line. 'It's different here, you couldn't possible let all the blacks think they were equal. They're not ready for it.' Meaning, of course, she's not ready for it.

*

There was a delightful smell in the kitchen. 'Stewed quinces!' she exclaimed, and Maria laughed at her pleasure. 'The most delicious thing I know and the worst to make. Auntie got me to help her one year and I'll never do them again. I've never known anything so hard to peel. Let me see your hands, I bet they're full of blisters.'

302

'I didn't do them today, klein mies,' Maria laughed. 'They were from the bottle. We made them last year, Miss Faure and me.' Auntie was the one white woman Maria did not call *ou mies* or *klein mies*, old madam or young madam. 'You know something?' Rachel said.

'Klein mies?'

'I'd love it if you didn't call me klein mies. How about Rachel?'

'Ee, klein mies!' Maria shook her head, giggling at the extraordinary and embarrassing suggestion. Rachel said, 'All right then, I'll stop calling you Maria. It's Mrs. Phokane from now on.' Maria's giggles mounted, threatening to overwhelm her. 'You know, Mrs. Phokane,' Rachel said, 'where I live now my friends wouldn't believe me if I told them that here women twice my age call me mies just because I'm white and they're black.'

Maria looked at her curiously. 'In that England, klein mies, I hear there is no apartheid?'

'That's right.'

'The people all live together?'

'That's right. And go to the same schools, and use the same buses. Everything. That's normal. It's only here that people think that's strange.'

'Ee, klein mies.' She shook her head, unable to take it in. 'Rachel,' laughed Rachel. 'Go on, just try.' Maria shook her head again, convulsed with laughter, unable to make herself say it. Rachel gave up. 'Tell me what happened to Martha,' she said.

'Martha, klein mies? She worked for ou mies Venter.'

'I heard. And I heard that Mrs Venter thought she was cheeky!' Maria looked at her, they both automatically checked the passage to see that her mother was not in earshot and then burst out laughing. 'I can't imagine anything worse than having to work for Mrs Venter.'

'Ai, klein mies, that one is terrible.' Maria shook her head, the tightly wound, brightly coloured headscarf waggling in emphasis.

'I went to Martha's house. I really wanted to see her. She's gone, and no one seems to know where.'

'She was sick, klein mies. Sick, sick, with the stomach sickness. She couldn't stay working.'

'So where did she go?'

'To her daughter, klein mies. Over there on the farm, near the border of Botswana.'

'What kind of sickness is it?'

'Ai, klein mies, I do not know the name. It is a sickness in the stomach, she couldn't work anymore.'

'Is she getting treatment for it?'

'Ai, klein mies, I do not know. On the farm I think there is no treatment.'

Sannie and her children arrived just before Sunday lunch, having driven out from Bloemfontein for the day. The little girl was big-eyed and silent in the face of Auntie's old, withering body, the two boys all elbows and knees, awkward and adolescent. After a few moments Sannie released them, telling them to go and find themselves something to do. Then she leant her head close to Auntie's face and said, raising her voice as if Auntie were deaf, 'Hello Auntie, *hoe gaan dit vandag?*'- How are you today? 'There's no need to shout,' said Auntie, suddenly lucid. 'I can hear perfectly well.' And then she returned to staring vacantly at the wall.

'When she talks to me in English I know I'm being ticked off,' said Sannie to Rachel, as if Auntie were not there. 'She's cross because I couldn't come last week.' And turning back to Auntie she raised her voice again though perhaps slightly less than the first time, 'Piet was away last week, Auntie. He took the Volvo and left me with the old Honda that keeps breaking down, so I didn't want to come out of town in it. Never mind, you've got Rachel here with you now. That's lovely isn't it?' Auntie continued staring at the wall and made no response. Sannie motioned to Rachel to come out of the room with her. Once in the passage she held her at arms length, taking a good look at her and said, 'So you've become a real Brit! I can't believe it.'

'Not me,' Rachel laughed, 'the moment I saw Duiwelskop again I wanted to kick my shoes off and start climbing!'

'You'll have to do it without me, I'm past all that!' She motioned with her head towards Auntie's door. 'Leave Maria with her and come over to my mother's place for lunch.'

'I'd love to, but Maria's got food prepared already.'

'Nonsense. You can't organise your life around the convenience of a servant. I'll tell her you and your mother are coming to us today.' Then, seeing Rachel's face, 'Don't be so ridiculous, Rachel, she'll be pleased not to have to bother with the two of you for once.' Sannie walked firmly off to the kitchen. Rachel went back in to Auntie. 'You're getting too fat, Maria,' she heard Sannie's voice, loud, uninhibited, personal. 'Ee, klein mies!' she heard Maria chuckle. 'And klein mies never gets fat, however much she eats!'

After lunch Sannie announced that her mother and Rachel's could have a little natter because she was taking Rachel off to show her the new sports centre. 'She's been here a week already and she's hardly been out of that house. We can't allow that!' Like most of Sannie's statements it required no response. It makes life very simple, Rachel thought, when you tell people what everyone's going to do and leave them to get on with it, without bothering about what they might want. But in fact Sannie's plan suited them all and the directness was refreshing.

'There's something I want to tell you,' Sannie said as she started the car, 'that I didn't want my mother to hear. Did you know Auntie is leaving you something in her will?'

'I didn't think she had anything to leave.'

'It comes from years back, though God knows how she managed to save on what primary school teachers got then. Now it probably won't buy a pair of shoes. Daniel will know, he looks after all their money. Quite the head of the family, our Daniel, taking over from Uncle Dirkie.' Rachel smiled but made no comment. Sannie was still getting at Daniel. Nothing much had changed. 'Anyway, when she broke her leg - at the beginning, when her mind was still clear - she called me to tell me she's left her life's savings to you and Jill.'

Rachel stared. 'Me and Jill? Not you? None of the boys? Why on earth?'

'There is a logic, a specifically Auntie kind of logic. Can't you guess?'

'I'm absolutely lost. I can't think of anything Jill and I have in common anymore. And if Auntie was going to single out anyone it ought to have been you.'

'I suppose that's why she told me about it. She said the only reason she had saved that money rather than giving it to people who needed it at the time was because the world is hard on women without husbands. As it turned out, she hadn't needed it so she thought it should go to Jill and you. Jill because she never married and you because your husband left you.'

'So she knew about Alistair? No one else seems to have.'

'She had guessed. Your mother used to read her bits from your letters, though she never gave her the whole letter to read. She worked out that Alistair must have left you because for the last couple of years there was never any mention of him or what he was doing.'

'But you didn't tell the others?'

'Auntie told me not to. She said it was for you to do.' They had reached the entrance to the sports centre. 'You're not interested in seeing this, are you?' Rachel laughed, 'No. I'm a lot more interested in what you're telling me. Let's sit out here in the sun while you go on.' Sannie said, 'She knew you would come, you know.'

Rachel could not speak for a moment. With difficulty she said, 'Well, she was wrong about me. I wouldn't have come if your mother hadn't summoned me. I'm ashamed.'

'It's a long way. No one expected you to. But I knew Auntie was holding on and I wanted her to be able to die. I told my mother she should call you.'

'What about Jill?'

'She hasn't been and she won't either, she and her beloved dancing. But Auntie wasn't stupid enough to expect her.'

'Why me, then?'

'I don't know. I just know she was waiting for you. '

'How do you know?' Rachel demanded, almost afraid.

'It's a funny thing, people dying. Half the time you think they don't even know you're there, they can't speak, they can't show on their faces what they're thinking. But every now and then you know they're giving you a message. It's impossible to explain.'

'I know. I've felt as if Auntie's been giving me messages ever since she broke her leg.'

'Well there you are, then,' said Sannie, very matter-of-fact. 'What was she telling you?' Rachel had to think for a moment how to say it. 'Not to back away from things.' Sannie looked as if she would like to know more, but for once didn't ask. Instead she said, her voice definite, 'I hope she knows you heard what she was trying to tell you, Rachel. It's time she died. Help her let go.'

Auntie was particularly restless that evening. 'Call me if you need help,' Rachel told the night nurse, and just before midnight she did so. 'She's asking for you.' Rachel came and sat next to Auntie, holding her hand and talking quietly to her, till eventually the restlessness diminished. Rachel drifted off into a troubled dream of the kind she had had so often over the last months but not at all since she had returned to Lourensrus. Something dreadful was happening to someone she knew and loved, but she couldn't work out who. She had checked that the children were all OK, and she knew it couldn't be Hassan, because his face kept appearing every now and then, close to her, and always at its most beautiful, calm and serious. She tried Hibo's flat, to find that it was empty. 'She's gone,' said the people next door. 'No one knows where.' She startled awake, and realised - of course, Martha.

She watched Auntie's face, shrunken and unlovely, the skin falling away from the bone even more markedly than when she had arrived a week ago, the flabby lips blowing loosely with each laboured breath. 'Auntie,' she said, so quietly that Auntie would not hear or be disturbed in her sleep, 'they've abandoned Martha, left her to rot with no money and no treatment.' Then she waited quietly, waiting to understand what Auntie would have done about it.

Daniel's telephone was answered by a bland, multiple-copy receptionist voice. 'I'm afraid Mr. Faure's with a client,' said the voice. 'I have instructions not to disturb him. Can I perhaps help you?'

'Can you tell him it's his cousin, phoning from Lourensrus? I only need a quick word.' There was a shocked pause. 'I can't believe it,' said the voice, now considerably more human - and definitely familiar. 'It's Rachel Leipoldt, isn't it?'

'Rosemary!' Rachel laughed, seeing a girl in school uniform with long dark plaits, whose father had travelled from farm to farm repairing tractors. 'I didn't recognise your voice under the layers of Smart Receptionist. How long have you worked for Daniel?'

'About four years. I was wiping babies bottoms until then.' When they had exchanged news Rachel said, 'Why don't you come out one day?'

'I'd love to, but I can't budge my husband.' Shades of Alistair. Rachel said firmly, 'You don't want to let that stop you. Come on your own.' Rosemary clearly did not regard this as a serious suggestion. 'That's married life,' she said. 'Hold on, I'll get Daniel for you.'

Daniel's voice came on the line. 'Yes, cousin from Lourensrus, what can I do for you? You've just made my secretary's day!'

'Daniel, don't call her My Secretary, I can't bear it. You were at school with her, for God's sake!' He sounded amused. 'Do you know, you've become like Auntie used to be!' She gave up. She couldn't take them all on, not on her mother's phone bill. She said, 'There's something financial I want to sort out. I was just checking that you're definitely coming sometime this week.'

'Are you really going to climb Duiwelskop?'

'That's what your crazy daughter says,' Daniel replied, putting his arm around his aunt's shoulders. Kind, patronising, head of the family, just as Sannie had said. Rachel's mother grumbled. 'I don't know why you want to go out in that cold wind when you could stay here in comfort with us.'

'Mom, we've been through all that,' Rachel said, as lightly as she could, and refrained from adding, at least three times. When she and Daniel were safely beyond her mother's hearing she said, 'She's driving me bananas. Anything I suggest doing that takes me one foot out of the house gets her immediate disapproval.'

'Mothers are like that.'

'No they're not,' she said indignantly. 'I'm a mother and I don't spend my time stopping my children from doing things. And nor did my mother when I was a child, you know that.' She saw that he was not interested in considering the matter further; anyway, she didn't want to waste this one afternoon with him arguing. 'Come, let's run!'

'What's the rush?' he asked, continuing to walk up the track towards the foot of the hill with firm, unhurriable tread, as she remembered his father walk. They reached the point at which the path began to zigzag in gentle stages up the hillside. She ignored the path, as they always had done, and headed straight up the hill. 'You can boulderhop if you want to,' he said, 'but I'm past it. I'm going up the path.' She couldn't believe he was serious. 'Come on, Daniel, what's happened to you?' He laughed with her, but simply continued on the path. After staring at him for a minute or two she gave up and came down off her rock to join him.

At the top they sat on the smooth table-like rock that had been one of her father's favourite viewing points, and looked out over the veld. The plain stretched endlessly to the west, a timeless semi-desert landscape, dotted at sparse intervals with small clumps of low buildings, and telegraph poles that got smaller and smaller until they disappeared into a shimmering haze of nothingness. 'Do you remember,' she said to Daniel, 'Auntie telling us the story of Jesus being taken up a mountain and tempted by the devil, who offered him everything he could see?'

'I remember Auntie telling us stories about Jesus, but not that one specially.'

'When she told it, I saw it as the view from up here. And I couldn't work out why the devil should have thought that was a way to tempt Jesus. Because anyone could have it, without selling their soul. Just by climbing.'

'And what did you bring me up here to ask me?'

'It's about Martha.' She told him what she had heard. He made no comment and she repeated herself, more forcefully. 'She's too ill to work so she's living off her daughter, and you know what farm labourers earn.'

'Rachel,' said Daniel, the accountant Daniel, the My Secretary Daniel, deliberately putting distance between them, 'I'm sorry Martha's ill but it does happen to people when they get older. What are you asking me to do about it?'

'She's not an old woman, she can't be more than fifty five. And Maria says she's not getting any treatment. She needs money.'

'Lots of people need money.'

'We owe her a pension, my mother and Matthew and I. I want you to help me arrange it.'

'There is such a thing as a state pension in this country.'

'Do you know how much it is?' It was not a question but an attack.

His voice was hard as he said, 'You have to work out what you've come back to do. I thought you had come to help your mother. I can assure you you will not be helping her if you suggest this. I don't know anyone who pays a pension to an ex-domestic servant. And Martha hasn't worked for her since your father died.'

'She worked for us all the years I was growing up. From after Ellen left. She must have been with our family twenty five years, almost her entire working life, except for one year being shouted at by that miserable Mrs. Venter. If she isn't entitled to a pension after that, then the entire world's crazy.'

'Maybe it is, but you can't go around personally righting all the wrongs you encounter.'

She was thinking, perhaps Alistair was right about Daniel after all, when the Daniel of her childhood made a hesitant appearance. 'I don't say you haven't got a point, but where's the money going to come from?'

'Sannie says Auntie is leaving me something. There's that for a start. And I gather you look after my mother's affairs. Do you know what she has to live on?'

'Yes I do and I don't intend telling you. It's not your money to dispose of.'

'All I want to know is, could she afford to part with a small regular amount each month?'

'Rachel, I'd like to help you. I was fond of Martha too. But you're going about it in the wrong way.'

'OK, forget about my mother. Matthew and I can do something alone. But I don't even have a bank account here, and I'm sure Martha doesn't have one, so I don't know how to fix it up. It's that I really wanted help with.'

'You and Matthew?' he raised his eyebrows. 'I didn't realise you had money to spare?'

'Compared to Martha I live in luxury. If Auntie's money isn't enough I can make a small regular transfer. And my impression of Matthew is that he's rolling in it.'

'You might find it a little more difficult than you imagine to get him to see things your way. The fact that people have money doesn't necessarily mean they're prepared to part with it. He hasn't shown an excessive amount of family feeling over the past few years.'

'Then I'll do it alone if that's the only way.'

'You are definitely becoming like Auntie.' He was laughing at her now, and despite her anger she could not help feeling a certain nostalgic warmth at the teasing affection. Then she thought with a stab of fierce longing of how differently Hassan would have laughed. Daniel's laughter said, look at my little cousin! Once she gets an idea into her head there's nothing you can do with her. Hassan would have laughed with pleasure to see her becoming more herself.

'Look,' she said, 'it doesn't really matter what you think about it. It's for me to work out what I'm going to do. All I'm asking you to do is to help me arrange it. Please.'

It was probably the 'Please' that did it, the fact that she, a mere woman, did not know how to handle the practical details of money and had to ask for his help. 'I'll help you fix something up,' he said. 'But just do me a favour and don't go ruining everyone's peace by talking to your mother about it now. Wait till Auntie's dead and your mother's had a chance to recover.'

'I'll wait. Thanks, I knew you'd help.'

'It's nice to have you back, Rachel, but I'll tell you I'm glad you don't live here the whole time.'

*

I haven't talked to anyone about you. Except Auntie, but that's a little different. With the others the question never arises. They accept me as the person they used to know but apart from asking about the children no one appears to be curious about my present life. Perhaps they just can't imagine in what ways it is different and so don't know what there is to ask. With my mother I continually bump up against ways in which I no longer fit into the mould she would like for me. For her sake I try to avoid making issues, but this feels a different avoidance of conflict from the one you and I talked about. I don't know how it has happened but I'm no longer afraid of what any of them think of me. Perhaps I had grown past bothering long ago, yet had to come back in person to discover it.

And then I think of you and all the others who have no chance of revisiting their own place, who will have to live as best they can with the tangled remains of unfinished relationships, of lives suddenly interupted. I think often of what you said just before I left, your fantasy about Mohamed freeing your father. There is nothing I long for more than that you should be relieved of the pain of his imprisonment and know he is free again and living in dignity, even if you can't be with him. But even if this doesn't happen, Hassan, I'm sure you will find a way to accept what cannot be changed and continue to be whole, as it seems to me you have always been.

I see you looking down at me, as you do when we have finished making love. Your mouth is still and serious, your eyes seem to absorb me. I want to touch your face.

5

Where had he heard those lines? They had come drifting into his mind, light as air themselves, as he sat here alone by the window.

In the first light of morning I find your face,
In the air, the touch of your breath,
In the stillness, your being in which I move...

They had come whole, as if he were hearing now someone recite, and yet he could not remember where or when he might have heard them. Whose were they?

Then he realised with a small shock of awe, they were his own.

When the phone call came he was in the middle of a chaotic session in the common room, with the television researcher trying to work out who he should be talking to between Hibo, Haleemo, Evelyn, Sophie, and at least eight children who never stayed in the same place, among them Ben, almost uncontrollably excited now that his vision of being on television with Ahmed was finally to be realised. 'Get the key people together in your office by four this afternoon,' his mother's friend Penny had said. 'A friend of mine's doing a documentary to coincide with the inquest verdict, that Kurdish asylum seeker who committed suicide, you remember?'

Jenny and Mike had come in to see what was going on. Hassan was still working things out with the researcher but overheard Hibo say to Jenny, 'You must come to the march. Bring your children!' Jenny said, 'I would if it weren't in work time.' Hibo said, amazed, 'A refugee campaign, and you can't count it as part of your work?' He looked up quickly to see both Jenny and Mike looking at him, and all three of them started laughing. Hassan said, 'You just trod on the ghost of an unsettled fight between Mike and me. It's time we put that item on the agenda again!'

And then Barbara came in to say, 'Call from South Africa!'

Hassan sped to his office. 'Rachel!'

'Hassan!' Her voice was as glad as his but much quieter. Other people listening? 'I have to stay longer than I planned. Auntie's going quite rapidly now, it seems the wrong moment to leave. The adjustment's going to be hard for my mother. If I stay a few more days

I can help with the funeral arrangements, clearing up Auntie's things; all that.'

'Of course,' he said. 'How much longer?'

'Next Wednesday. Have you got a pen? BA734, arriving Heathrow, 6.30, June the first. Can you be there?'

'I'll camp out the night before.' She started giggling and he felt wonderful. 'Can you phone Pat for me? Before I left she said to stay longer if I needed to.'

'If it's a problem for her I can stay with the children.'

'That's lovely,' she said vaguely, as if it were not really her business but something for him and Pat to sort out between them. 'Ask her to explain to the children, and the library, and Evelyn and the others.'

'There's no school next week. It's half term. Remember?'

'My God, I'd forgotten.'

'I'm enchanted at the idea that I know more about your children's arrangements than you do! What do you normally do with them during half term?'

'There's a holiday play centre for Ben and Simon. It's at a different school each term, Evelyn will have the details. Kate will want to stay home and do things with her friends.'

'We'll work something out. Don't give it another thought.'

'How are the children, Hassan? Have you seen them?'

'They're fine.' He was about to say, 'Rachel, the demonstration,' and at that moment she said, 'It's the march to the MP tomorrow, isn't it?' They both laughed. He said, 'We've got the television cameras coming!'

'You haven't!'

'We told you we wouldn't just sit back and do nothing, didn't we? They're filming Haleemo and the children at the school in the morning and they've already interviewed Sophie and Hibo.' He could see the delight on her face, so clear, so open. 'I want you back, Rachel.'

'Yes,' she said. 'Yes, yes, yes.'

'Go on saying that. For about ten minutes.'

She started laughing again. 'There's no one here as ridiculous as you. I miss it. Listen, there's something else, important.' Her voice became quieter. 'I want you to tell Pat and the children I'm coming back Thursday morning, not Wednesday.' He heard the words but he could scarcely believe what they said. 'Hassan, are you there?'

'I'm here. I'm recovering from shock. Did you just tell me to lie to your children?'

'You don't have to lie, at least not much. All you have to tell them is that I'm coming back to them on Thursday. Then you meet me Wednesday morning. I want time alone with you before I go back to all that. I'm hoping you can cancel all your appointments and take a day's leave.'

'Rachel, you amaze me. I would never have asked for this, and here you are giving it to me.'

'To us. I need it as much as you do. It just came to me, yesterday afternoon. I took an hour off to be on my own - I've been doing that every day this week, to keep myself sane. It's hard to describe what it's like nursing someone who's dying, you lose touch with reality. I climbed the hill behind our house, and I was standing there looking out at this view - Hassan, there is so much space, and every time I go up there, it's uncanny, I feel as if we're looking at it together. Sometimes I wonder if there's a place like it in Somalia, somewhere you've looked at. Anyway, I started thinking about how it would be when I got back to London, with everyone needing something instantly, and days before we could have any time alone together. And I thought, that's not on. We owe it to each other to make time. And if the children have managed without me for so long, one extra day isn't going to make any difference.'

'*Al hamdu lillah!*'

'My God, I've just remembered we're on a long distance line. It's so normal, talking to you again. Hassan, explain to Pat what's happening. We don't want her offering to bring the children to the airport! I'm sure she won't grudge me one extra day.'

'I'll bribe her, if necessary.'

She started laughing again. 'I'm putting the phone down.'

'No!'

'I am. Get ready - Bye!' And she was gone.

Since the phone call from uncle Ali there had been no news. That was the hardest part in a way, knowing things might be happening and having no way of finding out, simply having to wait for the next eruption. But it was just as difficult watching Nuh every evening, his uncommunicative mood becoming more entrenched as depression set in. There was little coming and going now with Aadan and his other friends. He was almost always at home, and alone.

On the day of Nuh's interview at Heathrow they had arranged that he would come to the ACRAS office on the way back, but he didn't appear. When Hassan got home Nuh was lying on the sofa, doing nothing. 'What happened?' Hassan asked tensely. But Nuh had nothing in particular to relate. It had been the same official, though this time the man had made no comment, just asked questions and written down the answers. 'And now?' Nuh asked.

'You wait. We're getting a lot of experience of waiting, you and I! Listen,' and this time it was an order rather than a suggestion, 'I'm going to see a friend of mine. Come with me.'

He had not been sure how Nuh would react to Jeyam's irreverence, but he need not have bothered. Jeyam's scathing comments about the immigration officials' determination to get rid of the Tamil refugees, far from depressing Nuh further, seemed in an odd way to release his own feelings. 'It sounds,' Nuh smiled ironically, 'as if your friends had the same immigration officer I had!'

'Plenty more where he came from,' said Jeyam.

Nuh turned to Hassan. 'What's the point of writing briefing papers for people like that?'

'You can't tell,' Hassan said. 'It's not a consistent picture. They let in some people and take a set against others. Anything's worth trying.' He turned to Jeyam. 'Tell him how the Tamil refugees got judicial proceedings started.'

'Do you think he can cope?' Jeyam asked doubtfully. 'All those legal complexities?'

'Don't listen to a word he says,' Hassan told Nuh. 'It's quite non-technical. The men staged a trousers-down protest.'

'A what?'

Jeyam took over. 'There were sixty of them, all arriving on one plane. They realised the immigration officers were going to send them back without even considering their applications so one of them managed to get a message out to a relative, to send a lawyer quick. Meanwhile it was crucial to delay everything till the lawyer got there. So when they were ordered back onto the plane, all the men took their trousers off!'

Nuh said, incredulous, 'And it worked?'

'Sure it worked,' said Jeyam. 'It's one thing to send someone back to persecution fully dressed, but you hesitate to be seen hustling a large group of naked men onto a plane!'

Hassan said, 'By the time the officials had forcibly dressed them all, the lawyer had arrived with a judge's order not to remove them until there had been a judicial enquiry!'

Nuh was laughing. He looked at Hassan and quoted something in Arabic. That's better, Hassan thought, that's more like it! 'It's from the Holy Qur'an,' he explained to Jeyam,

*Never will God change the condition of a people
until they change it themselves.'*

Jeyam said, 'I regret that particular action is not copyable. It depended on the element of surprise. By now someone will have issued official guidelines on what to do when asylum seekers pull their trousers down.'

Hassan said, with quiet emphasis, 'But it worked.'

*

Someone was calling him in his sleep. He opened his eyes, to see Nuh bending over his bed, shaking him gently on the shoulder. He stared for a moment, orienting himself, then propped himself up on his elbow. 'What's going on?' he asked. 'What time is it?'

'It's just after one. Wake up properly, I've got some news for you.'

He sat up bolt upright. 'I'm awake.'

'Aadan's just phoned. Some of the people at the SNM conference managed to get through to Dire Dawa. SNM troops have taken Bura'o. And the first thing they did was release all the political prisoners.'

Hassan became rigid. 'You're absolutely sure?'

'A hundred percent. It had already happened thirty six hours before any of us knew. Friday 27th May, 1988. Go and write it up on the walls of London, it's a historic date.' With a wild whoop of joy Hassan lept from the bed, and he and Nuh grabbed hold of each other and hugged and danced in celebration, till Hassan stopped and said, 'Mohamed. Mohamed must have been with them.'

'He was. Aadan checked specially.'

You were right, Mohamed. You were right, and I was wrong. It was the right time.

'And Hassan - they're heading for Hargeisa.'

If Hassan could have prayed, he would have. For what remained of the dark hours of early morning after he and Nuh had finally gone back to bed the incantations recited themselves in his mind, emerging like dreams from the recesses of his earliest memories.

> *I invoke the saints who keep the straight path,*
> *and the riches of the Sura of Yaasiin,*
> *May God, day and night, turn danger away from you.*

He could not pray in his own voice but he prayed through his father's; and the longer the voice continued the more he was sure that the news had got through to the people in the cells of Hargeisa Prison, and that his father was awake this night, praying for the men who were heading towards Hargeisa to release them. Praying for Mohamed.

> *You have collected together your weapons.*
> *Now as you leave my heart rejoices*
> *at the decision you have come to.*
> *When in the early morning, at dawn,*
> *you rise and go to mount your stallion,*
> *though sand and dust rise up around you, columns of dust,*
> *you will not lose your way on the road that you must follow.*
> *God who fills our waterponds will not make you thirst.*

He was not aware of having slept, but he woke. He sat up and stared around him. His own room, but something had changed. There was a terrible emptiness, a terrible sense of loss. He leant forward to reach the corner of the blind and lift it, to look out. Brilliant sunlight. Sunday morning quiet in the street outside. He looked at his watch. Just after eight. He let the blind drop back again, unable to stand the glare. He got out of bed and went through to the living room to Nuh, still sleeping on the sofa. He stood over him for a few minutes, watching his sleeping face. I need you to be awake, he was saying, without saying anything. Nuh opened his eyes. He looked blankly at Hassan, then said, 'What is it?'

'Mohamed is dead,' Hassan said.

Nuh jerked himself upright. 'When did you hear?'

'No one told me, but I know it. I have known it would happen ever since he left. This morning when I woke I knew it for certain.'

Nuh stared at him silently, then dropped back into a lying-down position on the sofa and with eyes once again closed he said, 'You don't know. Only God knows.'

'And if he has died, I suppose God planned it?' The bitterness in his voice shocked even him. For a moment he thought Nuh was going to lash out at him as his father or his uncles would have done. But Nuh said simply, 'Don't you want to go back to bed?'

'No,' said Hassan, his anger undiminished. 'I want you to answer me.'

Reluctantly Nuh pulled himself into a sitting position. 'We've been through all this before.'

'Mohamed had not died before. I want to know now how you can lie there and say, it is God's will.'

Nuh said, slowly, deliberately, 'If it has happened, it is God's will. Now go and put on the kettle and I'll talk more when I've had some tea. It's too early.'

The blinds were up, the light poured in. Through the window the new summer green of the leaves fluttered gently. Hassan comforted his hands around his mug and was no longer so completely convinced of what he had known when he had woken. 'I've thought of a poem for you,' Nuh said. 'It's a *buraambur* I heard a few weeks before I left, by Saido Haji. Composed after her brother was killed fighting -

He has gone to the Ganane River and to Garissa.
O God the Victorious, who took him there, help us -
The death they have reported, let it not have happened.'

*

Sunday morning. The church bells were ringing as Rachel wrapped her gown around her and went through to the living room. Her mother must still be asleep. She accepted the silence in the house gratefully and stood looking out of the window at the thin winter sun touching the top of Duiwelskop.

'Rachel.' She turned. Her mother was standing behind her, fully dressed. 'Auntie died, early this morning.'

It took her a second or two to take it in, then she went over to her mother and put her arms around her. They stood quietly holding each other. 'You said you would call me, Mom,' she admonished gently.

'There wasn't anything for you to do, and I thought you needed your sleep. The night nurse called me about four this morning. When I got there she was still breathing; a few moments later she wasn't. That was all. The nurse and Maria did everything that had to be done. I've phoned Aunt Anna. She's done it before for Oom Jan and she helped me when your father died.' Her voice trailed off, then came back at slightly more than normal strength, like a radio whose volume adjuster was out of control. 'They took her off to the mortuary about an hour ago.'

'And I slept through all that?'

'You were tired, girlie.' She hasn't called me that since I was about twelve, Rachel thought, and then thought of Kate and felt sad. Auntie needed to die, there was no cause to be sad, but there seemed to be intimations of other kinds of loss too. She did not want a time to come when she and Kate would stand as far apart from each other as she and her mother did today, reaching out hands to support each other across the distance of their so-different life experiences.

Her mother's body had become heavy in her arms, as if she were about to collapse at the knees. 'Come,' said Rachel. 'You to go back to bed again. Sleep now, for as long as you can. You've done what you had to do.'

In the event there was nothing for Rachel to do in planning the funeral. Daniel drove his mother over from Bloemfontein, and by Monday lunchtime she and Aunt Anna had it all organised, down to which hymns they would sing and whether the flowers on the coffin should be saved or cremated with Auntie. The cremation caused the biggest problem. Auntie's will had been brief, but definite - she did not want to be buried. Rachel could imagine her saying, I don't believe in filling up the ground with useless bodies. People need the space to grow food.

'But there are no facilities for cremation in Lourensrus!' complained Aunt Anna. Rachel knew what they were all thinking, though they would never say it now that she was dead - trust her to make a nuisance of herself to the last. To Rachel's pleasure Daniel stood up to them, firmly and without fuss. 'It's perfectly simple,' he said. 'We just arrange to send the body to Bloemfontein.'

'But then her remains won't be here, with the rest of the family!'

'If Auntie had minded about that she wouldn't have asked to be cremated.'

Rachel listened, knowing that there was nothing for her to contribute. Auntie was released, her mother could rest and start life again, the significant things had already been achieved. She had no experience of funerals and even if she had wanted to express an opinion she would not, like Daniel, have got away with opposing Aunt Anna. She had been away too long, had chosen to become a foreigner. She had surrendered her right to have anything to say in how things should be done here. She did not mind; it seemed to her appropriate.

Only once they were in the church did she realise that there was one thing she should have done. She was sitting with her mother and Daniel and the aunts in the front row, reserved for relatives, with Sannie and her family in the row just behind. None of the other cousins had come. Matthew was still in America. James had no one to leave in charge of the shop. Jill had a performance in two days time. Stefan and Willem were having trouble with the new pipes they were laying - there was a danger of flooding or air blocks or some such thing that Rachel did not understand and did not want to understand, but which meant that, much as they would have liked to be there, it was impossible for them to leave at the moment. Stefan said, on the phone to Rachel, 'Do you remember what Auntie always used to say about funerals?' Yes, she did remember, vividly. She remembered Auntie's scorn for people who came to funerals when they hadn't bothered to pay any attention to the person who had been alive and needing them until a few days before. Rachel wanted to say to Stefan, and where were you before? Or I, or any of us except Sannie? But there was no point. It was over.

So there she sat, in the front row with her mother and the rump of what had once been the family, looking straight ahead at the familiar wood panelling of this church that her great grandfather had helped to build, in which two generations of Faures and Leipoldts and de Wets had been christened, and sat obediently through services week after week throughout their childhood. The church that Auntie had attended every Sunday of her life till her legs would no longer take her there, even though there was never a minister who met her approval. 'That Dominee Venter,' she would say, 'he hasn't the least idea of what the love of God means.' Aunt Anna used to say, 'Then why do you keep going? Go to the Methodists if you think that will be better.' Auntie never replied, but they all knew, this had been her mother's church and she would not break faith.

Dominee Venter had gone long since. Now as minister there was an earnest young man who had been in Lourensrus only six months and had never known Auntie other than as one of the old ladies it was his duty to visit from time to time, to sit at her bedside and say a prayer with her since she could no longer come to church. 'Did Auntie like him?' Rachel had asked. Her mother replied, obliquely, 'Auntie wasn't really herself by the time he came.' Which probably meant she had said something pointedly rude about him which Rachel's mother preferred not to remember. Rachel had met him the day before the funeral. He seemed innocuous but conventional. Nothing more spiritually challenging had ever happened to him, it seemed, than a period of work in Johannesburg where he had been shocked at the low rate of church attendance among young people. What would this young man be able to say about Auntie that would bear any relationship to the kind of person she had been? She felt Auntie's mantle on her, as she had been feeling it for all the months since she had first met Haleemo. She felt that she ought to say to the others, 'Why are we letting this stranger take over? Auntie would have hated it. Let someone who knew her conduct the service, someone who knows what it is we're honouring in her.'

But she did not say it. Auntie was gone, beyond caring, beyond indignation at the stupidity of convention. This funeral was not for her but for the others, and they needed to do it in the only way they knew. Her job was simply to be with her mother, to help her get through it, not to make things harder for her.

Behind her the church was filling up. She would have liked to have turned round to look but she knew that her mother would think that inappropriate, so she stayed looking ahead. She knew there must be a lot of people because the organist went on playing for a long time. Despite what Auntie would have said she was moved to think that so many people had come.

It was only when they stood up to sing the first hymn that she realised who all those people were, for from behind her came not the expected tentative funeral sound, but a great swelling of full confident voices. When she heard it she turned - she could not stop herself - and she saw that the back of the church, the space behind the last pews, was filled to overflowing with scores and scores of black people, mainly women. Women who worked in the white houses of Lourensrus, women who had made the journey from the township and must have left early that morning for there was only one bus a day. No one had given thought to the special arrangments that would have been needed to make sure that all those whom Auntie had loved would be equally welcomed. No one had remembered that it would be necessary to instruct the church wardens that, regardless of normal practice, at this funeral black mourners were to be invited to sit alongside the relatives and white friends in the body of the church. So they had quietly filed in to the back, discreetly taking the places they expected to have to take, while she had sat there in the front row, her head bent down so as not to embarrass her mother, and had not even been aware that it was happening.

Now it was too late. For a few moments she felt utterly defeated by the knowledge of her failure - this one, small, significant failure, and all the others that it symbolised, from all the years she had lived here and never found a way to act. But the voices behind her soared with such strength, such love and such forgiveness, that she was carried with them; accepted, released, freed through the love of Auntie which she and they shared, freed to acknowledge her failure but to move on beyond it. 'That's just the way they sing,' Auntie had said, and they sang that way, their hymns that gave thanks for her life. They sang with power and conviction and sorrow and joy, breaking into spontaneous harmony that rose to the rafters and filled the church, till it spilled out, like the people, into the street.

6

For once going to Heathrow was pure pleasure. He was there before the plane landed, though he knew it would take her at least half an hour to come through passport control and collect her baggage. He stood in the crowd of people waiting - children climbing on the barrier to get a better view, men in slightly shabby suits holding up notices with the names of other men in smarter suits whom they had been sent to meet. Pakistani families in force, three generations. And he among them all, waiting for Rachel to emerge pushing her trolley of luggage, her face looking out for him. Her face as it had always been, would always be, time without end, amen.

She was there! And he had leapt over the barrier and was with her, his arm around her as they pushed the trolley together, laughing, holding tight against each other, their bodies longing, their spirits rejoicing. And then down the escalator to the underground station, and on the train and out, watching her exclaim with delight at the green, green of the summer leaves, the splashes of geraniums and pansies in the window boxes, as if she were seeing it all again for the first time. And then into his flat, dumping her suitcase just inside the door and straight to bed, to make love as if they had been deprived for years, and then to lie soft and warm and naked and wet, their bodies sweaty and satisfied and lazily stretched out, with not even a sheet to cover them.

He got up to make them coffee. She lay in luxury waiting for him to return, looking out of the window at the high wispy clouds. He came and sat on the bed next to her and she propped herself up on an elbow to drink. 'I want to hear everything that's been happening while I've been away.'

'What do you want me to start with?'

'The children.'

'They're thriving. Though Pat says Ben had a couple of moments when he just didn't understand why he couldn't have you back, now!' He grinned, 'I must say, I thought he had a point!'

'Simon?'

'Simon's fine. Do you know he's taken to me?'

'I expected it, from the moment I saw him watching you cook sabaayad.'

'We've expanded the repertoire. He now appears to regard me as an appropriate person to show his drawings to.'

'What about Kate?'

'You mean, how is Kate? Or how does Kate cope with me?'

'Both.'

'Kate in herself is fine, so Pat tells me. And Kate does not approve of Hassan.'

'No.' She sighed. 'I didn't expect anything different. But I thought, with me out of the way, maybe -'

'She didn't give herself a chance. I was there both weekends but when she wasn't out with her friends, she shut herself up in her room, reading.'

'I suppose that's one way of dealing with it. I forgot to tell you, my mother spoke about you, just before I left.'

'I didn't know she knew about me!'

'Nor did I. I'd told her in my letters about Haleemo and the campaign, and going into the ACRAS office once a week, but I wasn't aware I'd said anything more personal about you than that. It must have showed through. She knew.'

'What did she say?'

'She said, this Somali friend of yours, Hassan, is that a Muslim name? When I said it was she said, well, I don't suppose it makes much difference since you're not a believing Christian anymore. But he wouldn't do anything silly like wanting the children to become Muslims, would he?'

Hassan was laughing. 'Go on. What did you say?'

'I said, he's not a practising Muslim. He's just a very good and loving man.'

He stopped laughing. 'And?'

'That seemed enough for her.'

'She didn't say anything else?'

'No.'

'Aren't you surprised?'

'Not really. If I had said I was bringing you home to live in Lourensrus, that would be another matter! Anyway, she's had to cope once with my choosing an unacceptable partner, maybe it's easier the second time.'

'But a black lover! A white husband was respectable on two counts at least, even if she didn't like his politics.'

'It's not colour as such that's the problem. They all know my children go to a school where half their friends are black, and that doesn't shock them. It's too far away to concern them. But they would mind passionately if someone suggested they integrate the schools in Lourensrus. You're not a threat because you've never set foot in Lourensrus and have nothing to do with South African politics.' She paused. It was so difficult to convey to someone who had not been there, and she wanted him to understand the good things in her mother as well as the limits. 'I think she was trying to tell me she would prefer not to be excluded from what's important to me, and that if I say I love you she will try to feel happy about it.'

'And the rest of them? Will she tell them?'

'That's her decision. I really don't care. If the only way she can handle them is not to mention it, that's for her to work out.' She suddenly remembered, 'What did you do with Nuh?'

'I told him I needed to be alone with you today.'

'And tonight?'

'I gave him the choice of spending the night somewhere else or being here with us and not minding. He said he'd go to Aadan's.' He paused. 'His mind's on other things. Rachel, there's news from Somalia.'

She jerked herself upright. 'Why didn't you tell me straight away?'

'You wanted to hear about the children first.'

'I didn't know you had news. What's happened?'

'The SNM have crossed the border from Ethiopia, and attacked a town called Bura'o. They're heading for Hargeisa now. And one of the first things they did in Bura'o was to release all the political prisoners.'

'Hassan!' She swooped herself up and was dancing on the bed, pulling him up, spilling the remains of the coffee. 'Oh that's wonderful! Your father!' He caught hold of her, hugged her fiercely, then pulled her down with him so that they were lying together again. 'Take it easy,' he said, touching her face, looking into her eyes, making her still. 'There's a lot that can still go wrong.' She saw then that he was afraid. She felt a rush of protective love and wanted to stroke his hair, to calm him, to say, 'Don't be afraid!' But this was not the kind of fear that could be banished by love.

'There's Mohamed,' he said, as if he had heard her thoughts, 'and all of them. The civilian population. Last night we heard that the army has come back into Bura'o and has gone on a rampage, dragging Isaaq men out of their houses and shooting them point blank. Bayoneting boy children so they can't grow into SNM soldiers. They're giving arms to anyone who's not Isaaq and telling them to kill or they'll be killed. In Hargeisa people are fleeing. My father may be starving. I want the SNM to get there, I want it more than anything, but I'm also afraid of what will happen when they do.'

Half way through the afternoon Rachel said, 'Let's go to the Park. It's too beautiful a day to spend inside.' When they got back Nuh was there, standing at the window with his back to the door. 'Nuh Ali Dahir,' said Hassan, his voice light, jocular. 'We have the pleasure of your company after all!'

He had spoken in English. Nuh answered in Somali, and without turning round, 'No, I'm going. I just waited to see you first.' He turned, acknowledging Rachel's presence with a minimal, unsmiling nod. Something's wrong, Hassan thought, panic rising. Something's terribly wrong, and he doesn't want to have to tell me with Rachel here. In Somali he said, 'It's Mohamed, isn't it?'

All Nuh said was,

'O God, the Victorious, who took him there, help us -'

Then he turned his back on them again and continued looking out of the window.

*

The first evening home, the children hung about her as if to assure themselves she was really there and bombarded her with stories of what had happened while she had been away. She unpacked the *koeksisters* Maria had made for them - plaited strips of dough, deep fried and doused in syrup, sticky and delicious - and the presents that her mother had sent and the photographs from Aunt Anna. They sat on the sofa looking at them and asking her questions and listening to her stories, and she felt whole and contented.

Within a few days it was as if she had never been away. The same rush to get everyone ready in the morning, to do the shopping, to listen to Simon's complaints about how someone had pushed him in the playground while she simultaneously admired Ben's new reading book. The same mixture of chaos and creativity, the practical and the profound.

But with Kate things were different. It seemed to Rachel that in the time she had been away Kate, too, had crossed some private boundary. There was a reserve about what could and could not be said between them that had not been there before. It saddened Rachel, and also panicked her slightly. I have done this, she thought. By loving Hassan I have broken something between Kate and me, something that was precious and may never be repaired. She had no strategy for dealing with the panic except to tell herself, over and again, not to be afraid, and gradually it began to work. There were a hundred possible explanations for what might be going on inside Kate. Jealousy was undoubtedly one of them but it was probably not the only one, maybe not even the main one. The girl was thirteen years old, afterall. Even in two and a half weeks there had been visible changes in her body. She was fuller around the hips, her small breasts lifted more obviously under her summer tee-shirt. More significant, she carried herself differently, enhancing the message of her breasts rather than hiding it. Perhaps she was about to start her periods? Perhaps she had in fact started while Rachel had been away - and if she had, would she have felt let down that Rachel was not there to tell? Or relieved, to be saved the embarrassment? Rachel did not know, for they were on new ground - Kate, a sexual being, dealing with the new knowledge of her sexuality just as Rachel was celebrating the rediscovery of hers.

We need time, she thought. Maybe it won't ever be the same again, but perhaps this would have happened sometime anyway, regardless of Hassan. The important thing is not to panic, just to be here for her, to wait until she is ready to move on.

Of all her friends the only one who asked her about what it had been like going back to South Africa was Pat. The others asked after her mother and expressed sympathy about her aunt. Perhaps, like her people in Lourensrus, they could not imagine anything more and so did not know what to ask. Nor did she know how to tell them. But it no longer mattered that she couldn't share with them the experiences of that other life, for it no longer felt like 'that other life', far away, cut off. She knew now that she carried it with her, that she had lost no one.

From Hibo and Evelyn she heard in full detail about the march to the MP. 'He'll do anything to get his face on the box,' Evelyn said, both scathing and triumphant.

'What did he say?'

'Only some high-sounding waffle about the importance of family unity. But we got a promise out of him to meet a small group of us to listen to the details. We were only waiting for you to get back before we fixed a date.'

'You shouldn't have done that,' said Rachel. 'Phone him tomorrow and take the first appointment he can give us. If it's a time I can't go, someone else will have to.'

Time's running out.

In fragments, carried by wounded men and fleeing civilians, the news reached Dire Dawa and Djibuti and from there was telephoned to London - government forces had now firmly re-established control of Bura'o, what was left of it after the shelling. It was in attempting to defend it that Mohamed had been killed. Not on the Sunday morning when Hassan had been so vividly aware of his cousin's death, but the next day, Monday May 30th. And the day after that, SNM troops had attacked Hargeisa, quickly taken control of the northern parts of the city, but been unable to dislodge the army from its hold on the crucial government buildings - which included Hargeisa Prison.

The telephone lines were continually blocked. Even when people got through, no one could tell them for sure what was happening. In Whitechapel and Aldgate, Bethnal Green and Limehouse, Cardiff and Sheffield, desperately anxious people sought each other out, compared notes, tried to piece together what they could, to find out what was happening to their families. There was nothing to be learnt from the radio or the papers. When Rachel managed to get through to someone at the BBC to demand why a major civil war was going unreported, she was told that their news desk could not substantiate the stories they were receiving. They could not report rumours, only facts. 'That means,' she said, furious, 'that all an oppressive government has to do is to remove foreign journalists and then any atrocities it cares to commit against its own population will not have happened as far as you're concerned, just because you didn't have one of your own people there to see them?'

'In effect, yes,' said the man at the other end. 'And if you can think of another way, that still allows us to keep our reputation for only reporting the truth, please let me know.'

For Rachel there was little time to reflect and certainly none to waste on personal anxieties. Occasionally she thought back to the time when the campaign had just got started and remembered that she had felt busy then, sending out petitions and leaflets and organising a concert to raise funds. At the time these had seemed big things to aim at, each one a new departure for which she needed to get herself mentally prepared. It seemed a long time ago, a time when there was still time. Now there was none. Haleemo's children, Nafisa and Abokor, were probably cowering in an abandoned house while the adults who were responsible for them were being roughed up by soldiers and thrown into a truck, to be taken to a National Security prison, or mowed down while trying to leave the house at night to look for food. Hassan's father might be dead already. And if he was alive, he would be witnessing the horror of his fellow prisoners being taken out in batches to be shot, and awaiting his turn. This was not the time to be sending out leaflets. They needed something more than that, something far more powerful.

She sat up late, reading her way through the pile of completed petitions and letters that had come in her absence and that Pat had left stacked in two large cardboard boxes. She searched the names and addresses for any that might lead her to someone in a position of influence. Eventually she was rewarded by a petition with a cover-letter on House of Commons notepaper. An MP in Cardiff congratulated the committee on their action on behalf of Mrs. Warsame. He had in his constituency in Cardiff, he wrote, a large number of Somali voters, long term residents of this country. He considered it high time official recognition was given to what was happening in Somalia, and full Refugee Status accorded to the many Somalis who had a genuine fear of persecution. Britain was the natural country of asylum for people who had relatives long settled here. The present half-hearted approach to asylum applications was particularly regrettable given Britain's longstanding connection with what had once been British Somaliland. He presumed the committee was in touch with Mrs. Warsame's MP, but since there were implications for many other Somalis, he himself would be willing to raise the matter if they had not had any success in that area. If members of the committee would care to contact him... Yours etc. The letter was dated 26th May, before the attack on Bura'o.

First thing next morning she phoned Hibo. 'Will you come with me? We can officially hand over the petitions at the same time. There are already several thousand signatures.'

'Of course I'm coming,' Hibo said.

'I'll talk to Haleemo,' Rachel said. But when she did, she realised immediately that it was too late for anything that happened in Britain to make any difference to Haleemo. She looked as she had looked when Rachel had first seen her, as if concentrating on anything that was happening around her required an effort far greater than she was capable of. She scarcely listened as Rachel and Hibo made plans, or discussed the points they should emphasise when they saw the MP. *I must bring my children out!* Rachel heard her say - months and months ago, that had been. There might have been time, if she had acted faster. If she had not taken so long to get herself ready. If she had not had so many fears of her own to sort out. If she had been able to see then what she could see now, and had had the confidence to do then what she was about to do now, they might have got Haleemo's children out before all this had happened. She had failed her, and it was no use expecting Haleemo to have any further faith in what the campaign might achieve.

But that did not mean they would stop. Until they knew for certain there was no hope, they would go on. If Haleemo's faith had failed, they would simply have to buoy her up with their own. And anyway, events had moved the issue on, beyond Haleemo. Even if they could not save her children there would be others, those who managed to get out of Hargeisa alive and had to flee somewhere. People who would need asylum, who would be separated from their children, their husbands, their wives, who would live daily with the knowledge of their elderly parents abandoned somewhere, with no one to care for them. This had started as Haleemo's campaign but Hassan had said from the start that it would be for all of them. They would go on, more urgently now than ever before.

7

Afterwards Hassan could remember little of the sequence of events leading up to the 10th of June. Too much happened, too fast. He knew, of course, because he was dealing with the papers at work, that Nuh's letter from the Home Office had been dated 1st June, which was also the date that Rachel had returned from South Africa and the day on which they had heard confirmation of Mohamed's death. But after that everything became blurred, just as confused as the stories they were hearing from Hargeisa. He remembered Nuh coming back one evening - was it before he had had his Home Office letter, or after? - with a rumour that the most prominent prisoners were being transferred under armed guard to the maximum security prison in Mogadishu. And then another rumour, that each day batches of prisoners were being killed. In Berbera, it was said, the army chief had insisted that their throats be slit before they were shot, slaughtered as animals are in Islamic tradition.

'It doesn't make sense,' Hassan said. 'Why some each day, why not all at once?'

'Allah alone knows,' said Nuh.

And of course there were no names. There would just be bodies, dumped in piles in a shallow pit while the fighting continued in the streets of Hargeisa, and no one had any way of knowing who was alive and who was dead, let alone of sending a message to people waiting in the safety of London. If the SNM troops finally succeeded in taking the prison, he would hear if his father was still there. But if he did not hear? That would not mean for sure that he was dead. There would still be the possibility that he had been taken to Mogadishu. And if Sabah went to look for him there and there was no sign of him, even then they would not be sure, for there were a hundred other prisons to which he could have been taken.

He would not know, not for months, for years. Perhaps never. *Aabahay*, my father. Aabahay, presumed dead but perhaps still alive somewhere. Suffering, abandoned.

'There's a translation of a poem I want you to read.' He handed Rachel the book, ready open at the page. 'That one. *The limits of submission.* It's by one of the great poets of the north, Farah Nuur. He comes from a small tribe that was dominated for years by a more powerful one. The poem is about how they finally revolted against their oppressors.'

She took the book, but did not want to look at it. 'I thought Somali poetry had to be heard, not read. Aren't you going to recite it to me?'

'I can't. My voice won't do it. Read it.'

> *Over and over again to people I show abundant kindness.*
> *If they are not satisfied*
> *I spread out bedding for them and invite them to sleep.*
> *If they are still not satisfied*
> *I milk my camel three times, and tell them to drink it up.*
> *If they are still not satisfied,*
> *I kill the homestead's ram and the fat he-goat for them.*
> *If they are still not satisfied*
> *I offer them a beautiful girl and her bridal house .*
> *If they are still not satisfied,*
> *I lavish salutations upon them, 'Brother-in-law, Sultan, King!'*
> *If they are still not satisfied,*
> *At the time of early morning prayers*
> *I prepare the dark grey horse with black tendons,*

And with the words 'Praise to the Prophet'
I take the iron-shafted spear,
And drive it through their ribs so that their lungs spew out.
Then they are satisfied.

'Hassan, that's a terrible poem.'

'We live in terrible times.'

She was afraid for him. She remembered him saying, there are people for whom anger lasts so long that it devours them. Don't ask for it to last... 'It's a poem for Mohamed,' he said. 'His death has made certain things clear to me. I realise now that all the time he and I were arguing about SNM, all that time he was living in the aftermath of his own father's death. Mohamed used to look at me in a way that - he just couldn't understand what was missing in me that I didn't see things his way.' He paused. 'What was missing was the violent death of someone close to me.'

Rachel put the book down and came to sit close to him. 'Mohamed once said,' Hassan went on, 'after what has happened to your father do you really think it's enough to sit there behind a desk? To him revenge was the only natural response. But I was looking for another way, something guaranteed to get my father out of there alive. And of course there isn't such a way. There never was.'

Alone in her own bed, so far from Hassan's where she ought to have been, comforting him, she read into the small hours. Nothing moved, yet she became aware that there was someone else in the room. She looked up to see Kate standing at her door in her nightdress. 'Can I come into your bed?" Kate asked.

'Of course.' Rachel moved over to make room. It was a long time since this had happened. 'What makes you awake so late?' Kate said nothing but she accepted Rachel's arms around her. Rachel switched off the bedside light and they lay together in the comforting dark. Eventually Kate said, 'I had a postcard from Daddy while you were away.'

'And?'

'It said, Love from Daddy and Rita.' She must have given some sign with her body for Kate asked, sharply, 'Did you know?'

'I knew there was someone. I didn't know she was called Rita.' She was thinking, typical of Alistair to announce it in that way, simply to pretend the issue isn't there. She said, smiling in the dark, 'So both your parents are giving you trouble?' Kate said nothing. Rachel went on, 'Do you know, when I first found out about her, I was very upset.'

Kate demanded, 'Why?' accusingly, as if to say, what right have you to be upset?

'For no good reason. Just because it's hard getting used to anything new. But I'm glad now. If he and I aren't going to be together it's sensible for each of us to find someone else.' Kate lay still. 'Poppet,' oh hell, she doesn't want to be called that. Then some instinct told her that tonight Kate would be comforted to be called by the name that had kept her loved and safe all the years she could remember. So she said it again, 'Poppet, I should have talked to you properly about Hassan ages ago. I'm sorry, I think I've made it harder for you by behaving like an ostrich.'

'What do ostriches do?' Kate asked, momentarily distracted.

'They stick their heads in the sand when they see danger ahead. Then they hope that danger won't see them!'

Kate giggled, but at the same time her body had become tense again. Rachel said, in as matter-of-fact a voice as she could manage, 'I'm going to be staying overnight at Hassan's sometimes. Pat says she'll be happy to come about once a week till we all work out what's going to happen. You decide which evening you want your saxophone lesson - she says any weekday except Thursday.' Kate still lay rigid, saying nothing. Rachel went on. 'And Hassan will sometimes spend time with us here at the weekends.'

Kate burst out, 'I don't mind your going there sometimes but I don't want him here. It's OK if he comes when other people are here, but not just him. It's not like our family when he's here.'

'Our family can change a little and still be our family. Hassan being here sometimes won't take anything real away from you and the boys, just as your going out with Becky and the others doesn't take anything real away from me. We're the same for each other, there are just extra people added.' Then she had another thought. 'Have you noticed that Simon gets into a bad mood every time you go off on a Saturday with your friends?'

Kate was instantly defensive. 'He'll just have to get used to it.'

'That's right,' Rachel said and waited for the penny to drop.

*

The morning Nuh got his letter from the Home Office was also the morning the papers carried the extraordinary announcement of the inquest verdict. CORONER SLAMS GOVERNMENT'S TREATMENT OF ASYLUM SEEKERS, it ran. Verdict of suicide aggravated by official indifference and lack of care. Urgent need for comprehensive review of procedures...

And that same morning Nuh's letter arrived. Hassan was normally gone before the post came, but he had worked late the night before and was late leaving. He went downstairs and was about to open the front door, stepping over the brown envelopes that lay on the mat just inside it, when he saw the official Home Office stamp on one of them and bent to pick it up. Mr. Nuh Ali Dahir.

He went back up the stairs two at a time and into the flat, and without speaking sat down on the floor next to the sofa where Nuh was just stirring. As soon as Nuh's eyes were properly open he put the envelope into his hands. Nuh stared at it without making any move to open it. Hassan said, trying to keep things light, 'You didn't have to wait that long after all. It's only two weeks since your interview.' Then he thought, perhaps it isn't a decision after all, perhaps it's something quite different, another bloody form that needs filling in.

Nuh opened the letter, and before he silently handed it over, Hassan knew.

Mr Nuh Ali Dahir - You do not qualify for entry into the United Kingdom under any of the Immigration Rules. I therefore refuse you leave to enter. I have given directions for your removal at 1700 hrs on 8/6/1988 by aircraft to Nairobi, Kenya...

He remembered yelling, 'No, no, *no!'* uncontrollably, slamming his way around the flat, until something made him stop and look back at the sofa to see Nuh lying there - passively, not moving, not saying anything, all the fight gone out of him - and that frightened him more than anything he had ever experienced... Then sometime later that day in his office, saying over the phone to James Freeman, 'The Home Office already has one suicide on its collective conscience. Do you want another?' James had been gentle with him - he remembered that too, though at the time he could not receive it as gentleness, only as a refusal to be adequately moved - and his own voice had become more and more out of control in his urgency to get through that impassive blandness. 'There's been a gross miscarriage of justice,' he had said, 'the immigration officer took a hate to him before he even heard what he had to say. I saw it myself. What kind of a hearing is it when the prosecutor and the judge are the same person? I'm starting proceedings for a judicial review.'

Then everything became blurred again, blurred by his own frenzied activity and the constant awareness of Nuh's depression. Nuh did not even bother to get himself food. If Hassan had not put it in front of him he would probably not have eaten. All he did was watch television and wait for the phone to ring or people to come with news from home. Each evening Hassan would explain to him what he was doing about his case. They had no right of appeal against the decision, not until after Nuh had been removed to Kenya, which would of course be too late. But a judicial review could win them time. Time for what, Hassan did not say and Nuh did not ask.

And through all that miasma of anxiety, of furious activity alternating with hopelessness, there was Rachel. Rachel standing in his office - he registered vaguely that it was the middle of the morning, so it was impossible for Rachel to be there, but there she undoubtedly was with Hibo next to her, and she was saying, 'Just win us some time and we'll raise so much noise they won't have the nerve to send him back.' He looked at her incomprehendingly, as if she were talking about how things operated on another planet. 'We've got on to the television people,' Rachel was saying, undaunted. 'They're coming to interview you at four tomorrow.' And Hibo was talking about the meeting in Whitechapel. 'You have to speak,' she said. 'The whole thing is changed.'

'What's going on?' he asked.

Rachel said, slowly and clearly, as if trying to get through to someone who was only half-conscious, 'Hassan, we've had a meeting. Everyone agrees we can't proceed with Haleemo's campaign as it was, things have moved beyond that. We're demanding that there should be no removals of Somalis while the war continues, and full refugee status for anyone who manages to get here. Hibo and I are drafting a new leaflet. We need you to give us the details of Nuh's case.'

Another phone call from Djibuti, from uncle Ali, rousing Nuh momentarily into full concentration. Hassan, listening to him talking once again with vigour in his voice, wished that the conversation

335

would go on a long time. Eventually Nuh handed the phone to Hassan. 'He wants to talk to you.'

'Hassan?' It was the first time he had heard uncle Ali's voice since he had left Hargeisa, eight months ago. His last link with his father, almost severed. Uncle Ali had nothing to tell him. 'Ismail sends his salaams. I'll phone again as soon as there's any news.' Hassan put the phone down.

Nuh said, 'The government have airlifted all foreign personnel out of Hargeisa,' and he quoted, as if to himself,

Maybe the Europeans will go away
And then maybe the Angel of Death will get busy.

'What are you saying?' Hassan asked.

'I keep thinking about the wars of Sayyid Mohamed Abdille Hassan against the British. You know what defeated him in the end, don't you?'

'Nuh -'

'The British bombed him out. 1920 - one of the earliest examples of aerial warfare. They couldn't get him any other way. Whenever they thought they'd got him, he simply disappeared for a while into the interior and raised another army. In the end they had to bomb his movement out of existence.'

'Are you suggesting Siyad is going to bomb Hargeisa?' Hassan demanded. Nuh shrugged. 'It's different,' Hassan said urgently. 'The British bombed enemy fortifications, on enemy soil which they weren't trying to control. You don't bomb your own city, not with your own army controlling half of it!'

'Siyad's got to do something. And he's mad, madder than uncle Musa, by far.'

Two days later they heard that the bombing of Hargeisa had begun. People were fleeing, running out of their houses, out of the town, taking nothing with them except the clothes they wore, running to the Ethiopian border. The planes followed them as they ran, strafing the road. The bodies fell, and there was no time to stop to bury them, no cover in that vast, open expanse of dust and stones against the violence that attacked them from the sky.

*

They lay that night a long time holding on to each other, as if to protect each other. They lay in the dark and spoke very little.

For a while Rachel thought they would probably lie like that, without making love, until they fell asleep. She wanted more than anything for Hassan to sleep. She held him gently, occasionally running her fingers through his hair, but not moving her body in any sexual way, hoping that sleep would come for him.

After a long time he began to move a little. First just a foot, softly moving against hers, then being still. Then his arms loosened their hold, just enough to allow his hand to move on her back. His touch still did not feel like a lover's, more as if he were reassuring himself that she was still there, that there was still something good and loving and gentle left in the world, something that he could touch and know to exist. But the longer his fingers trailed her back the more electric her skin and flesh became, until she could stand the exquisite awakening no longer and was moving against him with her whole body, holding, caressing, devouring. They made love angrily, and with infinite gentleness, as if in doing so they could cancel out everything except their love.

Afterwards he lay for a long time on top of her, supporting himself on his elbows so as not to press down on her too heavily. Eventually he slipped down next to her, put his hand out to touch her face briefly, and then lay still. Now he'll sleep, she thought.

'Rachel.'

'Ssssh,' she said softly. 'We'll talk more tomorrow.'

'There's a poem -'

'Hassan, there's time. Save it, tell me in the morning.'

He lay still, but only for a moment. 'It's a special poem, I don't know why I haven't told it to you before. It's not long.'

'Go on then, but softly. Don't wake yourself up too much.'

'It's OK, I could do this one in my sleep. My father used to recite it to me each time I left him to come back to London, and he liked the English translation. It's a poem of farewell.' He was silent again. Then, 'Whenever I close my eyes I keep seeing the people fleeing from Hargeisa, women with babies and young children, with no food for them, old women like my grandmother who can't run, can't keep up -'

'The poem,' she reminded gently. He began.

Now you depart, and though your way may lead
Through airless forests thick with hagar trees,
Through places steeped in heat, stifling and dry,
Where breath comes hard, and no fresh breeze can reach -
Yet may God place a shield of coolest air
Between your body and the assailant sun,
And in a random scorching flame of wind
That parches the painful throat, and sears the flesh
May God, in His compassion, let you find
The great-boughed tree that will protect and shade.

By the time he had finished reciting his voice was calm again, with something like his normal strength. 'A shield of coolest air,' she repeated softly. 'It's what you do, in your work.'

'What is?' He sounded almost angry, as if she were belittling the poem by this comparison.

'You and the others. Me. Trying to provide that shield. With air - words - international conventions - loopholes in the law, petitions. Something as insubstantial as your own breath. It's you who taught me that.' He was silent. She lay still, hoping that perhaps now he would sleep, and rest, and in rest find the strength to start again tomorrow. She thought she heard his voice - so quiet it was scarcely more than breathing - saying, 'It's all we've got.' But she had not felt his body move and she did not know whether she had imagined it, if she was hearing it again in her memory or if he had said it now.

Author's note

I gratefully acknowledge permission to use the following translations, in a few cases with minor adaptations. Initials indicate the translator:

Faarah Nuur:	The country is snatched and divided	A/L
	Over and over again	A/L
Ilmi Bowndheri:	And I am forever a poet	L
Ismaa'iil Mire:	Everyone will receive	A/L
	I saw a man who will not live long	A/L
Raage Ugaas:	As swift as if hurled from a sling	A
	Like people journeying while moving camp	A/L
	When men closed their doors	S
Saido Haji:	He has gone to the Ganane River	A
Salaan Arrabey:	O clansmen, stop the war!	A/L
	When misfortune siezed me	A/L
	There is a time	S
Sayyid Mohamed Abdille Hassan:		
	Now you depart	L
	I invoke the saints who keep the straight path	A/L
	I have no forts, no houses	S
	Three things one does not recover from	S
	Must I from time everlasting	S
Siraad Haad:	You are the sky which gives no rain	A/L
anonymous:	You are like a place with fresh grass	A
	Maybe the Europeans will go away	A
	You are the risen sun	A/L
	My heart is single and cannot be divided	A/L
	For of course that life is sweet I grant you	A/L
	Woman, lovely as lightning at dawn	L
	Your bright mouth	L
	I long for you	L
	He who has lain between her breasts	L
	Since when you die	L
	If you, O Aynabo, my fleet and fiery horse	L
	My brother is there	D

A/L   B W Andrzejewksi and I M Lewis, *Somali poetry - an introduction*, Clarendon Press, Oxford,1964

A   B W Andrzejewski, unpublished, and one from Ruth Finnegan (ed), *The Penguin Book of Oral Poetry*, Allen Lane, London, 1978

L   Margaret Laurence, *A tree for poverty - Somali poetry and prose*, McMaster University Library Press, Canada, 1970

S   Said S Samatar, *Oral poetry and Somali nationalism*, Cambridge University Press, 1982

D   John Darnton, quoted in David Laitin and Said S Samatar, *Somalia, nation in search of a state*, Westview Press, 1984

The people in this novel are fictitious, the background of public events is not. For an understanding of events in Somalia I am indebted to the many refugees in London who have told me about their experiences, and to B W Andrzejewski, who gave hours of patient help to answering my queries and checking points in the manuscript relating to poetry, its role in Somali society and other aspects of traditional Somali culture. Sa'ad Ali Shire, Ahmed I Samatar and Idil Yayhe Ibrahim read drafts of the manuscript and made useful suggestions, and the writings of Rakiya Omaar, Said S Samatar and I M Lewis illuminated many aspects of Somali history, society and politics. For information on asylum procedures I am grateful to Mary Dines, whose work on behalf of refugees has given her a wealth of knowledge which she generously shared. Also to Ragnhild Witherow, Mark Ashford, Jaime Alvarez, for information on conditions of immigration detainees, Ian Macdonald, Nicholas Blake, John Macdonald, QCs, Tzeggai Yohannes of the Refugee Council, and staff of the Somali London Cultural Community, the Refugee Arrivals Project and Battersea Reference Library. For encouragement and advice on production I am grateful to Robert Molteno, Andrew Corbett, Aidan Lunn, Ralph Smith, Linda Wright, Barbara Dinham, James Alty and Helen Salmon.

My thanks to the many friends who read drafts of the book and gave me valuable comments, especially Joanna Rosenthal for fruitful challenging in the early stages and Ralph Russell for reading more drafts than anyone else would have tolerated. To Sharon, May and Robert, my special thanks for keeping my courage up and patiently accepting my inability to remember to turn off my bath.